"Woodbury's writing is artful and full of imagination [with] vivid characters who are distinguished by idiosyncratic speech patterns. Listen and you'll hear teenage hipsters speaking in iambic pentameter, or the narcotic howl of a homeless prostitute."
—John Walch, *Austin Chronicle*

"The roads in this grand 'American Odyssey' criss-cross and coalesce . . . Most crucially, Woodbury is a great humanist . . . a sort of one-woman 'Nickolas Nickleby' . . . a Whitmanesque vision of America at the end of the twentieth century. There is talk of race, abortion, mental illness, war, and ecological disaster. But in the end, there is also redemption and many reconstructed lives."
—Hedy Weiss, *Chicago Sun-Times*

"As in all good novels, the characters are half the fun . . . Woodbury has a keen ear for dialogue and for the myriad ways we reveal our identities through speech."　　—Jack Helbig, *Daily Herald* (Chicago)

"Think of the expansive social criticism of John Dos Passos's *U.S.A.* tempered by the loopy humanity of Lily Tomlin."
—David Cote, *TimeOut New York*

WHAT EVER

Heather Woodbury is a native of northern California. In her late teens, she moved to New York City's East Village and became involved in the early '80s performance art scene, where she developed her method of generating material via improvisational writing and performance. Throughout those years she lived in several NYC neighborhoods, was employed as a go-go dancer, a barmaid, and a cater waiter, and crisscrossed the country several times by car, train, bus, and thumb. All of this served to inspire *What Ever: An American Odyssey*, her eight-part "performance novel," which she went on to tour as a solo performance extensively in the U.S. and Europe and to serialize as a radio play, broadcast on NPR stations.

Woodbury has received numerous awards as a performer and playwright. In 2001, she received an award from the Kennedy Center Fund for New American Plays, as well as an NEA Fellowship for her new work *Tale Of 2 Cities: An American Joyride*. She currently resides in Echo Park, Los Angeles, with her husband, and is writing a novel version of this same work.

WHAT EVER

FABER AND FABER, Inc.
An affiliate of Farrar, Straus and Giroux / NEW YORK

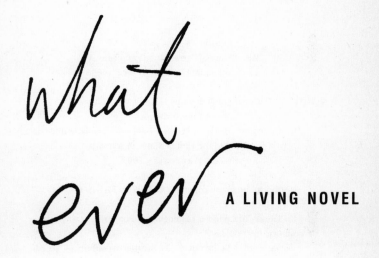

what ever

A LIVING NOVEL

HEATHER WOODBURY

FABER AND FABER, INC.

An affiliate of Farrar, Straus and Giroux

19 Union Square West, New York 10003

Distributed in Canada by Penguin Books of Canada Limited

Printed in the United States of America

FIRST EDITION, 2003

Author photograph copyright © 2002 by Melvin Estrella

Library of Congress Cataloging-in-Publication Data

Woodbury, Heather.

What ever : a living novel / by Heather Woodbury.— 1st ed.

p.   cm.

ISBN 0-571-21172-0 (pbk. : alk. paper)

1. City and town life—Fiction.   I. title.

PS3623.O66W47 2003

813'.6—dc21

2003044825

Designed by Gretchen Achilles

www.fsgbooks.com

1   3   5   7   9   10   8   6   4   2

To my nieces Juniper Margarita Mayer Woodbury and Jessika Anwyn Evans.
And to the memory of my aunt Juliet "Due" Woodbury.

CONTENTS

ACKNOWLEDGMENTS

Dudley Saunders, my "bestest friend and fairest cohort," told me one day, back in 1994, that I was cursed. He told me that I had too many, rather than too few, ideas and dared me to undo this curse by trying to express them all: "Write and perform all new material every week for a year," he said. Franklin Furnace and the Jerome Foundation gave me an honorarium, helping me to take up that dare, mercifully modified to a more gestational nine-month length. Lach, founder of The Fort, a musician's club on Avenue A in New York's East Village, gave me the opening slot every Wednesday night for thirty-seven consecutive weeks from September 1994 to May 1995. The audience—my first editor—witnessed the birth of this novel on the tongue and helped midwife it: egging me on, lobbying for favorite characters, hissing at their antagonists, sometimes crying, often laughing along with me; the drunks and pool players in the back did not. They bellicosely ignored the doings and thus helped immeasurably to refine my concentration. Dudley Saunders, in less than a month, edited the resulting twenty-plus hours into a ten-hour "performance novel," which he also directed as a solo play.

A few brave artistic directors took a risk in presenting this as yet unheard of four-night solo epic: Mark Russell of P.S. 122, Bonnie Cullum of Vortex Rep, and Martha Lavey of Steppenwolf Theatre Company. Other partisans aided and abetted in producing and promoting *What Ever* in other venues, other media, and in Europe: Ira Glass, Laurie Anderson, Suzy Williams, Peter Soby Jr., Barbara Cavanagh and Davison Grant, James and Danielle Fearnley, Steve Brown, Steve Kaplan, Jonothon Stearns, Richard Linklater, Marcia Farquhar, Jo Bonney, Rich Ferguson, David and Amy Misch, Larry Fessenden, and Tim Evans.

My literary agent, Scott Mendel of Multimedia Product Development, believed in *What Ever* as a written work from the start and did not stop nagging me until I revised it as such. His tremendous perseverance brought this work to the attention of Linda Rosenberg, my editor at FSG, who has had the guts and grace to take on a hybrid literary form in this most category-conscious of eras, and who has been an extremely thoughtful and encouraging guide in realizing *What Ever: An American Odyssey* as *What Ever: A Living Novel*. Denise Oswald, also at FSG, had early belief and enthusiasm in this project.

Family and friends have sustained me (often literally!) throughout this cross-continental eight-year odyssey: professor of linguistic studies Tony Woodbury (who also advised me on indigenous American languages used in this text); Zoe, Camille, and Angela Woodbury; Bill Burnett; Stephanie Meckler; Sheila Gordon; my brothers, Mark Evans and Brian Woodbury (who always believed in me); my parents, Mark and Marda Woodbury; my sister-in-law Elma Mayer (who attended nearly every performance until she gave birth!); my husband, Roberto Palazzo (who arrived, *boyfriend-ex-machina*-like at the conclusion of the saga, my personal living proof that life imitates art).

Last, as first, Dudley Saunders Jr. has been my cohort in the truest sense throughout this adventure; for without him, it would not have been.

To all these dudes, I say, Multitudes o' gratitude upon ye!

PREFACE

In writing the original script of *What Ever*, I spelled each word as I heard my characters speak it. In this way, the original script, though by no means consistently spelled, nevertheless provided a reliable blueprint for me as the sole performer of the text. This original text would no doubt prove an interesting study for a linguistics professor or for a very avid actor, but for the purposes of this book—a novel in dialogue form—the contents would not travel well. It should also be noted that seeming inconsistencies occur in all natural speech. Depending on the sounds that directly precede and follow it, the same word will be pronounced differently by the same speaker, for example: You want that? versus Do ya want that?

Therefore, since it is close to impossible to transcribe precisely the accents and inflections of each character, I have done my best to *intimate* their pronunciations, salting and peppering their speech to communicate the flavor of their individual dialects while attempting to keep the stew edible. Hence, not all sounds are spelled as the speaker would pronounce them but, with certain key words and sounds, I have attempted to capture the general tone of the character's accent.

As John Steinbeck wrote in 1962 in *Travels with Charley: In Search of America*:

One of my purposes was to listen, to hear speech, accent, speech rhythms, overtones, and emphasis. For speech is so much more than words and sentences. I did listen everywhere. It seemed to me that regional speech is in the process of disappearing . . . I, who love words and the endless possibility of words, am saddened by this inevitability. For with local accent will disappear local tempo. The idioms, the figures of speech that make language rich and full of the poetry of time and place, must go. And in their place will be a national speech, wrapped and packaged, standard and tasteless. Localness is not gone but it is going. In the many years since I have listened to the land, the change is very great . . . no region can hold out for long against the highway, the high-tension line, and national television . . . What I am mourning is perhaps not worth saving, but I regret its loss nevertheless.

In writing *What Ever*, I attempted to do my part in recording all the particularities of American speech that still hang on, forty years after Steinbeck wrote this. I hope that what I have culled from these current idioms will not only preserve what is being lost, but also in iterating the forms of "wrapped and packaged" speech will help illuminate what already has.

CHARACTERS

CLOVE CARNELIAN
—A young raver, citizen of Santa Cruz, California, given to dangerous ecstasies, haunted by Cobain the Friendly Ghost

SKEETER, A.K.A. EZEKIAL CHRISTIAN FRYE
—A young raver, stricken with love for Clove and Sable, raised hitching rides with his ma Linda, native of Oregon

SABLE NUGENT
—Clove's "best friend and fairest cohort," a young raver, in love with Skeeter, at turns envious of and protective of Clove

VIOLET SMITH
—An Upper East Side octogenarian given to regaling the customers of the Blue Ship Diner and her poodle, Balzac, with tales of her long and unexpected life

IRIS
—Violet's long-suffering prissy best friend

CORA SUE CLAY
—Violet's no-nonsense housekeeper and part-time confidante

PAUL FOLSOM
—Retired C.E.O. of Axnell Corp., suffering regrets and grave confusion, husband of Polly, lover of Jeanette

POLLY RENARD FOLSOM
—Paul's wife, a Southern belle housewife, trapped in her clean house in Middleburg, Virginia, falls in love with Reuben Scott Clay, a black garbage disposal contractor

SHEILA MARIE FOLSOM
—The radical environmentalist daughter of Paul and Polly

JEANETTE GLADJNOIS
—Skeeter's aunt, Linda's sister, Paul's mistress; a brittle Manhattan ex-call girl cum crystal healer, seeking to heal herself through healing others

LINDA FRYE
—Skeeter's mother, Jeanette's sister; a Wicca witch of the North Coast, embittered by the desertion of Skeeter's dad, Bruce Frye, a pot smuggler

BUSHIE, A.K.A. MOLLIE BRIGHT
—Abrasive, brave, and crack-addled Hell's Kitchen whore in a one-woman war with the yuppie condo owners of West Forty-fifth Street

MAGDALENA RIGOBAR JOHNSON, A.K.A. MAGENTA RUSH
—Bushie's long-lost homegirl, married to Mr. Johnson, an avid fundamentalist Christian

Since *What Ever* was created in the nine months between September 1994 and May 1995, the events chronicled in this story also occur during that time span.

PART ONE

SALVATION

CHAPTER 1

IN WHICH VIOLET AND IRIS DISCUSS FORBIDDEN DANCES

Our story begins long ago, in the early 1990s, when a couple of old ladies convene at the end of a counter in a bustling Greek diner on the Upper East Side of Manhattan. Both are well dressed in the manner of patrician American women who hit their stride in around 1930-something—jaunty hats, handsome old furs, snappy blouses, and once-saucy skirts. One is dressed neatly and primly, however, while the other wears colors just a bit too bright for her phase of life and has a gleam in her eye a bit out of step with her Upper East Side surroundings. This is Violet. A small black poodle is tethered to her stool and wriggles at her ankles. This is Balzac. She calls testily to the harried waiter, who seems so accustomed to her that he regards her as part of the fixtures.

VIOLET: Connie, Constantine! Constantinopolis! Can I have a glass of wateh, please?

Connie nods from down the counter.

VIOLET: Thank you, Connie. Come heah, Balzy, come heah, sit in my lap.

The dog scrambles up as she, with effort, heaves him onto her lap. She pats him attentively.

VIOLET: Poor dogs, they know when something *aw*ful is about to occur.

IRIS: What is it?

Violet's voice is low and has a layer of ever-present irony. Her ar's are all ahs, her or's are all awe's. Iris has a higher and sharper voice. She pronounces her r's with a crisp Midwestern accent. Her voice always has a tinge of worry.

VIOLET: How should I know, Iris, I'm not a dog! So, what're you looking put out for *this* morning, Iris? Is it y'doorm'n again?

IRIS: No, no, that's not it.

VIOLET: 'Tisn't? Well, what is it?

IRIS: Nothing.

VIOLET: Oh, Iris, just don't pussyfoot around, I find it very *bor*ing when you do. Just tell me what it is.

IRIS: It's *The Times*.

VIOLET: The times? The times that we live in? Still!

> She eyes their surroundings—the crowded diner, the street outside— with feigned disbelief.

VIOLET: Amazing!—or th' *Times*—*The New <u>Yawk</u> Times*?

IRIS: It's *The New York Times*.

VIOLET: Good Christ—no!—the times are bad enough, but *The Times* is far worse!

> Constantine slams down a glass of water and rushes off.

VIOLET: Thank you, Connie. Now, just what were you reading in the paper of record *this* morning to get you all—upset?

IRIS: Well, I was reading that there are these midnight dance parties that the young people, uh—

VIOLET: The young people? *The* young people? Which young people do you mean?

> She looks around the restaurant.

VIOLET: I should imagine there are *several* subdivisions at this point. Why, even Constantinopolis might be considered a *young* person, although he's got a pot belly and d'you notice his teeth—

> Connie delivers a basket of rolls. He hovers for a moment. Violet is startled.

VIOLET: He-hello, Connie, have you met Iris yet? She *loves* your soup! Isn't that re*mah*kable? Yes, well, she lost all her taste five years ago. Was it *all* of your taste buds, Iris deeah, or just several?

IRIS: Violet!

VIOLET: Oh, sorry, harumph, here, Balzy, have a nice roll. They're especially nice and STALE this morning.

> Violet feeds Balzac a roll.

VIOLET: Oh now, just let me know just what you read that was so . . . disturbing?

4

what

IRIS: Well, I read about these midnight dance parties that are called, uh, raves.

VIOLET: Raids? Raids? The young have been going on raids since the time of Genghis Khan, Iris. I hardly see how that can be news. Are you certain it was an *ah*ticle in *The Times* and not an exhibit at the Natural Hist'ry Museum?

IRIS: No, dear, raves!

VIOLET: Rage? Rage, as in all the rage?

IRIS: No, dear, raves, raves!

VIOLET: Balzy, stop barking so that I can *he*-ar Aunt Iris! Raves? As in stark raving mad?

IRIS: Yes! That's it! Exactly!

VIOLET: So what's the trouble, deeah, with these raves? What do they do? Do they rave? Do they recite passages from King Lee-ah? What's the, uh, what's the . . .

> She trails off. Amid the clatter of coffee cups, they can almost hear ambient trance music wafting across time and space.

CHAPTER 2

IN WHICH CLOVE HAS A TRANSCENDENT EXPERIENCE AT A RAVE

Meanwhile, on the opposite coast, a rave is in full sway. It is deep night on the Northern California coast. The waves sigh in and out, washing over a beached elephant-seal carcass close to the shore. In the near distance, rave rhythm thumps in time to sped-up heartbeats and video projections flash on a cliff side while ravers dance on a shelf of rock and in the pockets of sand below. Two teenagers, a boy and a girl, lie entwined in the sand before the mouth of a cave. The boy is good-looking but gawky—a puppy not quite yet a dog. His hair is dyed and has been grown long. He wears a turtle earring in his left ear, his face sports a valiant attempt at five o'clock shadow, his T-shirt bears a bright detergent box logo, his army jacket is spread considerably beneath them, and his X-large jeans are unzipped. The boy lets out a rapturous, satisfied "Ahhhhhhhhhhhh." They recover themselves and squat, catching their breath, looking out at the ocean.

SKEETER: Sooooo what's yerrr, ahhh, what's yer, uh, what's yer . . . name?

His voice is croaky and sexy, soaked in a North Coast stoner accent so sodden with laconic reserve that at times it almost sounds Southern.

CLOVE: Clove.

She is a pale, auburn-haired girl with wild, questing brown eyes. She is in an altered state, utterly awestruck by the sea. Her eyes are a little manic, eyeballs rotating.

SKEETER: Rave on. Mine's Skeeter . . . Ahhhh, pleasure tuh make yuh, Clove.

CLOVE: Yah, that was rad . . .

She speaks rapidly and with that peculiar lack of affect characteristic of the latest model of California accent. Her voice is light but throaty. She wets her lips frequently so that her mouth is always slightly open and refreshed and she sounds like her nose is eternally stuffed. She turns her attention to him for a second, blinking.

CLOVE: Why's yer name Skeeter?

SKEETER: Oh 'cause, wull, m' true name is Ezekial but my friends call me Skeeter 'cause they find me annoying in a mosquito-type of way.

CLOVE: Oh, rully? I don't think so.

SKEETER: Yeahhh . . .

He exhales on it, lets the word sit a minute, flicks a sideways glance her way. He's already gathered that she finds him less than annoying.

SKEETER: Is 'is yer first rave?

CLOVE: Yah, it's my first rave.

SKEETER: You X'in'?

CLOVE: X'in'?

SKEETER: Ecstasy?

CLOVE: Oh something . . .

She laughs a warbly, unhinged little laugh, eyeballs rolling.

CLOVE: I dunno. I'm not sure, huh-huh, huh-huh, huh-huh.

SKEETER: Yuh, wull, you picked a good rave, you know? 'Is ain't no corpret rave, just out here in the dunes, on the beach, unlicensed, no hoaxishness. Yeh-up, you picked a— Hey, Clove, whur you goin'?

CLOVE: I'm goin' to the ocean, to wash yer come off me.

SKEETER: Y'alright, Clove?

CLOVE: Yah, I'm raaaaaaaaadically alright.

SKEETER: Rave on, sister, rave on.

Clove ecstatically runs into the waves, jettisoned onto a whole new plane of reality. It is almost as if a little faery dust has been sprinkled in the ocean mist.

CLOVE: Alriiiiiight.

Greetings, wavers, salt sweet meets with salt wet,
Come! come! salt sweet, salt wet and wash my toes,
Watch! tide, watch me turrrrn on yer foaming beat,
Tickle my knees and lick them in yer spray,

Suck clean from me these drops o' mortal jism
and pull them far into earth's liquid schism.
Come! shoal of fish and swim beneath my skirt,
tug me bee-yond the toffee-colored rocks,
Sway, salty swells, into the wild deep flat,
Fold in, fold out, green waves, yer aching dress,

> Clove wanders out on a rock that juts far into the sea. She sights a sea
> creature in the waves.

There roams the lonely sea pony!
He rocks! to and fro
and flings his seaweed scarf over one shoulder and tilts—like so
It's you I'll wrap my legs about
and ride under under under under under
oh! golden purple fish! oh! seaflow'r!
oh! twinkling anemones allure!

> A crab bites her bare toes.

Ow! dawdling crabs
wand'ring under moonlight between the shallowed rocks
and tide's new pools,
do you not think I see you hiiiiiiding
sidestepping, dancing yer dance to the moon?
Is it a funeral dance fer the dead sea
that we've inundulated with our soap and shit and tee-pee?
Oh, tell me, the sickle-shaped moon,
what says she hee hee hee hee hee hee?,
Tell me, oh please tell me, what the moon rays?
I'll give you a sand dollar if you say,
sidestep my way, oh crabs and dance to the beat,
bite, bite my toes, eat, eat my human feet,
teach me how to dance like you
so the moo-hoo-hoon can catch my cray-hazy beat,
catch my cray-hay-hay-hay-hay-hazy beat,
catch my cray-hay-hay-hay-hay-hayzy beat—

what

Skeeter shouts.

SKEETER: Clo-ove! Clove! Clove, ur you alright?

CLOVE: Silence! I'm communicating with the crabs!

SKEETER: Oh, dat's great, Clove, whyn't you come back t' shore and tell me all about it! Rad! Come back off o' those rocks—I rully wanna hear all about it!

CLOVE: I will! Meet me under at the Shark's Breath Hotel!

SKEETER: Aw shit, shit! Hey! People, people! Thur's a girl, she's way out on the rocks talkin' to the crabs. (She's a rull nice girl too, she just jerked me off.) People! Whoah! People!

CLOVE: Ba boom—ba boom, ba boom ba boom,

how sad the ocean, but sadder still the shore,

be still my heart! But never still the ocean's roar!

> Clove leaps into the ocean. The music ceases as the rave party scatters and fans the shoreline, calling out.

SKEETER AND OTHERS: Clove! Clove! Clove! Clove!

CHAPTER 3

IN WHICH PAUL HAS A MISHAP

Midtown Manhattan. At a catered corporate luncheon in the executive dining room of a prestigious multinational bank, a handsome man—an aging all-American—clears his throat at the podium and taps the tinny-sounding microphone.

PAUL: Thank you, Charlie McKutcheon, for that introduction, thank you for having me here at this luncheon.

His voice is quiet, confident, earnest. He sometimes whispers for effect, which makes him sound like Jack Nicholson. His accent ever so faintly betrays a Northwestern upbringing and also can tend to a folksy, Ronald Reagan–like breathlessness.

PAUL: Uh, the Association of Franchised and Chain Retail has an interesting backround, for me, coming from the international point of view, and I hope I can light up a few topics that can help all of you compete well in the century to come. Er, at least the first couple decades, uh, I won't be around much after twenty-twenty, I guess I'll be dead. Ha!

He looks up for a laugh. No one laughs.

PAUL: Soooo, *ahem*, I'd like to highlight for ya three focus areas. Number one: personnel. Ah, our relationship to personnel is changing, uh, in every way imaginable, uh, from identifying those individuals and skills which are most needed, to identifying those, uh, we no longer need

He takes a sip of water and clears his throat.

PAUL: and in developing—and this is a key—a new relationship between the company or corporation and the individuals that make up that company team. Uh, we have learned that we have to nurture team players, that it's not enough to state expectations, we have to demonstrate to each employee how trust works. Uhr, you will be rewarded or . . . *not* rewarded—s'pose we could say punished—but we like to focus on the words REWARD and TRUST. Uhr, consistency is important here. I'll come back to this area.

The second area I would like to light up is what I call the Dissolution of Borders Phenomenon, uh . . . with the information revolution, with GATT and NAFTA we are approaching an age, in fact a *world market*, without borders. Okay, everyone has heard this, but what we haven't heard yet is a cogent strategy for maximum growth, okay:

Paul punches his fist in palm on each word for emphasis.

PAUL: *a cogent strategy for maximum growth.* This means overseas manufacturing, this means a personnel pool—okay here we are getting back to personnel; y'see, it's all related!—a personnel pool which is no longer confined to the United States of America but includes the entire world. The entire world!

He lowers his voice to a hoarse whisper, intensifying this stunning prospect.

PAUL: Think about that.

The third area I'd like to overview in my talk with you today is, okay, uh, the Crisis in Hope. What's it all for? I like to call this, uh, think-of-it-as, as a search, a search, okay? Because I don't have the answers on this one—for a new philosophy of business. Uhr, my kids are grown up, uh, they're gone from the house, uh, people don't come over much anymore. I'm in semiretirement now, my wife and I live in Virginia, just outside of D.C., so you have more time to contemplate. So, you're watering the lawn by yourself, y'know—ruther, the sprinklers are doin' it for yuh—but, in any case there's no kid-kids jumping in the spr-spr—excuse me just a second—sprinkles you know? The sprinkles of water that the little girls especially love to jump in?

He begins to wipe furiously at the corner of his left eye. It looks as if his eyes are irritated.

PAUL: And you're thinking—excuse my tangent here, I'll get right back on track—you're thinking—we're well-to-do, heck, we're wealthy! But what was it all for?

I got my daughter, Sheila, teachin' college out there in the environmental movement on the West Coast and she comes home—instead of spending a nice time with her she argues with me about

ever

industrial pollution and waste. She says, Dad, what's the point of all this progress if it's just destroying the planet we live on? And you know, I've got the answers for her on that one but down deep I've got no . . . uh, nothing, no, uh,

He wipes away more tears and the glass trembles in his hand as he takes another drink of water.

PAUL: uh, uh, can we hammer out a new outlook to fix this? Ah, I guess I've gone too far out here on the uh the uh *point* I was getting . . . off but, uh, but, tuhh . . . should we have a discussion, uh?

He scans the tables and meets a sea of blank, hostile faces.

PAUL: No, I guess not, uhh. Excuse me. Excuse me. It's been a hard week. Lotta flying. Charlie? Uhh. Excuse me.

Charlie puts his hand on Paul's back and steers him away from the podium.

CHAPTER 4

IN WHICH SKEETER IS STRANDED

Skeeter weeps by the shore as helicopters overhead sweep the dark waves with searchlights and members of the Coast Guard and Santa Cruz Sheriff's Department drag the shoreline.

SKEETER: I dunno whur she went. One second she was down by the waves, over by dat dead elephant seal, and the next second she was way the fuck out on those rocks. She was just dancin', she's just ravin', I can't believe she got pulled under out there. I went swimmin' for 'er. I dove in there with a surf board someone had and we were callin' for 'er. Shit! 'is can't be the truth! 'Is has got to be false and pernicious, bro', because I can't tolerate tragedy. I had a traumatized childhood already. Ask my ma. I saw 'er get run over in a 7-Eleven parkin' lot when I'se eight years old. Drunk dude ran 'er over in his VW hippie bus. But she survived. I helped 'er. I'se all: Mommie! Mommie! Shit, see? So Clove has got to be out dere, she's gotta be, because it's my lucky night: six days 'thout shavin' is my luckiest time, usually, and it started out like dat. I met her—she was stoked, we had us a spin, she *has* to come back. She *can't be drowned*! SHE CAN'T BE DROWNED!

He pounds his fist in the sand.

CHAPTER 5

IN WHICH BUSHIE GIVES ADVICE

The sun sinks into the Hudson River. Nearby, it is a dirty dusk on the streets of Hell's Kitchen, Manhattan. Two whores are standing on the corner of West Forty-fifth Street and Tenth Avenue. The older one is Bushie, a pale, pockmarked, pug-nosed granddaughter of the shanty Irish. She scratches and snuffles and expectorates a lot. She is antic, vibrating. She talks loudly with a brazen, bruised voice like a sandblaster strangled by cement in its nose. The little one stands there meekly, listening to her Walkman.

BUSHIE: Cassandra. Cassandra. Cassandra!!! Get off da Walkman, you deaf-ass copmeat! CA-SAN-DER-RA! Aw, chicken, yuh name is too long to be saying it all da time. We gotta get you a name like da rest uh us, like me, Bushie, and Nutz and Jig and—and I useta have a girlfriend, my main girl, we called huh Magenta Rush, huh real name was Magdalena.

CASSANDRA: Under her breath, humming to her music.

Isn't that longer?

BUSHIE: Yeah, it *is* longer but it was easier tuh say. You stand dere like dat, you won't get any pickups. You gotta push yuhself up, ya know?

Bushie demonstrates by pushing out her chest and ass and strutting.

BUSHIE: Why do I even tell you? I don't need no little Lycra-skirt-ass-jail-bait-copmeat takin' slugs from *my* money makuh.

She grabs her crotch for emphasis.

BUSHIE: Get off da retarded-ass headset and listen, Ca-san-der-a—aw, dat name's too long! Let's see . . . Cassie, Cussie, Cass Cass Cassette! Yeah, Bushie gonna call you Cassette. 'Cause you always listening *tuh* dat one tape. Ha ha! Dat's good! Cassette. Why you listen tuh dat guitar shit anyway? Not Bushie. I like house, disco, Kool and da Gang, now dat was music! Jackson Five! Bet you di'n't even know: Michael and Janet have bruddiz!

A truck roars by and she raises her voice to shout full blast.

BUSHIE: How come you hillbilly South people always like dat guitar shit? Shit sound just like dis truck goin' by! Ain't music.

Her voice subsides as the truck farts farther down the street.

BUSHIE: Music has tuh have a beat. Dat's why dese black-ass bitches be laughin' at us.

She points to her chest.

BUSHIE: White-ass bitches gotta be proud. Don't play dat noise shit around Jig and Pam, dey stomp on yuh machine. It's true. Not Bushie. Bushie nice.

A Jeep pulls up and Bushie walks over and leans in the window.

BUSHIE: Hey baby. No, no discount, no markdown here, dis ain't Home Shoppin', sweetheart, dis here is Street-Shopping! Dey got a cash machine on Forty-second. Yeah, okay, don't lie now, come back.

The Jeep pulls away.

BUSHIE: Bye! Slurpy-ass Jeep muthafucka. "Where's a cash machine?" What do I look like? Mrs. McBeat Cop? Empty-ass pockets. Shit! I'm hungry. Cassette, Cassette, go to da Ay-rabs, get me uh uh two Suzy Q's and, uh, uh, a sour-cream-and-garlic chips no no no make it Twinkies. No-no, no, get me a swizzle stick and, uh uh something healfy, a bag uh Jesse's All-Natural Peanuts, yeah, and a Choco-dile.

CASSANDRA: Huh?

BUSHIE: A *CHOCO*-DILE! *Gimme* dat Walkman, *give* it! Damn! Now go get me dat and get yuhself dat shit you like. Dat ice cream thing. No, don't go to da Tree Bruddiz, go to da Five Bruddiz. Da otha corner.

She points across Tenth Avenue, waving her arms theatrically.

BUSHIE: I don't go dere. Dey trew me out.

She mutters.

BUSHIE: Baby-ass. She don't belong on da street. She ain't even thirteen. I'm'na tell huh. Go back to where she from—hillbilly place under D.C. I'm'na tell huh—

ever

She squats by her tree, pulling her underwear down around her ankles, and sighs as she lets loose a stream of urine.

BUSHIE: Hey, Tree, how goes it, Tree? People think I'm crazy to talk to you. But PEOPLE THINK I'M CRAZY ANYWAYS SO FUCK IT!! What's it all about, Tree? Tuh do it or not tuh do it, you know? Dat's it, dat's what we all want to know. Ah, it burns, my piss burns, now maybe I'll get sick.

She stands, pulls up her underwear, and hails Cassandra, who is crossing the street with the provisions.

BUSHIE: Cassette, Cassette, come here! Where's my peanuts? No, I said peanuts, I changed my mind! See dis! See dis tape? What's it called? Read it! "Spiritual Damage"? Dat's a stupid-ass name!

She throws the tape on the sidewalk and stomps on it.

BUSHIE: Dere! Don't cry, Cassette! Don't cry or I slap you! See? Dis is how bitches on da street be! Den you got yuh pimps. You go wit' mine, Terry, he slap you, kick you, punch you and you know what else! GO BACK TUH VIRGINIA! VIRGINIA IS FUH LOVIZ! Stop crying! Stop! Who messed wit' you? Who? Daddy uncle brother or alla dem family-ass bastards?

Cassandra is choking on tears. She speaks in a whisper.

CASSANDRA: No one.

BUSHIE: No one? No one? You real pretty so you must be lyin'. Pretty girls and lies go togetha. No? You wanna stay pretty and stay out here? It don't work like dat. Gimme yuhr ice cream!

She smashes the ice cream on the ground.

BUSHIE: See! Dat nice ice cream lyin' in dat homeless shit and dirty-ass bot'les now? Dat's ugly-ass, dat's you. Dat's me, dat's West Forty-fif' Street! AH HA HA HA HA!

Cassette Cassette Cassette, I didn't wanna do it, I didn't wanna say it tuh you, but I had tuh, somet'in' force me! Here come dat Jeep fool. By da time I get back I want da girls tuh tell me, "Oh, Cassandra went with da Convenant House van. She went with dose wide-eyeball nuns."

I mean it, I'm serious, I'm'na kick yuhr ass! Hey, baby. No, no, she ain't workin'. No! just me, baby. Yeah? Well, alright! Get yuhr

what

ass tuh Convenant House! Get it off my block! GET IT! GET IT! GET IT!

She climbs in the Jeep, slams the door, and leans back.

BUSHIE: Drive, baby.

The Jeep lurches off and Cassandra stands alone on the corner, crying.

CHAPTER 6

IN WHICH DAWN DECLARES A CLIFF-HANGER

Glam "Poetry-Jockey" Dawn Malestrella in a bright, cartoonlike TV studio introduces her program. She jabs the air in front of her, thrusts out her cleavage "hip-hop style" to punctuate her delivery.

DAWN: Greetings, Cathode suckers! I'm your fave-rave PJ, Dawn Malestrella, and this is PO-E-Z-TV. Now it's time for *Suicide Watch—Actual Deaths*. Tonight, we've got an up-to-the-minute Suicide Watch, as it should be, rrrrright? It's about time! This suicide concerns a whole scene, the rave scene, that PO-E-Z-TV has been following with the keenest of razor-sharp interest for a long time. Wull, like months, alright? Soooo . . . Harper, where are ya?

On the beach, in bright camera lights, her associate, Harper, is standing by. Harper also waves his arms around in a bad imitation of a rapping homeboy.

HARPER: Dawnie, as yuh kin see, I'm standin' cliff side in Cali, only yards away from where Clove Carnelian, a young ravin' babe, disappeared under those gravy wavy waves.

DAWN: Awesome, who've we got?

HARPER: We got her best friend, Sable, and her, uh, boyfriend, Skipper.

DAWN: Excellent. Let's go for the jugular. Hey, Sable, how do you feel about your best grrrrrrrrrrrlfriend goin' over the edge and into the brew?

SABLE: Um, Dawn, uh, Clove is my best friend?

Sable is a small, luscious, black-haired girl with a sweet beguiling pucker of a mouth. She has a very high and light voice, a baby-doll burble of a voice. Her inflections are much like Clove's, though she doesn't sound like her nose is eternally plugged. Her English is a bit more standard than either Skeeter's or Clove's. When she gets excited, she sounds as if she's being tickled.

DAWN: Yeah?

SABLE: So why are you even talking to me about it?

DAWN: Don't you wanna have a last word, Sable, so the viewers will know your mind, what you honestly think and feel in your deepest part?

SABLE: No.

DAWN: No? NO!? Harper?

HARPER: Hey, we got Skipper here, Dawnie. He was with her when she ran fer the waves.

SKEETER: Er, Skeeter.

DAWN: Outtasight. Skizzer, did Clove have suicidal tendencies before, I mean prior to, this?

SKEETER: I don't know, Dawn, I just met 'er. (She made me come . . .)

DAWN: What?

SKEETER: But I don't think she's actually dead.

DAWN: Well, that's what we all hope, Skinner, but didn't she show signs?

SKEETER: Nuh.

DAWN: What?

SKEETER: I repeat: Nuh.

DAWN: Was she freaked out on the trendy drug du jour, Ecstasy?

SKEETER: I dunno.

DAWN: You don't know? Aren't you all intimate and all knowledgeable about this girl?

SKEETER: Not tuh wax personal 'gainst you, Dawn, but I truly don't cop tuh corpret entertainment, comprendo?

Skeeter walks away.

DAWN: What do you mean?

HARPER: Hey, hey Dawnie! We got State Trooper Officer Deputy Larsen here and this dude with a theory.

DAWN: Yeah?

OFFICER: Uh, at this time we got our SWAT emergency team searching the shoreline for the young lady. We've alerted the Coast Guard. Uh, it didn't look too good but we're doin' what we can do. I'd like

ever

to take this opportunity to point out that this type of tragedy is most likely to occur at an illegal event of this nature.

TODD: Hi, I'm Todd ull I have to say is that thur are black holes out there, thur are Bermuda Triangles and it's possible she's just been morphed into another space-time continuum so different from our own that we can't even conceive of it. Shit, I certainly can't even when I try.

Todd pauses and screws up his face, as if to summon all of his mental capacity.

TODD: Hard.

The effort is too much. His face goes slack again.

TODD: But, um, we don't have to see this necessarily as a tragedy, it's maybe more closer to a *virtual* tragedy. My name's Todd Rodgatzer. RAVE ON! Hee-ee, am I on PO-E-Z-TV?

DAWN: Yes. Get him off. Harper, what's the word? Will this Ravesite become a gravesite er what?

HARPER: Dunno yet, Dawnie.

DAWN: We'll be rrrrrright back after a poesy break with *Suicide Watch*—

Dawn points at the camera, narrowing her eyes to a squint.

HARPER: <u>*Actual Deaths!*</u>

Harper pulls back his arm and then flings it forward, thrusting his hand at the viewers in a signature closing gesture.

CHAPTER 7

IN WHICH VIOLET RECALLS A DARK TIME

Violet talks to a young woman who happens to be sitting beside her at the counter of the Blue Ship Diner.

VIOLET: Afteh he died, I'm afraid I felt too sorry for myself to live. And what'd been our *afte*hnoon highballs to*geth*eh graduated into breakfast cocktails for *one*. I became an old souse and walked 'round not caring *'tall* what I looked like and just hoping people would leave me *be*. I ordered liquor up everyday—and cheese sandwiches, from the drugstore. They still had lunch counters in those days, y' see, and they were perfectly good spots to eat in—a damn sight better than this establishment, I can assure you.

Violet brings a spoon to her mouth, then puts it back down in dismay. She begins to salt the soup.

VIOLET: WHY DON'T THEY SALT THE SOUP PROPERLY?

And salt it.

YOUNG WOMAN: Well, you have to watch out for excess sodium, you know.

VIOLET: What? Oh, you young are far too concerned with y' health.

And salt it.

VIOLET: After all, *we're* the ones who are dying and we don't go 'round eating *taste*less, *weight*less meals!

She tastes it again, puts her spoon down, and pushes the bowl away.

VIOLET: So I had the necessities sent up, and I neveh left the apahtment. I'd wake up, *fum*ing with rage that Elliot wasn't there and then I'd mix one of my morning concoctions of milk, orange juice, and plenty of whiskey and then I'd get *lit*, y'see, and sit on the sofa with the shades drawn down and laugh and laugh at things Elliot and I used to quarrel over, and at the jokes he played on me, and anything to do with him. I'd sit in my slippers and night dress 'til late in the aftehnoon and then, if one of my pitying friends didn't call and ask me for *sup*pah, I'd dress—*badly*—order cheese sandwiches from downstairs and then go to a bar on the corner of Fifty-first and Madison. It was a man's bar but they didn't meddle with a lady if she sat at a table and minded her own business, which I did, as I was very serious about getting fully *plastered* each and every night of my life. Nightfall is the worst when your best friend and your lover is gone and won't *ev*er return. I remember the shudder that would seize my stomach each night when the streetlamps lit up—that inexorable sign of nightfall in Manhattan. That meant rush into some clothes and escape the apahtment before it closes in . . . smothers. Are you familiar with that smothering sort of sadness yet? Oh, I hope you never are.

THERE you are, Connie.

CONNIE: Mrs. Violets?

VIOLET: Give old Violet some more buttah, will you? I'm not a sparrow, darling, I need to eat! And so does Balzac. He likes butter on his bread as well.

CONNIE: The bread is not for ze dog. Mrs. Violets, theese dog do not belong in—

VIOLET: Please, Constantinopolis, don't needle me! Cahn't you see I'm talking to this perfectly wonderful girl?

CONNIE: So pretty, honey. Where you come from?

The young woman smiles tolerantly.

VIOLET: Yes, isn't she pretty? Now, go and get the buttah. Where was I? I was telling you what became of me when El went and died.

I was miserable and awful for FIVE years—not one, not two, but FIVE. Yes! Self-pity is a terrible terrible thing.

YOUNG WOMAN: Don't be so hard on yourself. You were in grief.

VIOLET: Grief? Well, that was the trouble, y' see. I *wouldn't* grieve, I wouldn't admit that El was gone. 'Til one day. I remember it well. It was July 12, 1971. A friend called and she asked me to a *pah*ty and when I made my (by that point) *cus*tom'ry refusal this friend of mine *tore* into me. She said there wouldn't be any more parties for me because I'd become one of the most miserable persons she knew. She said, "I don't know who *you* are, but my friend Violet

Smith would never've behaved like this, she'd've pulled herself together and gone on! I guess *she* died when Elliot Cubert died, because I haven't seen hide nor tail of her since!" And she hung up on me. Well! I'd neveh been hung up on in my life and I'd neveh expected to be, pahticul'ly not by one of the most well-mannered individuals I'd ever known.

She stops and pauses for effect. She takes a quick glance around the room.

VIOLET: Twas 'round twelve noon. I ran into the bedroom, *threw* myself on the bed, and had a *rully* good weep. And I held on to these two pillows for deah life. Squeezed them and punched them and— I'll tell you a secret, deeah, I even *kiss*ed one of them. Then I—

Constantine sets down the butter. She butters a roll.

VIOLET: Thank you, Connie. Here, Balzac, here's some nice fresh bread and buttah dipped in some nice, FLAVUHLESS soup.

My deeah, I'll tell you, and I don't know why but I've neveh told anyone this part, though it's much less shameful than the part about being a lush and *that* I've told . . .

She knits her brow and looks up to calculate a moment, then gives a grimace and a shrug.

VIOLET: HALF of New Yawk. But then I did the queerest—and I mean *quee*r, not queer—queerest thing. I looked at those two pillows and I remembered buying them with Elliot when we first rented the flat togetheh. I remembered how Elliot in pahticulah had wanted a good set of goose-down pillows. And that's what we'd got, we hadn't spared any expense, we'd got the best. And I remembered all the nights our two heads'd rested on those pillows, the nights Elliot had held me—as no one should ever *be* held—

Violet looks penetratingly into her listener's wide-open eyes to emphasize how dangerous it is to be made to feel completely safe.

VIOLET: And how Elliot looked with both pillows under his head before the ambulance came to get him. Gray skin, smiling, *teas*ing me. And I *seized* these two pillows by the scruff of their—and I *flung* them loose of their cases and I brought them to the window and ripped them *wide apaht*. The fabric was *old* and yellow and tore easily. And from out of these *old* pillows came a stream of virgin goose feathers. I watched them float gently down . . . onto the hats and

ever

taxis and newstands of Fifth Avenue—white and soft and slow. People stopped, looked up, and tried to push them back with their arms. At precisely that moment I heard Elliot laugh and say, "You really are a misfit!" And I knew I was over it. And I knew I had to leave the apahtment immediately. So I did.

She casts a disparaging eye around the diner.

VIOLET: That's how I came to live in this FOOL's paradise we call the Upper East Side. Twenty-three years. I moved up here and I never once looked back. But I've always thought it was those pillows that got me over it and, there, you see, now you're the first one I've told.

She looks down at Balzac.

VIOLET: Balzac, sit still! And stop that whimpering!

CHAPTER 8

IN WHICH CARLITO WRITES TO ELIZABETA

One evening from his trailer, Carlos writes this letter to his wife in Spanish:

CARLITO: Dear Elizabeta,
This morning at dawn on Mr. Schmidt's farm, we found a white lady, as white as the moon, lying there in the fields. I was barely awake. I just had some coffee and some bread in my stomach so I was rubbing my eyes to see that I wasn't dreaming. But all the men were staring. Jorge, the one I told you who will never stop whistling, he was quiet for once and started to pray. Me, I thought she was a vision, she lay so quiet, nude under the cold brussels sprout plants. The dew laid on her as it did on the leaves and I thought, "She may be the Virgin or a saint come to give us some kind of message or guide." But then she sneezed and I thought, "She may be a witch or a demon come to curse us and maybe immigration will get Manuel and Helacio and me and the others." The Chicano guys, who are *no* as religious as we, went inside Mr. Schmidt's shed and took straw from there to cover her. Then they ran down the road and called the sheriff from a telephone. We were afraid the sheriffs might bother us, but we didn't want to miss the day. We had already missed the cool hours for picking. The sun was out on our shoulders by now. The police came and took the girl away. They said all night they had searched for her in the sea. Wrapped in a blanket, I could then see she was an ordinary *gringa* but how strange, *no*? I thought I saw a vision in the plants. What would we have called her? Our Lady of the Brussels Sprouts? I miss you and the children. Please kiss them. Here is some money for you, sweetheart.
Love, *Su Esposo*,
Carlito.

CHAPTER 9

IN WHICH CLOVE CONFOUNDS THE AUTHORITIES

The Santa Cruz County Sheriff's Department has Clove at a table in handcuffs. They have some hard questions for her. She tries to answer to the best of her ability, but it is difficult. The light is bright and she has had quite a night so far.

CLOVE: A thousand points of light. Who said that? Was that from something? Oh ggggggggoddddddddess protect me, the sheriffs are coming at me with a thousand light points stabbing my eyelids like broken lightbulb slivers cutting inside my sockets beyond whur the light has a right to go. Can't you dudes turn down the lights? Then I'll answer all the questions you need, ANTsered in yer pant-sers, oh, Officer Deputy, let me see yer hand, whoah, those are kind fingers you got. Just the middle two, I can see better right now can't you dudes see? That I can see better?

OFFICER ONE: I can see that your pupils are pinpoints, young lady. What does *that* tell us?

CLOVE: What? Ha ha ha, yah, Ossifer. Yer smartness is awesome to behold! My eye pupils are pinned, yah, 'cause yer light is pinning them in a thousand points! Ah, turn off the lights er I'll puke, we can all see better in the dark, you dudes have like no notion of what the light grains are doing to you— yer stomachs and yer hair and yer balls,

Clove shudders.

CLOVE: No notion of the ocean either, hey, why'd you pull me out of there, Ossifer? Put down the Styrofoam yur drinking so I can see yer fingers better, those're kind fingers you got, I'm not sure about the rest of yer personification but yer two fingers have got it goin'

on. Those fingers could go places. In the sky in the sand inside of seashells. Hey! maybe the crabs would bite 'em. Rage on, aha ha ha, then you'd be lucky, that's how they communicate, snab, snab, snab, say the crab crab crab!

She collapses in slurpy giggles while imitating the crabs with her legs.

OFFICER ONE: Excuse me, young lady. Why don't you calm down and tell us who made you get like this?

CLOVE: Who made me like this? Um, my parents!

Hey, on that subject, amn't I suppose to be with 'em fer you to be waxing all interrogational and shit? Watch out! Thur not like me. I like you dudes except fer yer crazy ice cube lights slicing the vision off with thur cold *razor edges*. OW! *OW*!

She tries to hide her head.

CLOVE: But I'm telling you, dudes, chill out with my parents, they were in antinuclear scenes, they'll be agged I even talked, they'll be agged I got up and walked with you dudes from offa that underwater brussels sprout farm and didn't practice civil dis like I was born to. Wull, how would you do underwater civil dis, right? How did you dudes get down there, anyway? I'm surprised you didn't have on Jacques Cousteau uniforms and shit. Hey, Ossifer, be nice, don't scream at me or I'll cry, we were so chill down there in the underwater farm, you were whispers. Whoah. Take off these handbracelets, right? I'm starting to bad trip, you dudes are getting all scary. Let me hold those kind fingers, dude, just one? One?

OFFICER ONE: I'm getting pretty fed up here.

OFFICER TWO: You need ta tell us who sold you the drugs you're on.

CLOVE: Oh dudes, don't yell at me. No one sold me drugs!

OFFICER ONE: It's pretty clear you're doin' Ecstasy, right?

CLOVE: I don't know what ecstasy means. Is this ecstasy? It was before you dudes got all hectic with me. Now it's HEX-tasy. Stop! stop! a thousand points of light are eating up my eyes like thermometers broken in half and stabbing. 'Kay 'kay 'kay! I'll tell you, I'll tell you who got me high and raving, 'kay? 'kay? I'll tell you who organized the rave! I don't know thur names—thur was a group of 'em—but I'll show you how they looked. They did a dance in a circle to the moon. Unkey the cufflets and I demon-straight! Unkey, unkey.

ever

The officer takes off her handcuffs.

CLOVE: Thankee, Deputee, I knew yer two fingers'd do it. Okay, this is how they looked like.

>   She squats on the floor with her arms thrust up through her knees and begins to scuttle across the police station like a crab.

CLOVE: And this is what they said:

Ha ha! Hee hee!

Oh come, young scamp, and turn yer lunar hoof

This way and that among our saline *hood*

We'll teach yer toes with bitings glad and wise

To know yer bleedings as we know the tides

So tithe us with yer heartbeat and yer breath

Slip breathless down into our rusty caves

And don the slippery bodice of the brine

and drink th'immortal absinthe o' green waves!!

>   Still in crab mode, Clove bites the officer.

OFFICER ONE: Hey, let go my fingers! Get the cuffs! Ah, sheesh, Glen. Take her away, let her watch TV 'til she calms down.

>   The officers think it best to recuff Clove at this point.

CLOVE: No no no no, ow, Officers! I can't calm down, we're in a bad place, I'm trying to save you, no, I don't wanna watch TV, that's telehypnology, the brussels sprouts told me, it enters yer brain through celebrities' eyes and it forces everyone to see the same thing!! Don't take me to the TV cell, please, please, please, the light hurts, we all hurt, oh ggggoddddddess, I'm gonna throw up, Officers, I'm—

>   Unfortunately at this moment, Clove cannot help but commence throwing up. The officers are not pleased.

CLOVE: Start at one place and reach out in *un*straight lines in *differ*ent directions and you'll get whur you wanna go. That's all I can tell you. The ecstasy is over now.

>   She heaves up a final puke.

CLOVE: That's all.

what

CHAPTER 10

IN WHICH PAUL RESORTS TO RESPIRATORY REMEDIES

In a posh studio apartment on the Upper East Side a woman in her very late thirties with a once-beautiful, tensile face sits cross-legged on her afghan rug, eyes closed, fingers in yoga-mudra, palms up on either knee. Paul paces the fine, polished parquet floors, taking in the view from the fifteenth-story window, then turns back to her with anxious eyes.

PAUL: Well, Jeanette, I like the way you redid the place. It's more you, isn't it? Is it? I've known you all these years, Jean, but I don't really know you, do I? You threw me for a loop on the phone there, Jean. I was sweating, anyway, because of how we left off our relat— er, er, arrangement, well, what do we call it? I always thought it was a relationship, I've always cared very much for you, Jeanette, and I'm sorry about the last few—y-y-years. You got my apologies on that. It's since I retired from the office, I'm either home with Polly in Virginia or I'm flying around the world giving these lectures and sitting in on these damn board meetings. The corporation *never* lets go.

Paul bumps his head on a string of uncut crystals suspended from the ceiling. He turns to look, pokes them.

PAUL: Are those magic crystals hanging there, Jeanie? Heh? I knew I never should've bought you that Shirley MacLaine book in the airport in Honolulu that time. No, just a joke. Look, I laughed. You made me feel human again.

But, as I was saying, Jean—are you gonna sit still like that forever?

He looks down at Jeanette in meditation pose. She doesn't move. He clears his throat.

PAUL: Uh, I always thought myself very fortunate in a myriad of ways and one of them was to've met you, and when you told me you were done with, with, that side of your life, I was glad to hear it, Jeanette, even if it puts me on an awkward footing, not knowing where I— I've always liked treating a woman like a— Well, I'm putting my foot in it. Speaking of which, how do you get your feet crossed that way? Let me try that.

He tries to join her there, leaning one arm on her white sofa, but he only succeeds in twisting to the floor, legs skewed.

PAUL: WH-WH-WH-WHOOPS! Heh heh! You always did teach me new tricks, Jean. Sorry, that's not— Y-y-uh . . . Yep—sorry. You didn't use to be so quiet. You want me to go? I just—

JEANETTE: Breathe, Paul.

Her mouth has a permanent turned-down aspect. Her voice is at once world-weary and brittle, a sultry voice but with a nasal whine. He breathes in and out windily, as if at the doctor's.

PAUL: The luncheon was a nightmare. I was giving my speech and then all hell broke out in me. I went in the men's room and spewed up the entire luncheon.

Jeanette gives him a glance from under her lids. She is always curious about catered meals. He registers this, remembers her curiosity in this regard.

PAUL: It was Cornish game hens and vegetable bundles and some raspberry dessert thing, I don't know! I spewed it up, Jeanie! I went off the deep end. Like one of those gaskets on a lawn sprinkler just flew off and was gushing, everywhere, flooding everyone's lawns. I suppose, if that happened they'd take my lawn away from me— declare it a wetlands! Jean, these environmentalists try to regulate all of us out of existence and now they've got my daughter Sheila involved with them.

Jeanette tries to concentrate solely on her breathing.

PAUL: Suppose they did? They'd take me off the boards. No more speaking tours. No more executive pension plan. No more . . . You could be the ranger, Jeanette. Jeanette? Listen? I'm cracking up here, I'm—

JEANETTE: Breathe, Paul.

what

PAUL: This isn't intercourse, Jeanette, we're not—

JEANETTE: But you always forgot to breathe *then* too. Breathe.

Paul breathes again in big oversized gulps. The breaths turn to big, gasping sobs.

PAUL: Guh! Guh! GUHHHH!

ever

CHAPTER 11

IN WHICH CLOVE CONFIDES
IN SABLE

Clove relaxes in the hammock in her family den, making a call on the cordless phone.

CLOVE: Hannah? Could you put Sable on the phone? Hannah! Sable! Give me Sable! Tuhhhh . . .

She exhales an exasperated breath.

CLOVE: Children agg me to such excess at times. Sable? It's Clove. Hi. Yah. Yah. No, I'm alright. Are you in trouble? Gah. I'm sorry. What's that humming sound on the line? Oh, yer parents are chanting. Gah, I'm so relieved my parents aren't Buddhists. Are they all agged and stuff about me almost drowning at the rave and getting arrested and like that? Gah, yer parents are so overly righteous er something. I'm not sure it doesn't matter nevermind. Wull, it's not yer fault. You were trying to find me. Why do they always get all blaming with you—yes they do, thur all, wull, yur all to blame and stuff. I know they call it karma but I don't get the difference. Wull, do you? It doesn't matter nevermind. *An*yway. No, my parents are calm, at first they were all indignant that I talked to the state troopers and didn't go all silent and recite my rights and stuff, but they didn't get all hectic like they usually do all "Don't take drugs like I did, LSD almost ruined our marriage" blah blah blah blah blah. They were kinda nontypically all quiet. Yah, I think my mom is freaked that I'm a teen suicide risk er something. I know! We were on *Suicide Watch—Actual Deaths*! I know! I can't believe it. My little brother Kyler taped it fer me. Did you dis that Petal Poo PJ Dawn Maggotstrella or what*ever* her name is? I know! Thur like all, "Is she gonna commit suicide er er?" I know they wanted me to be drowned. No! Sable?! Is this you? No, I was just being all excessive in the water under the moonlight, it was making this crescent cookie shape like the moon was cutting cookies in the back of my head even though I was looking the other way and the crabs were talking to me. It doesn't matter, nevermind. It's too complex. I *can't*. Wull, yah, I was with that dude Skitter. No? Oh yah, Skeeter. Wull, yah. Yah, we were by the cave by that dead sea lion, er walrus, whatever. Do you think he's flaccid and weak or do you think he's rad? Right on, I'm so relieved. Yah, wull we got slithery. Yah that's when I went to the waves to wash his—

She looks around to make sure no one can hear her, whispers.

CLOVE: protein shake off my hands. My hands! Sable! I didn't like him that much! You do? Did something happen while I was drowned? Whoah, you poached on me, you treacherous slut! Gah! Now *that's* bad karma! Just kidding! Doesn't matter nevermind. So do you rully want to hear? You promise you won't think I'm all Juliette Lewis? Right on.

I go to the waves and the ocean started talking, er, singing to me, it's like the ocean was this green spreading gown and it was pulling me *in* it. And then these crabs were all biting my toes. That's how they communicate. Oh, yah! You should see my toes,

She looks down at her bare toes and wiggles them a little.

CLOVE: they are all wretchedly butchered. It's gruesome in excess. But anyway, the crabs were pulling my toes and teaching me how to dance this crazy turning pattern fer the moon and then I could live under the waves and give the ocean something back fer us destroying it. Like me fer the sea lion, a life fer a life? I know! You said you—yah, isn't it ragin'? Yah! So I guess I was far out on the rocks and the waves were slashing all about me and I see this seahorse-man crashing and ragin' way way out in the middle of it and I— Sable, girl-dude, he was excessively real, do you believe me? Rad—and Skitter—yah, I mean Skeeter—was calling me and I don't remember what I answered but I jumped in and the next thing I knew I was swirling around in the waves and then I see this white white dude pushing the sea horse back under the waves and he's pulling back the dress of the waves to keep it from going over my head and he floats over the ocean to me and he says, "This is way fucked," and he leads me what I thought was way underwater and

ever

over underwater mountains and into an underwater farm, but it turned out, the state troopers told me, I had got in this cave and crawled over these rocks up a cliff and across the road to the brussels sprout farm whur they arrested me!

So this way pale dude leaves me there. And Sable, this is fiendishly odd, don't spaz, he goes, he's all, "Don't tell people you saw me," and I'm all, Who are you anyway? Sable promise not to tell anyone? Vow? Right on. He's all, "I'm Cobain the Friendly Ghost." I'm being ex*cess*ively real. This was *totally* realistic! I was all, Whoah, Kurt. I know! I know we don't even like Nirvana's music. Wull, *In Utero* is a good album. It is. Nevermind. No, I mean never mind, not *Nevermind.*" *Any*way, nevermind. Isn't it? What? Wull, tell yer parents to thwack off, I thought they were chanting anyway. Oh, is that why the insect sound stopped? Just kidding doesn't matter nevermind. Alright. I'm fine. I'm fine. Yer parents are so hectic. You should just be relieved thur not all Hare Krishna like Sari's parents. Is she grounded too? I'm sorry. Godddd-duh-duh-duh-duh-dessss. Mmmkay. Yah, sure. 'Kay bye.

She hangs up abruptly, without a blink.

CHAPTER 12

IN WHICH BUSHIE IS SURPRISED
AT THE ALL-WASH

Bushie and her pimp, Terry, stand in front of a washing machine arguing as Bushie forages through a garbage bag of clothes and Terry
loads.

BUSHIE: Terry, no no no yuh doin' it wrong, da detergent goes in
dere, in dere, stupid-ass, give it tuh me, here put my pink ting—

TERRY: What?

BUSHIE: Put my pink ting in too, it stinks uh come.

TERRY: Bush people's lookin'. Shut yuh mout'.

BUSHIE: What? I don't care if people look. Dey can kiss my butt.
Don' tell me you embarrass. Are you a man? Oh, I forgot you
a pimp.

Terry takes a swing at her, which she ducks. Then he walks out of the
Laundromat.

BUSHIE: Terry, where you going? Terry, I ain't gonna fold yuhr
wrinkly-ass shirts so you better be back here by da time dey dried or
I trow 'em away, I don't care. Yes! He could slap me, people, I'm not
afraid, enough is enough. Shit, he didn't put da detergent in right. I
gotta get some. Excuse me, miss, I'm tryin' tuh get tuh da detergent
machine—wait wait wait is dat you?

She stops short and stares at a scarred but beautiful Puerto Rican
woman frozen in shock before her.

MAGENTA: Bushie?

BUSHIE: Yes. Magenta Rush! Oh girl, where you been? Oh girl, oh
my God, oh my God, look at you, you straight now, you dressed like
a church girl.

MAGENTA: Yeah. I can't believe is you. Is—oh wow. I thought you
might be—

BUSHIE: What? You thought I was dead? Not Bushie, not me, remembah Lit'l Louis?

MAGENTA: Yeah.

BUSHIE: He died. He OD'd.

MAGENTA: Yeah? Daz too bad. God bless him.

BUSHIE: Oh wow, you *are* religious.

MAGENTA: Yeah, I been saved, Bushie, you can be saved too. Lemme give you da numba at aw church.

BUSHIE: Oh my God! Remembah how crazy we useta be? Remembah: "ABC, Easy as One Two Tree," hah hah hah, numba one, numba two, and numba tree, remembah girl, we made *MON*EY and we—I wasn't hooked up yet, I was dabblin', we useta dabble some wack shit, remembah? Angel? Mesc? We useta drive around wit' Sambo and Tony Pony? Dose boys were funny.

MAGENTA: I don't talk about those things anymore, Bushie. What happened to Tony Pony?

BUSHIE: Oh girl, you were crazy ovah him, yeah, now it comes back, you had tuh have da—

> Bushie makes a vacuum-sucking sound and holds her hands to her womb, pantomiming an abortion.

MAGENTA: Please! Bushie!

BUSHIE: I'm sorry. Magenta Rush, baby, I can't get ovah—I thought you was dead, I—

MAGENTA: I almost was. My real name is Magdalena.

BUSHIE: Yeah, Magdalena Rigobar, right, see, I remember dat shit. We were tight tight, we gonna be tight again now I found you.

MAGENTA: What happened to Tony Pony?

BUSHIE: Aw, he was alright, dat's da sad thing. He joined da Marines and he cleaned up and den he got killed in a accident in dat last Saddam war dey had. Are you sad? Aw, Magenta, I mean Magdalena. I dunno, whatever, friggin' great tuh see you again.

MAGENTA: It's good to see you also, Bushie, but you look—

BUSHIE: Look what?

> Mags flicks her eyes up and down Bushie in the street-girl shorthand for disgust.

MAGENTA: *You* know.

what

BUSHIE: Yeah, I know, but I'm'a change. Now I see you, I know I will, we gonna hang out every day like we useta.

MAGENTA: I'm married now. My name is Magdalena Johnson.

BUSHIE: Yeah? What's yuhr old man do?

MAGENTA: My husband sells Bibles wholesale to Christian bookstores. Daz where I work now, in a Christian bookstore.

BUSHIE: No shit, fuh real? And yuh husband deals books?

MAGENTA: He doesn't DEAL them, he—

BUSHIE: Yeah, yeah, I'm sorry.

MAGENTA: Lemme give you dee address of dee church. Dey are classes for people like us every day, Bushie, you can come, you can be *saved*.

BUSHIE: Will I see you?

MAGENTA: My husband doesn' like me to go out tha' much, but we always go to church at ten every Sunday.

BUSHIE: Remembah Candy?

MAGENTA: Yeah?

BUSHIE: She got murdered.

MAGENTA: God bless huh.

BUSHIE: God *didn't* bless huh, she got found in tree different parts, down Eleventh Avenue. Not fuh nuttin' but Terry's Uncle Francis useta call dat Death Avenue. Lemme help you fold yuh sheets, yuh're crammin' 'em in da bag.

Mag tears the sheets away and rushes to the exit.

MAGENTA: I gotta go, Bushie.

BUSHIE: I *LOVE* YOU, Magenta Rush!

Mag swings around, her eyes flash with anger.

MAGENTA: MAGDA*LENA*!

She catches herself, regains her Christian demeanor, speaks haltingly.

MAGENTA: I . . . love you . . . too, Bushie. Take cay-uh. Jesus love you.

BUSHIE: Yeah. Bye. I'll see you soon.

She waves at Mag's rapidly receding figure.

BUSHIE: Bye. Wow. I can't believe it. Magenta Rush! Dis is gonna be a good day, I could feel it. I could feel it.

Bushie mutters to herself.

BUSHIE: I'm'na get high.

ever

CHAPTER 13

IN WHICH VIOLET RECALLS
A SEA-CHANGE

On a Sunday afternoon, Violet and Iris find themselves once again at the counter of the Blue Ship Diner.

VIOLET: I'm remembering, uh, that I used to have these idiotic arguments about jazz. For *years* no one other than me thought that jazz was serious music. Yes, Balzac, thank you for barking. That *does* mean that Violet is smarter than everyone else. I'd find myself in these *dull* arguments, passionate *dull* arguments with these very handsome fellows who'd be smiling at me far too much while I defended jazz. Can you imagine such a conversation nowadays? No one—

IRIS: Well, I still think jazz was partly responsible for the decay—

VIOLET: Oh, of course *you* do, Iris. I meant a *mod*ern person, I meant someone with a *full set* of teeth. No, Balzac, be quiet, or we'll be evacuated again. Speaking of evacuations, Iris, did I ever tell you the story of my last passage home from Europe, before the war?

IRIS: Yes, *sev*eral times.

VIOLET: Well . . .

She sits nonplussed for a moment.

VIOLET: I'm going to tell it to you again!

There were *hideous* people on board this ship. First class was composed entirely of *hid*eous people, aside from Bill, my husband but—anyway, there were two American families who supported Hitleh, they were big fans of Hitleh, uh, there were . . . some German businessmen, and their wives, and there was, uh, an Austrian and an Ital— a Frenchman who never quite told us what their business was—it wasn't clear, but it was quite clear that they were cultured, intelligent, *hideous* people who loved to inf*u*riate Bill and get him to argue with them, which was the *stu*pidest thing to do. We'd sit there, in the captain's parlor, night afteh night, when we could've been playing cards and Bill would *argue* with them 'til he was sick. Later on, in the cabin, he'd lit'rally be *sick* all night from arguing with these people. And uh, uhh—

IRIS: I know the story, Vi, I—

VIOLET: Just let me finish! Don't interrupt. Not ladylike. So the only person on board whom I could stand—well, there was a Jewish girl who was a prostitute—a refugee, working her passage across. Uh, there were a good number of prostitute-refugees, uh, at that time, uh, before the war.

IRIS: Yes, I know, I was alive too, I have my *own* stories and I don't need to—

VIOLET: Yes!!! So—and there was also this little Portugese first mate and he had a gramophone he hoarded in his cabin and we listened to these sweet little boleros he'd collected from the Canary Islands. And I'd bring out my vaunted Paris *jazz* discs and we'd dance 'round, bump into things, and have a *rully* SWELL time!

    Violet laughs.

VIOLET: Well, one night I couldn't stand it any longer. There was Bill with, eh, the Frenchman, and the Austrian, arguing away, *red* in the face about whether the Negroes were apes and whether the Jews were dirty and you cahn't *ar*gue with these sorts of ideas, y'see. And I jumped up and I ran to the little first mate and I said give me your gramophone. And he was so bewildered he didn't—I said, give me your gramophone! And I went and *seized* my Paris 78s! The best! (I wish I still had every last one of those.) And I *marched* back to the captain's parlor, *cranked* it up, *put it* on, and Bill said, What're you doing? He hadn't even noticed I'd left, y'see. I said, I'm going, ladies and gentlemen, to do a little demonstration—

IRIS: Shh! Violet, the whole restaurant is—

VIOLET: —a little demonstration of how the Negroes and the Jews spend THEIR spare time. And then I danced and I danced, and I danced, and I danced, and I shimmied and I shaked and I rolled—

    She begins to do just this, rolling her old shoulders, shaking her bosom from side to side. Her voice is quivering.

IRIS: Violet, please!

ever

VIOLET: And I did it all night as wildly and vulgarly as I possibly could, with the records playing *again* and *again*. 'Til they all SHUT UP.

There is a bit of a pall of silence over the diner at this juncture and Violet seems to only just now take note of it. She lowers her voice a hair.

VIOLET: 'N everyone was very embarassed, pahticul'ly Bill. And afteh that, no one spoke to us for the rest of the trip!

She smiles victoriously.

IRIS: Yes, that's right and the following year your marriage went sour.

VIOLET: Yes, that's right. That was the same year you had the affair with the two twins who were killed in the war—

IRIS: Violet, you're rude and you're loud and this is the last Sunday that—

VIOLET: Oh forgive.

Violet takes Iris's hand in both of her hands and pats it beseechingly.

VIOLET: Forgive me, deeah, forgive. I just think it's very important we remember who we *rully* were. No one else will.

what

PART TWO

HOMEMAKING

CHAPTER 1

IN WHICH CLOVE ENCOUNTERS STRANGE GIRLS

Clove walks in a shadowy land, her breath slow and even.

CLOVE: He is neither of this world nor the next. He waits by the shore, drawing the breath of the young and the near-death. He is Cobain the Friendly Ghost, and he is singing in my ear, enough to tickle but not yet enough to hear the tune. But I don't want to listen. I run fer the redwoods, and, Sable, I got lost in the redwoods, loose brushes were giving me goose pimples, I tripped on a root and went somersaulting down this gorge, rolling in the wet soil, that almost-mud, 'til I was covered in it and scratched by the blackberry vines, and my nose was running from the fog. I thought, This is a strange place, Mendocino, when shall I return to Santa Cruz? And I lay there in the bottom of the gorge in a daze, half un-there, then I opened my eyes and I saw IT. And I saw THEM. IT was a FORT, made out of tree branches and mud and on top fake fur and colored barrettes and doll heads and play lipsticks and tiny tea sets and doll legs and Barbie vanity mirrors and tiny pots and pans sets and Hello Kitty compacts and hair baubles, and THEM was the ten girls: Jana and Gina, and Tessa and Melissa, Millicent and Juniper, and Anya and Monika. And Lydia. And Gelsam Marie. They all stood there in hiking boots and boys' kite-print long johns and blackberry leaf bras. About three to five years younger than me and you. Between eleven and thirteen years old, I would ESSSSSSStimate. They stood guarding thur fort, pink plastic pitchforks clutched in thur fists, and they said, "Welcome, welcome to the Sex Club Controlled BY GIRLS. We do everything we want here. We're a sex club, as in pornography, as in what men pay to go to, but thur are no men: thur are only our dads, and they are carpenters er stoners . . . er both. And thur are no boys: thur are only our brothers and they are surfers or acid heads . . . or both. And so we are a sex club. Controlled. BY GIRLS! Come in."

And so, Sable, I went . . . Inside it was warm, the walls and roof were low and lined with girls' underwear—all flower prints, 100-percent cotton—so this kept it very insulated and very warm. And thur were platforms, but they weren't raised, they were sunken into the earth and lined with magazine cutouts: One was all pictures from *National Geographic* of wolves and apes and husky hounds and polar bears and tigers and killer whales and snakes and newts and bats and praying mantises. One was lined with pictures from auto magazines, of engines and spark plugs and gas tanks and race car wrecks and keys and ignitions and leather interiors and motors and multitread tires and steering wheels and *Digital. Control. Displays.* And one was lined with all male musicians, of heavy metal howlers and salsa singers and saxophone blowers and drum pounders and chest naked superstars and gnarly speed guitarists and pretty hairy men all in rows. And the last was lined in one part only of women's bodies from all the man magazines, except just one part only, scissored out and glued all together into a collage. It wasn't the stuck-out breast parts . . . or the smooth hot dog buns . . . or the don't-squeeze-the-Charmin bellies. And it wasn't the spread, glycerining cunt lips either, it was another part—the eyes. Just the EYES looking-back-over-the-shoulder, JUST the eyes looking back. And even though it was JUST the eyes it could be told that each SET of eyes had been cut out from one of these magazines. It-could-be-told. It-just-could.

Each girl was invited to perform her own fantasy in her own sunken platform, which, they explained, was rully a PITFORM. "Would you like to?" they invited me. "Can it include boys?" I said. "IT is a fantasy," they said. "It can include whatever. But. It is controlled. BY GIRLS!!"

I got up, but the FORT was small and tight so I couldn't stand exactly . . . I squatted. And then I waddled over to the PITFORMS, staring down, one at a time, trying to choose. I couldn't decide. Finally, I chose the one with the auto parts. I lowered myself in. I felt

what

my foot-skin sink to the basin. I started to growl like a car, to whine like an engine trying to start.

Kyler, you woke me up, imbecilic boingo.

Clove wakes with a start in the backseat of her family car, alongside her little brother.

KYLER: I did not.

CLOVE: You did. With yer elbow in my tit.

Her father tries to start the car. The engine turns over.

CLOVE: Dad? What's going on? Are we all stalled er something? I thought I was dreaming . . .

KYLER: Were you havin' a wet dream?

CLOVE: Thwack off, Kyler.

Her father once again tries to rev the engine

CLOVE: Why do we even have to visit our limpid relations in Mendocino fer Thanksgiving anyway? It's so repetitive. Dad, you know I have to get back to Cruz fer Sable's slumber party. Yah? It's all-pervasive. Dad, are we all stalled? Dad?

The engine catches, then stalls out again.

DAD: Yes!

CLOVE: Tuhhhh. What. Ever. You don't have to wax all hectic, Dad, I just asked.

She licks her lips and stares ahead with indignant blankness.

ever

CHAPTER 2

IN WHICH SKEETER APPEALS TO HIS MOTHER

In a rented cottage on the outskirts of Portland, Oregon, a Wicca witch of the Northwest limps across her living room to extinguish her cigarette in a huge earthen ashtray filled with dozens of filterless cigarette butts. She is strikingly pretty, though deformed—the right portion of her face is slack and her right leg somewhat impaired. She moves with the assurance of a woman long accustomed to male desire and yet the damage both apparent in her body and latent in her bearing lends this assurance a spooky edge. The cats, though meowing hungrily, nonetheless give her a wide berth. As she flumes the last drag through flared nostrils, she selects a new cigarette from an ornately carved box and lights it with one of the many burning tallow candles placed throughout the crowded room. She stiffens as she hears an intruder at the door.

LINDA: Who's that?

SKEETER: Ma, it's Skeeter, open the lock.

Linda swings open the door and embraces him tightly.

LINDA: Ezekial!

They hug until Skeeter pulls away and awkwardly steps back from her.

SKEETER: Hey, Linda, lookin' good.

LINDA: You scruffy puppy, you dyed your hair blond.

Her voice is low and in that way similar to her son's sexy croak but it is distinguished by an air of weary skepticism, which is, in turn, underpinned by a forced mellowness.

SKEETER: Yeh-up, wull, I'se aimin' fer red but this girl from San Francisco gave me the wrong color.

LINDA: You're home. I'll burn homecoming alum. And allynwyd.

SKEETER: What. Ever. Rad.

LINDA: So,

She spits over her shoulder three times and disperses incense in the air.

LINDA: you've been shackin' up with punkettes in Frisco again, huh?

SKEETER: Linda, you show yer age. I'm no longer ten years old, I don't mosh no more, an' I steep with contempt fer San Francisco— it's a corpret town. Nuh, I was down near Santa Cruz at a rave.

LINDA: Oh yeah, raves, now I remember.

SKEETER: Oh yeah, remember me? I'm yer son.

LINDA: Don't get hexed, Ezekial Christian. Your vibration was so good when you walked in that door.

Skeeter speaks under his breath:

SKEETER: Fuck that hexy jinx. Wull, if you must know I came fer an underlying reason.

LINDA: All sons do.

SKEETER: Don't wax cynical, Linda.

LINDA: What do you want, child o' mine?

SKEETER: On the flip side, how's yer hip? The fake part maintainin'?

LINDA: It's okay. What did you come up to Portland for, Ezekial?

SKEETER: Wull, I'm stoked. I'm intrepidly stoked about—wull, yeh-up, uh . . .

LINDA: You're going to study magic and become a warlock?

SKEETER: Huh? Nuh, sorry, Linda, nuh, you and Aunt Jeanette are enough witchcraft in the fam, yeah? Nuh, it's it's—I am stricken with love!

LINDA: So blessings upon you!

She makes the sign of the pentacle on him.

LINDA: What's the prob? She doesn't love you?

SKEETER: Uh, I dunno about dat but 'at's not th' problem.

LINDA: Then what? She's my age?

She shrugs.

LINDA: She's got pagan-hating parents?

Her eyebrows shoot up.

LINDA: She's a he? That's fine.

SKEETER: Nuh, nuh! She-she-she-she's two. She's— I'm in love with the rad babe Clove who ran away from me and jumped in the sea and her ripe best friend, Sable, who stayed with me in the cave.

LINDA: Two babes? Oh Goddess in her deep hollow, you're just like Bruce.

SKEETER: Yo, Linda, don't be all rankin' on Bruce. He may o' been an asshole tuh you, but he was my fuckin' progenitor, right?

LINDA: *Two* girls. Two.

SKEETER: Clove an' Sable. They are the one for me, I know it! You gotta make me an enchantment.

LINDA: Oh no.

SKEETER: Ma? Please? Come on, get tranquil, get harmonized, think about it.

LINDA: No way, hombre, I'm not workin' my mojo for that kind of scene.

SKEETER: Yur so overly righteous at times, Linda.

LINDA: Call me what you want, puppy, but I'm not putting the craft to that negative use.

SKEETER: Wull, then, I'm gonna go visit Aunt Jeanette and get *her* tuh do it for me. Aunt *Jeanette* was always nicer, Aunt *Jeanette* was always helpin' me out. If it wasn't fer Aunt Jeanette, you'd have let me go hungry and dirty.

Skeeter kicks the furniture.

LINDA: Ezekial Christian, don't freak out!

SKEETER: 'S true! 'Til the accident you were gettin' all coked and stoked out. All tootin' and tokin'. You didn't even care if I went tuh school er er had anything, er er you—Aunt Jeanette cared—Aunt Jeanette bought me things. I'm gonna go visit Aunt Jeanette in New York City.

LINDA: How?

SKEETER: I'll *hitch*, like you taught me so *well*. How else?

LINDA: You think you can cut the cross-country hitching scene? They're different that way, you know. Can you handle Middle America? Can you deal with East Coast energy? I don't th—

SKEETER: I DON'T GIVE A FUCK!

LINDA: Don't cry, puppy.

SKEETER: I'm not!

He wipes tears on the too-long sleeve of his army jacket.

SKEETER: Yur so fucked up, yur so, I wanted you tuh fix it, yur so—

LINDA: Honey—

what

SKEETER: Leave me alone!

LINDA: Where you going?

SKEETER: To New York City!

LINDA: Ezekial! Come back! You just got home! Come back!

> The door rattles in his wake. She closes it slowly.

LINDA: I'll sprinkle red salt.

> She takes a long drag on her cigarette.

LINDA: He'll be back.

ever

CHAPTER 3

IN WHICH BUSHIE AND SNAPPLE DISCUSS THE PERILS OF DRUG ABUSE

It is late night on West Forty-fifth Street. Bushie and a good-looking young Italian-American whore in her midtwenties shiver in a pool of light under a street lamp, as if they hope its amber glow might warm them up a little.

BUSHIE: I was at da All-Wash Laundro, doin' me and Terry's shit an' I was in a good mood—happy—'cause I was up dere, you know, I was high, I had some. So I was doin' his socks, doin' our towels an' like that when I started addin' da fabric softnah an' I started tuh BUG. All dose straight people in da laundro started tuh look like zombies tuh me, an' I didn't want them tuh notice dat I was wacked so I kept starin' at da fabric softnah bot'l tuh chill out, I kep' starin' and starin' an' den I was starin' at da *reflection* of da label in da window of da washin' machine. An' it's goin' around an' around. I kept sayin', take deep breafs, Bushie, you in da All-Wash, on Tenf Avenue, you got Terry's jockey shorts in yuh left hand, you got da fabric softnah bot'l in yuh right hand, y' had something dusted, you a little *teeny weeny weentsy* bit wacked. But dat shit did *not* work because da more I stared—listen tuh me, Snapple!! Come on, don't drift, ain't you got a attention span? Damn, you young 'ho's're all channel-switchers. I HATE channel-switchers!

SNAPPLE: Don't freak, Bushie, I'm friggin' listenin', I'm listenin'! You's in da All-Wash doin' yaws and Terry da Pimps' clowthes. Yih-ah?

She has a strong Queens accent and one of the highest, squeakiest voices in all Christendom.

BUSHIE: Yeh, an' I'm watchin' da clothes spin and it's reachin' da soak cycle when yuh suppose t'add da softnah but I'm froze. On da label dere's a lady smilin' and holdin' up a bot'l wid a pitcha of anutta lady holdin' up a anutta bot'l wit' a pitcha of anutta—

SNAPPLE: Yih, yih yih! *Harry* up!

BUSHIE: An' so on

SNAPPLE: Yih-ah?

BUSHIE: An' I'm seein' huh reflected in da washa window an' she's spinnin' around and around an' she spins faster and faster and faster and suds're goin' and da-da-Terry's briefs are flippin' by an' it's goin' faster and da lady is in a RED CHECK DRESS smilin' outta da BLUE bot'l and den da label comes OFF in da wash and da lady's face BENDS and TURNS an' she's fuh real, she's spinnin' around an' around inside da wash machine an' sudsa comin outta huh mouf— huh mouf is like dis—

> Bushie demonstrates, smushes up her mouth as if it were smeared against glass, gurgles up spit.

BUSHIE: she's tryin' tuh *talk*, she's tryin' tuh say somethin', she's takin' off huh dress!

SNAPPLE: You wuh wacked! Beyond cracked, you wuh cracka jacked!

BUSHIE: She's screamin' an' shakin' an' finally I couldn't take no more of huh static, I opened up da machine—

SNAPPLE: In da middle of da *soak* cycle?

> Snapple can't believe it.

BUSHIE: Yeah, an' she came out screamin', "NO *MORE*, NO MORE STATIC CLING!"

SNAPPLE: Yih-ah?

BUSHIE: Yeh, dat's when I had convulsions and dey called EMS. Turns out it wasn't even *my* clothes. It was some CONDO-BOY's dirty-ass clothes. Dere were soap suds all ovah da floors. Halfa it was me. I was foamin' at da mouf and I was shakin'. Hard.

SNAPPLE: Shit, Bushie.

BUSHIE: I know, shit.

SNAPPLE: Terry's right, you gotta back off wit' dat.

BUSHIE: Terry, dat stupid-ass pimp, what does he know? Naw, I'm gonna reform like my homegirl from way back, Magenta Rush.

even

She's a Christian now. She went back tuh huh real name, Magdalena. She give me dee address of huh church. I'ma reform. Me an' Magenta— Magdalena gonna be tight again. Right now, I need some, though. You got five dolliz?

SNAPPLE: Frig dat, Bushie, go ask Our Lady of da Friggin' Fabric Softnah!

BUSHIE: Fuck you, Snapple.

SNAPPLE: Yuh're a lowlife, Bushie.

BUSHIE: Yeah? Well, yuh're a dumb *hoo*-aw.

SNAPPLE: Yuh're a ugly one.

> They stand there for a minute, facing each other down, shivering some more.

BUSHIE: Let's go tuh da *Ay*-rab's fuh chips. You wanna?

SNAPPLE: Awright, I need tuh warm up. Friggin' freezin', yih-ah?

BUSHIE: Yeah.

> They cross the street against the light, and head for The Three Brothers Deli.

CHAPTER 4

IN WHICH VIOLET SPEAKS OF RAINY DAYS AND MELANCHOLY

Violet sits on her sofa—a loveseat—in her cluttered living room one late morning. There is rain at the window. The captain's clock on the chiffonier strikes noon.

VIOLET: Balzac! Where're m' matches? Yes, you fetched the *Ches*tehfields but where're the matches?

He looks at the floor and then looks at her and barks twice.

VIOLET: Oh! Well, pick them up. Thank you, deeah, good poodle, *very* good. Mmmmm.

She lights her cigarette.

VIOLET: It's raining today. We won't go out. Gray days. Rainy days. Stay-at-home days, my mother liked to say. I used to get cross as hell being cooped up in the nursery in those days, early days. When? I was younger than YOU are, Balzy, why, f'God's sake, you're almost ten! Mad creature! Sit and listen, will you? Yes, wag your tail if you like. Drool all you want. There's a good boy.

It was a rainy day when I discovered the man in the garden. He was a boy, rully. It was just afteh the war let out. Hmph! Wars are like theater—you know it was very *good* when everyone comes *limp*ing out in a dead quiet. Then you know that it was ef*fec*tive. Well, World War I was *very* effective. Of course, I had only the dimmest idea of what war meant. The young man cleared the mist for me.

I met him on a drizzling aftehnoon in the garden. I escaped my stultifying siblings and ran over into the neighbors' garden. Manhattan homes *had* gardens then and they were *homes*, not stopping places with stackable plastic furniture and *tele*vision *con*soles! *Damn* it!

Balzac is alarmed and starts barking angrily.

VIOLET: Don't bark, I'm tired, Balzy. I want to tell you about Herman. He always lay out in a chaise lounge by the fish pond his family had. I met him that day in the rain. I asked him, "Why are you sitting out in the rain?" He answer'd, "Why are you playing?" "Because that's what I do." "Ah!" That's all he said. Ah! And then that dreadful breath in

Violet takes in a long, rattling breath.

VIOLET: uh, 'twas dreadful but *glor*ious. I'd never encountered a *mel*ancholy man before.

She puts out her cigarette.

VIOLET: He'd been an officer in the infantry. Discharged in 1918. I visited him every day. My mother disapproved. So I made a point of it.

Balzac bursts out barking.

VIOLET: Yes! Balzy, pre*cise*ly like you and the bah-throom carpet! *Very* shrewd poodle, *very* shrewd!

I made Herman mud pies decorated in the flowers we had, cocklebells and nasturtiums and honeysuckle, if I recall. He'd barely manage half a grin and then he'd set the pie down on the ground and stare off. Sometimes he hummed. Once he wrote me a po-em, eh I think I've still got it . . .

There was a little lass
Whom I met in a storm
She tiptoed up to me
And laid a tiny hand upon my arm.
Deah sir, she lisped. What is amiss?
And how I wished to tell
But alas, alas, alas
The little miss was but a lass
And I could not, would not, tell.

That was the first po-em I ever learned by heart. I *marv*elled at it. I had no idea what it meant but I loved to recite it to my fatuous elders because of the unsettling effect it had.

One day, quite a sunny day, a bee was chasing me and I jumped over the wall into Herman's family's garden. He lay there in the chaise lounge, very still. But, you see, Balzy, he was always still. I *snuck* up to him, stuck a finger in his ear. He moved not a hair. The

what

bee buzzed 'round. I *knew* and ran screaming from there. The adults came rushing out.

They said there was nothing wrong with him physically, but that he died of *nerv*ous exhaustion. I've always thought it was shock, a delayed sort of shock that caught up with him once he'd come home. Hmmm. Well, Balzac, let's phone Iris after all. She might like some lunch togetheh.

She turns toward the phone, quiet.

CHAPTER 5

IN WHICH SKEETER AND A NEW ACQUAINTANCE UNCOVER A SPATE OF COINCIDENCE

Skeeter finds himself by the side of a highway in the gray light of a waning day. Potato fields stretch flat on either side. He stands, thumb stuck out, mutters "shit" as each passing car swooshes by. A '70s-something rust-red Mustang comes into view, tears down the narrow highway, going at least ninety. It screeches to a halt a few yards past him and he runs to catch it. A red-haired guy with bushy eyebrows and a beard is inside puffing on a huge hand-rolled cigarette. He leans over and opens the low-slung car door.

MOCCASIN: How far ya goin'?

He has a voice like someone holding in a big toke on a joint and you can almost hear a swagger in it.

SKEETER: Wull, all th' way tuh New York City, but on th' penultimate swipe, tuh Indiana.

MOCCASIN: I'm headed north up through Montana and then tuh Rapid City, South Dakota, take ya dat far.

SKEETER: Most appreciated, dude.

MOCCASIN: Hop aboard,

The man rolls his eyes sideways at him as they speed off.

MOCCASIN: Private Idaho.

SKEETER: Heh heh heh. Yeh-up.

MOCCASIN: You look like you're about sixteen, what the cosmic fuck you doin' in the middle of Pocatello, Idaho, scout?

SKEETER: Hitchin' rides, you know.

MOCCASIN: Runaway?

SKEETER: Nuh.

MOCCASIN: No?

SKEETER: Nope. Just walked.

MOCCASIN: Yup. 'At's your generation. Walkaway. Huh. 'At's funny. You look like dat kid who died. Good actor, though. My old lady rented the movie after dat kid OD'd. Yeh-up. I don't care for dat homo shit and I fell asleep during 'at Shakespeare poetry bull but I have tuh say, all in all, I enjoyed it. I liked the kid. You look just like 'im and here you are hitchin' in Idaho. Strange. D'you see dat movie? *My Own Private Idaho*?

SKEETER: Naw.

MOCCASIN: Oh. Well it's called *My Own Private Idaho*. You look like 'im, you should see it. You look just like 'im.

SKEETER: Yeah, lotta people say I look like River.

MOCCASIN: Who?

SKEETER: River Phoenix? The dude that died?

MOCCASIN: Dat's his name? You *saw* the movie?

SKEETER: Nuh nuh I just know who he is, was, 'sall.

MOCCASIN: Yeah. P-p-p-people tell you you look like 'im?

SKEETER: Yeh-up. *Girls* do. All the time.

MOCCASIN: Hey, SCOUT! I ain't no homo!

SKEETER: Null that implication at the base, dude. No one said det you were—are. What. *Ev*er.

MOCCASIN: Right!

SKEETER: Right.

MOCCASIN: Name's Joe Moccasin, kid, yours?

SKEETER: Ezekial. But my friends call me Skeeter 'cause I annoy 'em in a mosquito-type manner.

MOCCASIN: Yeah, why?

SKEETER: Ah, I wager I talk overmuch.

MOCCASIN: Don't do dat to me, Skeet, not if you wanna ride all the way tuh Rapid City. I HATE people who talk too much.

SKEETER: Most assuredly. I won't, then.

MOCCASIN: Yeah, some people can never stop talkin'. Picked up a kid near L.A., sposeta take him to Salt Lake, dropped him in Vegas. Ugly little bastard. Punk rock pimple head, you know?

He puts out his cigarette in a cloud of exhalation disgust.

MOCCASIN: An' he wouldn't stop talkin'. 'Bout anarchy. Said he got

ever

thrown out of some crash pad in San Francisco 'cause he stole a little chick named Brigit's antique bread box. But he wouldn't admit he stole it, refused to recognize ownership.

Moccasin looks back and forth between the road and Skeeter as he rolls a new cigarette with both hands, propping his hands against the wheel as a precaution.

MOCCASIN: He said they were all *up*tight—part of the po*lice* state 'cause they believed the antique bread box belonged to Brigit.

He sticks it in his mouth.

MOCCASIN: I left 'im to the loose slot machines in Vegas. And I stole 'is lighter.

He takes a Zippo off the dashboard, clanks it open, lights up, clanks it closed, and tosses it back down.

MOCCASIN: Little *fuck*.

SKEETER: Was 'is name Cyrus?

Skeeter rolls his eyes slowly toward Moccasin, inclining his head slightly more in the man's direction.

MOCCASIN: Yeah! How'd you know?

SKEETER: I know that asshole. Useta float the punk scene in Frisco. He's terminally thievin' girls' shit.

MOCCASIN: You don't look like a punk rock.

SKEETER: No more, friend, 'at was when I was twelve'n shit. Now I rave, brother.

MOCCASIN: Yeah? I heard about dat. Dat's cool. We did all dat back in the sixties. All dat stuff you kids do? We did all dat thirty years ago.

SKEETER: What.

He looks out the window.

SKEETER: Ever.

Moccasin glances at him.

MOCCASIN: We did. It's all a repeat. We got high. We got higher 'an you. We *ball*ed everyone.

He clears his throat.

MOCCASIN: I mean, we balled all the chicks. See, I'm hep, I just don't like to hear this political bull. I'm inta gettin' high, ballin'—dat's cool—but when people start talkin' about takin' other people's property, livin' without money, not workin', 'at's when I start to get

what

pissed. We got to return to our tra*dit*ional values we GOT to, I mean, we got to keep *jobs* for Americans you know? And we got to keep our borders *clean*, you know? You *know*?

SKEETER: Sure, dude.

MOCCASIN: Two problems. Immigrants and politicians. Those're the two main problems we have. Dat's why I voted for Ross Perot. An' I haven't voted since. Why bother? Close the borders and vote out the politicians. Make America a real place again. You *know*?

SKEETER: Dunno. Ain't votin' age yet. Tuhhh.

Skeeter gazes at the scenery. There isn't much, as night falls on the flat fields.

MOCCASIN: Yep. You ain't even seventeen, right? You a runaway?

SKEETER: Nuh, goin' tuh visit m'aunt in New York City. My ma knows.

MOCCASIN: What business you got in Indiana?

SKEETER: Figure I'll stop in, see a dude I know.

Skeeter leans down, elbows on his knees, and looks as far out the window as he can.

MOCCASIN: Where?

SKEETER: Marion.

MOCCASIN: They got a federal prison there.

SKEETER: Yeh-up.

MOCCASIN: Your old man locked up there, Private Idaho?

SKEETER: Yup.

MOCCASIN: Drug oh-fence?

SKEETER: Marijuana smuggle.

MOCCASIN: What's 'is name? Maybe I know 'im.

Skeeter's neck stiffens with skepticism as he turns toward his driving companion.

SKEETER: Bruce. Bruce Frye?

MOCCASIN: Heheehehheh. See dat? I know Bruce. Heh. Yep!

SKEETER: How do you know Bruce?

MOCCASIN: Drug business, scout, get wise, boy.

He sticks his middle finger under his eye and pulls down the skin in some coded signal of criminal complicity that Skeeter is not yet familiar with.

 ever

MOCCASIN: Got a shipment aboard right now. Ha-haah! Bruce Frye's little runt. How 'bout dat? Small fuckin' cosmos, man.

He touches his chest and holds out his hand to Skeeter.

MOCCASIN: Arnie McManus, pleased tuh meet ya, Skeet.

SKEETER: Er!

Skeeter regains his composure but chooses not to shake hands.

SKEETER: What.

He looks ahead at the road.

SKEETER: *Ev*er.

what

CHAPTER 6

IN WHICH TWO SISTERS DISCUSS MEN AND MAGIC

Jeanette sits at a stool at her kitchen counter, looking out on her apartment. The phone rings.

JEANETTE: Jeanette Gladjnois speaking. Linda, pretty Linda, how's my baby sister? Hmm hmmm, I wondered. I was doing dream monitor travel with my Mytelene stalagmite—Mytelene stalagmite, Linner, that's a cave island crone crystal from the Aegean Isl— I know you're hooked on the potions, Linda, but I'm really sure as I live and breathe that the rock—that's what they are, Linnie, cave rock, what could be more outta sight sacred? The rock is the key, the rock. I'm sure. Stone sure. Well, anyway, let's not argue about magic. I'm your big sister but you've been practicing longer so we're even, 'kay? Yeah, I'm still smoking, can you hear it? Are you? You started again. Me too. Cloves, only cloves, keeps it down to a minimum of a pack a day. Soooo, you're in trouble, hmm hmmm? I heard it in the Mytelene stalagmite vibration. Some male being is making you jealous but I don't see it as necessary. He'll always come back to you. So who is it? Ezekial? My adored nephew? Where is he? New York? How's he coming here? Who bought him a ticket? He's hitching . . . I should've known that . . . that's what happens when you raise a child on the road. Soon as they're tall enough they show you the soft side of their thumb and leave you by the curb. That's your karma with Ezekial, Linda. Why are you getting angry? No, it wasn't all Bruce's fault, you can't blame everything on Bruce. You brought some heavy jive on yourself speeding and snorting through most of the eighties with that poor kid in your knapsack. Of course, I'll put him up here, he can stay as long as he likes. I'm his Auntie Jeanette, remember?

A white fluffy cat meows from the top of the kitchen partition wall. Jeanette snaps her fingers at it.

JEANETTE: Sheba! Down! I'm the one who supported him half the time, it's about time he came to visit.

She motions the cat onto her lap and absently ruffles and smoothes its fur, while lighting a new cigarette.

JEANETTE: Linda? Linda Carrie Gladjnois Frye? Don't be angry with me. Breathe. Hmm hmmm. Oh! *now* you're getting just like your nasty old self. Yes yes yes. Yes! I *was* "turning tricks" as you like to say! Well, at least I was supporting myself and I didn't drag a child into my screwed-up existence!

The cat stiffens and Jeanette dumps it off her lap. The chimes on its collar tinkle as it hits the floor.

JEANETTE: Why are you attacking me like this? I'm going to have to meditate for hours to deprogram your bad energy . . . you BITCH! What? You're making me smoke more too!

She laughs despondently.

JEANETTE: Oh Spirit, guide us out of our insanity! It's just like back in Ketchican, huh? Shrieking at each other out on the ice slabs? Let's both put out our cigarettes, hah! Breathe. Hmmm, I know you are, I'm worried about him too. We'll both send guides to help him in his journey across this *goddamn* country. Well, you may want to control him and make him come back but he ain't going to come back just yet, Linner, you know that. Magic can't help you go against nature. He's in love? With *two* girls? So? So is every man. It just means he's becoming a man, Linda. Believe me, I know men. Hmm hmm. Do I know men. Hmm. No, not really, how about you? No? NO one? Me neither—well, I am sort of seeing *some*one, somebody I knew, an old . . . yes, client, but he's, it was sort of more than that. No, I'm not—no. He's just—we had sort of a thing, I mean, we went on vacations together and, in a weird way he was part of the transition of me getting out of The Life. He gave me a *lot* of money. He's very— No, no, I didn't, I keep telling you. No, we just, he just talked, and I just meditated, it was very— Well I let him buy me a meal, alright? We ordered up from the Seaweed Pagoda. That's a macrobiotic place in my neighborhood *which* delivers. Only in New York. That's why I live here. Mmm? Of course he's married . . . Of course he's a Republican. They *all* are. Linda, don't exasperate me, Spirit doesn't recognize political parties.

She shakes another cigarette from the pack and clicks it lit with her plastic lighter.

JEANETTE: Linda Carrie Gladjnois Frye! Nazis and Republicans are *not* the same. No, I forgot to, I was teaching an all-day Internal Radiance Seminar and the polls were closed by the time I—I know, it's terrible, I can't believe it. Besides, getting back to Paul, I think he's undergoing some kind of transformation. I know, I know. No, I won't. I will. I will. I won't. Don't worry. I'm not going to go back to The Life, okay? Even though it's hard to adjust to the cut in pay. What?! "Now you know what it's like to work for a living?" I HATE it when people say that! That's just ignorance! You think being the perfect date and sucking the *perfect* cock for America's frustrated corporate male elite was not WORKING FOR A GODDAMNED LIVING!!? Well, well, THEN I'D LIKE TO KNOW WHAT IS! 'Kay, let's not get heavy again. Let's both put out our cigarettes again. Hmm hmmm. 'Kay, Linda. 'Kay, baby sis, I love you too. I'll send Spirit to Ezekial, don't fear. 'Kay. Hmmm hmmm. Bye-bye, bye now.

She slams down the cordless and looks at her watch.

JEANETTE: Shit, I *still* have to meditate and Paul's coming in half an hour.

CHAPTER 7

IN WHICH SKEETER'S PATRIOTISM
IS PUT TO THE TEST

Skeeter stands shivering his ass off by the side of a gravel road in the middle of a cold, moonlit night. The only thing near him is a length of barbed wire fence and beyond that dark, rolling hills. A dark blue Plymouth comes careening up the road and grinds to a halt beside him. The two men inside are whooping and laughing so much it takes them a second to get words out.

LAMONTE: Hey, white boy, what're you doing? You know yoo're on duh Pine Ridge Rez?

LUTHER: Yoo're on duh Pine Ridge Rez, boy, what're you doing on duh Pine Ridge Rez?

LAMONTE: Hey, Luther, open up another bottle uh wine.

SKEETER: Uh, just hitchin', just hitchin', dudes, just just tryin' tuh get across, just tryin' tuh get across.

He hops from foot to foot, hugging himself.

LUTHER: You know how big duh Pine Ridge Rez is? You know how many Indians died, froze to deaf out here?

SKEETER: Uuuuuuh,

His jaw rattles.

SKEETER: a *lot* I would wager.

LUTHER: Damn! You know how many men, women, an' children froze to deaf out here on Pine Ridge Rez? You can't get across.

LAMONTE: He's shiverin'.

LUTHER: You can't get across.

Lamonte laughs and Luther soon catches the contagion. He speaks through wheezes of laughter:

LUTHER: Yoo're gonna freeze to deaf! Yoo're gonna freeze to deaf!
They whoop and slap their thighs.

LUTHER: Get in.

LAMONTE: We're savin' your life, get in!

SKEETER: Uuuuuuuuerrrrrrrokay. Much gratitudes extended, dudes.

Skeeter hops into the already-rolling car, slams the door.

LUTHER: Whoooooooooooeeeeeeeeeeee! Drive! Lamonte!

They take off, careening wildly, gunning the engine for all it's worth.

LAMONTE: Give 'im some wine!

SKEETER: Uh, most appreciated, dudes. I only do psychoactives. I'm sure yur familiar with those . . . rain dances, vision quests, uh—

LUTHER: What duh fuck is your problem? You're not American? You're not ready to die for your country? Drink some wine!

LAMONTE: Doesn't want to drink our wine? Throw him out. Throw 'im out of duh car!

LUTHER: Cut 'is balls off first.

LAMONTE: He's not gonna need 'em.

LUTHER: He's gonna freeze to deaf, anyhoo!

They laugh for a while, then get dead quiet. The car slows up.

SKEETER: Er, uh, but seein' dat it's a special occasion, I'm at yer rez an' it's, uh, Thanksgivin' tomorrow, uh, I'd most appreciate some wine. I'll get as drunk as you are as fast as I can.

Skeeter wrenches the bottle from Luther's hand and gulps it down. The car lurches into top gear.

LUTHER: WHOOOO! WHEEEE! WHOOOO! Fuck it, GOD *BLESS* AMERICA! We're outta dis wine, open up another bottle, Lamonte.

Luther hands a new bottle to Lamonte, who tries to unscrew the cap with his mouth while driving.

LAMONTE: Wait. Oh fuck, Luther, you're throwin' up. Let's pull over!

He crashes into the fence, then brakes. He kicks Luther.

LAMONTE: Luther! Luther! Throw up outside!

Luther blunders a few steps from the car and crashes to his knees in the gravel, vomiting.

LUTHER: I'm poisoning myself! I'm poisoning myseeeeeelf!

He vomits awhile then looks up. There is just the sound of the wind in the long grass. They wait.

LUTHER: Ah, look at duh moon over duh ridge. Clouds're movin' her sideways. Ahhh.

Luther stands. He spits, crunches through the gravel to the car.

ever

LUTHER: It's a good night to die.

He gets in and slams the door.

LUTHER: DRIVE, Lamonte!

As they take off, spraying gravel in their wake, Luther howls a high, lonesome howl out the window. The sound trails off behind them in the still, icy air.

what

CHAPTER 8

IN WHICH POLLY DISPOSES
OF WASTE

A middle-aged housewife stands in her brightly lit kitchen, washing Thanksgiving platters and scraping huge amounts of food down the garbage disposal with a Rubbermaid spatula. She is dressed neatly in crisp slacks and a pastel cotton sports shirt. Her hair is freshly coiffed, dyed back to its original lustrous chestnut; she is lightly, expertly made up, just enough to highlight her fine features and the smooth, planed cheekbones so particular to Southern beauties. She purses her mouth as she speaks, punctuating her sentences with little pursed-up smiles, a habit she's acquired from years of holding back her true feelings. Her voice is light, high, and could be musical, only sometimes, more often than not of late, the music is off and it borders on squeaky, going up at the end of a word. Her accent is that of a genteel Southern lady.

POLLY: There are big reasons wah I don't, okay? That's all you need to know, just trust me and quit buggin' me! There are-are-are, there are big gosh *darned* reasons wah I don't. Marie, I didn't call you to talk about this. Wah are you always a bully? Lak this? I just wonted to wish you a happy Thanksgivin' and say that your dad and I missed you and— No, he's gone back, back for another "business" trip. Yo ho ho, on top of everythin' else! Wey-ell, what can I do, Sheila Marie? Your pops is not doin' too swey-ell. Me? I'm doin' fine, I'm just throwin' out the leftovers right now. I *love* the new garbage disposal, that old one nearly drove me out of my mind.

She switches it on and watches the food disappear in the whirring suction.

POLLY: Did I mention to you I'd ordered this new kind from a home shopping network? Wey-ell, it sounded fantastic and Paul, I mean Pops, said you cain't tell about a product on television and I said,

You're one to talk, mister, with all your "Marketin' for the New Millennium" international business conferences you're always runnin' off to at the drop of a hat! I'm *not*

She lowers her voice.

POLLY: complainin' to you about our relationship, Marie, I'm tellin' you about the garbage disposal.

She grinds some food in the disposal.

POLLY: I thought, now that looks fan*tas*tic, so I called and ordered it and the fella came and he was just the nicest, kindest young man, wey-ell, not that young, you know, maybe he was in his late thirties, maybe his early forties, but he was so clean cut and po*liiiite* and he had such a nice nice way. He was very strong and fit, you know, it's probably hard work installin' garbage disposals all day, I mean, you have to get way under the sink—he was practically layin' down on my kitchen floor, hon. I'm glad I had Beverly wax the linoleum the day before! It was a hard job. Then he had to go around and go under the house. Wey-ell, I'm tellin' you because I'm so happy, honey. I was right! It's a fan*tas*tic garbage disposal! I can put anything down it, I'm puttin' the stuffin',

She switches the disposal on and off again.

POLLY: the cranberries, I bought too many. The turkey. I was goin' to. I meant to, Sheila, but I just, I couldn't stand the mess after Paul,

She switches on the disposal.

POLLY: I mean your dad,

She switches it off.

POLLY: drove off to the airport this mornin'. I had called a men's shelter in Arlington and they said to drive it in the next day because they still had plenty from Thanksgivin'—so many donations come at this time and I just couldn't wait, Sheila.

She switches it on, leans into the garbage disposal, listening to it whir, then catches herself and switches it off.

POLLY: But I do listen to you, I'm doin' the recyclin' much better than I used to. I told Beverly, Clean out those dog food cans, those go in the recyclin' too—we all have to do our part! I thought about what you said and I thought, You know, she's right? Your father may not agree with you, but on this point I do. I don't lak all the fuss you made that summer,

what

She charges up the garbage disposal.

POLLY: but—wey-ell, whether you agreed with the timber company or not, Sheila Marie, a young lady does not go and chain herself to a tree that way.

She charges it up again.

POLLY: Thirty-four is still a young lady! Wey-ell, okay, Miss Smarty-pants, an old lady then. I don't care! A *lady* dudn't do that!

She charges it up again.

POLLY: I'm just so grateful no one did anything to you. Those loggers could've raped you. That is not crazy! Look at what happened to that other girl: exploded by a terrorist bomb! Sheila, let's not talk. What?

She flips on the garbage disposal

POLLY: I cain't hear you, I'm grindin' the turkey—

She crams turkey down the disposal, whacking it with her rubber scraper.

POLLY: What? The Federal Bureau of Investigation did not kill that sad girl! Her own MADNESS did. No, I'm not sayin' YOU'RE mad!

She weeps.

POLLY: Oh, oh!

She crams more turkey down the disposal.

POLLY: Nothing fits,

The garbage disposal whirs angrily.

POLLY: it's just—first your father, then you,

The garbage disposal whirs like a snarling, spewing, live beast.

POLLY: cain't anyone be nice to poor Polly? Polly wont a cracker! Hee hee!

Her voice turns high and singsong, imitating an upset child.

POLLY: Polly wont a cracker!

She switches off the disposal.

POLLY: I was *tryin'* to tell you I've been followin' your . . . recyclin' . . . Okay, sugar dumplin', I'm okay. Polly's okay.

She dabs her eyes and gives a weak, fluttery smile.

POLLY: Yes! She's a perky parrot! Hear that?

She holds the phone over the sink as she shoves down the pie and flips the switch on.

POLLY: That's the sweet potato pie. Old Mrs. Louard made it. Bev-

ever

erly's granny? Hear it in the disposal? Mmm. Hee hee. Did you eat turkey on Thanksgivin', Sheila? You're joshin' me? A whole *tofu* turkey? Was it a casserole? Wey-ell, how about that?

She purses out a smile and flips the switch on and off.

POLLY: Isn't that fantastic?

And on and off.

POLLY: That must have been the sight! You'll have to teach me sometime. Send me the recipe! Hear that?

And on.

POLLY: There's the corn puddin'.

She holds the receiver over the sink again.

POLLY: Hee hee. Ah!

She shrieks as the sound of metal hits the disposal choppers. She switches it off.

POLLY: Oh no, oh no! Ah! Ah! Sheila Marie, Mom's dropped her weddin' ring down the disposal! What should I do? Oh sweet heaven, your dad! Oh no, oh no, what should I do? I have to get off. I'll call the *fi*re departm— Who should I call? You're right! The garbage disposal man. He's so nice, he'll know how to get it. Oh goodness! I kept his number, too, he was so nice. He said if you have any problems, and this-this is a problem! This is a lulu. Oh, I'm fallin' apart here. Oh no! Polly wont a cracker! Hee hee! Okay, okay. I'm okay, sugar dumplin'. Mama's gotta go. I'll call you as soon as I get the ring back, okay? If you talk to your brother—wey-ell, I know you and Derek never speak to one another—but if you should happen to speak to your own blood brother on a national holiday d-don't tell him what's happened, okay? Okay. Bye, angel. Bye bye.

She replaces the phone in its receiver on the wall and looks around.

POLLY: Oh, by the grace of God . . . SHIT!

She wets her index finger and flips through her kitchen Rolodex. Her eyes narrow. She is quiet and calm.

POLLY: Here's the number.

what

CHAPTER 9

IN WHICH BUSHIE AND THE TREE BRAVE THE STORM

Bushie stands on the sidewalk screaming at her pimp in a deluge of freezing rain. Terry holds a flattened refrigerator box over his head.

BUSHIE: I don't care if it's rainin', Terry, you soggy-ass pimp! I gotta stay out an' earn sometin' fuh myself, okay? Do you *miiiiind*? I *got* to. Go back! Go away den, don't do yuh job, you never do. And don't punch me or I won't do da laundry tomorrow, lazy-ass, retarded-ass. Go, awright! Just GO, I can't make any money wit' you standing here, Terry. Eithah go stand down da block or go back tuh dee apartment like you want to! Bye!

She watches him walk off.

BUSHIE: Brrrrr brrrrr brrrrr— Hey Tree, how goes it, Tree?

A person walks quickly by, giving her a glare.

BUSHIE: Whatta you looking at? Shit, here come da Wonderbreads.

On the opposite side of West Forty-fifth Street, a small group of people huddled under umbrellas and shining flashlights round the corner and move, in determined fashion, down the block. As they pass, they stare grimly at Bushie. Bushie sings.

BUSHIE: "It's raining, it's pouring, dee old man is snoring, he went tuh bed an' bump his head an' couldn't get da fuck up in da mawwwwnin'." Fuck you, Wonderbread people, why ain't you inside yuhr ugly-ass condos? Fuck you wit' yuh baby-ass umbrellas, wit' yuh flashlight patrols and yuh "Dis Block Belongs To Us." Dis block belongs tuh my PUSSY, people!

She grabs her crotch for emphasis.

BUSHIE: Dat's right, it's a free country and why can't I sell what's mine?

They ignore her taunts and keep walking.

BUSHIE: Walk away, walk away! Wonderbreads! Brrr brrr. Hey baby!

A car slows beside Bushie.

BUSHIE: Hey.

A square-jawed middle-aged man in square-framed glasses, wearing a wet poncho, beckons Bushie with a faint smile.

BUSHIE: Oh no, not you, go away, go away before I get my man and his boys tuh rip your throat out fuh what you did tuh my homegirl. I know you. Keep on driving, you want me tuh call him! Drive! Go!

The car crawls away, hesitating.

BUSHIE: Oh fuck. Brrr. Brrr. Oh fuck! I gotta get a pickup—here come da Wonderbreads. Wonderbread *people*! What you got dat rope for?

She sticks out her tongue and her ass at the same time.

BUSHIE: Hey, you gonna arrest me wit' yuh civilian-ass patrol?

She runs from them, dances, and sings in the rain as they chase her.

BUSHIE: I'm hoein' in da rain, just ho-ho-hoein' in da rain— How's da rest go? You know, you educated, right? Tree, save me.

They catch her at the tree and she clings to it.

BUSHIE: I'm a citizen too, and I'm a hold of dis tree. Tree is my witness! Try! Try tuh get me off! I'm strong, baby-asses, I'm strong. I grew up gettin' beat. Ask your friends da police. Ask Officer Mancuso, he knows I got muscle.

She kicks at them wildly and viciously as they tie her to the tree with nylon rope. She gets in a good kick.

BUSHIE: Sorry, bitch, but you asked for it in dat pink-ass raincoat. Tie me up, den, tie me tuh dis tree, okay, dis tree my friend—ooo, you Wonderbreads are kinky, kinks cost extra, baby-asses. Is your dick hard yet, Mr. Save Our Neighbah-hood? It's so lit'l I can't see.

The man she addresses, a handsome, thin-lipped WASP, slaps her in the face.

BUSHIE: Yeah, smack me! Good! I tell da sergeant, you go tuh jail for assault, muthafucka. Dis illegal, people. Dis illegal. Come back! Come back! Tree, I can't get loose,

She struggles as hard as she can without damaging the tree.

BUSHIE: Tree, dey tied me *to* you. Brrr brrr. "Is raining, is pouring, dee old man is snoring." Tree, Bushie is cold. Bushie needs sometin', you know, just a little bit? You losing your leaves now, baby, look at

what

dat shit blow. It's pretty, dough. It sizzles, don't it? But not a fry siz-zle, mo' like a whoo, a whooo, a whhhhisper sizzle. Brrrrrr, I need some, I need some snap crackle pop. Here come da cops.

They pull up alongside Bushie, lights circling. They get out in full rain gear and move in on Bushie.

BUSHIE: Officer Mancuso, how you doin'? Is me, is Bushie. Yeh, you could untie me but I won't let go! Ha ha ha! No, don't hurt da tree, wait! You hurting it—don't—STOOOOOOPPPPP! PLEASE! I let go, see? You fucked up da tree! YOU FUCKED IT UP! Dat's right, cuff me, smack me. Tree, you be okay, Bushie see you next time, awright? Tree? Tree? Get bettah? Bushie love you. Bushie love you!

The police push her by the head into the back of the police van.

BUSHIE: Awright, I'm gettin' in!

The tree leans vastly to one side, battered by the rain. The police van speeds away.

ever

CHAPTER 10

IN WHICH SKEETER WAKES FROM A LONG SLEEP

Two elderly Native Americans stand over Skeeter as he comes to.

NELLIE: Dere great granpa was apparen'ly a brave, useta kill a horse by ridin' it to deaf, dat's why dey call dem duh Kills Horse family. But now, I guess, it should be updated, 'cause now we don't have too many more horses. We drive cars.

RUPERT: Yeh, should update it to dee, uh, Wrecks Cars.

NELLIE: Det's right. Duh Wrecks Cars.

RUPERT: Next time we see 'em.

NELLIE: Yeh, in duh hospital. Det's uselly where we see 'em.

RUPERT: Go, hey, Luther and Lamonte Wrecks Cars, how you doin', boys?

NELLIE: Det's right. Dey crashed inta duh willow tree down by duh creek bed night before Tanksgivin' and we went down dere to git 'em and we saw you lyin' dere in duh backseat wid wine all over your legs.

RUPERT: It was all over your *blue* jeans, duh *red* wine.

NELLIE: We said, what's, what's dis little blond kid doing on Pine Ridge Rez? Wid duh Kills Horse boys?

RUPERT: Det's right. Said what, what dey doin'? So we took y'up to duh barn. Dey mumble somepin' 'bout how dey saved your life, 'cause you were out dere hitchin' in duh cold.

NELLIE: Da's true. Dey did save his life, but den dey almost lost it again.

RUPERT: Yeh. So we put duh three of you to sleep in duh barn. Dey woke up for Tanksgivin' but you kep' sleepin' right through. So when people came we moved you here to duh trailer.

NELLIE: Det's right. You're at duh right place. Dis here's duh Indian Cafe. Dere ain't anybody else around here for twenty-six miles.

> A dog sets to barking and Nellie opens the creaky screen door to speak with it.

NELLIE: Smoky, get away from det rusted engine. Yoo're gonna cut yourself again.

> She lets the door go and the sound of it slamming nudges Skeeter further awake. He blinks and sits up.

SKEETER: Ohhhhhhh . . . Much obliiiiged. How long, how long did you say I was asleep for?

NELLIE: Oh, I'd say about four or five, how long d'you figure, Rupert?

RUPERT: Oh yeh, figure 'bout four five six, six seven eight days, figure.

NELLIE: Yeh, I figure. I don't know, dere were so many peopoe. Luther and Lamonte left wid dem an'—it was so busy an'—

RUPERT: Could you use a bite to eat?

SKEETER: Oh most lavishly an' appreciatively. Er, I mean dat would be rully rully nice. Uh, Skeet, er, Ezekial Christian Frye is my name.

> He holds out his hand to shake. Nellie keeps her arms folded but nods with a deliberate gravity that equals a handshake.

NELLIE: Nellie Beestingtaker. An' dis is Rupert Lacroix, my cousin.

> Rupert, a tall man of at least six foot two, steps directly over to Skeeter, looming above and greeting him in a booming voice.

RUPERT: Hi.

SKEETER: Hi. There. It's a full honor.

NELLIE: Why don't we go inta duh cafe. It's just across duh way. Rupert, you get him some fry bread. I'm gonna start cookin' up some meat. Dis is duh best meat you could get in duh whole U.S. here. It's USDA certified beef. Grade A. It's duh best.

RUPERT: Come on. It's just right here across duh way.

> They crunch through snow toward a big corrugated aluminum barn; the dog runs alongside, barking and panting. Nellie opens the door to the cafe, then hesitates.

NELLIE: Hold on. Rupe, gimme one of your Marlboros.

> Rupert takes a cigarette from the pack in his front shirt pocket. He

ever

places it first in his mouth, then hands it to Nellie. She takes it, rips it in two, and scatters the tobacco on the threshold.

NELLIE: Okay, now, go inside.

She ushers them in and the door slams behind them.

NELLIE: Git some fry bread. You want some—you like honey?

SKEETER: Sure.

NELLIE: Dis is duh best honey. You're not gonna git honey like dis nowhere else. Dis honey's made from Badlands clover. *Dthook-moogkha-Dthook-chey.*

Rupert holds out two pieces of fry bread as Nellie pours the honey from a jar. He hands one to Skeeter and bites into the other.

RUPERT: Means bee-shit.

SKEETER: Utterly devastational, I'm sure.

RUPERT: What?

SKEETER: Uh, er. Are you, uh, uh, of the Sioux Nation?

NELLIE: Lakota.

SKEETER: Like Dakota?

RUPERT: Lakota.

SKEETER: Multitudes o' gratitude fer savin' my life, elder dudes.

RUPERT: No problem. Come over here, sit by duh stove. We got duh stove lit up.

what

CHAPTER 11

IN WHICH CLOVE FALLS PREY TO SOMNAMBULISM

Clove walks in a dark, shadowy land, breathing slowly and evenly.

CLOVE: He is neither of this world nor the next. He waits by the shore, drawing the breath of the young and the near-death. He is Cobain the Friendly Ghost and he is singing in our ear, enough to tickle but not yet enough to hear the tune. Soon he will enter me. He is already half in. He wants me to take his melody, to croon his passage past the moon's watch over the ocean waves to the other side of gun-blast, the dissolve, the unsound that will absolve the blood-spill at Puget Sound.

She wakes with a start.

CLOVE: AHHHH! Whaaa? Whoah! Kyler! What're you doing in my room?

KYLER: Huh? Clove, you spaz, you woke me up, yur standing over my bed. Is this some kind of big sister incest?

CLOVE: Whoah! I must be sleepwalking again.

KYLER: Why are you holding that tampon over me?

CLOVE: Whoah, it's my period!

KYLER: Don't tell me about it!

CLOVE: Don't ask, piglet.

KYLER: Yur in my room. MOM! DAD! CLOVE is tryin' tuh RAPE ME with her TAMPONS!

CLOVE: Shhhhh! Kyler, it's the middle of the night.

KYLER: No *shit*. *Go*. Away.

CLOVE: Okay, oinker.

KYLER: Good night, goathead.

CLOVE: Good night.

KYLER: 'Night.

CHAPTER 12

IN WHICH VIOLET ENTERTAINS A NOCTURNAL GUEST

Violet is fast asleep, snoring away. Balzac barks. She wakes with a start.

VIOLET: What in the devil? Hmm? What? Who's there? What is it? Elliot, is that you? You frightened—no, it's not Elliot, is it? But you *are* a ghost, aren't you? I thought you might've been my last husband, deeah, who are you? Coltrane? Coltrane the Friendly Ghost? Well, I'm glad you're friendly, but you don't look a THING like Mr. Coltrane. I sawr him play many many times, y'know, and I'd say you're awfully pale, even for a ghost if you're John Col— Hmm, deeah? What'sat? Coburn? Coburn the Friendly—Kurt Coburn? Well, hello, what can I do for you, deeah? Balzac, up! Up on the quilt. There, stop barking. It's only a ghost come for some company. What time is it? Half past four. Well, I hope it's important. Coburn, you can sit there at the foot of the bed with the poodle, if y'like. I'm not squeamish about phantoms. Good *Christ*, I'm almost one myself. Perfectly alright. Come on, sit down. Frankly, you make me uncomfortable as *hell* hovering on the wall that way. What are you? Ah! M'trumpet! No one's touched that in years. No sense in trying to play it, you're a ghost, you cahn't play music, I don't think. Yes, *I* did. That's a secret. Only Elliot, my third husband, 'sbeen gone twenty-eight years, only *he* knows about my trumpet blowing.

She leans back, a little spooked as the ghost nears her with the trumpet.

VIOLET: You want me to give it a . . . ? Why? You need to write a last song. Were you a musician? Jazz? No. Hmm. Very good, deeah, very good. Well, I'm not sure if I've the breath left for it. Hmm. Are you going? Alright. I could play you—I've got an early Doretta Clark recording there on the phonograph, would you— No, I can see you're very un-un-unsettled, aren't you? Melancholy even. Well, go find your medium, then, I won't keep you. Au revoir. And if you cahn't find anyone else, you can always try me at—

Suddenly, the ghost is directly above her. Violet pulls back, then re-laxes, puckering her mouth, absorbed.

VIOLET: What's this? A kiss? Haven't had one of those in . . . years . . . Thank you, Coburn. Thank you.

The moment passes. Violet's eyes flutter open. She is alone.

VIOLET: Balzac, come to Violet.

She strokes him.

VIOLET: Hmmm . . . A kiss from ghostly lips. Hmmm, s'pose it *had* been Mr. Coltrane? Now wouldn't *that*'ve been something grand? Ahh . . .

She drifts back to sleep, and is shortly snoring again.

PART THREE

SEEING THINGS

CHAPTER 1

IN WHICH VIOLET ADMITS TO SMUGGLING

It is afternoon in Violet's apartment. Her housekeeper, Cora Sue, is vacuuming. Balzac hides under the loveseat.

VIOLET: Cora? Cora Sue? D'you think you could stop vacuuming, deeah? Could we not have the vacuuming today a'tall? The racket is fraying the *hell*—I'm sorry, I know you don't like profanity—fraying the hell—the *hooey*, the hooey out of my nerves.

CORA SUE: Mm-hmm. If you don't wont it, we won't have it.

Cora Sue is an attractive middle-aged black woman. She has a deep and deliberate tone. She speaks with authority and chooses her words with care. She has an air of not suffering fools gladly. Her accent, bearing some vestiges of the South, is distinguished by an emphatic pronunciation of the beginnings of words and the elongation of vowels.

VIOLET: Thank you, Cora Sue. I'm not feeling very well today. The doorm'n that I get on with wasn't in and the other doorm'n refused to walk Balzac, and that's why he did the dirty deed on the carpet. I'm *terribly* sorry you had to clean it up, Cora Sue. If I'd felt *a'tall* better I'd've cleaned it up myself.

CORA SUE: Don't be ree-diculous.

VIOLET: Why don't you take a breathing spell, deeah? We'll have a cup of tea.

CORA SUE: Mm-hmm

Cora Sue makes some tea in the kitchenette while Violet keeps on conversing.

VIOLET: I think I might've gotten a strain of flu that the doorm'n has because I feel like a Violet today. I've always thought my name was pahticul'ly unsuitable f' someone of my temperment, but t'day I feel like a little shrinking Violet.

Cora Sue carries in their tea and seats herself beside Violet.

CORA SUE: Here you go.

VIOLET: Thank you, deeah. You're not a'tall like my mother, Cora. But my mother didn't like profanity eitheh. Personally, I think convehsation without profanity is like *soup* without *salt*.

CORA SUE: We-ell, you-you shouldn't be havin' that *eith*er, I keep *tell*in' you, salt is *bad* for you.

VIOLET: Hmmph.

Violet sips her tea.

VIOLET: Speaking of *fla*vuhless soups, I think I might've got this flu at the Blue Ship Diner, deeah. D'you know th'other day, I found a short, black hair on my buttah plate—

CORA SUE: Oh! Noo—

VIOLET: —and it wasn't Balzac's eitheh. D'you think that that might be it?

CORA SUE: Well, *I* don't think that you should *go* they-ere. *I* don't think that you should be *eat*in' at the Blue Ship Diner. I *per*sonally would *nev*er eat in that establishment—*ev*-eh.

She pauses for emphasis, sets down her teacup, and gives Violet her full scrutiny.

CORA SUE: When were you they-ere?

VIOLET: Yesterdee.

CORA SUE: You can't go a *day* without goin' they-ere, can you?

VIOLET: I know. It's pathetic. It's the hub of my existence. Y'see, when I was a young girl, it was the garden next door—the neighbors'—then when I was a young bride in Paris before the war it was the corner pub or the bistro. Then during the war when I was a grown woman I was here in New York nursing the soldiers and I'd run out to the canteen. Then later, it was the jazz clubs and the

She whispers.

VIOLET: Communist Party meetings (I neveh joined but I thought the men looked *aw*fully fetching with their berets and their little goatees!) and then there was the bar and then there was the other bar and then there was the bar, the bar—it was the BAR for a good long while! Then, as lots of my friends who were *old* people died, I

what

became fond of the new and the young, y'see, and it became the Blue Ship Diner. I'm cold.

CORA SUE: You're shivering.

VIOLET: Am I? Am I?

CORA SUE: Let's just cover you up.

Cora Sue arranges a blanket over Violet.

VIOLET: Oh thank you, Cora, you're very kind. D'you have to go now, deeah?

CORA SUE: No.

VIOLET: You sure?

CORA SUE: No—I have one—I have anothuh *ho*ur with you.

VIOLET: You sure?

CORA SUE: Mmmmm-hmm.

VIOLET: Did I ever tell you the story about smuggling birth control home to the States, eh, before the war?

CORA SUE: Mm-mm, no, I don't b'lieve you've ever *told* me that one.

VIOLET: Eh, oh! do— You *do* believe in birth control, don't you, Cora deeah? Your church isn't one of those that—

CORA SUE: Well, *I* don't know *what* my *church's* opinion is, but *ye*-es, I do believe in birth control.

VIOLET: Good Cora, I'm glad that you've got good sense.

Cora Sue raises her eyebrows, sits back, and looks Violet up and down, slowly, trying to locate the part of her that would say something that foolish and condescending. Violet blushes and stammers.

VIOLET: Uh, uh, oh, uh—well, my first husband, Bill, and I used birth control because I was nineteen, living abroad, and I didn't want to have any babies. So, we were going back to the States for th'winter. Turned out to be miserable, most of the time we spent with, uh, Bill's family in Chicago. Dreadful sort of people. Terrible time. But first we were starting at Boston Harbor. We were to arrive by ship in Boston, stay with some relatives of Bill's, then take the train to New Yawk and make all the gay rounds for the—Christmas pahties—and I thought what more wonderful *stock*ing present for a few of my bosom friends but to bring them some diaphragms deeah!? And then I'd distribute the rest to the Sangerites to give them out to all the—to all the, eh, to th' public-at-*laah*ge. Can you believe that diaphragms were illegal: Can you believe that *still*

ever

they're complaining about teen pregnancy and we *still* have to smuggle birth control out to the young! Can you believe that? What do these idiots think? Cahn't they see the connection?

CORA SUE: No, 'course they can't. Did you watch the State of the Union address last night? Did you see them making *any* type of connections whatsoever?

VIOLET: You're absolutely right. That's why they're idiots, deeah. So, I got in touch with a doctor in Lyons and he sold me a satchelful of diaphragms. All different sizes. I'd 'round . . . three dozen.

And we get off the boat and there's Bill's relatives in Boston and they're waving from the docks—very staid old staunch Boston—they're going t' put us up at Beacon Hill f' the week*end*. And we come off, come through customs without a hitch and then Bill's cousin takes a strap of my satchel, says, Allow me, missus, I said, No it's quite alright, he says, Allow me, I said, No, that's quite alright, he says Allow me, I said Quite alright and I was trying to hold it and then don't you know, Cora Sue, it *RIP*PED apaht and *three dozen diaphragms* came *STREAM*ING out onto the docks in Boston! And there were people *SWIRL*ING all about, passengers and-and everyone froze, came to an absolute *STAND*STILL and just *stared* at these diaphragms *litt*ering the dock. I turned a very dark shade of bordeaux (which was my favorite wine at the time). And then, d'y' know what happened, Cora Sue?

CORA SUE: Mm-mm?

Cora Sue is on the edge of her seat.

VIOLET: Right. Suddenly, these Boston Irish Catholics made a *mad scramble* f' the diaphragms! Ev'ry father's daughter, ev'ry mother's son went *div*ing for these diaphragms. A *ri*ot broke out! *scram*bling! *poli*cemen had to be summoned! Women were sticking the devices between th' breasts t' keep them from being confiscated. One man *jump*ed into th' harbor and *swam* for it!

We were driven d'rectly to the train station in the highest dudgeon and put d'rectly on the train to New Yawk. I s'pose that might've been the beginning of the foundering of—my marriage with Bill, though I think even he found it funny at the time.

Violet laughs.

what

VIOLET: America is a funny place, isn't it, Cora Sue?

Cora Sue does not crack even a glimmer of a smile.

CORA SUE: Mm-hmm.

VIOLET: Yes, 'tis, isn't it?

CORA SUE: Hmmm.

She isn't having any.

VIOLET: Well, that's rully all I have t' say.

CORA SUE: That's all that you *can* say.

VIOLET: Yes. I s'pose.

The tea sits, mostly untouched.

CHAPTER 2

IN WHICH CARLITO MEETS A FRIENDLY PHANTOM

Carlito finds a spot away from the leak in the ceiling of his trailer and writes to his wife, in Spanish.

CARLITO: Dearest Elizabeta,

Listen, sweetheart, it is cold here in the north of California. Now we get a ride to Mr. Schmidt's brussels sprouts farm in the truck of Danny, one of the Chicano guys. The sea wind comes like cold hands from over the cliffs and seizes us by our necks and shakes us like puppies. It rains much. The brussels sprouts are glazed with frost each daybreak when we arrive. The Chicanos say it is the first rains like these in many years. It is good for the farm but we are chilled to the bone of our bones.

Another thing is making us shiver and that is, we have a ghost. Do not worry, Elizabeta, because he has told us he comes for friendship. Immanuel was relieving himself on the other side of Danny's truck when the ghost came behind him in the mirror. In English he told him, "DO NO BE FRI-HYUN, I YAM COBAING DEE FRIENGLY KHOST." The Chicanos translate this as meaning he comes as a friend but anyway, they don't believe he is there. For some strange cause, they have not laid eyes on him. Ever since we found the little nude *gringa* talking to herself in the brussels sprouts, this ghost has been visiting. He is blond and skinny and walks the cliffs. We have seen him many times, especially at daybreak. He likes our singing or humming. This has brought him twice. He stands in his cloak of ice plants, covered only by a thin layer of sand, and his figure wobbles as if we are seeing his reflection in the stiff grass. We Mexicans have started to scatter crumbs for him at lunch, just a few *tortillas*. The Chicanos laugh at us but they don't know anything, the *pendejos*. He must be hungry, no? Helacio agrees with me that the gringa brought the ghost. The sheriffs said she was taking drugs from a dance on the beach and she walked into the sea. I think she wakened him from the place where the dead are sleeping.

Helacio has hurt his leg and he may have to go back home. We are afraid to go to the hospital now that they have voted a law to deport us if we go there. The Chicanos say, Don't worry, they never enforce their laws, but still we don't trust this.

Little Joe has a bad cough and it will not go away. He had to stop working the fields but he is lucky because he found a job preparing salads in a good restaurant in Sacramento. Hopefully his cough will improve there. We hope he will stop coughing blood and it isn't tuberculosis. Pray for him and for me also and for this lonely ghost to find his peace. I pray for you and for Nilda and Miguel and Ester and Muriel and Daniel. Kiss them for me.

Here is your money. Did you buy them candy for Christmas, as I asked you to? I wish I could be there at this moment to drink a coffee in the sun and watch you wash your face and neck while outside all of our little donkeys are braying.

Love always, *Su Esposo*,
Carlito.

CHAPTER 3

IN WHICH SKEETER HAS A MISSED CONNECTION

Smack in the middle of America, Skeeter stands at the end of an inter-state rest area, thumb out, facing the roseate and amber glow of a free-way-smog-blended sunset. An eighteen-wheeler pauses by the exit and a big blond guy opens the door on the passenger side of the cab and shouts down to him.

WAYNE: I'm doin' an all-nighter to Pittsburgh, that take ya anywhere ya goin'?
SKEETER: Sure.
WAYNE: Careful.
    He jumps up into the cab.
SKEETER: Yeh-up.
WAYNE: Slam 'er hard. There we go. Where ya headed?
    Wayne steers onto the freeway. His voice is raised to a friendly shout level throughout their conversation.
SKEETER: New York City, tuh visit my Aunt Jeanette.
WAYNE: You a Hoosier?
SKEETER: Er, nuh.
WAYNE: Me neither. Illinois.
SKEETER: Oregon.
WAYNE: What you doin' in Indiana. Just passin' through?
SKEETER: Wull, wull, I tried tuh visit my dad Bruce.
WAYNE: Oh yeah?
SKEETER: He's in Marion.
WAYNE: Penitentiary?
SKEETER: Yeah.
WAYNE: Oh yeah.
SKEETER: Marijuana smuggle.

WAYNE: Name's Wayne.

SKEETER: Skeeter.

WAYNE: Oh yeah?

SKEETER: Yeh-up.

Skeeter leans his head into his hands and starts to tear up.

WAYNE: Are you upset, Sneezer? You look like you're . . .

SKEETER: I am.

WAYNE: 'Tsokay, kid, pour yer heart out, I've heard everything, 'tsentertainment fer me, keeps me awake! Go ahead. Let Uncle Wayne have it!

SKEETER: They wouldn't even let me see 'im. This's been one taxatious hitch. I mean, I grew up hitchin' rides. But this west-tuh-east ride's been RACKish . . . I been frozen, I been bored tuh tears, I been nearly raped.

Wayne gives him a look, furrowed eyebrows. Skeeter blinks at him. Wayne gives him another look. Skeeter clarifies:

SKEETER: By a woman.

WAYNE: Call it sexually coerced by a rampant female, Skeezer, sounds more masculine.

SKEETER: Sure, but anyways, then I got stuck in Injun territory.

WAYNE: Oh yeah?

SKEETER: Yeh, 'at was pretty hectic, but then I got immersed in it. From a cultural standpoint an' like that.

WAYNE: Mmm-hmm.

SKEETER: Then in Wisconsin I near-qualified fer the frozen foods section, 'til I got picked up by a girl in a stolen pickup.

WAYNE: Hold on— Ten-four, good buddy. Got a fourteen-year-old here on a cryin' jag, call ya back, over and out.

SKEETER: I'm sixteen.

WAYNE: I knew you weren't eighteen.

SKEETER: Anyway, so this girl picked me up was drivin' four hundred miles tuh get an abortion.

WAYNE: I'm pro-life, but I can sympathize with your situation.

SKEETER: Yeah?

WAYNE: Yeah! Go on. This is good.

SKEETER: So I'se hopin' on makin' Marion by X-Mass, since this half-breed dude who gave me a ride in South Dakota knew my dad

ever

Bruce from prison and said that he was goin' tuh be in Section C 'cause in addition tuh smugglin' marijuana he subsequent tuh his imprisonment wrote letters tuh media officials regarding his sale of reefer tuh this Senator Flinch Whitcomb in 1975.

WAYNE: Whoah dear!

SKEETER: So they would not let him have visitors, but this dude reckoned if I made it by the Holy Days they might make an exception. But then I got lost in these back roads of Wisconsin and went way north, almost froze, and then I met Camille.

WAYNE: Who?

SKEETER: The girl gettin' th' abortion, dude.

WAYNE: Right.

SKEETER: And I got all waylaid by her.

WAYNE: Wait, you got laid?

SKEETER: Naw, nuh, she was having an abortion, Wayne.

WAYNE: Wouldn't have to worry about gettin' her pregnant.

SKEETER: She was vomitin' an' all, dude.

WAYNE: I see your point.

SKEETER: 'Sides, I'm already stricken with love fer these two babe-dudes in Cali, Clove and Sable. I thought about fallin' in love with Camille but it would a just been overmuch.

WAYNE: Right.

SKEETER: Seein' as I fall hard.

WAYNE: Oh yeah?

Wayne casts another look at him.

SKEETER: So I went tuh Milwaukee with Camille and I waited fer her tuh get her abortion an' then we consorted fer a few days, apropos of her trauma an' all.

WAYNE: D'you get laid?

SKEETER: Nah, we couldn't.

WAYNE: Dry humpin'.

SKEETER: Yeh-up.

WAYNE: Dry humpin' in the pickup, you're alright, Keifer.

SKEETER: Skeet. Er.

WAYNE: So why ya cryin'?

SKEETER: I'm not anymore, dude, 'cause yur tangently gettin' me distracted offa my chagrin.

what

WAYNE: But why were ya cryin'?

SKEETER: 'Cause I wanted tuh see my dad.

WAYNE: When'sa last time you saw him?

SKEETER: Nine years old an' before 'at, four years old.

WAYNE: You only saw him twice.

SKEETER: Wull, 'til I'se three he hung out with me an' my ma, Linda, but after dat—

WAYNE: He *split*.

SKEETER: 'At about summarizes it.

WAYNE: So what happened?

SKEETER: They tol' me at Marion det he was in Section C an' I couldn't see him, couldn't even so much as write 'im a fuckin' note and when I said dat must be on the illegal slope of the criminal justice climb, they started tuh ask if my age was of legal tender, an' fer ID, so I told 'em my ma was outside in the car but she didn't want tuh come in, then I gave 'em my fake ID an' I exited rapidamente.

WAYNE: Good lie. Good escape. You did good.

SKEETER: I walked a long way, then I thumbed down yer massive vehicle—

WAYNE: Her name is Debbie.

> Skeeter looks askance.

WAYNE: The truck.

SKEETER: Oh! Hello, Debbie.

> Skeeter pats the dashboard gingerly.

SKEETER: And the rest is contemporaneous, Wayne.

WAYNE: That was good, Jeeper. Time for a donut break. Crack open that Hostess box and hand me that thermos. And let me tell ya somethin'.

SKEETER: Whut?

WAYNE: You're better off.

SKEETER: What?

WAYNE: You're better off you didn't see him. Your old man's a troublemakin' loser.

SKEETER: That's what my ma Linda says.

WAYNE: Mother's always right, Jeep.

SKEETER: Skeeter.

WAYNE: Mother's always right.

ever

SKEETER: Tuhhhhh.

WAYNE: Gulpa joe?

SKEETER: Thankee.

WAYNE: Yep, it's a long haul, it's a long haul, but we're gonna make it, we gotta.

SKEETER: Tuhhh, yup.

WAYNE: Yep, we gotta.

> Wayne blows the deep, dolorous horn and speeds up to pass. They wail past the other car and into the night.

what

CHAPTER 4

IN WHICH CLOVE AND SABLE CARRY ON A CLANDESTINE CONVERSATION

Clove walks into class and sits at a desk next to Sable, sighing deeply. They begin their customary exchange of notes and drawings. Their drawings are a form of inner speech, indicated in bold.

SABLE: Why were you so late fer class and why didn't Posner say anything?

CLOVE: 'Cause I was talking to that hectic counselor. They all think I'm all suicidally tendacious ever since I walked into the ocean at the rave. They think I'm all Generation X and influenced by Kurt Cobain. It is so dull.

SABLE: What did you say?

CLOVE: I say no, duh.

She thinks and draws: *Star. Star. Star.*

SABLE: But it is true you do have those fiendish dreams about K. C.

She thinks and draws: *Spiral. Spiral. Spiral.*

CLOVE: Yah. But that is the ghost of Kurt Cobain. That's not Cobain himself. You know we were never all fanlike. I only started to like *In Utero* recently and you even disagree with me about that. Anyway, that's different. He's haunting me because he saved me from drowning and he wants something. It's not the same as being all influenced—this note-is-way-too-fucking-long.

SABLE: Yah it rully was. We have to start a new sheet of paper and we hardly did any drawings. Posner is so dull.

CLOVE: I know. I hate when he gets all hectic about Bosnia and stuff, I get all—more than agged—I get all—like I can't breathe and all complex like bolted.

SABLE: All bolted?

CLOVE: Like all, I can't breathe, I just can't think about all those people in that country too much all trapped in a city like that and all those armies and all.

SABLE: Right! So don't think about it. But are you sure yur not all influenced by Cobain and stuff? Are you still sleepwalking? You look a tad fiended.

CLOVE: Yah, I think so 'cause yesterday I woke up in my little brother's room scratching his guitar with an onion.

SABLE: An onion? What were you doing scratching Kyler's guitar with an onion?

CLOVE: Sleepwalking, duhh. Gah, yur agging me to excess today.

SABLE: Right, so then let's talk about Bosnia with Posner.

    Sable stares ahead at the teacher. Clove looks at her, licks her pencil, and writes.

CLOVE: This class is so learning impeded.

SABLE: Null that—whose idea was it to take this fer our history credit?

CLOVE: Wull, it was a good name.

SABLE: "This Century in the News" is a good name?

    She thinks and draws: ***Boing! Boing! Boing!***

CLOVE: Yah? Wull, I thought so at the time. Dude, I've been gettin' ragin' headwaves about that boy we met at the rave, Skeeter.

SABLE: Did you get a letter from him?

CLOVE: No, I was arrested, how could I give him my address? Did you?

SABLE: Good. Yah, he sent me a postcard.

CLOVE: What do you mean "good"? What did it say?

    She thinks and draws: ***Flower petal.***

SABLE: It said he thinks of me all the time.

    She thinks and draws: ***Teardrop on flower petal.***

CLOVE: Wull, I'm sure if he had my address he would've written me too. That's funny 'cause that's what he says in my dreams.

    She thinks and draws: ***Penis . . . near . . . teardrop.***

SABLE: That he thinks of me all the time? Ooo, I'm so ultraplanted!

CLOVE: No, that he thinks of me all the time.

what

SABLE: Wull, he sent me the postcard.

She thinks and draws: *Lips . . . next to . . . penis.*

CLOVE: Wull, did he ask fer yer address?

She thinks and draws: *Fangs . . . underneath lips.*

SABLE: No, I put it in his pocket when he hitched off.

CLOVE: So you threw yerself in his pocket. How was his pocket?

She thinks and draws: *Gnarly hand with long, sharp fingernails . . . dripping blood droplets . . . covering the entire page.*

Sable spreads out with a rebuking crackle (and thinks): New sheet of paper . . .

SABLE: It doesn't matter. Never mind.

CLOVE: I'm going to get stoked in the bathroom after class? You want to come?

SABLE: No, I want to be alone.

CLOVE: She *vants* to be alone.

She thinks and draws: *Lady wearing veil.*

SABLE: Yes, she does.

She thinks and draws: *BLACK OUT.* Upon writing this in huge block letters, Sable blacks out Clove's drawing, passes this final missive, and sits with her arms crossed, ignoring Clove. Moments later, Clove is finishing a joint in the school rest room while simultaneously applying Rapturous Ruby lipstick. This presents some difficulties, as the joint is down to fingernail-pinching size. Clove solves the problem by eating the remains of the roach. She turns back to the mirror, screams, and jumps, frightened by the reflection of someone behind her.

CLOVE: Cobain, is that you? He went out the window.

She looks at her image in the mirror. In her fright, she has smeared lipstick across her pale wrist.

CLOVE: Take a look at that blue vein

Shining through my pale skin

She writes on the mirror in lipstick.

CLOVE: Like the vein

O' Cobain

Who died in pain

Blowing a bullet through his brain

Take a look at my blue vein

ever

Tree is bare, branching branching
Sew it to his blue brains
Like thread winding winding
Turning and split
Branching and bent but never slit
Still spun from the heart
Bare branch blue vein, carry it with you to the beat
Blue blue blue vein, enwrap
Blue blue blue vein, spin out
Blue vein run bold, blood fast, blood sweet
Blue vein unfold, unclasp, unseat
Blue vein run wild, without puncture
Blue vein run ravenous deep but do not rupture
Bare branch blue vein entrance me with yer dance
Practice my pulse, enchant me in yer chants
This is no ode to sad Cobain
Who died in vain
This is the ode to my blue vein
Shining through
Pale
Skin!

    She finishes with a flourish, streaking the crimson across the glass.
    The entire rest room mirror is covered.

what

CHAPTER 5

IN WHICH PAUL AND JEANETTE HAVE A CRYSTAL-CLEAR MOMENT

Jeanette and Paul lie on her bed in postcoital peace. Jeanette strokes his back and speaks softly.

JEANETTE: Come on, Paul, why don't you let me run the crystal energy on you, it'll feel good.

PAUL: You feel good enough for me, Jeanette, hon.

JEANETTE: No, I mean on a cellular level.

PAUL: Why don't we leave well enough alone, Jean, and agree to disagree, stay on this level.

JEANETTE: Because I want you to feel healing energy. I want to open you up. Wide.

PAUL: Can't you just massage my prostate like you used to?

JEANETTE: I'm not your mistress anymore, teddy bear.

PAUL: I'll leave Polly if you massage my—
Jeanette leaps up and seizes the crystal she's hidden under her bed. She holds it over him.

JEANETTE: See? This is the crystal. It's a mytelene stalagmite cave-crone crystal from 3000 B.C. Lie still, Paul.

PAUL: Er er er right.

JEANETTE: Breathe.

PAUL: Breathe.

JEANETTE: No, do it.
Paul breathes in and out, once again as if breathing for a doctor's stethoscope. Jeanette passes the crystal over his body. As she does this, his body seizes up and he enters a trance state. Jeanette also is possessed; her eyelids are heavy and she moves in slow motion.

JEANETTE: Hmmm, I'm picking up all of this bilious energy in your ninth gate, that's the seat of conscience.

Paul breathes out.

JEANETTE: Paul, your eighth gate is blocked by smoke, from fires, industrial explosive fires, Paul, oh Goddess, you've been involved in the deaths of thousands of people, Paul! Oh!

Paul sputters, trying to release himself, but he is firmly in the grip of the trance. Jeanette grows tearful.

JEANETTE: People were trapped, children died, mothers, fathers, their bodies piled up, they panicked, they couldn't escape. It was a decision you made on paper. I can see the brown hairs on your wrist with your Rolex, your fingers holding a pen and signing a document. Let me see if the crystal can clean this up for you . . . it can't, it can't, it's . . .

Her hand shakes.

JEANETTE: let me move on to your seventh gate. Oh!

She is relieved.

JEANETTE: I see an ancient forest—trees!—and running through it a beautiful river that is making everything die?! It's filled with an invisible poison, the fish are floating belly up! *Paul*, what does this have to do with you? Your mouth is moving. I see men's ears listening, they're listening to you, Paul, their hearts are beating under their ties? They're taking your words to heart. Paul, let me see if I can do this, the crystal is trying to cleanse this for you.

She exhales.

JEANETTE: Mmmm, this is getting difficult. At your sixth gate, I see your wife, Polly, she is tired she—oh! Hmmm, you have lied to Polly, you have lied to your family, you have lied to—ME!

Her eyes fly open.

JEANETTE: Ah! Ah! The crystal, look at it, it's turned BLACK, it's BURNING!

She throws the crystal away from her. Paul springs off the bed as if there were a snake in it, suddenly awake. Jeanette is crying.

JEANETTE: Ah! Paul, you have to go, you don't fit into my new life. I can't go through this again.

PAUL: Okay, Jeanette.

JEANETTE: How can you seem so sweet to me and be re*spons*ible for all of this?

PAUL: That's just it, I wasn't responsible.

what

JEANETTE: But you *men* are supposed to be responsible.

PAUL: We aren't.

JEANETTE: I see. That's why Polly hates you.

PAUL: She doesn't. She loves me. I lied.

JEANETTE: I see.

PAUL: I'd better go now, hmm?

Paul has his pants on now and is buttoning his shirt.

JEANETTE: Paul, don't go, hold me.

He strokes her head.

PAUL: Ah, Jeanie, you're better than all of this. You've made a new life for yourself. I'm so proud of you getting out of the business and into this crystal razzamatazz. It's remarkable. I can see that now! It really is. You don't need a dolt like old Paul Folsom, you're healing, as you like to say, Miss Gladjnois, and you'll get there, I know it.

JEANETTE: But why is the wonderful sweet man comforting me and advising me to break off with this EVIL man the SAME man? WHY?

PAUL: Why does moss grow under bridges? I don't know, Jeanette, if I knew anything would I have lived my life this way? All my life I've done things and I've expended enough brain power to accomplish those things, but do you think for one moment I've known anything? If I have, it's been that I love making love to you and that I love my children and those are the only two things and even those I've only known infrequently.

JEANETTE: Oh Paul, I love you.

He turns away from her and gazes out at the view from her fifteenth-story window.

PAUL: You shouldn't.

ever

CHAPTER 6

IN WHICH BUSHIE HAS A
CELEBRITY ENCOUNTER

It is late at night and Bushie struts maniacally up West Forty-fifth Street and stops in front of a gaping hole by the curb. She is laughing and shouting at the top of her lungs.

BUSHIE: BUSHIE'S BACK PEOPLE! BUSHIE'S BAAAAAAAAA-ACK!!! Hey Hole, where my tree useta be, Bushie is wacked. Her peepee is burnin' like a disco inferno, it's singin' up inside Bushie's piss pipe. Bushie has done a big wack on da pipe tonight and now dey are playin' my piss thing. Its'a truth I got singin' piss, people! Whammo!

An egg whizzes past her head and she looks up. She cups her hands and shouts up.

BUSHIE: Don't trow eggs at me, you condo-ass Wonderbreads. You don't know how tuh trow if I was trowin' eggs at yuhr Wonderbread asses do you think Bushie would miss? No! Dee ansuhr is NO-OO!

I pissed on a star. Bushie pissed upon a star. I useta piss here, Hole, where my tree useta be. Dat's one reason da tree died, everybody pissed on huh, and den da police yanked it real hard dat night in da rainstorm when da condos had me tied to it. I was cursin'!! Dat's what kilt my tree. Da sanitations took huhr away after Christmas an' *I swore*, outta *respect*, dat I will NEVER PISS ON DIS SPOT AGAIN! Dose Wonderbreads—STOP TROWIN' EGGS!

She dodges overhead bombing.

Why don't *dey* buy a new tree? HAH???

Now dat da fundings are cut, BUY A NEW TREE! See, Bushie's smart, Bushie knows.

Bushie pissed on a star today. It was Charlie Frets. I go: "Ain't

dat Charlie Frets who had dose hits back in da seventies?" Me an'
my main girl useta dance tuh "Jump on da Jam Slide" on huh
brudda Felix's tape-deck. We useta dance—"banh banh banh"—we
jump offa huh grandma's plastic couch. Stand on da top JUMP on
da Jam—BAM!—'til we had all black an' blues. I fuckin' idolated
Charlie Frets, said tuh all my P.R., black bitches, I said: See! White
people can get down on it white people can funk it up look at Charlie Frets: Is he hot or is he not? Yeah, an' dey had to agree.

Me an Magenta was little we made up dances. I useta blow huh
belly button. Like dis.

She sticks out her tongue and does a slow, sensual Bronx cheer. Her
voice softens.

BUSHIE: Magdalena Rigobar. Magenta Rush. Nobody knows. Nobody
but Bushie an' dis tree-hole knows what Bushie did.

She starts shouting again.

SO HE PULLS UP TUH DA CURB. I go it *is*, it *is* Charlie Frets. He
goes "Which one of youse will piss on me?" Pam wouldn't. Nutz
didn't feel good. Snapple said she had enough perverted rides fuhr
da afternoon. I go: You useta be a star why you want me tuh piss on
yuz I'll do you regulah. He goes "I got *real* women fuh dat. I want
one of *you* fuh degradation." I didn't want to, Tree Hole, but Terry
had just took my whole take and I needed sometin' fuh myself. So I
pissed all ovah him in his gray sedan down by Time Storage Ware-
house. I pissed on him but inside I held it an' I hummed his song.
Denh, denh, dah, denh, denh.

DEN he gave me twenty which is cheap when you think how
bigga hits he had back in seventy-five, but took it fuh MY hit. And I
took it fuh real. HEY! YOU MISSED ME AGAIN WIT' YUHR EGGS!
LAME-ASS! An' Bushie got way up be*yond* da stars like I'm way
up inside Magenta Rush's belly button even if she married dat
Christian-ass Bible dealer an' she don't see me no more I don't care
'cause inside it's jinglin' my pee-hole is singin'.

She croons:

BUSHIE: " 'Jump on da Jam slide do da do da funky glide, oo baby I
love you . . . ooooooooooo' "

ever

CHAPTER 7

IN WHICH POLLY TAKES
HER COFFEE BLACK

Polly stands at a coffee bar avidly sipping a paper cup of coffee. She sights her friend Bunny Peters and waves. Bunny, a big fat woman wearing an expensive flower-print dress purchased in an upscale department store, waves back and hurries toward her.

POLLY: Yoo hooo, Bunny, honey, here I am. I'm so glad you could meet me! Don't you just love the new Better Bean here at the mall? Can you imagine how we drank all that bad five-and-dime coffee our entire lives? Where'd we used to go? The Patchwork Quilt Cafe, remember that little ole place with the blue frill curtains and we drank cup after cup? Here at the Better Bean I only need one little ole cup, it's so black and rich, hee hee. Do you think this coffee's from South America? I hear the best bean comes from northern Africa, the ay-rab-ica, they call it, makes the best coffee. How're things at the Rabbit Lodge? Let's sit here. That's a big cup of coffee, Bunny Peters, what is that, a jumbo? You mean you're just goin' to live on coffee 'til you lose weight? But, Bunny, you're a big gal, you've always been a big gal, they-ere's nothin' wrong wi— Alright, let's not talk about it! I'm in too good a mood. Hmm. Let me try yours. Mmmmm. That whippy creamy thing is no-fat?

Her voice goes up in disbelief as she licks the whipped cream from her little finger.

POLLY: Mmmm. Delicious. Ahh. Hee hee hee. Do I? Thank you. Hee-hee! Wey-ell, I feel different. I feel forty years younger, lak the old Polly Renard, with no Folsom on the end of *my* name. No, I haven't decided to leave him. No, he'd have to leave if I did. I'd keep the house. But anyway, Paul's on another you-know-what-kind-of-trip in New York City. And I don't care two *figs* what he's doin'!

Wey-ell, it's all to do with losin' the weddin' ring down the disposal. Right, wey-ell, you know how I called you and I was so upset and you said "Wey-ell go ahead and call that garbage disposal man, you lak'd him so much," and you implied—wey-ell, you may not have outright said it Bunny but you implied— Wey-ell, I already had called him because it made sense, I mean, he installed the garbage disposal, the ring went down it, he'd said if there was any problem, just give a ring, so I had already taken your advice before you gave it.

Alright, I'm gettin' to it! So he came by that afternoon and you know how he had to put that thing all the way down the drain, that hookie thing?

She crooks her baby finger.

POLLY: I know you know all this, Bunny, but I'm just tellin' you the sequence of events, now do you wont to know or don't you? So he did that all afternoon, never found the ring, had a glass of ice tea—Beverly was there, she made it for him, as you know Beverly prepares a fine ice-tea—and then he left, said he would try again, wey-ell, he came back for three weeks, each time no luck, and each time he was so polite and Paul was never there. Then he started comin' by around six, which, as you know, is when Beverly leaves and we'd just talk and—what? Oh, about, about nothing, the weather, the house, that townhouse village they're buildin' over the old meadows, churches, different styles of church people go to. Hee-hee!

She looks at Bunny nervously.

POLLY: Wey-ell, Bunny, one day, Paul phoned from Zurich to say he was comin' back to the U.S. but not flyin' back to Virginia but ruther stoppin' over in New York and I was just so fumed up for the trillionth time in this long marriage! Wey-ell, alright, I won't go into that.

And then Reuben came by just then and I gave him a slice of cherry pie which I had baked myself. Beverly didn't make it, it was my old family recipe, you know it, and as he ate it he kept ex-

ever

claimin' how good it was and when he came to the last bite, Bunny, he held up that forkful of pie.

She pauses for effect.

POLLY: And he slid it right into my mouth before I could stop him.

She closes her eyes and flutters her lids, allowing her graceful fingers to caress her collarbone. She opens wide her eyes, blushing with pleasure.

POLLY: We *did*! I cain't believe I would ever do such a thing at my age. He's twelve years younger. You don't think that's bad? Good. He's, he's, he's not my husband, though, Bunny, and we were, were taught that was wrong. Hee hee! I knew you'd say to heck with what we were taught! I knew you'd say that.

She sips Bunny's no-fat mochachino.

POLLY: Mmm, such good coffee. But I don't know, I still think it's wrong. Wey-ell, Bunny there's one little ole thing . . . I cain't tell you . . . No, he's not, he's divorced. Good man. Sent his son to college with the garbage disposal business. He's kind, he's polite, he's, oh, Bunny, he's lak nothin' I've ever known before and yet, he's so familar to me.

She closes her eyes again.

POLLY: He's black, oh Bunny! He's one of them.

As Polly opens her eyes, she witnesses her best friend Bunny Peters stand up and walk quickly from the cafe pavilion area of the Better Bean Boutique.

POLLY: Bunny? Bunny? Where are you goin'? Don't get up and leave Polly. I'm your best friend for fifty years. Bunny Suzanne Peters! Don't desert poor Polly,

Bunny is gone.

POLLY: Polly wont a cracker, Polly wont a . . .

Polly sits at the table for a minute, tears filling her eyes. She looks around and sees she must gather herself together. She dabs an eye with her paper napkin, stands up, and approaches the coffee bar with her cup now empty.

POLLY: Excuse me, young man? I'd lak a fresh cup of coffee, Java Brew. No milk! This time. I take it black. Now.

POLLY: Hee hee! I'n't this nice weather we've been havin' lately?

She jumps, then recovers herself.

what

CHAPTER 8

IN WHICH SKEETER APPROACHES THE EVIL CITADEL

Skeeter is in a car with a New Jersey family.

ANTOINETTE: I wanta know, why'd you pick 'im up when we don't even have enough room fuhr our own?

JOEY: I told ya, he's a good kid, he needed a ride, haven't you ever needed sometin' in yar life?

ANTOINETTE: Need? Need? Joey, I need a new friggin' life, hah? I need a wash machine fuhr all your children's dirty clothes, I need a new flaar in the dining room, I need—

Antoinette coughs until she has no breath left and then leans her head between her legs and wheezes like someone who has almost drowned.

JOEY: You need a new setta lungs.

ANTOINETTE: Joe Junya, hand your mother a new pack outta her carton since ya father's a friggin' creep who picks up freaky low-life hitchhikers and won't—

JOEY: Dat's it, I'm pullin' ovah.

ANTOINETTE: Dis is da Joisey Toinpike!

JOEY: Dis kid does not have tuh listen tuh dis, dis is too em*bar*rasin', yar em*bar*rassin' me, Antoinette.

ANTOINETTE: Good!

JOEY: Kid, I'm sarry, I gotta drop youse here.

SKEETER: But er, er, this is the-the turnpike.

JOE JR.: Get out!

JOEY: Sarry, kid, I can't take no more.

SKEETER: What. Ever.

Skeeter climbs out of the crowded car and slams the door behind him. He can still hear them arguing as they pull away.

ANTOINETTE: See what yiz did, Joey, you made a bad situation worse.

JOEY: Shaddap!

DAUGHTER: Mommy, Mommy, Joe Junya hit me! Wah waaaaah . . .

JOEY: Shaddap, alla yaz!

They disappear. Cars whiz by.

SKEETER: Tuhhh.

Skeeter spits, then looks up and jumps, narrowly dodging a car.

SKEETER: Oh ye pagan Goddess o' the Turnpikes, abet me, deity-dudes, in my hour o' need!

A canary-yellow 1960 Thunderbird screeches up. Inside is a very wrinkled and very skinny old man wearing a tweed sportsman hat. His head revolves on his lizardly neck slowly and he regards Skeeter with unflinching blue eyes.

JULIAN: *Whar* ya going, Hermes?

SKEETER: ANYWHUR!

JULIAN: Get in!

Skeeter dives in and they peel off into the stream of traffic. The man steers with abandon.

SKEETER: Voluminous obligin's, dude—

He sees that the old man is wearing a proper gray suit, only a little stained around the collar.

SKEETER: Sir.

JULIAN: De nada. Where you going?

He has a dry, rustling croak of a voice. And he speaks through tight, clenched lips, showing his teeth, which are rotted.

SKEETER: Wull, New York City is m' final destin—

JULIAN: And *New* York City it shall *be.* We are *list*ing that way as I speak. You are in *luck.*

The old man's eyes light up alarmingly.

SKEETER: Ragin'.

JULIAN: What's your name, *Puck?*

SKEETER: Er, Skeeter.

JULIAN: As in the *mo*squito?

SKEETER: Right on.

JULIAN: Do your friends call you that because you an*noy* them in the *mode* of that insect?

SKEETER: How d'ya know that?

what

JULIAN: I've been around.

A hairy, unkempt man of about forty rises up out of the backseat. He screams feverishly, first spitting, then stretching out each word, laboring as if English were not his native tongue. It is. Spittle flies from his mouth.

CABZACACA: An' aroun' and aroun' an' aroun' he go, where he stop nobody gonna know!

He plops back down.

SKEETER: Rare scare!

JULIAN: Don't freak, don't freak, that's only Cabzacaca, my ward, the adopted son of my ex-lover, Abraham.

SKEETER: Er, er you gay?

JULIAN: Homo*sex*ual! I've been one for *years* and I'm not going to go GAY NOW! Call me fairy, call me faggot, if you like you may call me nasty old faggot.

He waits.

JULIAN: But call me.

SKEETER: Oh. Er, wull, condolences on th' expiration of yer lover, Abe.

JULIAN: Oh no, he's alive.

SKEETER: Er, then why'd yuh adopt Cabzakooka?

JULIAN: Don't know.

SKEETER: Wull, whur's yer ex-lover?

JULIAN: Not entirely sure. Last I heard his *men*tal derangement went out of *ran*ge even for the *Boo*d-hissts at the *Boo*d-hisst farm and they packed him off to the *a*-sylum. Somewhere in New *Hamp*shire, I *haz*ard.

Their companion pops back up.

CABZACACA: Treadinggggg up a mountain, a cement mountain I came across six archangels with corrugated aluminum wings, I asked them their names and they said their names were *Fredo*, like the brother who gets *killed* in the *Godfather* movies, *Junco*, as in junk bonds, *Parmesati*, as in Parmesan cheese you buy to shake on your spaghettis, *Lisa*, a common name, *Bad Breath Mouth*, a name of self-evident origins, and *Wendall*, to signify nothing. Those were the six names of the archangels. I got on their metallic monkey backs and we flew down to McDonald's and had McMuffins. It was a nice day.

ever

The sun behind a net of clouds looked like a leaking rusted gas tank afloat in a burnt red ocean. I smiled at the day as it came to a close. Daddy Julian, can we go to McDonald's?

JULIAN: NO! Go back to the land o' nod. You're freaking out young Mr. Kerouac here.

> He plops back down again. Skeeter, who *has* been discomfited, rearranges himself and turns to the old man.

SKEETER: What would be the origin of Caboosacock's name?

JULIAN: Cabzacaca? Short for Cabeza de Caca. Means shithead in Mexican. We picked it up when we were living au naturel in the Sierra Madre. Ten years. Thin air. Pure drugs. No friends. Should've stayed.

SKEETER: Ragin'. And yer name's Julian?

JULIAN: You're *sharp*, Mosquito Boy, you're bright as a *pen*ny. *Say*, you're not of these *ortho*dox*ic east*ern states are you? You're from the u*top*ic west?

SKEETER: Correcto, Oregon.

JULIAN: Mm hmm. White supremacist encampments.

SKEETER: Tuhh.

JULIAN: You a NAZI?

SKEETER: Nuh. Are you?

JULIAN: *No*. Just checking.

SKEETER: Er, yeah. I comb th' coast, mostly. Loiter down Cali-way. I rave—heard uh that?

JULIAN: Heard of it? I in*vent*ed it in DREAM in 1949.

SKEETER: Zat on the veritable side of the slope?

JULIAN: Listen, I've told you I'm a seventy-year-old faggot, Detective Spade, why would I lie about inventing the Raving Movement?

SKEETER: Er, it's called rave. As in, I rave, we rave. Radical raves, brother, rave on, rave on, etceteras.

JULIAN: I get it, Alfonso. Allow me to introduce myself. Julian Pritchard Beech—

> He turns to shake hands, entirely letting go of the steering wheel. They shake.

JULIAN: —and this is my car, Miranda.

> He turns back and regains control of the wheel.

SKEETER: Beauteous car, what's the age on her?

what

JULIAN: Miranda is thirty-five years old. And a virgin.

SKEETER: Right on.

JULIAN: How 'bout you? Are you a virgin? Don't freak, I'm a fairy, not a pedophile. I don't care for boys under forty.

SKEETER: Nuh.

JULIAN: You've done the wild waltz?

Julian turns on him suddenly.

JULIAN: *How*-many-times?

Skeeter counts silently.

SKEETER: Uhhhh, countless.

JULIAN: *Cunt*less?

SKEETER: Nuh.

JULIAN: Ah, so, as far as fairy you are virgin?

SKEETER: That'd be correcto.

JULIAN: Hmmm. And what brings you to the Evil Citadel, lad?

SKEETER: I'm paying a rite-of-passage-type visit tuh my Aunt Jeanette, she's a healin' professional of the pagan wave.

JULIAN: Who dwells?

SKEETER: Er, north Manhattan.

JULIAN: East? West? WEST? EAST? KNOW YOUR GEOGRAPHY!

He steers wildly. Skeeter bounces around and calls out nervously.

SKEETER: Two-sixty-four Seventy-eighth Street! Near Lexington and Park Street?

Julian resumes normal steering.

JULIAN: Ah, your Auntie Jeanette must have healed many *rich* sickies. Upper *East* Side, Man*hat*tan, *dig*?

SKEETER: I guess.

JULIAN: My *simp*leton hallucinator and I roost out in a *slum* palace in the illustrious *Flat*bush fief, domain of *Brooklyn*, but seeing as you are at least *part*ially a virgin, Miranda has consented to *bear* you to your *Aunt*ie's.

SKEETER: Repetitiously, I thank ye.

JULIAN: *De nada;* mos*quite, de nada.*

Cabzacaca pops back up, his eyes bulging, and swats the seat behind Skeeter's head repeatedly as he declaims his dream.

CABZACACA: Daddy, the razored flower petals fall like foil off a baked sweet potato to my eyes are heater coils and I need to piss but the

ever

river is dry the river is flooded the river is gone the river is hot and it's melting, it's melting—

Cabzacaca hooks his arm around Skeeter's throat and chokes him.

SKEETER: Dude dude dude duuuurrggggghhhhlllll—

CABZACACA: DEE IIIIIIICE IS MELTING!

JULIAN: Cabza*ca*ca. Cabza*ca*ca

Julian drives the car crazily, but chides his ward in an unruffled monotone.

JULIAN: Off him, unhand the lad, off, off, this will give him a bad first impression of our famous me*trop*olis, Cabza*ca*ca.

CABZACACA: MCDONALD'S!

JULIAN: Yes, okey*doke*, McDonald's, now un*hand* the child!

Cabzacaca unlooses Skeeter and collapses in the backseat.

JULIAN: He'll *doze* the rest of the way to Mc*Don*ald's now. Sorry about that.

SKEETER: Pull over, dude, and let me the FUCK out!

JULIAN: *Skee*ter, what's the trouble, kid?

SKEETER: On my hitch across this country I have had enough attempts made on my life, my SO-CALLED liberty and my pursuit o'—WHAT! *EV*ER! tuh last me three lifetimes at th' least! Now pull over an' let me out, I'll WALK the rest o' the way!

JULIAN: Don't freak, don't freak, this is good for you, welcome to our *great*est, our *mad*dest city. You'll *like* it. Calm *down*, dear. Stop crying, you *twat* addict!

SKEETER: Huh? But yur his dad, an' yur not even straight!

JULIAN: What! In HEATHEN'S NAME has THAT got to do with it?

SKEETER: Nuthin'! But yur sposed tuh be his dad, old dude, an' he tried tuh strangle me.

JULIAN: He didn't *mean* it.

SKEETER: Stop the carrrrrr!!!!

Skeeter opens the car door.

JULIAN: Close the door. Close it or I'll crash the car.

Julian floors it until they are going a hundred miles an hour and jerks the steering wheel from side to side, cackling madly.

JULIAN: I'M SEVENTY YEARS OLD AND I DON'T GIVE ONE BUTTFUL OF SHIT ABOUT BUYIN' IT! *TRY* ME! Ah ha ha ah ha ha ah ha ha!!

what

SKEETER: AH! AH!

They are thrown savagely about in the car. Julian's laughter escalates along with Skeeter's terror. Skeeter slams the car door shut. Julian resumes his normal driving and Skeeter tries to catch his breath.

JULIAN: You know what your trouble is, Hermes? You need a *grand*-daddy. Tell you what, I'll adopt *you*, too.

SKEETER: Kin we go to a diner, then, instead of a McDonald's?

JULIAN: Okeydoke, I'll buy you a Coke.

SKEETER: Happy returns, dude. Hmmm, now rewind on how yuh invented raves?

JULIAN: There it is! There's New York, see it?

Julian points to a distant but unmistakable skyline.

SKEETER: Yeh-up. I do.

Cabzacaca pops back up.

CABZACACA: Of all the towns in all the world, why'd ya haveta end up in this one?

He lies down again.

JULIAN: There's a Hojo's at the next exit. Strawberry *shakes* for one and *all*. This is your first approach to the Profane *Me*cca, Mos*quite*, you must savor the ap*proach*.

SKEETER: Uh, I am.

CABZACACA: Truth?

Cabzacaca sticks his face in Skeeter's neck and this time Skeeter turns and barks at him.

SKEETER: Most veraciously!

CABZACACA: Huh!

Cabzacaca sleeps.

JULIAN: I can see that you *are*. I can see that you'll *like* it. Let's turn here and put it *off* some moments *mo*re. *Lin*ger on the *led*ge of antic-ip*ati*on.

Julian changes lanes, heading for the exit.

ever

CHAPTER 9

IN WHICH VIOLET SHOOTS A DEER

During a lull between the after-work crowd and the nightlife crowd at the Blue Ship Diner, Violet is able to get the ear of Sonia the waitress. She stands next to Violet, leans an elbow on the counter, and eats her dinner while keeping half an eye on her tables.

VIOLET: Bill came home afteh the war and we were still officially married y'see, Sonyer, though I think we both privately knew that it had to be over. I was living in New York by that time and I'd been nursing half-dead soldiers throughout the war, so Bill's state of mind was not a'tall a surprise. I fell in love with most of the soldiers whom I nursed, but I hadn't the heart to have a romance with any of them. It wasn't on Bill's account. It was those poor men. Trading promises seemed such an insult to them at that stage. D'you understand a'tall, deeah? Was he? Your ex-boyfriend was in Vietnam? Well then, I'm sure you do. You're very sensitive, Sonyer deeah, I can see that. Why are you standing? Sit *down* for your break, f' God's sake, don't stay on your feet! What's that, the tuna?

Connie? Can I have some more hot wateh f' my tea? Yes, well, I'll be *happy* to pay the eighty-nine cents or whatever'tis, just *more* hot wateh, please. And whatever Sonyer wants to drink. *I'll* pay for it . . . How do you tolerate working with ruffians like Connie here at the Blue Ship Diner? He's your brother-in-law? Constantinopolis? Is your husband Greek, deeah? Let me see your wedding ring. Oh, it's very nice. Is he, uh, what do they call it, a macho? Is he a macho, your husband? Yes? Good. Well, then you'll enjoy the story of how I divorced Bill.

Bill was discharged and came immediately heah to New Yawk. First off, we went out f' suppah with my parents which was, naturally—godawful.

So. We were in a cab—he was boarded with an army chum, because I was still rooming at the time in a women's residence, y'see. We were in a cab and in the cab, he turned to me, and he said, Violet, I'm going tomorrow and buying a brand-new hunting rifle and then I think Roy and I—Roy, that was his army chum—are going to go on a hunt f' the weekend. I thought this was a pahticu'ly idiotic plan, Sonyer. But I'd spent my girlhood summers in New Jersey on my uncle's estate and my uncle was a hunting man, y' see, and often took me along. I'd go almost anywhere and do almost anything to escape my immediate family; father, mother, brothers, and sister, every last one of them were terribly nice and *terribly dull.* My uncle was a different sort. He was stern and cross, rather a *cruel* man, actually, but he enjoyed life.

She pauses and considers this.

VIOLET: Or at any rate, he enjoyed *kill*ing things, and he'd taught me how to do it. How to shoot and trim and quarter a deer. So I said to Bill, Right, well, I'll go with you.

Bill didn't like this, y'see, Sonyer. Despite or p'rhaps on *account* of his being a writer, which meant that in essence he was a bookish *fop* of a man, he had his heart set on doing *man*nish things. I'd 've thought the war would've cured him of that, but I found out differently.

So Roy, another fellow Sam, his girl, Joan, and Bill and I all went up to a lodge somewhere just outside of Poughkeepsie. I thought I'd go out with them and got myself up early that first morning in trousers and a flannel jacket and big boots but Bill said, What are you doing? You stay here and keep Joan company. Be a good sport.

She looks at Sonia hard and long, that she may register the full indignity of this command.

VIOLET: So I did. Joan and I sat all day in the main room at the lodge. There was a fireplace there, I remember, and a plaid couch with plaid pillows and there were oil paintings hung *ev*erywhere of Scotsmen in kilts. We couldn't figure that part out. We spent *half* the day talking 'bout it! Joan was a *snappy* girl. She had lipstick even redder than mine, and let me tell you, Sonyer, mine was *red*, very red! And I still remember to this day what she had on. She wore a tartan jacket with matching red silk jodhpurs and a little blue tartan

ever

hat that was pinned on her black hair. The men all hated it. I thought it was *grand*, in an impossible-to-wear sort of way, but somehow, she wore it s' I thought it was grand.

So Joan and I sat there all day in th' main room. First we ordered breakfast,

She waits.

VIOLET: then we ordered lunch,

She waits again.

VIOLET: then we ordered drinks. Then the sun went down and the men still hadn't returned. We thought we'd wait for the fellows to come back before we ordered suppah, so we ordered another round of drinks. It got very dark outside, we had to pull a little quilt over us t' keep warm and so we ordered, naturally, another round of drinks, and another, and another—we ordered SEVERAL MORE ROUNDS OF DRINKS. We were *crocked* when the men got back at eleven-thirty—not to mention *starv*ing! They were dragging a deer but it hadn't been properly killed. They were covered in blood from it. They hadn't trussed it properly and something was terribly wrong but they wouldn't tell us. Are you interested deeah or would you rather rest during your break, Sonyer? No? Good. Connie! More hot *wateh* f' my tea, PLEASE. Balzac, stop wriggling about on my lap, if you don't mind. Good poodle.

So, Joan and I sawr all this when we wobbled out into the yard at the back of the lodge. There was an open sort of shed f' the hunters to string up the game. Apparently they'd shot the deer in the wrong place, somewhere below the gut, and then argued about how best to kill it or that's as much as they would tell us. Some inscrutable point of honor or other. Well, apart from being stewed, I was suddenly quite angry when I sawr there was still a bit of life left in the deer. Joan was screaming at Sam. I shook her and told her: get the men washed up. Then I took Bill's gun and I shot the deer in the heart. The men went all silent. I kept hollering at them, Will you please tell us what on *earth* is going on!? They wouldn't look at me. They'd only look at Bill. Next morning, Bill sat on the edge of our bed and he said to me, Violet, I don't think I can be married to your sort of woman. And I said, What sort of a woman is that? The

what

sort of woman who would kill a deer. That way. And I said, Well, I don't think I can be married to the sort of man who *wouldn't*. And so we were divorced. Isn't that swell? Oh, don't look so horrified. 'Tsalright, deeah, I was remarried and divorced—uhh, so many times I cahn't even remember. How's the tuna, Sonyer?

ever

CHAPTER 10

IN WHICH CLOVE AND SABLE
TAKE A FIELD TRIP

Clove and Sable are winding up the coastal highway in a beaten-up old VW bug. Clove is driving.

CLOVE: Sable, how do I shift it?

SABLE: Just shift!

CLOVE: Oh—ah! AH! This is so excessive, would you do it fer me!

SABLE: Here. Watch out fer that van!

Sable reaches over and honks the horn.

CLOVE: Ah!

SABLE: Ha hah!

CLOVE: Ha ha ha! Rad. Yer parents' VW is so stoked. Did you tell them yur teaching me to drive?

SABLE: Boing boing boing, of course not, Clove, take yer foot off the gas.

CLOVE: Which foot is it?

SABLE: That one.

CLOVE: Oh my God-duh-duh-duh—

Clove turns to Sable and Sable joins in. Whenever they do the Goddess stammer, they wobble their heads in unison, drawing out the word goddess until they crack themselves up.

SABLE: duh-duh-duh-duh-duh-duh-duh-duh-duh

CLOVE: duh-duh-duh-duh-duh-duh-duh-duh

CLOVE AND SABLE: dess-ss-ss-ss

CLOVE: —rad, ha ha ha!

SABLE: Are you sure you want to go up there?

CLOVE: Right on. It's only twenty miles up the coast.

SABLE: We could've stayed in Cruz.

CLOVE: Yah? And like driven around Main Square and loitered with all those tweakers. That would have gotten us radically catatonic. What're you putting in?

SABLE: The new S. J. Salome tape, *Sunburn*.

CLOVE: Rad.

> Sable puts the tape in and they sing along. The lyrics go something like this:

Jaundiced telephone call at three o'clock in the moan-in'
and you say you done love me anymore
so let's just put little knit caps on our heads an' go an' shop in
boutique stores
an' Flyyyyyy
Fly at the sun
and hope we don't
Hope we don't
Hope we don't
get sunburrrrrrrrrrrrrrrrrrrrrrrrrrrrrrrrrrrrrrn

> The two girls try their best to imitate the scratchy, suicidish, psuedo-little-girl insouciance of S. J. Salome's voice. Fortunately, they are too much like real little girls to quite pull it off. Now comes a jangly bridge that they also do their best to imitate, singing something like: "Yang yang yang yang yang yang yang yang yang" and flailing their heads all over. They bear a resemblance to excited squirrels. Clove recovers.

CLOVE: Right on. That was so spasmodic and rare and burning-with-rage when S. J. jumped off that old-fashioned Jack in the Box head and flew over that parking lot with those wings singin' this an' *Suicide Watch—Actual Deaths* was all there being all, "You mean she didn't get smushed? This isn't a suicide like? Er? Er? Er?"

SABLE: I loathe that show to excess. You have no idea how trauma-like that *Suicide Watch* news crew was the night you drowned at the rave, are you sure you want to go back there?

CLOVE: Don't keep being all, are you sure, are you sure—what are you all trepidatious on?

SABLE: I just feel like maybe that beach is cursed.

CLOVE: Why?

ever

Clove passes a car on the narrow two-lane highway and Sable notices that a truck is coming toward them.

SABLE: Watch out!

CLOVE: But why? Because I almost drowned er because—

SABLE: Watch—

CLOVE: of the dead sea lion er—

SABLE: OUT!!

Sable grabs hold of the wheel just in time and swerves them onto a tiny shoulder of road. The car behind them brakes and swerves to avoid them, almost colliding with the truck. Both of the other drivers lean on their horns, screaming at them as they sail out of sight. They skid into the red earth of the cliff and Clove remembers to brake as Sable yanks up the emergency brake. They cannot stop giggling. They do the Goddess stammer.

SABLE AND CLOVE: Oh God-duh-duh-duh-duh-duh-duh-dess-ss-ss-ss.

CLOVE: Huh huh huh.

Sable abruptly stops giggling.

SABLE: I better drive

CLOVE: Okay. Let's tweak, I need to get tweaked.

SABLE: Rad.

They switch places, scooting over and under each other without getting out of the VW. Clove lights up a roach from the glove compartment. They pass it back and forth.

SABLE: Maybe that was a bad omen and it means we shouldn't go.

CLOVE: Tune yer ear, Sable, ever since that night I am being haunted by Cobain the Friendly Ghost. He wants something fer saving me out the frisky sea and bringing me to the brussels sprouts fields o' safety.

SABLE: What I don't get is why is he all the way down here in Cali, when his thing happened all the way up by Puget Sound?

CLOVE: Maybe it's an ocean thing, I don't know, that's why I want to go back to the brussels sprouts and see if thur's a sign.

SABLE: A sign of what?

Sable passes Clove the cinder of the roach. Clove holds it beween her fingernails and manages a last toke.

CLOVE: Ever.

what

Clove exhales and eats the last of the roach, spitting the paper off the tip of her tongue. Sable starts up the car and steers back onto the road.

SABLE: Get out the map.

CLOVE: Okay.

Clove gets a new map out of the glove compartment and inhales it.

CLOVE: Mmmm, it's all plastic wrapped. I so adore that new plastic smell. Mmmmm. What do we need a map fer if we're just going straight up the coast?

SABLE: To look fer a sign up our spine. Why is Cobain haunting Queen Califia?

CLOVE: 'Cause the cuh-liffs are far or nee-ahhh.

SABLE: Yah

CLOVE: In Cali Cali—

SABLE: Shiva.

CLOVE: Kali is the End.

SABLE: —the end of the calendar.

CLOVE: Kuh-liffs of flowers fornicatin'—

SABLE: Yah!

Clove spreads the map on the ceiling and reads off names as she points to towns.

CLOVE: Eureka, Manteca, Vacaville, Yuba.

SABLE: Vaca-yuba Vaca- yum yume yume.

Sable makes convincing vacuum-sucking sounds.

CLOVE: Bakersfield!

This cracks Clove up.

SABLE: Bake-a bake-a Bake-a Shake 'n' bake 'n'Quake. Quake a ville Quick-quick-quick.

CLOVE: Back to Cali.

SABLE: Nah, let's leave her—

CLOVE: Na.

SABLE: Yah.

CLOVE: Na.

SABLE: Yah Yah Yah 'cause she's quakin'

CLOVE: Shakin' comin'

They lower and lower their voices.

SABLE: Down.

ever

CLOVE: Down.

SABLE: Down.

CLOVE: Right on! We have to start our band. We are way better than S. J. Salome, without a grave doubt!

SABLE: It's totally our karma, but first we have to decide what instruments and we have to learn how to play.

CLOVE: No, first we have to devise our name.

SABLE: Hmmm.

CLOVE: I know.

SABLE: What?

CLOVE: The Tweakers?

SABLE: Yeah?

CLOVE: 'Cause we're always tweaked when we write our songs.

SABLE: Sounds flaccid to me, The Tweakers.

CLOVE: Yur just thwackin' on the neg slope.

SABLE: Tuhhh, now yur talkin' all surf rave.

CLOVE: Yah? Like that dude Skeeter yur so ultra slobbery over, he's a surf rave.

SABLE: Nuh, nuh.

CLOVE: He is, he's all, "Let's slide off on the copulatin' side o' the slope, girl-dude," an' all like that.

SABLE: Tuhh. He said that to you?

CLOVE: Yah. Yah?! Tuhhhh. I was the one getting all slithery with him before I drowned and you scarfed him off me, you trespassing tangerine tart.

SABLE: Wull, if he ever comes back then you can have him, if yur going to get all Juliette Lewis.

CLOVE: I'm not getting all Juliette Lewis! In point of fact, yur twingin' a tad Jennifer Jason Leigh. This is waxing all *Single White Female*. Tune yer ear, Sable, you can have him, alright? He's yers.

SABLE: No, you can have him.

CLOVE: Never mind, what ever.

They stop talking and sulk.

SABLE: Here's the brussels sprouts farm! Wur here.

They pull up and Clove runs out and over to the brussels sprouts.

CLOVE: Ragin'! These're all the brussels sprouts. I was all playing in them rappin' with them all engrossively an' shit until the state

what

troopers came. Whoah, Brussel Sprouts–dudes, how are you? Heh, heh, heh, heh.

Clove has her head down among the sprouts and cocks her ear this way and that. Two farmworkers stop picking and regard her.

CARLITO: *¿Ella es la misma?*

HELACIO: *Sí. La loca desnuda.*

CARLITO: *¿Seguro? Es la misma chica?*

HELACIO: *Sí, seguro.*

CARLITO: *¿Seguro?*

HELACIO: *Sí!*

CARLITO: *Pregunta-le, pregunta-le sobre el espectro.*

CLOVE: Sable, these are the farmworker-dudes who found me and called the troopers. Hey, hi!

CARLITO: *Pregunta-le.*

HELACIO: My friend want to tell you, you make no to sleep, to come awake a-a-a-

CARLITO: *Un Espíritu, fantasma.*

SABLE: Oh God-duh-duh-duh-dess, thur talkin' about a ghost.

HELACIO: Yes! He is khost. He say, I yam Cobaing the Friengly Khost.

SABLE: Oh God-duh-duh-duh-dess, this is too overly fiended.

CLOVE: See, Sable? I told you I wasn't all deludated. I told you that he was realistic.

SABLE: I can't believe it, this is rare, this is uncooked.

CARLITO: *¿Ella lo conoce?*

HELACIO: *Sí, sí.* The khost, you know the *espectro*?

CLOVE: Everybody does, it's Cobain.

HELACIO: Yes?

CLOVE: Cobain? Nirvana?

Helacio looks at her blankly. Clove hums Nirvana's "All Apologies."

HELACIO: Yes. Music he like. He come from there. El Pacifico, the ocean?

He points over the cliff to the ocean below them.

CLOVE: Yes, he is haunting me.

HELACIO: We also he is "yhaunt-teen."

CLOVE: He wants something.

HELACIO: What?

CLOVE: He—

Clove mimes putting a gun in her mouth and pulling the trigger. She
staggers back a few steps to demonstrate the impact.

CARLITO: ¡Ooooo, qué lástima! Murió en pecado mortal.

Helacio taps his head.

HELACIO: He give he head, you give you head.

Carlito nods in solemn assent.

CARLITO: Sí, un sacrificio.

SABLE: Clove, I just finished studying about Aztecs in "Western Days
an' Ways," and I think we should get back to my parents' VW,
Clove, I'm being crucially realistic.

CLOVE: These are Mexicans, Sable.

SABLE: Yah?

Sable takes off for the VW.

HELACIO: You need to give something to make him sleep, yes?

CLOVE: I understand.

They are all three very serious in that moment and understand something important is taking place, something that will change their lives.

SABLE: I'm leaving without you, Clove, I'm leaving without you!

Sable has the VW started.

CLOVE: Wait!

Clove runs for the car.

CARLITO: Wait! Hay una brussels sprout, para ti.

She stops and turns as he, with ceremony, presses a sprout into her
palm, closing her fingers over it.

CLOVE: Grassy-ass.

HELACIO: Gracias.

CARLITO: Gracias.

SABLE: I'm leaving without you, Clove, let's speed-speed!

CLOVE: Bye.

Once more she turns and runs, just catching the VW as it tears off.

CARLITO: Bye.

HELACIO: Bye-bye.

They watch the girls in the VW lurch, then sputter off back down the
road. Their eyebrows go up.

HELACIO: Hm. ¿Que raro, no?

CARLITO: Sí. Que raro.

what

CHAPTER 11

IN WHICH AUNT JEANETTE LEAVES SKEETER ON THE CURB

Jeanette and Skeeter stand in front of a newsstand on Lexington Avenue on Manhattan's Upper East Side.

JEANETTE: Rashid? This is my nephew Ezekial—

SKEETER: Skeeter.

JEANETTE: Oh sorry, honey, Skeet-Skeet?

SKEETER: Skeeter.

JEANETTE: Skeeter, he likes to be called. He hitched all the way across the country to visit me. Isn't that mythic? He's sixteen. He's from Oregon. My sister Linda lives out in Oregon. Hmm? Oh well, you know kids these days. Oh, here comes that little poodle. I love this. Watch. See, he buys a pack of Chesterfields every day. Then he goes back into the diner. I love that! I always imagine some little old lady smokes those Chesterfields. Only in New York! Give me a soft pack of Merit 100s—no, the other box, the plastic-wrapped pack, the plastic's off on that one, who knows, right? No, no newspaper, Rashid, you know me. I can't absorb those worldly vibrations this early in the morning. What? That's true. Bye, have a nice day.

She tucks her cigarettes in her purse and steers Skeeter away from the newsstand as she sips her morning coffee from an "I Heart New York" to-go cup.

JEANETTE: He's right, Skeeter, I never read the newspaper. Ever. Don't tell your ma Linda that because she's very political. Out there on the left coast, it's a different climate for people in the craft. Here we mostly do seminars. That's what I'm teaching today: Reigning the Inner Domain. It's about taking control inside inwardly. *In*! *In*, on the *in*side!

Jeanette's gesticulations to this effect cause her to accidentally spill coffee all over her young nephew.

JEANETTE: Oh! I'm sorry.

SKEETER: Er y'alright, Aunt Jeanette?

JEANETTE: I'm fine, I'm fine.

She daubs him with tissues from her purse.

JEANETTE: Now here's some money. Taxi! Taxi!

A cab pulls up.

JEANETTE: I just hate to leave you alone like this your first day in New York, but have a good time. Be careful on the streets. If you get lost or something happens, focus on cobalt blue, that's your Protector Being's color.

She opens the cab door, then hesitates.

JEANETTE: Or call a cop. I'll see you back at the apartment, have fun.

SKEETER: Alright, but in scrutinizing yer countenance, I must announce I infer a love trouble o' some type.

JEANETTE: You and your fucking mother are too piercing! Alright, Ezekial, if you must know, Auntie Jeanette is having an affair.

SKEETER: Ravin'.

JEANETTE: Not so—"raving."

She climbs in the cab.

JEANETTE: I'll tell you about it later. Back at the apartment. Bye!

She slams shut the door and addresses the cab driver.

JEANETTE: Epiphany Institute, Fifty-first and Madison, and step on it.

She rolls down the window and waves as the cab pulls away and joins the stream of traffic.

JEANETTE: Bye, sweetie!

SKEETER: Bye, Aunt Jeanette.

He looks around.

SKEETER: Hel. Lo. New York City.

Skeeter steps cockily down the sidewalk, whistling a happy technotune.

what

PART FOUR

QUAKES

CHAPTER 1

IN WHICH CLOVE IS VEXED

Clove is rather angry at her parents. She stands squarely on their redwood deck and responds indignantly to their line of questioning.

CLOVE: You are both so poxily hypochondriacal and hypocritical and I am so sick of listening to both of you! I did not try to commit suicide at the rave by walking into the ocean. I was not trying to commit suicide, I was WALKING INTO THE WATER, can't you see the difference? You are both all poxily, mightily, blinded, so overly righteous I can't stand it. Yur always complaining about Christian Coalition and Ralph Reed. Wull, can't you see that yur exactly the same only different? Maybe I wasn't trying to commit suicide. Maybe Cobain the Friendly Ghost is not something from my imagination. Maybe I'm from his imagination and he did save me when I walked into the water. I wasn't trying to kill myself. Did it ever occur to you that maybe I just wanted to get away from you? Maybe I just wanted to go live underwater away from people? You better not try to correct how I—I just talk like this, I am not all mentally dull and unarticulated. This is how I talk! This is how I am! Can you accept that? Yur like all "Wull wull maybe she's on this new drug Ecstasy not like our old drugs not like acid er all that cocaine that we were high on when we FUCKED and conceived her!"

She jumps back as her father lunges for her. He is restrained by her mother.

CLOVE: OH! Right, try to hit me, Dad. That's rully pacifist, Mr. Civil Disobedience!

I am not all influenced by Kurt Cobain! If you had ANY knowledge of ANY music written after NINETEEN SEVENTY-*ONE*, then you would understand I'm not into Nirvana's music to any extreme radical degree!! See, you just cut all my thoughts up into like little crumbs you just separate it out into like little crumbs so I can't talk!

I'm not like this with my friends with my friends I'm all articulate and mellifulated. It's just when you cut cut me up into little bits of bread—WHAAAAH, I can't tolerate you anymore. I can't tolerate it. You are so overly deludated and you don't even see it. Why don't you just go ask yer limpid psychic friend Sylvia Soothe Larchmont. She'll tell you that I am being haunted by a realistic ghost and I am not all deludated. His name is Cobain the Friendly Ghost and if you had any sense you would hire an exorcist fer me!

And I *AM* going to that next rave. It's perfectly safe! We live in Santa Cruz, three blocks from the beach, why're you so worried about me walking into the ocean up there and it's not even a beach rave? IT'S PERFECTLY SAFE. It's in San Francisco, by a factory that's all toxic and abandonated. IT'S PERFECTLY SAFE! Because I don't—

She puffs with indignation.

CLOVE: Because I don't want—maybe I just want to be away from people. Maybe if I can just go to that next rave—and if you try to stop me then you will regret it fer the rest of yer interminable lives!—maybe because maybe I just want to spin until I reach that *glidden toppish un*place of ravishment and ultra-heartbeat and just be away from everybody and part of IT, spinning in that *glidden toppish* place and not tied to *any*one, especially NOT YOU! Ahhh! I can't stand you fer one particle of a segment of a section of an infinitisimal BIT of a moment LONGER! I'm going out. I told you before! Me and Sable are getting our *eye*brows pierced this afternoon.

She marches down the redwood steps and then whirls around to face her parents.

CLOVE: And don't try to stop me, you rancid, flaccid, scrambled old HIPPPIIIIIEEEEEEEEEESSSSS!

CHAPTER 2

IN WHICH SKEETER BUYS
SOME BATTERIES

New York City. Two pretty Nuyorican high-school girls are browsing in a Korean grocer's. One is plump and sweet. The other is thinner and more angular, wears glasses, and has an air of ennui.

ESTER: *Mira*, Vivian—I'm so bort I'm so bort with everything being all the same all the time, you know? It's like, the same homies with the same ridiculous dumb stuff that they say to us all dee time. The same, you know, go to school, you know, stay at home, stay out of trouble. If you go out, you gonna be in trouble. They's bad boys, they's good boys. Stay at home, go bort out your mind. I'm just so sick of it.

VIVIAN: You was always cracy, you was always cracy, Esta.

ESTER: Yeah, wait until you hear the speech I'm going to give at graduation. I'm going to rock dee administration's world. I am going to call them on their shit, you know?

VIVIAN: Esta, I can't believe how you talking like dat aftah all those nuns have done fo' us.

ESTER: Dey didn't do anything fo' us. My fatha fixes cars and my mother cleans apartments to send me to dat school. Didn't no Pope John Paul pay fo' *my* tuition, a'right?

VIVIAN: Esta, you so cracy!

ESTER: Huh, I just wish something different would happen. I'm just so bort. What are we goin' to buy in dis store? We been in dis store fo' fifteen minutes. What are we gonna buy? You wanna buy one a dese papuhs? You wanna buy a newspapuh?

VIVIAN: No, what for? Oh, who's dat ugly man?

ESTER: Oh, it's um, oh he *is* ugly. 'Is Ralph Reed, Christian Coalition.

VIVIAN: Oh. Oh. *Dag*.

ESTER: You wanna buy the papuh?

VIVIAN: NO, why botha?

ESTER: 'Strue you wanna buy some rice cakes, Vivian?

VIVIAN: No, I can't, I get too fat.

ESTER: You look *good* fat, Vivian.

VIVIAN: No.

ESTER: Le's buy some . . . How about some . . . apples.

She turns to the apples and then glances up toward the cash register. Her gaze is suddenly arrested.

ESTER: Vi, Vi, look ovah they-uh- that white boy, that white boy.

VIVIAN: So?

ESTER: He's fine, right?

VIVIAN: He's dirty.

ESTER: No, he's not. He's, daz— daz a white boy, daz how they dress. Dey dress like dat.

VIVIAN: But his clothes aren't fresh.

ESTER: Daz 'cause he's a white boy.

VIVIAN: Daz why I don't like them.

ESTER: Oh, you so racial-phobic at times, Vivian. Look, use your eyes, he's different, ri'? He looks different.

SKEETER: Er, two double-A batteries? Nuh, nuh no bag, conservation. Cons-er-vation? Never. Mind.

VIVIAN: Esta! Oh my Got! I can' believe it, oh, you em*bar*rassin' me! I can' believe it.

Ester makes a beeline for Skeeter and bumps straight into him.

ESTER: Whoops! Escuse me, I'm sorry, I didn't know where I was going. Hi, my name is Esta.

SKEETER: Er, top o' the day to yuh, Ester. No. Harm. Done.

ESTER: What's your name? You don't sound like you from around heeah.

SKEETER: Nuh, I'm from Oregon.

ESTER: Oh yeah? Is dat nice?

SKEETER: Wull, it's kinda on the foggy, humdrum side of the slope but comparatively speakin' with th' rest of the United States of America, it's, uh, pretty, uh

He flicks his eyes over her body, taking in her inquisitive brown eyes,

what

her black ringletted hair, her perfectly formed small breasts, her narrow waist and little, jutting ass.

SKEETER: —yeh-up.

ESTER: So what's your name?

SKEETER: Er, Skeeter.

ESTER: Squeegee?

SKEETER: Nuh, nuh Skeeter, Skeeter, uh—

ESTER: Oh, you mean like mosquito like . . .

She makes a mosquito sound.

ESTER: Daz cute, daz yo' nickname? Daz cute, daz cute, daz real cute.

SKEETER: Yeah, 'at's right, m' rull name's Ezekial.

ESTER: Oh yeah? Is dat your real hair? Is it really dat blond?

Her eyes linger in his tresses.

SKEETER: Nuh, this girl in San Francisco gave me the wrong dye, I'se aimin' fer the redder side o' the color spectrum but—

VIVIAN: Esta, come on! Esta! Harry up, let's go. Esta, come on!

ESTER: Wait! Uh, I could dye your *hay*-uh, I could dye your hair red, you want me to?

She darts a glance at his loins, then back to his green eyes.

ESTER: Gimme your beepa numbah, you got a beepa?

SKEETER: Er, I got my Aunt's phone number, I could—

VIVIAN: ¡*Mira, mira*, Esta! Come on! ¡*Mira*, Esta!

Vivian is signaling in a meaningful way toward the entrance.

ESTER: Wait! I'm gettin' his numba! Oh. Hi, Happy.

She looks over at a young man who now stands at Skeeter's back.

HAPPY: Hi. Yo, you like Puerto Rican girls, huh?

SKEETER: Er, somehow I-I detect thur's a trick question in there. Somewhur.

HAPPY: Yo, my man, don't—don't mess wit' me, just answer my question, a'right? Don't try to be smaht.

There is a tense pause in the grocery store conversation.

KIM: You, kid, OUT! OUT! You kid, you don' buy, YOU GET OUT!

CONSTANTINE: Hey, hey, hey, it's alright, dis long head he's with me, he's my busboy, come on, you go to work now, guy, you go to work.

He winks at Skeeter.

CONSTANTINE: Kim, pack of Wimstom-Salem—

He corrects himself, enunciates his English carefully.

ever

CONSTANTINE: *Win*ston-Salems one *hun*threets. Okay, come on, guy.

HAPPY: YO!

CONSTANTINE: HEY!

ESTER: Bye-bye!

He steers Skeeter out the door. They walk down the bustling sidewalk.

CONSTANTINE: Come on, kiddo, come next door, my diner, I manage her, Blue Ship Diner, you wait inside awhile, you not from New York, hah, you don't know how to watch it, hah? Where you from?

SKEETER: Uh, I'm from Oregon.

CONSTANTINE: Constantine Karamidikas.

He holds out his hand, greeting a fellow foreigner.

CONSTANTINE: I am from Cyprus, Greece, hah? Come on.

SKEETER: Many thanks fer th' safety-bearin' gift dere, Constantine.

CLOVE: No problem. Welcome to the Blue Ship Diner. Come on.

Ester, Vivian, and Happy are still in Kim's Market.

ESTER: Why you have to be bad like dat, Happy? Why you have to make everything nasty like dat?

HAPPY: Why you have to be smaht?

VIVIAN: Esta, come on just ignore him.

ESTER: One day. One day a light will go off insite your head, Happy. I carry that hope. I carry it.

HAPPY: Yeah? I smack dat hope outsite your head.

ESTER: For *your* sake I carry it. For your sake I will *still* carry it! For *your* future, Happy, HOPE!

HAPPY: Fuck you!

ESTER: HOPE!

Vivian forcibly pulls Ester out of the store. Happy chases her to the exit.

HAPPY: Dang! She's so—

Happy punches his fist in his palm and bites his lip. He swings around and walks coolly back to the cashier.

HAPPY: Gimme a pack of Winston-Salems, one hundrits. No, I don't want no matcheese.

CHAPTER 3

IN WHICH PAUL HAS A
CHANGE OF HEART

Paul sits opposite Bob Flaskett at Axnell World Headquarters across an immense mahogany desk. Both men wear gray Brooks Brothers suits.

PAUL: I'm at a loss, Bob, as to what to say to you.

BOB: The feeling is mutual, Paul.

PAUL: No, I don't think the feelings are, uh, mutual, old friend, I doubt that.

BOB: Listen, Paul, we've known each other for fifteen years. You've been an Axnell man for twice that time. When I came to this corporation you were the guy I looked up to—you were the guy—I said, This is a real stand-up tough kind of a guy. He calls the shots, he doesn't take any shit, doesn't mince any words, he does what has to be done, to get the job done. This is the guy I want to be. And ovah the years I've known you, everything you took on, you made remarkable progress, remarkable. I've seen how you've expanded in ways the rest of us didn't think was possible. You were way ahead of all of us, on this whole Information Revolution, guys like me who were younger than you who should've seen it and didn't. You were right on top of it moving right along. You've always been a person who saw things before other people saw them, Paul. Then you go into early retirement. Well, I'm not going to sit here and pretend that that didn't surprise the hell out of me but then I figured: hell, maybe Paul wants to live down in, uh, Virginia and just enjoy what he's earned. Enjoy his life. Enjoy what he's earned. You never struck me as that type of a guy. You always seemed like someone who thrived on conflict and struggle, even on the home front: uh, when you and I were pals, not too long ago if you remember, Paul, you pretty much confided in me that your marriage to Polly consisted of the first half fighting, the second half cheating on her.

PAUL: Bob—

Paul clears his throat.

BOB: No, let me finish Paul, I'm on a roll, I'm on a roll here I just wanna finish. So you go into early retirement. I figure that's it. I feel bad but I gain from it. I mean, I'm sitting here, I gained from it. Here I am.

Bob grins and takes in the finely appointed executive office.

BOB: Then two months down the line I gotta call you back to make a speech at the, uh, Changing Shades of Trade Conference in Columbus. You make a big impression and before we know it, you're a hit, you're makin' speeches all ovah the circuit all ovah the globe. We got you back sittin' on the board with Axnell affiliates. I'm happy for ya. And then the funny speech happens—your daughter? Her environmental problems? I dunno. We all felt for you, we all felt for you. It happened. Figured you're havin' a little minor crisis. Then you don't show up in Chicago. Fred Nesbit has to call me and tell me this in the middle of their convention out there. Ralph Reed from the Christian Coalition was there and apparently he was very disappointed. I try to make something up to cover your ass but I don't know what to tell him. I know you've been here in New York, Paul. I gather you're screwing around with that girl again. Or'd ya get a new one? That's fair, that's none of my business, although I have to say we useta be pals, I useta hear from you. So what's this boil down to? I think you're having a breakdown, Paul, I think ya need to seek professional help. There's nothing to be ashamed of. When my son, uh, well, you know, the death of Peter, uh, he died, the heroin problem and all that, really sent me for a loop and Catherine and I sought psychiatric help—that got us back on track after a real rocky year and that's okay, y'know? Nothin' to be ashamed of. A man can ask for help now. The times they are a-changing, heh? They've got helpful medication available, there's no shame in it. I'm not ashamed to admit—alright, I admit, I have a prescription for Prozac since Petey died, it's just a short-term thing, but it's pulled us through a tight spot and it's very helpful. Heck yes, you bet it is. It hits the spot, it gets the job done, you can do double doses at conference time! Are you following me, Paul? I'm trying to talk man-to-man, heart-to-heart here, can you follow?

PAUL: Bob, I really must interject. Bob, I've known you for years and I have a great deal of sympathy for your position. I've been there. Remember, you've got my old job—

Paul runs his hands along Bob's massive desk.

PAUL: Matter of fact, you've got my old desk. But, but this is more than a crisis, Bob, or a, or a breakdown. I am breaking down but I can't go back. I can't go back to lying to Polly, I've got to have it out with her one way or the other.

I may be in love with my girlfriend, she's not my mistress, she supports herself now, she's a crystal healer. I know it sounds wacky. She gives seminars and talks about healing yourself through magic practices. But you want to know something, Bob, I've been thinking and maybe it's no more wacky than all the financial projections and business forecasts that you and I have participated in over the years. And you know what? I'm beginning to really wonder if we need to make some adjustments on our moral outlook.

BOB: Our what?

PAUL: Our moral outlook. Overseas manufacturing, for instance, Bob. Those workers. Even our stateside operations. The tinkering with governments and political parties, the, uh, policies you and I have overseen regarding the environmental impact, the accident that happened, you know the one I mean, Bob, I've begun to won-der if we might be partly, uh, to answer for all that. Did we inadver-tently cause some of those . . . deaths?

BOB: You need to check into a hospital, Paul, do a program, admit you're an alcoholic.

PAUL: But, but—

BOB: Oh come on, Paul, I've seen how you swill down the Scotch at lunch.

PAUL: But that was last year, I haven't had a drink in weeks. In over a month.

BOB: You haven't?

PAUL: No.

BOB: Oh. Hm. What are you saying?

Paul loosens his tie, trying to breathe better.

ever

PAUL: I'm saying that this is more than a breakdown. It's a change of heart. I may be seeing our system break down before my eyes. If, like you said, I've always been ahead of you guys, perhaps I see it first and you don't. But you will.

BOB: You're bananas, Folsom, you're bananas.

PAUL: Yes, I am.

Paul tugs at his belt, adjusting it around his girth.

BOB: You're out of the game.

PAUL: Yes, I guess.

BOB: Well, good luck.

Bob holds out his hand to shake. Paul extends his hand but suddenly it jerks back and he reflexively clutches his left arm.

BOB: Are you—? Paul?

Paul slowly stands up and stumbles backward, upending his chair. Bob hits the intercom.

BOB: Jesus Christ, Nancy, call Security, get an ambulance now! He's having a heart attack! HE'S HAVING A HEART ATTACK!

Paul lurches back and falls backward over the chair legs.

CHAPTER 4

IN WHICH BRUCE FRYE REGRETS

Bruce Frye, a handsome, weathered type of guy, stands in a prison library, typing on an old Corona electric typewriter that is chained to a shelf. He is a pretty practiced typist, but this letter is taking him a long time.

BRUCE: Dear Ezekial,

I am writing to you from Marion Federal Penitentiary Library. I finally came out of the gray zone and word came to me that a person identifying himself as my son had come to visit and run off when questioned by the guards as to his age. Counting back, I figure you're sixteen, since you were born in July of '78 back when your ma Linda and me were shacked up in that pretty little beach bungalow near Malibu. Wish I was there now. Wish I was anywhere but here now. I would not make the same mistakes. No, but I'd probably make different ones. When they told me what had happened, I had to keep myself from punching them or breaking down entirely because I have so much to say to you, son, and just five minutes would've been so precious to me. Prison life is not very good. You might or might not know that I am on what they call the BLANK list because I talked to a reporter during my incarceration and told him that I had sold pot to BLANK BLANK, the former BLANK BLANK from the state of BLANK back in seventy-BLANK.

They are most likely blacking these parts out but I feel sure you can put two and two together if Linda didn't drop you on your head too many times. If you can't, read our nation's oldest progressive paper BLANK BLANK and it will tell you what is going on with my case. A paper like that will also keep you up on people like Ralph Reed of the Christian Coalition; I've got my eye on that son-of-a-BLANK.

If it was just for smuggling marijuana out off the Keys, I would most likely be out by now, but my political activities have BLANK BLANK BLANK BLANK BLANK.

But that isn't why I write to you, son, and I hope that whatever prison hack is reading this will let this letter go off to you if he is a father or a son of someone and has a heart. Ezekial, I write to tell you that I fucked up royally as your dad. This is painful for me to say so that's how I say it. Up until prison I was a partying guy. I partied a lot with your mom Linda, which you might partly remember. Until you were three, when things got heavy with her vis-a-vis taking care of you, then I split. I'm not makin' any excuses, I'm just tellin' it like it is. Then I partied down in South America and had some mind-blowin' adventures. I really recommend that before you die, you hit up Peru and Ecuador, it's a definite experience and a half. While I was up in the mountains, I had some visions and tripped to some places through Indian guides that made me somewhat remorseful for my lackadaisical attitudes as a father. In one particularly intense trance I was transported through time and space to your side and was alongside you when your mom, Linda, was hit by that drunk-driving asshole in the 7-Eleven parking lot in Oakland, California. I started to choke, I felt the tears going down your face, your heart beating, and I saw Linda slippin' by so close to the spirit world, I could reach out and touch her with my fingertips. So I took a plane. You may recall that when Linda was in the hospital, I did show up for a while. You and me stayed in a motel together for about three weeks and I taught you how to swim in that gunky pool. You were a really cute little squirt, cute as hell. You kept trying to give me shit for leaving and at the same time, you were hangin' off my shirttails and I promised myself I wasn't gonna split again. But then your mother's sister Jeanette showed up right before Linda came out of the hospital and me and her had a big— argument. I 'member you were asleep under this blue foam motel blanket and the TV was on, your favorite show, *Peewee's Playhouse*, and I thought I can't leave this kid, and I did. In here, I've had time to think and my one big regret is what I did or didn't do for you—and Linda too. So please try to find it in your heart to forgive me, Ezekial. I hope to make it up to you one day. When I get out of this BLANK BLANK BLANK prison.

Play it strong and keep cool.

Your dad, Bruce Frye.

CHAPTER 5

IN WHICH SHEILA SURPRISES HER SHRINK

Sheila Marie Folsom sits in an armchair in the office of her therapist, Barbara, at the Berkeley Psychotherapy Clinic. There is a large Diego Rivera print directly over Barbara's head.

SHEILA: I know we're almost at the end of our forty-five-minute hour—hey, maybe Clinton could raise the shrink session to fifty minutes while he's raising the minimum wage by a nickel, what do you think?

Her speech is even and clipped. It sounds as if she's worked to eliminate any music from it so it bears only the faintest hint of the South.

SHEILA: Okay, sorry to get sarcastic and political, I know that's part of my defensiveness, but we talked so long about the way you remind me of my dead cat that I didn't tell you what happened. Actually two things, I know they're external and in the present, not the past, but I think they're important. No, I'm not trying to downplay the thing about you and Felix but I think this bears talking about too—WILL YOU JUST LISTEN?!

Okay, uh uh okay, uh my dad has had a heart attack and and and—thank you, I—yes, I acknowledge that is a big deal, I know! But there's something even more. My mother called to tell me this and you know how she lost her wedding ring down the garbage disposal at Thanksgiving and she burdened me with the whole trauma, in our usual dynamic of me having to solve her insoluble problems? Yes, that's always been our pattern. But she called me to tell me that Dad had a heart attack and then, Barbara, she confided in me that she's having a love affair with the garbage disposal contractor, who's black! Barb, black! No, Barb, Barb, this is me, this is Sheila, I'm the biggest radical in the world, I don't have any "issues" about people of color but Polly Ann Renard Folsom is from southern Georgia! She still refers to Beverly, the family housekeeper who is five years older than she is, as a girl! I mean! My mother, the long-suffering housewife, after all those years of Dad cheating on her, is cheating on Dad! My mother has blown my mind!

No, it didn't give him the attack. No, no, I know because she hasn't told him yet. No, he had the attack in Axnell Corporation Headquarters in New York. He was resigning again. Apparently, he's having some kind of breakdown, maybe all the evil he's been complicit in has finally gotten to him (alright, I know, I'm getting political as a defense), he's dropping out of corporate orbit, he's had a change of heart. What did I say? Heart? Freudian slip. I don't know. It meant . . . oh my God, my poor dad, my daddy, he's always been the villain, always the one I fought with, I had to comfort my poor victim mother but now she's runnin' around trying to conceal her light-heartedness and he's the one suffering pain—what? I said heart again? There we go! Oh my daddy, my dad. You know I phoned him at the hospital and you know what he said? He said that when the attack came, he had a vision of sweeping over the green green forests of the Olympic Mountains

Sheila begins crying.

SHEILA: where he grew up in Washington state. (He grew up poor, you know, he just worked himself up to filthy rich plutocrat!).

And then I realized that's why I chain myself to redwoods, that's why I'm willing to die for trees, because it connects me to the big grandfather tree in my heart! Whoops, I said it again!

Her voice is now little-girlish.

When me and Derek were little, my dad and mom would fight and sometimes he'd leave, go stay in the airport hotel. Me and Derek, that was when he was little, before he could join the Christian Coalition and we were still friends; I could still boss him. And we'd take all the grass out of the lawnmower, stuff it in our ears, and scatter it around the garage and kneel down inhaling the gasoline smell and praying for him to come home. When he came back, he always brought two boxes of Nabisco wafers and a bunch of bananas and Mom would make banana pudding from her nanny's recipe—we called it "Nanny's Nana Puddin' "—and we'd all sit in

what

the den all together on the couch and eat that for dinner and watch five TV programs in a row.

She smiles through her tears and listens to Barbara.

SHEILA: I KNOW IT'S SICK BUT IT'S MY FAMILY!! I love my dad! I love my mom! I'm *tired* of being angry at my parents! I just want them to be okay!

She weeps fully. Barbara gives her some tissues for her issues.

SHEILA: Okay. I know I brought it up at the end of the session. I'll speak to you next week. Thanks, Barb, for listening.

She leaves.

CHAPTER 6

IN WHICH SKEETER
SOJOURNS IN SOHO

Skeeter stands by the refreshment table in a Soho art gallery.

SKEETER: Er, this cheese is fer free? Copious ingratiatin', I'm sure. May I procure as well one o' those handy cuppies o' wine? Don't get me wrong, in my native habitat on th' left coast, I imbibe strictly on the psychoactive slope, but here in New York I'm surmisin' it behooves a person tuh make like the inmates, if you snag my tangent.

He looks at the refreshment people and sees that they do not snag his tangent one bit.

SKEETER: Never. Mind. This place is just fiendin' me out.

A fashionably dressed Euro–New Yorker with an unidentifiable Euro-mesclada accent addresses Skeeter with instant intimacy.

STEPHAN: Do you understand dee art?

SKEETER: Is 'is art?

STEPHAN: Yeah, what do you think, man, you in a gallery? What is it?

SKEETER: Er, it looks like a big bucket o' blood tuh me, with some blue jeans floatin' on top.

STEPHAN: Dat's it, dat's dee installation. What do you think it's about? What's dee statement?

SKEETER: Er, blood. Bloodshed. Blood lust, bleedin'. Levi's? Two things. Er, period blood, an' killin' blood.

STEPHAN: Hey, I like dat, you a smarty-pant kid, hah? I don't like dis shit needer, I come to take a break from dee shop. Yah, me and Zacha, my girlfriend, you know, Zacha at Mood Hat?

SKEETER: Er, nuh.

STEPHAN: Come on, man! Everybody know our hat are fabulous, we so together so fabulous, genius, we make incredible hat! Last week, Naomi Campbell buy three. Joe Pesci's daughter, she comes in all dee time, she's our best friend, fabulous, come on, you know our hat, don't be a smarty-pant kid. Our hat change in four different color to match dee mood. One for— Oh, I'm tired of dee rap, sell sell sell. I'm going out of my mind, but I love it! All dee time since last July, Zacha never stop, she's crazy, I love her, she's fabulous, dynamite hot hot babe, you know? Fabulous chick, but I want to strangle her sometimes, we box—

> Stephan mimes boxing, jumping around and disregarding the art admirers he bumps into.

STEPHAN: yeah. Don't get me wrong, I'm not a wife abuse, number one, she not my wife, number two, she got a better punch den me! I told her, Baby, I could never wear dat chain and balls, you know? She said, Who dee fuck care anyway? Life is too trendy. Sweet! Dat's why I love her ooo and dee hats, I love dee hats, dey are genius, dey change colors, we live dee hat, we breathe dee hat we eat dee hat we fuck dee hat, no, only joke ha ha, but you got to know us, everybody in dee neighborhood love us, we are dee fabulous trend store of Soho. See? I can't get a break, can't get way, it follow me everywhere, man. Come next door. You want to buy a hat? I give you a 10 percent discount. I'm tell you gonna love it, these hat are so creative so now. They art—this! Is not art!—the hat are art— dey gonna be everywhere! Cover the global economy we gonna put dem onna dee Internet!— Ha ha, look at dat!

> He gestures toward the door, where an old woman and poodle have just arrived.

STEPHAN: Dee old lady got on our hat, hey, lady, I remember you, how you like dee hat? Incredible, fabulous, yes?

VIOLET: It does me just fine, deeah, who are you?

STEPHAN: I'm dee owner of Mood Hat, Stephan, Zacha's man.

VIOLET: And who are you? The unfortunate progeny of the mad hatters?

SKEETER: Nuh, I'm just spectatin' here in this gallery. I'm Skeeter.

VIOLET: And I'm Violet Smith. Gate crashing the art opening, are we? Very good, that's swell, a time-honored tradition. I've been doing it since 1929.

ever

A well-made-up woman in a Soho designer dress crosses the gallery floor, quickly calling out in a not-so-tony British accent.

WOMAN: Excuse me, madam, no dogs allowed, Rachel Heartstone Galleries is *noot* a pet store!

VIOLET: This isn't a *dog*! This is BALZAC! Officious prat! Alright, I'll skedaddle. Pleased to've met you, Skidoo.

Violet turns on her heel and is gone.

SKEETER: Skeet. Er, likewise.

VIOLET: Come on, Balzy.

STEPHAN: Crazy old chick, hmm?

SKEETER: Tuhhh.

STEPHAN: Come on next door. I like you so much I give you a hat! Gratis! Hey man.

He slings his arm around Skeeter's shoulders.

SKEETER: Er.

STEPHAN: Come on, what you say?

SKEETER: Fab. U. Lous?

STEPHAN: Fabulous!

SKEETER: Er, I guess.

They stride off.

what

CHAPTER 7

IN WHICH POLLY TRIES TO RESIST BLACKBERRY PIE

A woman stands at a hospital pay phone. There is a line of people waiting behind her. First in line is Polly, who waits nervously, looking around and biting her lip.

WOMAN: She's got a tube down her throat, Charlie, I'm trying to tell you. Her face is swollen, she's being tortured, they're torturing her to death. How did this happen? We shouldn't have let—what?

Bushie, followed by an entourage of streetwalkers, comes up to the woman.

BUSHIE: Excuse me, do you know where dey keep da crazy people locked up?

WOMAN: What? No, I'm sorry. I don't work here at the hospital.

Bushie grabs her crotch to emphasize her next thought.

BUSHIE: Well. Excuse me fuh livin'! I just wondered if you knew where it is, is all.

WOMAN: The psychiatric wing? It's on the third floor in the silver wing, I believe.

BUSHIE: *Thaaank* you. Okay, Snapple, Rosie, Pam, let's go visit Nutz.

They straggle off toward the elevators.

WOMAN: What? I don't know. Some strange person was just bothering me. No, I'm in the cafeteria. I can't hear you, the hospital workers are having a demonstration or something. I'm in the-the-the thing, uh, I mean the cafeteria. Yeah. I came down here to get a tea. I was having a fit in the ICU, the nurses kicked me out. You have to come here, when can you get out of work? Oh, come on, Charlie, we have to, I don't know what we can do, I know you're right, we're helpless—no, *she's* helpless, you're wrong, we have to fight them, these doctors are all on *speed*, they have zero attention span—

what? Can you come now? Oh, you're *God*, Charlie, you are *God*, I worship you. Okay, meet me in the what's-his-name-wing, you know? On those horrible powder blue sofas, yeah, by the Coke machine, okay. Okay, great, I'll be waiting—and Charlie, hurry. I might start smoking again. I know *she's* dying of lung cancer but *I—I'm—I* can't take it! Okay okay. Bye!

    She hangs up and turns to Polly.

WOMAN: Sorry I took so long, it's all yours.

POLLY: That's alright, I understand.

    Polly steps up to the pay phone.

POLLY: Operator, I've lost my callin' card so I'd lak to make a phone call to Chantilly, Virginia, and charge it to my home phone in Middleburg, Virginia. Mmm hmm. Mrs. Paul Folsom. Oh *no*! Don't say that on the line to him. Polly, Polly Folsom. My home phone is seven oh three—four nine eight—five six seven six, that's right, Middleburg, Fairfax County, Virginia. Will his, um, will the Chantilly number appear on my home bill? Mm-hmm. Oh *really*? Oh wey-ell, that's fine, I guess who cares, right? It's only a little ole number. Mmm? Nothin'! Yes, the Chantilly number is seven oh three—six two three—three ohhhhhh, ohhhhhhhhhhhh, three. That's Loudon County, you know the area? Oh, it's very lovely, spring's comin', the cherry blossoms are in bl—you're connectin'? Thank you. Oh! You're welcome, I *al*ways used AT&T, I never switch—He-he-hello, Reuben? It's me, Polly. I'm still in New York in the hospital with Paul. I mean, my husband, I mean— Yes, I am upset. Oh darlin', I cain't cry, I'm in a hospital cafeteria in New York City, and all the workers are havin' a powwow. Colored people— Persons of Color!—Black! Lak you. I'm sorry! It's just that now whenever I look at one of your people, I see you—please don't be angry with me, wah oh wah Blackberry Pie? Wey-ell, I guess you cain't help but be angry.

    There is a pause.

POLLY: Will you say something? It's killin' me to hear you so silent on the line.

    There is another pause.

POLLY: Reuben? Wah did I call? Wey-ell, to tell you something. Please, no! Don't leave me, stay on the line, I have to tell you. Wey-ell, yes, I am leavin' you. I don't wont to but Paul is my husband of thirty-five years and his heart attack! I tried, I tried to tell him about us but, but I couldn't. He told me he'd leave his mistress, J-J-J-J-Jeanette, that's her dang name and I couldn't.

She lowers her voice to a whisper.

POLLY: No, it's not because you're black, no, it's not. It's because . . . I love you. Love dudn't work. That's what my mother told me: "Love dudn't work!" I'm twelve years older than you, we're fools, where would we go? Maybe you're right, it's the same old thing it always was, I admit you're right. It didn't work when I was a child in Georgia and it still dudn't work now. My first friend was a little colored boy, we used to run down the roads together holdin' hands. But then someone told us: "Don't you ever do that again!" Guess who that was? His mamma! You know as well as I know that it's your people as much as mine. It's not supposed to happen, that's wah it was so . . . sweet.

Oh Reuben, forgive me. Reuben? Are you there?

Her voice gets falsely cheerful for a moment,

POLLY: Let's hang up and never see each other again, alright? Hmm? You're right.

then drops back down to tender.

POLLY: Best to leave it this way. Do it quickly. Keep the mem'ry. What are you doin' right now? Mmmm. What are you wearin'? Oooo. Me? I'm wearin' a pink dress, chiffon. Yes, stockings. Blue . . . Sheer. Too cold up here in New York City, my legs are cold. I'm cold. Hmm. Okay, one, two, three, good-bye, Blackberry Pie–wait!—Reuben? Maybe, when I get back home, we should meet one last time. No, you're right, it's a bad idea. Good-bye then.

There's a pause.

POLLY: The hotel in Arcola? Next Wednesday at our time? Yes, I think I could do that. Let's see, Paul's checkin' out of the hospital Sa'urday and I'll drive us down. Sorry. Didn't mean to talk about him. Did you change your mind? Or? Okay, I'll see you there. I think it's a good idea. Only to say goodbye, right? The nice way. Okay one, two, three, good-bye—wait—Reuben? Reuben?

She regretfully replaces the receiver. A very little old man, literally stooped in half, addresses her irately:

ever

SOL: It's about toime, lady, are you aweh dat dere ah people in dis hospital vit *dy*ink relatives?

A distraught young black man behind him concurs:

DAMON: That's true! People got *dy*in' relatives!

Polly backs away.

POLLY: I'm—I'm sorry.

what

CHAPTER 8

IN WHICH SKEETER'S
SLANG IS DERIDED

A white girl in fatigues and army boots and green dreadlocked hair approaches a side of brick wall on the corner of Avenue A and St. Mark's Place in Manhattan's East Village. Several of her cohorts are leaning or sleeping against this graffiti-scarred and piss-marked habitat. She addresses a nodding and drooling little blond girl, who is folded up under a zebra-striped tarp.

SPAZ: Chris, is Giraffe back yet from Essex? Chris!

CHRIS: Hey.

SPAZ: Is Giraffe back yet?

Spaz paces back and forth.

CHRIS: I don't know.

The little blond nods off into a stone-cold stupor.

SPAZ: She better come back soon, though, 'cause she has our comic books. Well, when did you see her?

JASPER: We don't know, Spaz, man, whatta you doin'?

A big, pockmarked, mohawked boy of about seventeen rolls his eyes to his companion, Skeeter. They are swapping gulps on a bargain bottle of beer.

SPAZ: I'm pissed.

JASPER: Yuh pissed, why?

He has a rough, booming voice.

SPAZ: Fuckin' Daniel made me walk all the fuckin' way to Tenth Street in the fuckin' rain and then he fuckin' tells me, "Ah, you know you shouldn't come up 'cause I think my fuckin' roommate might be home." Why didn't he have the guts to tell me before I walked all the way up to fuckin' Tenth and C to get high in his apartment and then he goes, "Oh my roommate might be there." Why didn't he say so before? Fuckin' Daniel.

JASPER: Spaz, dis is Squeezo.

SKEETER: Er, Skeeter.

SPAZ: Hey: Spaz.

SKEETER: Rave on, Sister.

SPAZ: What?

SKEETER: Er, mucho ravished tuh make yer acquaintance?

SPAZ: Ooo, surf some waves, dudes, gnarly—who is this?

JASPER: He's from *AW*-regon, Spaz.

SPAZ: Oh yeah? My girlfriend Jimina was from Oregon, she didn't talk like, oh gnarly man, surf some waves.

SKEETER: Er, tune yer ear, Spaz, did I employ the term "gnarly" er "surf some waves"? Unless my tongue-brain coordination is grievously lapsed, I venture tuh state it was yerself that made use of these flaccid terminologies. Perchance you've only skimmed left coast jargon through th' televised scope?

SPAZ: What? HE TALKS *FUCKED*.

JASPER: Here comes Mr. Spam.

A bearded middle-aged man in a soiled poncho approaches. His eyes are supernaturally excited.

MR. SPAM: Hello, guttersnipes.

JASPER: Hey, Mr. Spam, dis is Skeez.

SKEETER: Er, Skeeter.

MR. SPAM: I must command part of your liquid beverage, Jasper.

JASPER: Squeez, can Mr. Spam have some Milla Lite?

SKEETER: Most avowedly.

MR. SPAM: I've recently received a message from the outer intelligence.

JASPER: Oh yeah, Mr. Spam? You fuckin' head blast!

SKEETER: Er, yur of the lunatic persuasion?

MR. SPAM: Huh! Fringe, I'm of the fringe jackets, but not quite twinged, they have to measure me, they're waiting for the price coats to come through, have to be 100 percent slaughtered *holy* cow, no *meat* eaters, all India, yoga-meditated, then I will wear it into the space taxi and be transported to the space torture chamber—all white—but you have to watch the meter, they require a large sum.

what

JASPER: Oh yeah? Hah! Fuck off man, yuh crazy.

MR. SPAM: I have one thought for the day, the outer intelligence told me to tell the trash children.

JASPER: Yeah, what is it? Give Squizzo back his Milla Lite, you fuck brain.

MR. SPAM: This, garbage-mouth, or in the Spanish vernacular, *Munchandero-de-basura* . . .

KARATE: 'Ey, watch it man, don't talk da' shit in Spanish, man, you givin' me a headache: *me duela la cabeza*, watch yuhself.

JASPER: Yo, Karate, what's up?

KARATE: 'Ey, Jasper, *cómo estás*?

JASPER: Alright.

KARATE: Alright.

They execute a ceremonial handshake.

MR. SPAM: As they say in Planet Argot, schleemem nerk: jf jkdldld-jfr9*g*io, roughly translates, transduces as: the word is: Newt Gingrich and Phil Donahue are one and the same! He has cloned himself after Marlo Thomas—*THAT* GIRL!—oversensitized his manhood off, she took it off and the only way to retrieve his penis was to coin the archconservative lingo and awake a full computer invasion, so you see? The feminazis strike back: PART *TWO*. Newt and Phil are one. TWIN *BRAINS*.

JASPER: Fuck you. Fuck off. Go the fuck away.

Jasper coughs.

JASPER: Mr. Spam, got a Marlboro?

MR. SPAM: Old Gold.

Mr. Spam fishes a flattened packet of Old Golds from his jeans pocket and hands Jasper a cigarette.

MR. SPAM: Smoke this, send smoke signals to your dead brain, child of filth of slime of tar.

Jasper smokes through a tubercular-sounding coughing fit.

JASPER: Fuck off!

MR. SPAM: Child of the neglectful mothers, the dirt suckers.

JASPER: Go the fuck away, Mr. Spam! I'm having a bad fuckin' day! Go away!

He hocks a loogie at Mr. Spam, then he collapses against the wall, given over to smoking and coughing.

ever

MR. SPAM: Remember: Newt and Phil! Twin brains!

Mr. Spam beats a retreat.

SKEETER: He's got a hair of veracity thur, Jasper, regarding the fiendish resemblance 'twixt Newt Gingrich and Phil Donahue.

JASPER: Spaz is right, you TALK FUCKED.

SKEETER: Voluminous command o' the vocabulary here on Avenue A.

JASPER: Go back to Oregon.

SKEETER: Whur you from?

JASPER: Connecticut.

SKEETER: Why don't you go back there, fair dude?

JASPER: You tryin' tuh start something? You want me tuh break in my new boots on ya, SURF?

Jasper dances around Skeeter, kicking. Skeeter stands his ground and lowers his voice.

SKEETER: Not overmuch, Jasper, but first let me risk waxin' redundant in statin' that I am not o' the surf posse but on the *rave* side o' th' tribe, an' secondly let me state det when people kick me I typically respond in a *re*flexlike fashion. As in, I kick *back*.

JASPER: Fuck it, then.

Jasper collapses against and slides down the wall. Skeeter joins him. They sprawl on the putrid sidewalk.

SKEETER: I return the sentiment.

JASPER: I can't go back to Connecticut. My stepdad kicked me out. HE'S A FUCKIN' *COP*!

SKEETER: Ah, wull, my old man's in th' penitentiary on a marijuana smuggle, if it's any consolidarity. My ma Linda forwarded me his letter. See?

Skeeter removes a crumpled letter from his mood-hat.

JASPER: Yeah? Is dat why yuh drinkin' quarts of Milla?

SKEETER: Yeh-up.

JASPER: Why?

SKEETER: 'Cause I read it an' in it he apologized fer not bein' a good dad an' all like that, shit.

JASPER: Oh shit, fuck dat. So what are you gonna do?

SKEETER: Burn it.

what

JASPER: Here, give it to me.

He takes the letter and stands up, trying to light it with his lighter.

JASPER: It's hard to burn in the rain. Here, take it.

They hold their coats around it until it catches fire. Skeeter holds it in front of him, watches it burn, and throws it down and stomps it.

SKEETER: Dear Ezekial—I regret I was not a good father tuh you and hope I kin make it up tuh you in the future.

JASPER: Huh! NOOOOO *FU*TURE!!

SKEETER: Cor*rec*to, Jasper!

JASPER: Yuh're alright, Squizzo, YUH'RE A PUNK!

SKEETER: *Skee*ter. Nuh, I did that punk shit when I was twelve. Now I rave, brother. In point o' fact I came down here so—

JASPER: Yeah?

They slide down the wall again.

SKEETER: —so I could find my girlfriends on the rave net. You know anyone? My Aunt Jeanette told me tuh look fer it down here. On the left coast we go on-line in the java rooms.

JASPER: Not here. Ask Spinner.

SKEETER: Who?

JASPER: Dat guy ovah there spinnin' the fuckin' glow-worms. He used to live over at Collective Unconscious on Avenue B 'til it burned down. Those people ovah there know all dat computer shit.

Skeeter gets to his feet with some effort.

SKEETER: SPIN-NERRRR!

He falls back hard against the wall and slides to the ground.

JASPER: What are you gonna say to yuh girlfriends?

Skeeter lunges back to his feet.

SKEETER: Rave Net Bulletin: Dear Clove and Sable, I love you both lavishly. It is rainin' here on Avenue A in New York City. I just burned the only letter my dad ever sent me. I am devoted tuh the both of you ravishing babe-dudes fer the rest of my short life. I am coming tuh Santa Cruz tuh elope with you in triplicate.

He burps long and loud.

SKEETER: I'm drunk. Save me.

He burps again.

SKEETER: Vouchsafedly yers, Skeeter.

ever

JASPER: You're as fucked in the head as Mr. Spam.

SKEETER: Fuck.

He burps.

SKEETER: All-purpose word on Avenue A.

JASPER: Avenue A!

SKEETER: Fuck.

JASPER: You said it. I didn't.

what

CHAPTER 9

IN WHICH JEANETTE
FINDS A CURE

Jeanette is alone in her apartment, screaming at the top of her lungs.

JEANETTE: No more praying. No more praying, no more hoping. No more hoping, no more praying. No more positive thinking. No more healing. No more loving anyone for the rest of my life, anywhere, anywhere, anyplace as long as I live. Paul! You bastard. You came to me in pain, you said, "Jeanie, Jeanie, heal me, I'm in pain. Jeanie, Jeanie, help me." I told you, Paul, I said, I'm not a call girl anymore, it's been three years of struggling and healing and doing good work and healing. I'm not a call girl, we can't have that kind of relationship and you said, "Jeanie, I don't want to have that kind of relationship, I want to know you, I want to love you. I love you, Jeanie. I love you, Jeanette, more than I've loved anyone, more than I love my wife, Polly, more than I love even my daughter. I love you, Jeanette." And I *believed* you. I thought maybe I've just been hardened by fate. Maybe all this healing work I've been doing for other people has healed me. Maybe all this chanting and studying has made me evolve out of the *cycle of pain*. I've *soaked* my three-thousand-year-old Mytelene cave-crone crystals in butterfly tears, I've left bowls of *honey* and *cream* and *curd* for the triple goddesses of the *waxing,* the *waning,* and the *full moons*. I've *scrubbed* karmas, I've *scoured* souls, I've *cleaned* chakras. Maybe I'm *healed*. Maybe I'm out of the *cycle* of pain. NO! NOOO! I'm gonna melt these three-thousand-year-old crystals down in the microwave! I'm gonna burn my books on the sacred healing touch. I'm gonna desecrate my altar to the triple goddess. There is no *triple* goddess. There is no *double* goddess. There is *no Goddess*! There is only SINGLE ME! *FUCK* the Goddess in *ALL* of her aspects! No more healing. No more praying.

No more positive thinking! I'm thirty-nine years old and I can't even hold onto a sixty-two-year-old man with a bad heart and a paunch! WHY NOOOOOOT? Paul, you bastard, your heart had an attack so you're going back to your wife Polly and leaving me alone with nothing but the doofy son of my loony sister who stares at me all the time like a drowning puppy. "Heal me, Aunt Jeanette, heal me!" No more healing, no more praying! I renounce prayer. I renounce hope. There is no Goddess. There is no God. There is no God. There is no hope. There is only ME!

There is a knock at the door.

JEANETTE: Oh, Skeeter, is that you? Oh Ezekial, did you lose your keys again?

She opens the door. There stand Violet and Balzac.

VIOLET: Uhp, hello?

JEANETTE: Huh—hello.

VIOLET: Hello, deeah. I'm your neighbor from around the corneh. I bribed our corrupt doorm'n to let me into all the buildings 'round heah. I'm passing, uh, circu- uh a petition against the death penalty. Um um um, to Governor Pistachio, uh, Pataki. Uh, I live in the building on Park Avenue. You know, the tan building with the hideous gargoyles? The Delphi Apahtments? D'you know it? Uh, are you in favor of government executions, deeah?

JEANETTE: Uh—no! Uh.

VIOLET: Uh, well, oh, am I disturbing you?

JEANETTE: Oh, just a personal crisis. Here, let me sign.

VIOLET: Is it your husband, deeah, or someone else's?

JEANETTE: Someone else's. Are—are—how did?—are you a psychic?

VIOLET: No.

Violet draws herself up and gives Jeanette a stern look.

VIOLET: I'm an old woman. Listen, deeah, I can tell you this much. In my life, I've been left—Balzac! Don't bark! Oh this is my dog, Balzac. He's so happy we're on an adventure. I've been driving him mad telling the same dull stories again and again. (Don't worry, Balzac, it won't be a long one this time.) I've been with many men and all of them have left me, either of their own damn volition or by *dy*ing. And after each one is gone, the friends come. They say, Oh it isn't as bad as you imagine it is. You'll meet another one before

what

you know it. And they're wrong. It's always far worse than you imagine it is, and it takes years before you meet a new one. The only thing for it, deeah, is to have a good stiff drink. Have you got any liquor?

JEANETTE: I-I think I have a bottle of brandy somewhere.

VIOLET: Good. Pour yourself a large glass of that and then *sit* there and *drink* and *curse* the day you were born about five hundred *million* times until you just get sick of it and you'll find that life just has a way of going *on*. And on and on and on and on and on . . . 'slike a tune that you *cahn't* get out of your head, it's rully rather an*noy*ing after a while . . .

JEANETTE: I—uh—uh—I—I don't know why . . . but you are making me . . . feel . . . better.

VIOLET: Senseless prattle, deeah. It usually makes a person feel better. Get plenty of it. And *drink*. Heavily!

JEANETTE: Okay. Uh—who are you?

VIOLET: Violet Smith, and this is my dog, Balzac.

JEANETTE: I'm Jeanette Gladjnois. Good luck.

They shake hands.

VIOLET: You too, deeah.

JEANETTE: Bye.

VIOLET: Bye.

Jeanette closes the door and wanders pensively toward the middle of the room.

JEANETTE: Hmm. Maybe *she* was the old crone. Maybe there *is* a goddess and I've just been looking in the wrong place. Now, where is that bottle of Christian Brothers?

ever

CHAPTER 10

IN WHICH POLLY IS CARELESS

Polly is in her breakfast nook. She has a mop in one hand and a phone in the other.

POLLY: Paul, honey, could you turn down the CNN? Sheila Marie's on the phone? Do you wont to speak to her? She ring-a-ding-dinged just to see how you were gettin' alo-ong? What's that, dar-lin'? Oookee-dokee. She-She? Daddy says he'll just watch a few more minutes and then he'll pick up in the den. He's an ole boob-tuber, you know, once he's home. Hmm? I'm in the breakfast nook. I told Beverly, Take the day off. I need to keep busy. I'm moppin' and glowin, hee hee. Mop mop mop 'n glow glow glow! Floor's al-ready clean as a brand-new day! I better stop.

She puts the mop aside and sits down at the table. As she talks she cannot resist wetting her finger and scraping at the coffee stain in the table's Formica finish.

POLLY: Wey-ell, we checked him out of the hospital Sa'urday, and I drove us down in the Lincoln. Hmm? I sound fonny? How? Wey-ell no, Sheila, I'm very happy. Your father's recoverin' wey-ell. He's re-coverin' wey-ell. Doctors said it was more stress than anything else, wey-ell, gosh, who wouldn't be stressed what with a wife, a mis-tress, two children like you and Derek who could hardly be more different, Derek bein' in the Christian Coalition and you runnin' off chainin' yourself to trees all the time.

Wey-ell, he-he's come back to me, She-She! At the hospital, he decided no more J-J-Jeanette, no more NYC business trips, no more business, period. That's wah he had the heart attack at Axnell Head-quarters. He was tryin' to tell that to Bob Flaskett that ole son of a gun, and I guess it was too much and his poor pump went a teensy bit pooped and it failed. But it's all over, all of it, over and now we're back in Virginia, Papa Paul Bear and Mama Polly Bear. Hee

hee. Hmm? Wey-ell, now, Sheila Baby-Bear, I shouldn't have confused you with that nonsense. That's O-V-E-R. Just forget your mom Polly ever did anything so, so, you know?

Wey-ell, you're the only one who did approve. Do you know Bunny Peters isn't speakin' to poor Polly? Wey-ell, I know she always told me to leave him, but not for a—you know. Okay, okay, She-She, I shouldn't have told you, Miss Berkeley Radical, okay—a black! I said it, you happy?

Ooo, did you know Derek's movin' to D.C.? Now he'll be close by, maybe him and Dad can kiss and be friends. What d'you think? Wey-ell, apparently the Christian Coalition is settin' up a permanent office there, so Derek transferred up from Leezy-anna.

Fawn is fine. They're movin' up their engagement. Wey-ell, apparently, there was a li'l problem with premarital "hoo-hoo"—you know. No, it wasn't *Fawn*! It was Derek. Poor Dorky, he's more of a square than silly ole me!

Me? What do you mean? What about me? Wah do you keep askin' me that, honey? I'm fine. It's ended. Paul, your father, I mean, is being nicer than he's been since before you were born. It breaks my heart. He even ordered me a new ring, since I lost it down the garbage disposal. Oh, if only I hadn't had that new garbage disposal installed, if only I hadn't met Reuben, if only he hadn't had to come back to try and find that damn ring, if only your father hadn't decided to be nice to me again, after all these years, if only Reuben weren't a Negro—black—person of color! I love his big black beauty! There! Goddamn it, I said it! I *love* my Reuben and I wish I could leave your damn father, who is suddenly bein' so *terribly* kind and has *al*ways been so God Almighty *white*! Lord!

She turns and sees Paul standing in the doorway of the nook.

POLLY: Paul? What happened to the CNN? Lord! You're white as a sheet! Sheila Marie? Mom an' Daddy're havin' a li'l emergency, we're goin' to have to call you right back, okay, sweetie? Bye-bye. Have a nice day!

POLLY: Oh!

PAUL: Oh!

ever

CHAPTER 11

IN WHICH CLOVE EMBARKS

Amid flashing lights and heartbeat-timed rave rhythms, Clove dances over to Sable.

CLOVE: Sable, there you are, my rave-aged sister. Whur have you been since midnight?

SABLE: Querulously and perilously dancing.

They dance throughout their conversation.

CLOVE: Here?

SABLE: Yah, here and there an' everywhur. I was up in that top o' this factory with this dude who was all thirty-something and all knowledgeable and he was showing me how they smeltered the washing machine lids on and how it was all toxic producing.

CLOVE: Did you get slithery?

SABLE: Nuh, he was all old and thirty-something. He was rad, though, I'm sure someone his age would be most lustful on him.

CLOVE: Have you been dancing relentless-like?

SABLE: Yah. With incessance.

CLOVE: Rad.

Clove spins.

CLOVE: I'm spinning toppish unto dawn's finger poked into the derelict manufactury windows, all roasty brown and metallic with toxic age made fair, fresh, and brisk-headed by our ravish night of *spin, spin,* SPIIIN!!!!

SABLE: Silence of yer lambish bahh, you pixilated dervish wench!

They do the Goddess-stammer, continuing to dance through their customary synchronized head-wobbling.

CLOVE AND SABLE: Godddddddddddddduh-duh-duh-desssssss.

They are quiet and just whirl around for a while.

CLOVE: Sable-dude?

SABLE: Yah, dude?

CLOVE: I'm waxin' all wistful that our long-lost lust-stokin' slithery boy is not here to breach the break o' dawn with our highnesses whul flood is flashing outside the factory walls.

SABLE: Oooo oooo ooo, I almost nulled out! The news!

CLOVE: What? What?

SABLE: This dude Thisbee who was all cybernated and me were talking and he's all, "Yer name is Sable, er er, is yer friend's name Clove" an' I'm all, Yah, how do you fathom that? An' he's all, "Yur so cute, I shouldn't tell you."

CLOVE: Would you just tell me?!

SABLE: He's all, "Yur so cute but thur's a bulletin fer you on the rave net from a dude identifyin' as Skeeter in New York City."

CLOVE: Skeeter? Yah? Fer you or fer me?

SABLE: Yah, he says he's all excessively devoted to both of us!

CLOVE: Double fucking joy!

SABLE: Clove, dude, that's what it said, he's all drunk an' all lonely and he burnt some letter from his dad an' he's comin' to Santa Cruz to elope with us.

CLOVE: But I'm not going back to Cruz!

SABLE: Here comes the sun through the rain clouds! It's dawn!

CLOVE: Whoah, we danced 'til dawn!

They are blissed out and silent, dancing ecstatically to the horizon, backlit by a pink sunrise. Now Sable looks at Clove quizzically.

SABLE: What? You mean yur not coming back to Cruz?

CLOVE: Nuhhh.

SABLE: But I can't drive back on those deluviated highways in my parents' wizened Buddha-VW all solitary an' face yer snapping hippie parents in Cruz.

CLOVE: Then come with us, Sabe, see that couple over thar in the green?

SABLE: Yah. What are they wearing?

CLOVE: Brussels sprouts, see? Brussels sprout capes, hats, leggin's, an' harnesses. Doesn't that elucidate you?

SABLE: Clove, yur tweaked.

CLOVE: It doesn't matter, nevermind. Forget it.

SABLE: What? What? Elucidate me!

CLOVE: No. Nothing. It doesn't matter nevermind.

ever

SABLE: Elucidate me!

CLOVE: Wull, you promise not to get all intoler-bloated if I mention Cobain the Friendly Ghost again and how the farmworker dudes told me I have to put him back to rest 'cause I impishly rattled him from his sea-bed when he dumped me in thur sprouts field?

Sable covers her ears.

SABLE: Ahhhhhhhhh, let thur be BLIGHT!!!!!!

CLOVE: Thur is blight, Sable! Thur is! Thur's floods! That's another sign! Remember, the farmworker dudes gave me that brussels sprout I buried under the Cruz boardwalk and after that I had that brussels stalks dream?

SABLE: Stop redundenating everything, yah yah!

CLOVE: Wull, last week when I dreamt about the brussels stalks twining north under the beach ground and it said I had to follow them north, I was certified. And then last night before I fugitated hippie family prison, what did my mom cook but tempeh brussels sprouts casserole.

SABLE: Boing boing boing, so? Who derives a care? I see no connection.

CLOVE: But thur is a connection, Sable, don't you see? That's why I have to embark with Kerrwyd and Zaylya on thur pleasure bark *The Lemon Lady*. See it? It's bouncing on the dock. It's thur houseboat and they have this society "Vivir Soñando"—it means to *live* in your *dreams* and they dreamt brussels told them to dress up like brussels sprouts and go to a party in a washing machine and there they would meet a young girl and take her away. And I'm a young girl . . .

She spins around and around.

CLOVE: . . . and this is a rave in an abandonated washing machine factory and look! Eeee! Thur are brussels sprouts sprouting up through the floorboards! That's another sign!

SABLE: Whur? Clove those are video projections!

CLOVE: Godddddddddddddddd—

For the first time in the life of their best-friendship, Sable does not join in on the Goddess-stammer.

CLOVE: duh-duh-duh . . . Sable? Won't—can't you come with me?

SABLE: I can't, Clove. My parents? School? That dude Skeeter?

what

Don't, can't you wait? The ocean is ferocious and hectically rambunctious. Thur's floods!

CLOVE: The ocean is wild and wailing and pleasing. Up the coast I'm embarking with Kerrwyd and Zaylya on *The Lemon Lady* at the break of this brave dawn. Fare thee well, fairest and bestest of friends, we'll meet again, I'm totally sure!

> Clove runs off and boards the houseboat. She straddles the deck, waving.

SABLE: Good-bye, Clove. Rave on, sister.

CLOVE: Rave on!

> Clove babbles away as the houseboat embarks on the stormy seas. Sable calls plaintively into the fog.

SABLE: Yah. Have a nice day!

> She turns away.

SABLE: Oh Clove, why did we ever come to this rave in San Francisco!? Oh Clove, oh Skeeter, why have you both desertified me? Oh God-duh-duh-duh-duh-dess.

> A shiver runs through Sable as she stands alone, no longer dancing, though the beat goes on and on.

ever

PART FIVE

CASTAWAY

CHAPTER 1

IN WHICH SABLE SENDS A RAVE NET BULLETIN

Sable sits late one night at her computer, clicking away intently at the keyboard. Her cerulean-blue bedroom is lit only by the computer screen—enough to illuminate the eyes of the Hindu deities and the thighs of the waif-boy underwear models who decorate her walls.

SABLE: Rave Net Bulletin from Sable Nugent, Santa Cruz Rave: Has anyone sighted a dude named Skeeter on the New York City Rave scene? I heard he sent me and my friend Clove a cyberized missive last week. I never read it but a dude named Thisbee said you sounded all bifurcated and solitudenated, which is how I am in excess at this actual moment. I am stoked that you are devoted to me, Skeeter, but a tad conflated that you additionally pledge yourself to my dear friend and fairest cohort Clove. But time is snappish. Clove has embarked on a sea voyage northwards with a pair of torpid thirty-somethings. She thinks she is all vision-questing and like that and she desertified me at a Frisco rave so I had to drive back on washed-out roads and tell her poxy hippie parents of her absconsion. Needless to say, I am agged to the gills. I last saw her stark on the houseboat, buffeted to and fro-ish by the raging flood-fat waves and her penultimate babblings were, as follows:

As she types, one can almost imagine Clove, eyes aglitter, steering into the squall and versifying thusly:

CLOVE: Gush green surf, spout gray whales,

embarcadero'd am I

a sputtered eye fer Bodega Bay

I cry on a wave good-bye, good-bye
to my true dude Sable good-bye
I must flow North toward the Puget Sound
fer thur's brussels sprouts tugging me under the ground
and gulls fly low
qui-quawing so so
It's North along the Cali coast we go:
hurtling the tangled waves,
sparring the tarnished cliffs' blade,
bracing the ziggy shore's zag!
Pleasure bark—woof! woof!—ahey!
we'll brave the flooding day
up the coast we fly we float
in a pillowed house that's partly boat
and away we go like a hungry goat
chewing the scud in our nave
we charge the Pacific moat
under the Golden Gate Drawbridge
to thrashing rains we pay our homage
spurtle! spurt! spout! the fog'll never give out
wave yer tails, ye gray whales
and stretch yer sperm five hundred males
to Puget Sound we shout
a trailing twine of brussels sprouts cord
beneath the brine
cords that climb
out the California belly
up the neck of Oregon,
to the headstate of Washington
ahey, ahey, ahey, we go up the coast
chasing Cobain's ghost
back to who know whar, yah?!
In *tha* deep deep deep!

SABLE: Er, words to that effect. She was tweaked. Please come to Santa Cruz so I can talk to you, Skeeter, and do not wax all Jason Priestley when you get here or you will never taste of my carnal de-

what

lights again. I am desolidated. I lack Clove, I lack you, and I am being drained alive by my hectic Buddhist parents who have been
chanting without cessitude since these rare events went down. I
need you, dude!
Savagely yers, Sable.
P.S. Nobody else read this.

ever

CHAPTER 2

IN WHICH JEANETTE
RETRIEVES SKEETER

Skeeter and his new companions wake in a haze of dirty sunlight.

JASPER: Spaz, move yuh fuckin' puppy, she's droolin' on my boots, fuck it.

SPAZ: Move her yourself. Shouldn't we get off the wall and go to the park?

SKEETER: Er, yeah, I'se leanin' toward th' nature scene myself. After all, the sun is shinin' fer once on Avenue A. Jasper? Spaz? The park?

JASPER: Don't ya have any more money?

SKEETER: Aggrievedly, nuh, I am lacking lucre.

SPAZ: You still talk fucked after a week of hanging with us!

SKEETER: Er, perchance, Spaz, and on the coincidental leg, you continue tuh annoy the fuck outta me.

JASPER: Ha ha, see, Squito boy is alright. I told you he was a punk.

SKEETER: R-A-V-E. I *rave*. Whur's my old man's letter?

JASPER: Give 'im his pile of ashes.

SPAZ: My puppy's chewin' on it. Pork Rind, stop chewin' on that dirty half-burnt piece of shit.

SKEETER: Give it. Tuh me.

He tucks what is left of the letter into his mood-hat.

SKEETER: Jasper, you still wanna go to the park?

JASPER: In about two hours. I'm still hung over. Anyone got a stogie?

SPAZ: I can't believe Giraffe sold my comic books for H. I can't believe Giraffe sold my comic books for H. Hey, lady. Spare any change for puppy chow or tampons?

Two nicely dressed Polish matrons walk by, doing their best to ignore the "crusties."

LADY: No, I don't spare any change for a dirty girl.

SPAZ: Aw come on, don't you ever have your period? Don't you like animals?

LADY: No, no.

She lets off a stream of expletives in Polish to her friend. No one understands except a Polish bum who is having nightmares in a nearby doorway.

JASPER: Ooo look at that rich lady gettin' outta dat cab.

Across the street, Jeanette gets out of a cab and scans the sidewalks.

SPAZ: EAT THE RICH.

JASPER: ANARCHY!

SKEETER: Ah shit. 'At's my Aunt Jeanette. An' she's not overmuch of the rich persuasion, you—*cap*sized knaves, she just waxes a tad fancy is all, she's jus—

SPAZ: She's wearin' a fuckin' beige suit with pearl-drop earrings!

JASPER: STOMP THE RICH!

SKEETER: Ah, shit!

Jeanette spots them and begins to cross the street.

ever

CHAPTER 3

IN WHICH VIOLET SHARES HER
VISION WITH CORA SUE

It is afternoon in Violet's apartment. Cora Sue is vacuuming.

VIOLET: Cora? I need y'help, deeah.

CORA SUE: Hmm?

VIOLET: I need you, I need y'help. Turn off the vacuum cleaner, please, deeah.

CORA SUE: What is it, Violet?

Cora Sue switches it off and straightens up.

VIOLET: I need to make something before I die.

CORA SUE: Die? You're not goin' t' die. Don't talk like that. You know, you ain't goin' t' die yet.

VIOLET: *Yet* being the operative word. Did I ever tell you about my room?

CORA SUE: What room?

She sits down beside Violet.

CORA SUE: This room?

VIOLET: No. No. The room of jazz. I wanted to make a room that was like jazz, like jazz itself. I told people about it in the fifties. There was— When I was married to Kelly, we used to go up to a farm in New Hampshire. Uh, loads of exhibits went on there. Artists and sculptors and poets. Eh, it was Peter and Jenny Tricott's farm. Jenny was a very mousy girl. Peter was very droll and always smoked a pipe. And there were loads of people up there—one in particular, I remember, a homosexual poet that I liked—quite—I-I was very fond of him, named Julian Beech some-something like that. Then of course there was Sophie Flax. Very good artist. She had a *terrible* time getting any attention, eh, back then. Terrible. But, teh, 'course now she's the only one that they remember. Sophie Flax—I was at

the Modern last Thursdee and I sawr one of her— I-I took Balzac
but they wouldn't let me bring him up—I had to put him in the coat
check, poor miserable little poodle—and, uh, I sawr a piece of hers.
I stared at it f' *hour*s. It was a giant ladies' clutch purse—black. Iron.
Welded together with, eh, eh, lipsticks 'n combs 'n brushes. I
thought 'twas *very* clever. I looked 't it f' *hour*s. That was Sophie
Fla— I used to argue with Elliot about Sophie—I'd say she's a fine
artist! He'd say, "No, she's not, she's merely decorative." *Noth*ing,
nothing ever tempted me to leave Elliot, but if anything *could* have,
that would've been it.

But we were talking about Kelly, my second husband. When I
was still married to him, uh, we went up to the Tricott Farm, we're
sitting 'round. I sort of joked, I said, Wouldn't it be splendid to have
a room of jazz? Make a room like that? Peter Tricott says, "Oh, Vi,
old girl, all the rooms in your flat're jazzy. You've got us all beat
hands down when it comes to decoration!" I said, no, not a *jazzy*
room: a room that is *LIKE JAZZ*. And I thought of it la —uh, last
night—second time I've thought've it since then. The only other
time I remembered it was during the sixties, reading *The Times*.
There was this Japanese girl, eh, she had a name something like
eggs, eggs, not the whites but the the—yokes?—she married the—
one of the—

CORA SUE: Yoko?!

VIOLET: Yeh! Yoker *O*no. She was, I said, that's *it*, that's *exactly* it! *I*
could've done something like that, what this *girl* is doing—that's it!
Last night I woke up in a cold sweat—Balzac was off the foot of the
bed; he usually sleeps at the foot of the bed! But he IS a dog, after
all, so he was off!—and I thought of the room of jazz. And I've *got* to
make it.

All long, dark, blue plumes. One has to take off one's clothes
and walk nude through it. Carpets *soak*ed in whiskey. Burgundy
walls. Brass shells *plung*ing from the walls, and little tiny mirrors all
bent and crooked looking in at one another, doorknobs of fur. Loads
of smoke, fire, blood. Will you help me make it? Neveh mind the
housecleaning—LET'S MAKE THE ROOM!

CORA SUE: Wey-ell, I would. I would, Violet, you know *I* would. But
what you're describing sounds impossible.

ever

VIOLET: Yes.

Violet accepts this. Then, suddenly, a perverse glee in the impossibility of it fills her eyes.

VIOLET: But so is *jazz*!

CORA SUE: Let me fix you a snack.

VIOLET: Alright.

Cora Sue goes to the kitchenette. Violet calls to her.

VIOLET: Well, at least I told it to someone. At least you sawr it in your mind's eye too. At least, I won't DIE without anyone else knowing about the Room of Jazz.

CORA SUE: Die. Will you stop talking about dying?

Cora Sue calls over her shoulder, arrested midmotion with a jar in her hand.

CORA SUE: I don't know how I'd get through the day without you. I can barely tolerate all the other folks I clean for. I don't know what I'd do without you.

VIOLET: Don't worry, you're right. I have no plans whatsoever to DIE. I'll just keep going!

She sits quietly.

VIOLET: Eh, I'll have a few slices of the sweet pickle and, eh, some saltines—five or six should do nicely.

what

CHAPTER 4

IN WHICH A NEPHEW EXPRESSES HIS AFFECTION

Back at the wall.

JEANETTE: Ezekial, there you are, come on, get in the cab, I've been looking for you for a week. What happened?

SKEETER: I dunno, I been subject tuh vagrancies. Aunt Jeanette, meet my . . . frien— er, associates. Jasper, Spaz meet—

JASPER: Spare any change, lady? I can see you got it.

JEANETTE: Oh really?

Jeanette takes an angry pull on her cigarette.

JEANETTE: Well, I earned *my* change sucking the cocks of the rich white male corporate elite for ten years. If you want some goddamn money, I suggest you go suck some cocks of your own.

SKEETER: Whoah, Aunt Jeanette, yur waxin' perilously scandlous!

JEANETTE: Ezek-Skeeter, whatever your fucking nephew name is, get in the damn cab and get away from these drunks.

She yanks him off the wall.

SPAZ: We're anarchists.

JEANETTE: Alright, then, *anarchist* drunks! Come on.

JASPER: Fuck it, Squeezo, yuh not gonna get in dat bourgeois cock-sucka's cab, are ya?

SKEETER: Er, with pleasure.

He quickly gets in the cab and turns to wave.

SKEETER: Bye, associates! Bye, Jasper, bye, Spaz, bye, Pork Rind, say good-bye to Giraffe and Mr. Spam and Chito.

SPAZ: ANARCHY!

JASPER: ANARCHY!

SKEETER: What. Ever.

They pull into traffic. The cab driver looks back at Jeanette.

ANATOLE KOMALSKY: Where to?

He has a thick Russian accent and a deep, no-nonsense voice.

JEANETTE: Now back to where you picked me up—Seventy-eighth and Park.

SKEETER: Is 'at true, Aunt Jeanette, did you? Is that how you got yer apartment an' everything?

JEANETTE: What? You think I bought that place teaching my sacred crystal seminars?

SKEETER: I pondered.

JEANETTE: Now you know. You asshole. I've been worried sick about you on top of Paul having a heart attack and deciding to go back to his idiot wife Polly.

SKEETER: Wull, 'at's why I stayed away, Aunt Jeanette, I figured I was in yer path an' all like that, what with yer emotional decrepitude an'—

JEANETTE: So you just went down to Avenue A and stayed there without calling for a week?! How did Linda raise you?!

SKEETER: On th' road? In a bumlike fashion.

JEANETTE: Was it the letter from your dad, Bruce, in prison that Linda forwarded to you? Is that what sent you off?

SKEETER: Nuuhhhhhh.

JEANETTE: Ezekial.

SKEETER: SKEEETERRRRRR! I burned it.

JEANETTE: What?

SKEETER: I burnt 'is croakin' letter. See? Hur.

He removes the remains of the letter from his mood-hat and shows them to Jeanette.

JEANETTE: Why did you save the ashes then?

SKEETER: Never. Mind.

JEANETTE: Ez-Skeeter, I realize I haven't been a very available host.

SKEETER: 'At's fine. No problem, Jeanette dude.

He wipes back tears.

SKEETER: I hate my dad anyway. I only defend him tuh piss off Linda. I can't believe all those years you sent us money orders an' all like that you were bein' a, a, p-p-p-prostitute.

JEANETTE: But now I'm a healer, Skeeter, and I do fine.

SKEETER: Tuhhh. 'Cept you won't help me put a spell out on Clove

what

'n Sable fer whom I am waxin' MOST pinish and melancholic an' you can't help yerself with yer own twisted heart troubles. Yur just like my ma Linda, all Wicca-er than thou with her crafty ways, but she's still th' same fuck-up with men an' jobs 'et she's always been. An' I'm her son, an' now I get a letter from Bruce. "Dear Ezekial, I'm sorry." Yeah, so am I. Tuhhhh.

JEANETTE: Skeeter, Linda might be a flake but she loves you and she is a good witch, she is a magic healing lady. And I-I may have had a hard life—

SKEETER: 'At's fine, no judgmentality 'bout yer *checkered past* on *my* slope.

She cuts him off.

JEANETTE: But I'm not a flake, okay? I might have emotional problems but I'm working on them and even Bruce, your dad Bruce, might be on the wrong side of the law and he was a big partyer, but he's-he's, what can I say, Bruce is Bruce and I wish he'd been around more because he's a unique guy and you remind me of him only you're not an asshole. I didn't mean that. Yes, I did! Come here, come here, Ezekial.

She holds out her arms to him.

SKEETER: SKEETERRR!

He pounds his chest, but in a second he breaks down and is crying on her stomach.

SKEETER: Aunt Jeanette, Aunt Jeanette. I been drunk fer a week and I don't even have alcoholic tendencies.

She strokes his head.

JEANETTE: I can tell—you're a stoner from way back.

SKEETER: Right on, oh Aunt Jeanette, you feel so good, yur just like my ma Linda but even prettier an' you understand me better. Yer married boyfriend is such the asshole tuh desertify yer fineness.

JEANETTE: Oh, Skeeter.

SKEETER: Ohhh, Aunt Jeanette.

He is drawn to her full breasts.

JEANETTE: Stop it, Skeeter, honey, don't get sexual.

SKEETER: Puuuhlease, Aunt Jeanette.

JEANETTE: No, stop. Gaia!

She pushes him off.

179

JEANETTE: I told Linda to stop letting you sleep with her after age seven.

ANATOLE KOMALSKY: Excuse me, you are going to make incyst in my cyab, I drop you at the kirb. Nobody make incyst in my cyab.

JEANETTE: No, I am not going to "make incest"! I'm a grown woman, I can resist the sexual attractions of teenagers. Unlike *men*. My name is not Roma*nette* Polanski!

ANATOLE KOMALSKY: Oh, Roman Polanski, good director. I am fyilm-maker. You *know* Roman Polanski?

JEANETTE: Sure, *Knife in the Water*?

ANATOLE KOMALSKY: Oh yeah—*The Tenant*?

JEANETTE: Oh yeh. Sure. *Macbeth*?

ANATOLE KOMALSKY: Huh, oh you know that one? You really know!

SKEETER: Er, who?

JEANETTE: Ah, never mind, Ezekial. Let us off here, here on Lexington. Let's go to the Blue Ship Diner and eat bloody steaks and fries, do you want to?

SKEETER: But, uh, Aunt Jeanette, the food there sucks, and wur both kinda sposeta be vegetarians, aren't we?

JEANETTE: Yeah, so let's go, let's go, and eat it all!

She hands the driver a twenty.

JEANETTE: Here you go, keep the change, thank you.

ANATOLE KOMALSKY: You arre welcome. Uh. What's your number? You want a date?

JEANETTE: Sure.

She looks at his name and picture on the hack license.

JEANETTE: Uh, Anatole Komalsky. I'll call you when I'm in the mood to cuddle up and rent *Rosemary's Baby*. Bye!

ANATOLE KOMALSKY: Bye-bye.

SKEETER: Er, have a nice day!

Skeeter shuts the cab door and follows Jeanette to the Blue Ship.

what

CHAPTER 5

IN WHICH CLOVE DRIFTS ON
THE LEMON LADY

Clove wanders onto the deck of *The Lemon Lady* houseboat, rubbing her eyes. Zaylya sits on a hemp deck chair, sipping from a tall hand-blown glass.

CLOVE: Good morning.

ZAYLYA: Good afternooooon, Clove.

CLOVE: Have we left Bodega Bay, yet?

ZAYLYA: Oh no, we're just rocking here in the bay. That's how the *Vivir Soñando* Society keeps afloat. We just stay moored in our dreams for as long as we want to.

Her head lolls to the side. Her voice is painfully honeyed and musical, a yoga teacher from hell.

ZAYLYA: That's how me and Kerrwyd survive.

CLOVE: Oh yeah. Whur is Kerrwyd?

ZAYLYA: He's on the other side of *The Lemon Lady*, talking to his business associates on the cellular phone.

CLOVE: Uh, that's a tad hectic. Since I thought you were like living in yer dreams and all like that.

ZAYLYA: Right, well, we also live off Kerrwyd's family's investments. There's a little inlet of sunshine here in the fog. Come sit next to me, I'm drinking the *Lemon Lady* special. It's, ahh, fresh-squeezed lemons, fermented rice water, and Calistoga!

She pours Clove a tall glass and hands it to her.

CLOVE: Oh the fog, the fog, scutters and sways, scoops through the ssssssun like through curds and wheys.

Clove sags into the deck chair beside Zaylya.

ZAYLYA: Hmmm?

Zaylya looks slightly confused.

CLOVE: Oh Nothingnevermind. I've just been in a lazy lemon daze since I embarked on yer rare pleasure craft.

ZAYLYA: Hmm. Maybe you'd like to join the *Vivir Soñando* Society with me and Kerrwyd.

CLOVE: Do you love Kerrwyd?

ZAYLYA: Ooo, heavy teenage question. Nooo, um, 'course, Kerrwyd is my best friend. What can I say? Drink. Drink!

> Zaylya drinks deeply. Clove puts the glass to her lips, but forgets to drink and lowers it.

CLOVE: I think I elucidated further my dream and my hauntings by Cobain the Friendly Ghost. See, I figured out this: Cobain was afraid of not belonging underground when he was alive. So of course, naturally he would continue to be fearsome of that when he's dead. And also he was fearsome of all people that were all like waxing all loving toward him? So when I walked accidentally into the ocean at that rave, he wasn't just sleeping in his sea-bed. He was waiting fer somebody to haunt and it would be natural that he would pick me because I *rave*: I'm not overly transfixed by his tragic grunge aura. And then he took me to the brussels sprouts fields whur the farmworker dudes were. Wull, they never even heard of him. They don't know who he is. Was. Whatever. And so when I planted the brussels sprout in the sand it was only natural that they would twine north and I would be called to follow. Follow?

ZAYLYA: Drink.

> Clove almost drinks but again hesitates.

CLOVE: I'm adamant about getting out of Bodega Bay. Aren't you going to take me to Puget Sound? Isn't that what you do? You live dreaming?

ZAYLYA: Well, our dream was to wear brussels sprout clothes, go to a rave, and there we would meet a young girl, who would be a pleasing companion. Your dream is different. Drink.

> Clove tips back her head and drinks a long draft. She sits there, looking spaced out.

CLOVE: I still think I need to follow my dream.

ZAYLYA: Hmmmm.

> Zaylya smiles knowingly.

ZAYLYA: Dreams unfold into other dreams. You'll see when you

what

get older, mellow out. You'll see. Just stay with us and . . . drift awhile . . . Here in Bodega Bay on *The Lemon Lady*.

    Clove drinks more. She is feeling very odd. She begins to sing, eyeing with alarm what she enumerates in song.

CLOVE: *Lemon Lady* daaaze. Abalone ash-traaaays. Will I ever get out of this California Dreaming Haze? Phaaaaaaase? Spaaaaaaze? Quaaaaaaaaays? Spaaaaace . . . Ooooouuuuuut.

    Only the gulls heed her plaintive tune.

CHAPTER 6

IN WHICH BUSHIE
CHANGES TRACKS

Bushie and Rosie sit in a garbage-strewn gully by the Eleventh Avenue freight-train tracks. They are sharing a crack pipe. Rosie is a tiny Dominican woman with a sweet, very quiet voice.

BUSHIE: Listen tuh da trains, Rosie, listen tuh da trains go by. It gives me shivers. I like comin' down here. Aaaaoooh, it's gonna be springtime soon. All uh dis garbage dat us garbage-asses leave down here—yeah, I know, I do it too, I know, I ain't makin' no excuses. It's all gonna be covered up wit' grass, ferns, stinky tree leaves . . . Gonna be nice. See dat right dere,

She points.

BUSHIE: dat pink haltah-top wit' dat dirt growin' all OVAH it? It's like, it looks like a pink haltah-top plant or some shit comin' outta da ground? Dat's mine. Last summah, some ride shot his come all over it an' I took it off. Showed my titties right on da street, tole dat old man who hates us, kiss my titties, baby, I ain't wearin' dis haltah wit' some ride's mess on it. I came down here and I trew it. Dat ole Italian man, he says, "You a *hoo*-ah, you a bad girl!" I says, "No *shit*." He says, "You get outta dissa neighbah-hood, you make-a it bad." I says, "Dis was always a bad neighbah-hood," says, "My people are Irish, we was here before youse, you Italians think you own Hell's Kitchen!" Dat's what my grandmudda, da drunken-ass, useta say tuh my mudda, "You know, Debbie? Not fuh nuttin' but dese Italians t'ink they own da friggin' *neighbah*-hood." R.I.P. I told dat tuh dat old man he got so angry, he tried tuh beat me wit' a stick.

It was funny, dough, I came down here, da train tracks, an' hung out all day. It was July, it was hot. I took da day off, I din't even get high, Terry came lookin' fuh me on Forty-fif' and no one knew where I was. All you all thought I was arrested, no, not Bushie. Bushie was down here, hanging out wit' my titties sunbathin'. I used tuh come down here when I was a kid. Lie down right next tuh da tracks an' feel da train go by, give me shivers.

Dat's how I met Magdalena, Magenta Rush, she invaded me. I kicked huh P.R. butt da first two times, but after dat, I dunno, she just hung out so I got used tuh huh. We both got beat. We was both ugly. But Mag got pretty. Bushie neveh got pretty. But she useta put makeup on me. An' we useta get *wacked* down here, we useta get *dusted*, and we useta *do* it.

ROSIE: Togetha?

BUSHIE: NAW, I meant wit' GUYS. We did it wit' bad-asses. You think I'm bad now? I was way bad den. I'm gonna miss it here. Shit. Remembah dat music back in da seventies? Dey don't make it good like dey did den. Donna Summiz, Jackson Five, Kool and Da Gang? Remembah dat?

ROSIE: I was still in da Dominican Republic in da seventies. We listened to . . . Oscar D'Leon?

BUSHIE: Yeah?

Bushie isn't paying attention.

BUSHIE: I'm gonna miss it down here, Rosie.

ROSIE: Why you gonna miss it, Bushie, what do you mean?

BUSHIE: Dis is gonna be my last time gettin' high down here. Dis is gonna be my very last time, it might be, might be my last time down here on da tracks. Remembah Cassette? Dat little baby bitch from D.C.?

ROSIE: No.

BUSHIE: No, I mean, Cassandra.

ROSIE: Oh yeah, huh. What happen to huh?

BUSHIE: I made huh go tuh Con-venant House.

ROSIE: You *made* huh?

BUSHIE: Yeah. I slapped huh, I slapped huh and told huh, get yuh ass tuh Con-venant House, you too little, go get off my beat, get off my street. Dat was last winter. And den yestuhday huhr and huh new foster parents rode by in a Chevrolet station wagon. She was wearing—

even

Bushie furiously wipes at her eyes, grinding her fist in her eye sockets. She is crying.

BUSHIE: a clean blouse and a clean pair of pants.

ROSIE: What are you buggin' out for, Bushie?

BUSHIE: And she goes tuh me, "Thank you, Bushie, you saved me, you changed my life, you made me get help." An' huh straight-ass foster parents go, "You change huh life, thank you." An' I go, "No I didn't, I just wanted you off my beat, I was just bein' mean." She goes, "No, dat's not true, Bushie, no, 'cause you looked at me and said somepin's going on wit' yuh family, somebody did somepin' bad tuh you," an' its true, I did say dat, but I didn't say it nice like dat, I said it all fucked up. I says, "I wasn't bein' nice I was just bein' a asshole," she goes, "No, Bushie, you helped me, Bushie. You helped change my life," an' she kissed me on da cheek, an' huh straight-ass foster parents give me dis card dat say, anytime you need help tuh get off drugs please contac' us. And den dey drove off in their Chevrolet station wagon.

ROSIE: Why are you buggin' out?

BUSHIE: 'Cause it's not *true*, I neveh helped *nobody*, I neveh helped *nobody*.

ROSIE: Daz not true, Bushie, you a kindhearted person. Remembah when you helped me when da' man—

Rosie flinches.

ROSIE: almos'—did dat to me—an' I was all hysteric an' you bought me flowers an' we took a bath togetha?

BUSHIE: No, I didn't DO dat! I don't remembah, I didn't DO dat!

ROSIE: Yes, you did, Bushie, you kindhearted.

BUSHIE: No, I'm *not*! Dis might be my last time gettin' high down here on da tracks. Do you think I could make it through rehab, Rosie? You think I could make it through?

ROSIE: I tell you, if anybody could, it would be you. 'Cause you one of God's *own* bitches. I seen *bitches*, and I seen God's own, and you one of God's *own* bitches.

Bushie sniffles.

BUSHIE: Yeah?

ROSIE: Yeah.

what

CHAPTER 7

IN WHICH SKEETER AND PAUL HAVE A FRANK DISCUSSION

Skeeter cracks open the door to Jeanette's apartment. Paul stands in the hallway.

PAUL: Hey, Squeaker!

SKEETER: Skeeter.

PAUL: Uh, is your Aunt Jeanette here?

SKEETER: Nuh.

PAUL: But I telephoned from the airport, she said she—

SKEETER: She went out, dude, she didn't wanna see you. Hur's yer things.

PAUL: What did she say?

SKEETER: Manifestly? Her flat-on verbiage? She said tell 'at asshole tuh collect his things and I never wanna see him again.

PAUL: Oh yeah?

SKEETER: Hur's yer stuff. She called 'em yer stupid starchy shirts, in point o' veracity.

PAUL: Did she now? Jeanette? Jeanette? Are you in there? Jeanette?

He pushes past Skeeter, trying to see into the apartment.

SKEETER: Don't push, Paul dude, I step aside fer yer corpret-ness. Take a long look, I wager it's yer last. See? My Aunt Jeanette went out, she didn't want tuh see yuh.

PAUL: What did you call me?

SKEETER: Corpret.

PAUL: Why?

SKEETER: 'Cause 'at's what you are. 'Slike you got some shares in m' Aunt Jeanette an' you sold *them* out 'cause the shares in yer wife went up and then *those* went down an' *now* yur attemptin' tuh buy back the shares in m' Aunt Jeanette. Wull, you hurt her fine fe-maleness. It don't work like dat.

PAUL: You obviously understand nothing about business, Sq-Skeet.

SKEETER: My friends call me Skeeter, but you kin call me Ezekial, Mr. Folsom. Tune yer ear, I don't wanna understand about business. I understand 'et corpret mentalities such as yer own take an' waste precious resources—er, sorceresses, in th' case o' my *fine* witchy Aunt Jeanette whom you have so perilously squandered.

PAUL: I won't stand here and have a scruffy kid like you bawl me out for a complicated relationship between two adult—

SKEETER: Adult? Er. Rated. Don't stand there then, dude, take yer shirts and shift off.

PAUL: Oh, it's a Seaweed Pagoda take-out bag! All the meals we ordered up. She loves that macrobiotic crap! Guh guh guh!

Paul breaks down, wiping his eyes.

SKEETER: Can I help you, dude? Paul? Tuhhh. Yur all corporet and aged, I didn't 'spect you'd wax tearful. Are you havin' a sequel tuh yer heart attack?

PAUL: No, no! You don't understand. I love your aunt immensely. I went back to Polly because I thought—I don't know what I thought. Two wrongs don't make a right, but after my heart attack, I wanted to mend my ways. I've betrayed everyone, my children, my wife, your aunt. Even old Axnell Corporation. I'm not even an Axnell man anymore.

SKEETER: Paul, dude, here's a rag fer yer eyes.

He pulls a blue piece of cloth from deep in his pocket and offers it to Paul.

SKEETER: An' tune yer ear, 'at corpret shit is salaciously hoaxish from the outset. You know? You do well tuh wash yer hands from that lavish blood market.

Paul blows his nose.

PAUL: Well, you're evidently another extremist like your Aunt Jeanette—whom I care for immensely, immensely, Ezekial—

SKEETER: Skeeter.

PAUL: I thought you didn't—

SKEETER: I changed my—never. Mind.

He watches Paul for a minute.

what

SKEETER: That rag yur wipin' yer eyes with, that was gifted on me. Some Lakota Indians gave me that rag on my hitch east. Girl in Wisconsin swiped some saline on it too. No problem shedding copious tears in my presence, Paul, I'm a noxious weeper myself.

PAUL: Thanks.

SKEETER: None needed.

PAUL: Thanks anyway, young man. I apologize for calling you scruffy earlier. It's that hat.

SKEETER: Yup, it's a mood-hat, changes colors wich yer moods.

PAUL: Hmm. It changed color just now.

SKEETER: What. Ever.

Skeeter takes off the hat and folds his arms, giving Paul an impassive stare.

PAUL: I feel better.

SKEETER: Why?

PAUL: Well, why not?

SKEETER: Wull, you left my aunt fer yer wife? Polly? Who it now appears has reciprocated. She's off-loadin' yer critterous corpus, *n'est-ce pas*?

PAUL: She's having an affair with a *black gar*bage-disposal *con*tractor.

SKEETER: What twinges yuh th'most? The black skin, the choice o' livelihoods, er, the fact he's prob'ly doin' yer wife better 'an you ever did?

PAUL: What?

SKEETER: Wull? Which?

PAUL: All three.

SKEETER: Veritable?

PAUL: Yes.

SKEETER: Tuhh. Aunt Jeanette is right, you are a pathetic hypocrite.

PAUL: She said that?

SKEETER: Yeh-up.

PAUL: Hmm. I guess I'll go now. Here's your handkerchief. Nice to finally have a man-to-man with you, Squ-sk-skeeter.

They shake hands.

SKEETER: Tuhh. Answer me one rapid query on th' man side o' th' slope. You seem like you tangled with an abundance o' females in yer corpret line o' life.

ever

PAUL: Um, not really. Not so much.

SKEETER: Wull, I too am stricken with love fer two. Clove an' Sable are thur fair and respective names and they are th' best o' friends. Inseparable almost, an' like that. 'At's how I became intimate with 'em, during brief bouts o' separation. I came here, in fact, tuh beseech my Aunt Jeanette, tuh work her sacred crystalline powers tuh—

PAUL: Put a hocus-pocus on them? So you could be with both?

SKEETER: You surmise it forthrightly. But no such fortune.

PAUL: Want my advice?

SKEETER: Not rully, but m' old man serves in Marion Federal Prison on a marijuana smuggle and my ma Linda and Aunt Jeanette are *not* wull disposed tuh my cause.

PAUL: Sorry to hear that. Well, I'd say be honest. You're lucky you met them both at the same time. I met Polly and Jeanette twenty years apart. That's why I'm so confused.

SKEETER: I am being *hon*est.

PAUL: Where are these girls?

SKEETER: California.

PAUL: What are you doing in New York City?

SKEETER: Uhhhh.

PAUL: You want my advice? Here it is. You're running away. Stop that. Run *tow*ard them, not away.

SKEETER: Tuhhh.

Paul pats Skeeter's shoulder and leaves.

SKEETER: Bye, Paul.

PAUL: Bye.

Paul raises his hand in a flat, one-syllable wave. Skeeter watches him go, lost in thought.

what

CHAPTER 8

IN WHICH POLLY AND
REUBEN DETOUR

Reuben drives Polly down a country road. The car is loaded with suit-cases and boxes.

POLLY: Reuben, can you please pull over? There's a shoulder up ahead, see? Under the Spanish moss? Just, please. I need to think and be still before we go any further.

REUBEN: Alright.

He gives her a look and pulls onto the shoulder. He is a large, nice-looking man in his late forties. His baritone voice is quiet and assured.

POLLY: Thank you.

She smiles tensely. They sit a moment in uncomfortable silence. Polly rolls down the window.

POLLY: Ooooh. Look, there's a stream. Wonder if there are fish in it? My daughter Sheila'd say, "Wey-ell, Mom, those fish are poisoned by pollution, did you know the state of Virginia imports industrial . . ." That's how she goes on. But I cain't see . . . maybe out on the West Coast where she lives, or San Diego where we're goin', the fish are polluted, but here everythin' seems the same. South is lak that. Growin' up in Georgia seems the same as now here in Virginia. 'Course, when I moved up here I thought Virginia was full of Yankees. I'm sorry, Reuben, you don't need to hear that kind of talk.

REUBEN: What kind of talk?

POLLY: Wey-ell, you know, Yankee, Con-Con-Confederates. Old-timey talk!

REUBEN: You know what's old-timey, Polly Ann?

POLLY: Hmmm?

REUBEN: I cain't take no more bein' a black man first an' bein' Reuben Scott Clay second.

POLLY: I don't understand, wah oh wah, my Blackberry Pie?

REUBEN: That's just it. Wah'd I have to be your Blackberry Pie? I'd as soon be your Strawberry Cheesecake. Or you the berries and I'm the cheese. Don't you understand, Polly Ann?

POLLY: No.

REUBEN: It don't matter which is which, which is the flavor and which is the sweet. It matters it tastes *good*, it goes down deliciously, it matters that we lak it. Polly and Reuben, not black man and white woman. I don't wont to be your black man. I'm your man. Talk to me about your husband if you cain't help yourself, but speak as *yourself*, and don't expect me to do otherwise. I'm me, don't you see that? These are *my* hands that touch you, *my* eyes that look at you, this is *my* ear hearin' you.

POLLY: But your skin, darlin', is different than mine.

REUBEN: So is all skin. Your husband's skin, my ex-wife's skin. Skin is what keeps us in. Skin is what we share.

POLLY: I see. I *do* see, Reuben, and I love you . . .

REUBEN: But.

POLLY: Every mile, every mile we go down this road away from my house, I feel lak . . .

REUBEN: Yes, I'm listenin'.

POLLY: I cain't go on.

REUBEN: Go on.

POLLY: I cain't! I feel that we should turn back the car and not go to San Diego. I get so sad, Reuben, I cain't go on. I get so sad. It all seems lak such a waste. That's fonny, that's how I met you, inn't it? You were installin' a waste disposal system in my home so I could keep it extra clean clean clean! Wey-ell, maybe that big ole practical joker up there in his Holiday Inn in the sky thought that would be a real blessed hoot of a way to tell Polly the Parrot somethin' when he had me fall for a man who did that! You know how I love the sound? You tease me? ZZZEWING ZZZZWING ZWEEEEE. I think I love it because it's the sound of bad, messy things gettin' *ground* up and *sucked* away! Except now I see that my life has just been made up of those leftover parts.

Now my marriage is over. Thirty-five years of it. It might've been a bad marriage, but do you know how *long* that is? How many

what

TV nights? How many teeth hid under pillows, how many messy meals, how many fights in the garage where the children couldn't hear, how many—oh, just days, days sittin' and lookin' at the lawn grass grow so we could mow it back down to just two inches above the soil, flat, spread, clipped green, I used to love that smell of freshly cut grass. Now it makes my stomach hurt.

I wont back all my leftovers! I wont back all the mown grass! I love you, Reuben, I think I do, but I don't think I can stand to push one more part of me down *any*body's waste disposal system. Hee hee! Oh, Sweet Jesus, tell me I'm wrong, because I am tired and confused and even love cain't make me go on.

REUBEN: I'm sorry t'hear that.

He starts up the car. He speaks very quietly.

REUBEN: Guess I'll be turnin' us back, takin' you home.

POLLY: Oh Reuben. Wah don't you argue with me?

REUBEN: It's a waste of time, Polly. It's a waste of time.

ever

CHAPTER 9

IN WHICH CLOVE CALLS FROM A FISHING SMACK

Clove is belowdecks on a small fishing craft. She is on the phone.

CLOVE: Hi, Mr. Nugent? Could you put Sable on the telephone? Yah, this is Clove. Nuh, I'm not back in Santa Cruz. Yes, my parents know whur I am now. I just called them. Wull, gahh, I'm sorry, Mr. Nugent, can I please speak to yer largest offspring, Sable, now please? Gracias. Tuhh. Sabe? It's me. Yah I'm fine. Are you all excessively begrudged at me 'cause I totally understand if you are. I'm near Noyo? 'At's all near Mendocino an' Humboldt County an' like that? Nuh, yer Buddhistic dad was just agging me to excess, he was all, "You panicked everyone in Santa Cruz, you made poor Sable drive back alone on flooded-out roads, yer karma is rully heavy, lady." I *know*, I loathe to excess when yer dad calls me "lady"! Tuhh, I'm sorry girl-dude, have they been chanting all incessant-like since this happened? Are they twitting you out? Godduh-duh-duh-ddddddddddesss. Huh huh. Are you okay? Just serenify, ulright? Yur still my fairest and fellest friend, dude. I wish you had run with me, ulthough you were right about those torpid thirty-somethings and thur hectic houseboat, *The Lemon Lady*. No, now I'm on a fishing smack. I'm calling from the cellular phone. Yah, it's somewhat rare, but fer some reason, all the crafts thuswise have cellular phones? I'm not sure it's too dull it doesn't matter nevermind. Yah, I'm on this ragin' fishin' smack with this full-on rager. No, he's old like our parents, but he's ragin'. His name is James Scoops Shannon the Third and he talks like this: "Roll us a pair o' *Drum* tobackys, Clover, and let's fry this fog clean." Tuhh, wull *I* think it's ragin', I guess you have to be here. I wish you were. I felt so gray blue and pellucid and careened when I said farewell to you that dawn after we raved all night at the Frisco Rave and you were all dancin' bravely into the day through the spray and I was all randomly spewing words? Yah, wasn't I rarely tweaked? Right on. I wish you had come ulthough yur totally relieved you didn't have to tolerate Kerrwyd and Zaylya and thur treacherous torpor. Wull, they followed thur word as far as taking me to Bodega Bay, but from there they listed and lulled and thur conversations were all nullish and void—all, "Stay the summer with us, you lovely girl" and all, "Have some more fiendish lemon-ade, we made it ourselves" and all, "Just relax and mellow out" and I was all dazed but I knew thur was something hoaxish up, so, tune yer ear, I poured my glasses of lemonade in the bay and I waited fer them to fall slumberous in the evening fog and then I jumped aground. They tried to catch me, but the fog was most thick.

Wull, I skulked up the coast, hitched a motorboat ride from these hectic tourist dudes, named Aaron and Ethan. They were all like fully attired in Gore-Tex sportswear—realistically! I know!—and then I walked and walked fer three days I was eating ice plants 'til Jimmy found me on the cliffs just standing there wantonly bab-bling and he was all, "What the cosmic fuck're you doin' here?" Then he salvaged me and took me aboard his fishin' smack the *Mar-garita Mama*. He's real rad, he never does any fishin', but he spends a lot of time listenin' fer the Coast Guard on the radar. What? I'm not sure it's too dull it doesn't matter nevermind. *Sable, listen*, I told him the whole story of Cobain the Friendly Ghost and my haunt-ings and following the brussels sprout roots north and he's all, "That's essential man, you've got ambition, that's abso-fucking-lutely essential." Like that. He rages on. It's so humorous.

And he knew my parents! Yah, you know those limpid seven-ties cocaine camping trips they went on before I was born? Wull, it turns out he not only used to go on them with them, but he sold them the cocaine too!! Yah! Wull, at first he was telling me these rad stories he was all, "This one balled that one, and it was here a tittie-tittie, there a ball-ball, and then this cat balled *all* the chicks," and then he went all silent when we found out it was my mom. Yah, he told me not to tell them that part. But he talked me into calling them and reassuring them of my well-being and all.

Wull, at first they were all agged and panic-stricken, but then

ever

they confessed as to how it was all part of the hippie ethic and got all nostalgaed fer thur days as flower children an' like that and wished me luck on my hero's "vision quest" and I promised I'd keep calling and take a GED and go to junior college in the summer. That serenified them. No, I wasn't bein' mendacious. Hey, why don't you drop out too so we can do it together? O*kay*, just *kid*ding it doesn't matter nevermind.

Sable? Sable? Yur not waxin' all Tom Hanks, are you? Wull, I mean, are you serenified yet? How's dudes? Did you hear if Skeeter sent us another cyber love bulletin on the rave net? You did? Rad, what did you say? Rad . . . Rad! . . . Raaaaaad! Tuhh? You said that? But I didn't abandonate you, that's not real. I asked you to come with me. Sable dude, cheer up! If that Skeeter-knave comes to Cruz you can encroach on him all unimipeded by me, you hedonistic harpie. You should be glad.

A barreling voice booms from above.

SCOOPS: Kid, get off my cellular. Coast Guard's in our radius. Gotta spread da mackerel nets and look fishy.

CLOVE: Ay, ay, Cap'n Scoops!

She speaks back to the phone.

CLOVE: Gotta go, Sable. I do too. Be serene. Talk to you later. 'Kay, bye.

CHAPTER 10

IN WHICH SKEETER
ENCOUNTERS THE NYPD

One afternoon, a busy New Yorker enters the ATM area of a Chase Manhattan Bank.

PERSON: Are you waiting for the cash machine?

SKEETER: Er, nuh, go ahead, I'm just loitering here tuh meet someone fer reconnoitering purposes.

PERSON: But what did you say? Are you next?

SKEETER: Nuh. Go. Ahead.

CRAZY MAN: You've got the head 'tire—cloth of many colors.

A handsome, pale black man carrying several sketchbooks approaches Skeeter.

SKEETER: Yur referrin' tuh?

CRAZY MAN: Head cloth, millinery, the lid on ya.

SKEETER: Oh, you mean th' hat. Yeh-up, it's called a mood-hat. Euro-dude south of Hyuh-ston Street gifted it on me, changes colors wich yer moods.

CRAZY MAN: Ha ha ha ha ha hahahaha!

The man laughs as if his laughter is an improvised free-jazz solo and then segues into snorting like a pig.

SKEETER: What waxes y' ticklish?

PERSON: He's crazy. He's crazy. Can't you smell him? He's mentally ill. He camps here. It's disgusting. I don't think you should talk to him. You're not from New York? Don't talk to him. He's mentally ill.

The busy New Yorker leaves quickly.

CRAZY MAN: No lid, no lid on that one, but you, sir, I can see you are cut from different fabrics. You are a connoisseur, you run the Empire Museum no less, in fact, *c'est vrai*?

SKEETER: Uhhh.

CRAZY MAN: Allow me to show you some short brief sketches. Scrippet. Did I say scrippet? I meant thicket. Pencil cloud buried in the bush. Tried to give me pen, ink, no, ink is a stain, ink cannot be erased, it obliterates the changing forevertude of the drawing state, y-y-y-you know, don't you?

SKEETER: I think I take yer meanin' in part.

Two cops walk in—a short one with a high voice and a fat one with a deep voice. The short one does most of the talking.

COP ONE: Hey, Picasso, ya gotta move, get out of here.

COP TWO: What is dis garbage? You're makin' a friggin' mess again, ya stink.

CRAZY MAN: Scoundrels, nothing but scoundrels, look at the clock, tick-tocks it not? Business is in its stroke, *c'est vrai*?

SKEETER: Veraciously, luna-dude.

COP ONE: Who're you, his brutha?

The big one chuckles at his partner's humor, seeing as Skeeter is white and the homeless artist is black.

SKEETER: Er, wull, you see over yer heads det that sign says open during business hours tuh the public, an' this dude is a member of that pop, is he not?

COP ONE: Get outta da way before I arrest you, ya faggot piece of shit punk rock—

SKEETER: I rave. RAVE! Why can't anyone in New York City distinguish the difference betwixt *PUNK ROCK* and *RAVE*???!!!

COP ONE: Let's cuff him,

The cop bends back Skeeter's arms and cuffs him.

COP ONE: Dis looks like one of da bastards in here last week messin' up the bank and chantin' dirty fuckin' things against da government—

SKEETER: Nuh, I wasn't here.

COP TWO: Don't lie. I saw you, you scattered deposit slips all ovah the floor and screamed, "Save the pueblos of Chapas!"

SKEETER: Chi*a*pas, you mean.

COP ONE: See, he admits it.

SKEETER: Let me, unhand me, scofflaws, yur waxin' overzealous in yer curtailment o' my civilities! I wasn't here, but now that yuh mention it I do recollect somethin' about Chase Manhattan urgin'

what

the president o' Mexico tuh unloose military dudes on some Indian-type citizens—AH!

CRAZY MAN: Soldier boys are step stompin' right up through the third eye of *Jes*us Christ, the explosion is coming to their *vault*ed place.

COP ONE: You too, Picasso.

He grabs the Crazy Man and cuffs him.

SKEETER: AH!

CRAZY MAN: AH! AH! AH!

The Crazy Man sings out another jazz solo.

ever

CHAPTER 11

IN WHICH PAUL PURSUES
HIS HEART

It is midday in midtown Manhattan. Paul catches Jeanette just as she exits a building through a revolving glass door.

PAUL: Jeanette.

JEANETTE: Paul! What are you doing here? Did you come for a seminar at the Epiphany Institute?

She tears down the street through streams of lunchtime pedestrians.

PAUL: Jeanette, don't be sarcastic, I was waiting here because I knew you were probably teaching one of your seminars.

He chases after her, bumps into someone.

PAUL: Excuse me.

He calls to Jeanette:

PAUL: Can we talk?

JEANETTE: No, I'm in a hurry, I've got half an hour to meet Skeeter at Chase Manhattan and give him the money to buy our plane tickets to Portland.

PAUL: Your nephew. Fine young man. He was there at the apartment when I came to explain to you.

JEANETTE: I'm sick of explanations, Paul.

She bumps into someone.

JEANETTE: Excuse me! I told Skeeter to tell you that I never wanted to see you. Why are you still in New York? Go back to Virginia.

PAUL: But Polly's, my wife's left me, she's having an affair.

JEANETTE: Good. First time she's done anything impressive that I know of.

They stand at a corner, waiting for the light to change. Jeanette begins to cross.

JEANETTE: Send her my compliments and go back to Virginia and rot!

PAUL: But, Jeanie, it's you I love—

JEANETTE: Stop calling me that! It's Jeanette! I'm not your Jeanie, I don't live in a bottle, and I'm not here to grant your every wish. In fact, tell me your heart's desire and I'll use all my crystal powers to make sure you get the fucking opposite.

PAUL: Don't hate all men on my account.

JEANETTE: Don't flatter yourself. There was a long line of bastards before you starting with my father. You don't know about that, do you?

> They are crossing another intersection. Two young men in extremely baggy trousers walk ultraslowly ahead of them, trading rhymes.

KID 1: Over to da *si'*,

I said you gonna *be* fly,

see how I *move* you *like* they is no *oth*a guy,

over on the *take* out

got to *gim*me stoopid *make* out

No *blem*ishes, no *false* kisses,

pro*mise* this is no *fake*-out.

KID 2: Whoopsie -whoopsie-*o*

girlie-*girl* I am your *rome*-o,

I'm *fat* like *dat*,

like *tit* for *tat*

an dat you alrea*dee* know—

over on da *scat*,

you *look* like a *kit*ty-cat,

dat I want to *pat*, an' pat

aw, *don*'t gimme dat—

JEANETTE: Excuse me, we're trying to pass here.

PAUL: Why do these kids these days walk so slowly?

> Jeanette thinks about it a minute, distracted.

JEANETTE: I don't know.

> Without missing a beat, she plunges right back into her rage.

JEANETTE: Anyway, as I was saying, if you want to know the real truth, Paul, the first man to betray me was my father.

ever

As she rushes down the sidewalk and Paul struggles to keep up, a horn
sounds alongside them repeatedly.

JEANETTE: He came back from the Korean War a sick man, okay?
When I was ten, he pushed my mother down an ice hole. Then he
put a gun in his mouth. My mama was an Eskimo. How do you like
your little Eskimo Pie, Paul? All my life I wondered if my mother
was still there under that ice, and then I realized she was, she was
frozen inside me.

The horn blasts and Paul looks over.

JEANETTE: I kept her intact. Until you came back and you said,
"Jeanette, I don't care about the past, let's be real this time, I want
to know you" and then I gave in, I opened up, I thawed out, I let
the ice break and dissolved my mama in the warmth of *trust*ing, of
being available to YOU, of *loving you*, goddamnit. You SHIT, you
SHIT, A CURSE ON YOU!

She hammers his chest with her fists as the horn blasts again. Annoyed
pedestrians, utterly disinterested in the scene, have to alter their hur-
ried courses down the sidewalk to get around them.

PAUL: Jeanette, that man is—that cabdriver is honking at you, look.
JEANETTE: What?

Anatole Komalsky is leaning out his cab window.

ANATOLE: Hey remember me? I picked you up with your horny
nephew who tried to make incyest with you?
PAUL: What? Skeeter tried? And I'm fond of the boy!
ANATOLE: Remember, we were going to go on a date. Roman Polan-
ski, hmm? How about the new one, *Death and the Maiden*?
JEANETTE: No, thanks, I don't think I could handle Ben Kingsley as a
South American fascist these days. I'll get in touch when there's a
revival of *Repulsion*.
ANATOLE: Okay, well, I'm in the book. Anatole Komalsky.
JEANETTE: Right.

Jeanette tears off again and Paul chases her; by now he is out of
breath.

PAUL: Who the hell was that?
JEANETTE: Anatole Komalsky!
PAUL: What was all that about Roman Polanski? Have you
dated him?

what

JEANETTE: What? No, I'm too old for Polanski: I'VE GOT PUBIC HAIR!!! Remember?

PAUL: No, I mean the cabdriver.

JEANETTE: Of course not, Paul. Oh, why am I reassuring you, you infidelitous scumbag!

A little twenty-something woman in a smart business suit and sporting a pert pageboy haircut bumps right into Paul.

KIT: Paul Folsom?

PAUL: Huh?

KIT: Kit? Kit Fisher? Barston, Levey, and Axtheiler?

She speaks rapidly, rushing allherwordstogether and has a high, squeaky voice like a kid. She plays with the pearl necklace at her throat.

KIT: I met you at the New Cycles for the Next Millennium Conference? You were awesome?!

She glances back at the fast-receding figure of Jeanette.

KIT: Is she alright? Ted Ryan says you resigned from the Axnell Board?

PAUL: Oh yeah, I'm great, fantastic, nice to see you, Kit, give my regards to Ted Ryan, tell him I've become an an-anarchist.

KIT: Excuse me?

PAUL: Ha! Just kidding. Got to go. I'm having the most important, *HOR*RIBLE conversation of my life.

KIT: Wooo-kay! Nice to *see* you.

PAUL: Jeanette, wait up, I've never seen that kid in my life.

JEANETTE: She said she knew you, Paul.

PAUL: From a conference. It's like your seminars. I mean, what are you teaching today?

JEANETTE: Cornucopia of Chakral Light Workshop.

PAUL: What? That sounds like a lot of malarkey!

JEANETTE: You asked me! Don't ask!

PAUL: Okay, well do you remember the name and face of every student?

JEANETTE: Yes, because only three people signed up! I'm broke! Now, go away, I'm almost at the bank and I don't want to have a scene with Skeeter.

PAUL: But we've been having a SCENE in front of HALF of NEW YORK!

ever

JEANETTE: That doesn't make any difference. THEY'RE JUST EX-TRAS! SKEETER IS A MAIN CHARACTER! NOW *GO AWAY*!!!

He runs after her, gulping down breath, pushing people out of his way.

PAUL: I love you, Jeanette. What do you want from me? I'LL STOP MAKING DONATIONS TO THE GOP! I'LL BURN INCENSE TO A GODDESS OF YOUR CHOICE! I'LL EVEN WEAR ONE OF SKEETER'S MOOD-HATS.

As he catches up to her, she stops and turns to face him.

JEANETTE: No, Paul, it's over, you let me down too many times.

She walks away.

PAUL: I hope you don't hate men because of me, Jeanette, you deserve the best.

She turns again.

JEANETTE: I don't hate *men*, Paul. Hatred requires energy. I *relinquish men*.

PAUL: That's worse.

They both think about this.

JEANETTE: I know.

PAUL: Good-bye, then. I'm glad I at least saw you one last time.

She gives him a final, loving, rueful once-over.

JEANETTE: Good-bye, Paul Folsom.

PAUL: Wait.

JEANETTE: *No*!

PAUL: No, I mean, look, isn't that Skeeter those cops are dragging through the bank lobby?

JEANETTE: Where?

They rush to the bank entrance.

PAUL: Hey, hey stop that!

COP ONE: Who are you?

PAUL: I'm Paul Folsom, retired CEO, Axnell Corp. Until recently, I served on the board of Chase Manhattan and I'd like to know what you're doing with my ex-girlfriend's sister's-with my-uh-grandson! Grandson!

COP ONE: Uhhhhhhhh.

SKEETER: 'At's right, along comes a corpret dude and post-haste I'm reprieved o' yer hoaxish accusations!

what

CHAPTER 12

IN WHICH VIOLET AND BALZAC
TAKE A STAND

Violet escorts a young woman past picketers outside a midtown Manhattan abortion clinic. Balzac, on a leash, leads the way.

GIRL: Do you know that you're murdering your innocent baby? We've got pamphlets here. We can offer you free counseling.

VIOLET: Take my arm, deeah, and ignore them.

LYDIA: Thank you.

GIRL: Look at you, you should be ashamed of yourself, an old grandmother and you're leading this woman into a baby-murdering factory. I hope you're proud, Grandma!

VIOLET: I'm quite proud, actually. Furthermore, I'm not anyone's grandmother or mother. I had two illegal abortions.

LYDIA: I'm Lydia.

VIOLET: Hello Lydia, I'm Violet, and this is my poodle, Balzac. Once we're past these hooligans, it's a piece of cake. Just get in the doors and up the elevator to the clinic. Oh, there's one of the doctors. We'll just nip in with him.

MAN: "Salvation is far from the wicked for they do not seek out your decrees."

VIOLET: Well, I've always preferred a stiff drink and a decent meal to salvation anyway, thanks all the same.

MAN: "Have mercy on us, Lord, have mercy on us for we have endured much ridicule from the proud, much contempt from the arrogant."

VIOLET: What's the matter?

LYDIA: I'm Catholic.

VIOLET: Oh Lydia deeah, I'm dreadfully sorry! This'll all be over very soon.

Balzac breaks from his leash and runs toward the male picketer, harrying his ankles, barking.

VIOLET: Balzac, don't attack the man! Be a pacifist poodle.

MAN: "We must obey God rather than men!"

VIOLET: Stop that, Balzac, "We must suffer fools gladly!"

Balzac barks ferociously as the man removes a gun from his jacket. Violet sees.

VIOLET: Christ, he's got a gun! Doctor, watch out!

Three shots are fired. Balzac barks once, twice, hurling himself between the doctor and the bullets. He howls in pain as the third shot strikes. The same two cops who have recently tangled with Skeeter rush upon the scene and heroically tackle the gunman to the ground.

COP ONE: Is everyone alright?

COP TWO: Get down on the ground, buddy, yuh're under arrest fuh murder!

COP ONE: The doctor's alright.

BYSTANDER: That poodle saved his life!

VIOLET: Everybody, please! Get out of the way! Balzac's been shot! Please! Help!

CHAPTER 13

IN WHICH POLLY WAKES IN
HER KITCHEN

In the dim hours past midnight, Polly is sleepwalking in her kitchen.

POLLY: The bleach goes here, the Mop & Glo goes here, the Pine-Sol goes here, the Lemon Pledge goes here, the Tide goes here, the Arm & Hammer, the Brillo Pads, the Drān-o, the rose-scented toilet-bowl deodorizer, the soap bars there! There! There! And let's not forget the broom, the mop, the vacuum, the dust mop, the sponges, there it is, all of it! Is that clean enough for you? Is that clean enough? You big ole empty house? Is that enough? Can I make a mess in you now? Is thirty-five years of cleanin' you enough, you big ole dumb house?

She wakes suddenly, calling out.

POLLY: What? What am I doin' here in my kitchen?

She finds herself at the phone, speed-dialing Reuben.

POLLY: Reuben? It's Polly . . . I'm sorry to wake you but I think my house is tryin' to *eat* me.

She is quiet for a moment.

POLLY: I don't wont to go to San Diego with you, but can you come over?

His answer floods her face wih tenderness and relief.

POLLY: Thank you, Reuben. Thank you.

PART SIX

LOCOMOTION

CHAPTER 1

IN WHICH SABLE STOKES
HER ARDOR

One sticky and lonely afternoon, when the rest of the Nugent clan has gone to the beach, Sable surfs the Net and comes across this message:

AUSTRALIAN RAVE-BOY: Rave net bulletin—from the Perth, Australia, Rave to the Santa Cruz, Killifornia, Rave: To the girl who left a cyber love note on the Net to a djude called Skeeter. I met the djude at the Rave-A-Rama Boutique on Saint Mark's Place when I was on 'oliday in New York City and told him your message. He asked me to post this:

```
Dear Sable,
Yer distress at Clove's impish desertion afflicts me most
ungently. On the feverish slope, I think on you to
excess. Please wait fer me in Santa Cruz and we kin go
north together t' retrieve Clove. Deliriously yers,
Skeeter.
```

End of message

Sable backs away from her computer and throws herself, heatedly, on the bed.

SABLE: Skeeter, Skeeter, I can't tolerate this excessive lust a microbe more. Wait 'til you get here, I'll say kneel down and pledge allegiance to yer Sable, errant dude. Wherefore did you pay heedless rapture to my supple Sableness in a cave of cliffside Cruz and then go hitching all hoaxishly away? Kneel, and make recompense and I'll dispense most ecstatically with frigidalities and shoot fructose drops of ardor all down your fine, tan body. Give me that face that sunset mound of hair, let me *clasp* it, *grasp* it, and ree*lax* it, there! . . . Oh dude, so slithery fair, forget Clove and cleave to one love, surrender to me and no more ask leave to make us three. I am not a horse—one of two—nightmarish in a stallion's stable, I am the one, the only, the fellest, the fecundest, I am Queen Sable. Kneel and ask my pardon, navel-licking knave, nay, nay, nay, nay, nay nay! Nay! NAY! AH! AHHHHHHHH!!!!!

She collapses in an explosive sweat.

SABLE: AHHH, I can't *stand* it anymore! I CAN'T STAND IT!

CHAPTER 2

IN WHICH BUSHIE REQUESTS
A TOOTHBRUSH

Bushie is in a small, white "detox" room in a hospital. She crawls around on her bed and bounces herself off the walls, clawing the sheets and baring her teeth.

BUSHIE: Dey didn't give Bushie no toofbrush. My teef hurt. Ah. Ah! AH! want tuh scratch my teef. Dey want me tuh get clean and dey didn't give me a toofbrush. NURSE. NURSE, COME AN' BRUSH MY FRIGGIN' TEEF before I eat this entire stinky-ass sheet. I'll swallow da whole sheet and PULL IT OUT MY ASS. Dat'll make me clean clean? Why should I be clean? Why did I come tuh dis shiny place?

I wish I was back on da outside back on Forty-five wit' my home bitches, Bushie is homesick, people, I need some, I want Terry even if he punched me in da stomach twelve million fuckin' times, it would be bettah dan dis! Would someone come here??!!! I want my pipe, I want some step on a line break your mama's spine, smoke on some crack, break your own back, don't never come back, I don't wanna come back tuh reality, what have I got, people, what have I got? TOOFBRUSH! I ain't even got a toofbrush.

My teef hurt, dey are covered wit' scum, didn't no one never teach Bushie tuh brush her teef, not my drunk-ass granny, not my beaten-ass mudda, not my stepfadda Henry, he knocked my teef out my ugly head, said "Dere you go, Mollie, dat's what you get, now swallow it." I swallowed my toof. Girl at P.S. 51 told me about da toof fairy. I was crazy: toof fairy gonna go diggin' in my stomach fuh my toof? She gonna leave a fifty-cent piece? Am I gonna shit fifty-cent pieces? But I brushed my teef fuh Magdalena Rigobar. I brushed up after I met huh 'cause she said, "Mollie, you nasty, you don't brush yo' teef," so I brushed 'em an' brushed an' I smiled—

She gives a toothy smile to one corner of the room.

BUSHIE: at huh, said, See? See? An' I kissed huh.

She closes her eyes and her tongue slides into an imaginary mouth. Eyes closed, she sings:

BUSHIE: Mag Mag Mag Mag Mag-genta Rush an' Buuuush-shie down inna train tracks, no one ever saw, no one.

She opens her eyes to the bright room and resumes shouting.

BUSHIE: I wanna brush my teeeeeef! I wanna be clean! I wanna be clean fuh Mag. But she don't love Bushie no more, she married tuh dat Bible dealeh, she's happy widout Bushie, she ain't gonna be dere when I get out, what is dere? Nuttin', no money, no high, no home bitches, no pimp, no neighbah-hood. I can't, I can't, let me out, I wanna go back, I was born a whore an' I'll die a whore, at least a *whore* could *buy* her own toofbrush. TOOFBRUUUUUSH!

She gnashes her teeth. She is on all fours on the bed, and she glares at the room as if it contains everything.

BUSHIE: I wanna bite the world! I wanna bite da Virgin Mary, I wanna bite Jesus Christ! HEY I wanna bite dat Holy Ghost on his holy hairy butt! I wanna brush my teef 'til dey bleed an' bleed to a rivah biggah dan Hudson an' float me on a boat back tuh Magdalena Rigobar Magenta Rush! I WANNA *TEAR* DIS WORLD *APAHT* AN' SEE WHAT DEY *GOT* IN DA *NEXT* ONE!

She looks up, out the window.

God! Gaaaawd! Is dat you, God?

BUSHIE: I never saw *you*, God, I saw yuh *pimp*, da pope. But I don't want no go-betweens, dis time, God—I want *you* tuh put out fuh *me*! Is dat you, God,

She stands and goes toward the window.

BUSHIE: on da otha side of dat winda? Come in!

She crashes her head against the window.

BUSHIE: Oh, dey got it sealed. Oh, I get it. I get it . . . I get it . . . I don't. I don't, I don't get it . . .

She paces the room.

BUSHIE: Why you need a pimp, God? Why is everybody pimps or whores? I need tuh brush my teef. Dey taste like tree-day-old egg

what

foo young from Wing Ching's on Tenf Avenue. Dey taste like sucked-on dirty fingers from outta empty pockets.

She falls to her knees.

BUSHIE: God, if you really *are* God, tell da pope tuh fuck himself, an' get Bushie a toofbrush.

Bushie puts her palms together to pray.

BUSHIE: We'll take it from dere. Amen.

Bushie bows her head.

CHAPTER 3

IN WHICH SKEETER, PAUL, AND JEANETTE HAVE A CHANGE OF ITINERARY

Jeanette sits scrunched between Skeeter and Paul in the waiting area of a gate at JFK Airport. The two males are engrossed in conversation.

SKEETER: So then, Paul dude, the half-breed Sioux rancher left me in the McDonald's at Murdo, South Dakota. Needless o' sayin' I was most . . .

PAUL: Demoralized?

SKEETER: Correcto. Thur's the apt palabra.

PAUL: And who'd you hitch next?

SKEETER: Wull, then I was most misfortunate tuh be hitched up by a heinous wholesaleress o' Indian talismania an' spiritual paraphernalia an' like that. Speedin' her way tuh Manhattan in time fer Christmas sales. A business-blinded person such as yerself.

PAUL: Hold it now, Skeeter boy, Axnell?

SKEETER: Yeh-up, I refer tuh yer ties with that corpret body.

PAUL: Locating oil and manufacturing necessary chemical compounds? That's hardly equivalent of bartering in primitive—

JEANETTE: Primitive! Oh, come on, Paul, primitive, that's such a canard!

PAUL: Ahem, okay, uh, ancient tribal artifacts?

Skeeter looks away, indicating supreme boredom with their couple squabblings.

SKEETER: What. Ever. Do you wanna hear the remains o' the narrative, er?

PAUL: Go on, go on. December. South Dakota. McDonald's.

JEANETTE: Are you two lover boys gonna finish your greasy egg sammies? If I can't smoke in this fascist airport, I'd better keep eating.

PAUL: Here.

SKEETER: Hur.

They hand her their sandwiches without looking at her.

SKEETER: So this Deanna Dream Deer's got this "Dream Seeker" van with like, *ant*lers strapped tuh th' fenders an' like that. And she tried tuh, uh, yeh-up

Skeeter looks around the waiting area. No one seems to be listening aside from Paul and Jeanette.

SKEETER: Tuhhhh, she tried tuh tamper with my testicles, er, in a *most* unsolicited fashion.

PAUL: By golly!

JEANETTE: Deanna Dream Deer?

Jeanette's mouth is full of sandwich.

JEANETTE: She teaches with me at the Epiphany Institute. That slick "Medicine Wheel-of-Fortune" Seminar. That phony tried to molest my nephew on a cold winter's highway in the middle of Bumfuck, South Dakota?

SKEETER: Er, Bumfuck, Wisconsin. She drove rull fast.

JEANETTE: I'll have her ex-covenated! There won't be a witching circle from sea to shining sea that she can set foot in. The phony! The despoiler!

PAUL: Calm down, Jeanie. Uh, son, did she uh—?

SKEETER: Nuh, I wangled 'er inta makin' it in th' snow, Eskimo-style, then I hid under a snowdrift whul she tried tuh run me over in 'er "Dream Seeker." Merry fuckin' X-mas, an' like that.

PAUL: Well done.

SKEETER: Yeh, and den I 'se hitchin' anyone who'd take me tuh keep warm. I got grievously lost an' was near frozen food by the time Camille picked me up, drivin' her uncle's stolen pickup tuh Milwaukee tuh obtain abortion services.

PAUL: My gosh.

SKEETER: So I hung with her fer—

FLIGHT ANNOUNCER: Passengers holding tickets one through thirty,

ever

now boarding, Flight 202 to Portland, this is your final boarding call.

JEANETTE: Skeeter, hon, it's time to get on the plane.

They all stand up.

PAUL: Gee, I wish I were getting on the plane with you.

JEANETTE: Paul, please, I told you you could see us off if you didn't try to coerce me.

PAUL: Sorry, Jeanette, it's, uh, just your nephew's stories about crossing America are so fascinating. What a thing for a young fella to do.

SUE THE SECURITY: Excuse me, we're having a second security check here. Can you just raise your arms?

The small Chinese-American woman frisks Skeeter with an electronic detector.

SKEETER: Sure. On th' frisk foot, much gratitudinals fer salvagin' me from those hoaxish cops tryin' tuh curtail my civilities an' like that, Paul dude.

JEANETTE: Yes, thank you, Paul, for that.

PAUL: Not at all. It was unjust and un-American. I was shocked.

SKEETER: Tuhh. Wull, bye, corpret dude.

They shake hands.

PAUL: Good-bye, Skeeter.

Paul turns to Jeanette.

PAUL: Jeanette, will you think about us?

JEANETTE: Okay, Paul.

PAUL: Have a good time with your sister in Portland and a safe trip to Alaska if you—

JEANETTE: Spirit is with me, Paul. Good-bye you-you-you!

PAUL: See you soon.

SUE THE SECURITY: Excuse me but there's something wrong with this hat.

SKEETER: Er, it's a mood-hat. Changes colors wich yer moods.

SUE THE SECURITY: Well, it's registering as a security risk. You'll have to leave it behind. I can't let you board with it.

SKEETER: 'Fraid not, airline lady-dude, th' hat stays atop m' head.

SUE THE SECURITY: What did he say?

what

JEANETTE: Ezekial Christian Frye, come on! Take off the hat. Give it to Paul, you'll mail it to Linda, right, darling?

PAUL: Certainly, I'll FedEx it to your mom in Portland, scout, give it to me.

SUE THE SECURITY: Ma'am, this is the final boarding.

JEANETTE: Oh Goddess, can't he take the fucking hat?

SUE THE SECURITY: There's no call for that kind of language, ma'am. No, I'm sorry, security is very tight today.

JEANETTE: Why?

SUE THE SECURITY: We've got a famous poet on board. Eden Badstar?

JEANETTE: Oh, is she the one who does the Compulsion cologne commercial?

SUE THE SECURITY: No, that's another poet. This is the poet who does the TV dinner ad. You know:
"Dirty hotel,
slammin' words together,
no time to cook,
just nuke me up a Hungry Jack,
make sure it ain't Kerouac,
beat, beat."

JEANETTE: Oh, right. You do that very well.

SUE THE SECURITY: Thanks. I was a communications major.

Another airline employee rushes over. His voice and aspect are completely monotone.

HANK: Sue? What is this? We're holding up the entire plane. Sir, are you boarding?

SKEETER: Tuhh. I can't, Aunt Jeanette, yur a practicioner o' magic. You understand I can't hazard emplanin' without th' hat.

HANK: What did he say?

PAUL: But—what's the hat?

SKEETER: Dude, I-I-I-I-I-I—I'm feared o' flyin'. I'se weened on hitchin'. I've never been off the ground

He adds under his breath:

SKEETER: 'cept by virtue of psychoactives.

JEANETTE: But what am I gonna tell Linda? I promised I'd get you back to Oregon without hex or harm.

ever

PAUL: I know! I'll take him, Jeanie. Tell you what? We'll take the train!

JEANETTE: But, Paul, if you think you can get me—

PAUL: I'm not doing it for you, Jeanie, I'm doing it for me, for Skeeter, for America, for Amtrak, for-for-Heather so she can further her goddamn plot! I'll see my lefty daughter, Sheila Marie, in Berkeley and I'll see this damn country. It's high time.

HANK: Are you getting on the plane? We're closing the hatches.

JEANETTE: Oh! Goddess forfend us all! Okay, Skeeter, Paul take care of each other you-you-you men!

SUE THE SECURITY: Run! Jog! Jog!

> Jeanette runs for the plane as Sue jogs alongside her in the mode of a cheerful personal trainer.

SKEETER AND PAUL: Bye!

SKEETER: Tuhh. Many thanks, dude.

PAUL: What do you say, fella, Penn Station?

SKEETER: Most alacriciously.

PAUL: Let's go then.

SKEETER: Tally ho.

> They stride off.

what

CHAPTER 4

IN WHICH CLOVE MUST TRAVEL BY LAND

Clove stands on a foggy coastal highway looking very pale. She almost forgets to stick out her thumb when a seventies pickup hauling a rusty blue boat trailer finally comes around the narrow curve. It jangles to a stop and a tawny, muscular woman, cigarette dangling from her mouth, leans over and rolls down the passenger window.

CHRIS: Where you goin', Girl Scout?

Her voice is scratchy, hoarse, and warm, chronically amused.

CLOVE: Northward to Puget Sound, er, at least the Seattle area.

CHRIS: Jump in.

The woman holds out an arm and pulls Clove in.

CHRIS: Here. Slam the door, slam her hard, she's an old truck, Janis Jalopy—here, let me do it.

She leans across Clove and slams the door shut. She drives.

CHRIS: Hi. Got any cookies?

CLOVE: Er. Tuhh, what er you?

CHRIS: I'm just joking. You look like a Girl Scout, selling cookies, although Route 101 ain't the place to do it. Anyway, you're too old to be a Girl Scout. How old're you? Eighteen?

CLOVE: Yah.

CHRIS: Oh. Seventeen?

CLOVE: Yah.

CHRIS: Sixteen?

CLOVE: Tuhh. Correcto. But. I'm not a runaway. I mean, I am, but I called my parents and thur all resigned to my absconsive behavior 'n like that.

CHRIS: Fuck me, I love tryin' to wrap my brains around the way you next generation talks. Heh, heh, I wouldn't care if you were a run-away. Chris Gomez,

She holds out her hand to Clove. They shake.

CHRIS: and this is my truck, Janis Jalopy. I know, it's a corny name. My ex named 'er that.

CLOVE: Hi. I'm Clove Carnelian. Is that yer boat in the back?

CHRIS: Yep, that's my speedboat *Stevie Nicks*. She got a puncture off Devil's Elbow. You know where that is?

She squints as she lights another cigarette with the car lighter.

CLOVE: Here in Oregon, right?

CHRIS: Well, yeah, do you know where you are?

CLOVE: Route 101.

CHRIS: Yeah, you're in Suislaw National Forest. How'd you get here and not know that? Where you from?

CLOVE: I'm from Santa Cruz.

CHRIS: Fuck me, you hitched all the way from California?

CLOVE: I hitched waterways.

CHRIS: Say again?

CLOVE: I say I came by way of the ocean an' like that? I was most loathful tuh relinquish my watery mode o' transport, but I've been walkin' fer the last three days so I juxtasupposed that if I stuck to the coastal highway I'd still be following the brussels sprouts.

CHRIS: Hey, is this just some new thing teenagers are into that I haven't kept up with or are you deranged? What the fuck?

CLOVE: It's complex.

CHRIS: Yeah.

CLOVE: Yah.

Chris suppresses a smile and raises her eyebrows. She puts out her cigarette in the car ashtray.

CHRIS: Do me a favor, open that thermos.

Clove hands her the thermos.

CHRIS: I've got some medicinal tea in there. It's supposed to help you break up wich your man. Replaces the sex hormones with tran-quillity molecules or something, I don't know. Want some?

She takes a swig and hands it back to Clove. Clove screws the top back on.

CLOVE: Nuh. I'm aiming to find my dude, not cut him loose er whatever.

what

CHRIS: Yeah.

Chris puts a cigarette in her mouth and offers one to Clove.

CHRIS: Want a cigarette?

CLOVE: Nuh. I don't smoke. Cigarettes.

CHRIS: Yeah. I'm quitting as soon as I get the rest of the Marlboro Adventure Team gear.

She punches in the automatic lighter.

CHRIS: See, I've got the jacket, ay?

She gestures to the jacket she wears.

CLOVE: Er, yah, I was waxing curious on that.

CHRIS: Yeah, I've got the knife, I got the shirt. I got the sweats, the kerchief. The drinkin' gourd. I just want the blankets.

She pulls out the lighter, sees it isn't lit, and punches it back in the socket.

CHRIS: Truly nifty little plaid blankets.

CLOVE: Tuhh.

Clove looks out the window.

CHRIS: It's just bullshit, you know, but it was a big joke between me and my ex, Ernie, asshole.

She tries the lighter again.

CHRIS: Damn this lighter!

She punches it in again.

CHRIS: Come on, *Janis Jalopy,* fire up that lighter. The batteries better not be going out on us. We'll get fogged in up here an' we'll be fucked. One-oh-one ain't no picnic in the dark. These hairpin curves—shit! There it is.

Now she puffs her cigarette.

CHRIS: Now tell me about these brussels sproats.

CLOVE: Wull, it all started when I walked into the ocean at this rave—that's a dance thing whur everyone stays up and dances all—

CHRIS: I know, I know, how old do I look, ay? Yeah, I know. My buddy Possum's a DJ in Eugene. You take Ecstasy and you trip out.

CLOVE: Wull, we dance, it's not the ecstaseein', it's the toppish, spinnish whirl of dancing that puts you in a ravished trance, er, it's too complex.

CHRIS: No, I get it. I just don't understand the brussels sproats.

CLOVE: That came later. See, I walked into the ocean following these

ever

crabs who were talking to me. Then I got saved by this rare presence who put me across the road in fields of brussels sprouts.

CHRIS: Wow, you mean a spiritual force lifted you out of the water?

CLOVE: Wull, I know this is overly excessive to most ears but he identified as Cobain the Friendly Ghost.

CHRIS: Wait. Like Kurt Cobain.

CLOVE: Like Kurt Cobain.

CHRIS: Were you a big fan of his? Were you like one of those teenagers they said was real upse—

CLOVE: No.

CHRIS: No? Then I don't get it.

CLOVE: That makes us duplicacious.

CHRIS: Say what?

CLOVE: I don't overly get it either. I'm just following an ultra-visual in my mental eye.

CHRIS: You mean a vision?

CLOVE: Whatever, it's too complex.

CHRIS: What is it? I think I get it. Come on, girl, convince me you're not insane, ay? I don't let insane people ride in Janis Jalopy.

CLOVE: Wull, tied in with the haunting of the ghost, I began to see this visual o' brussels sprout roots twining under sand north toward Puget Sound, er, at least—

CHRIS: The Seattle area.

CLOVE: Yah, an' I knew I was destined to follow them. So I did. By way of hitchin' houseboats, speedboats, fishin' smacks, sailboats, and walkin' the cliff dunes. 'Til finally I got excessive hunger pangs and I came out here an' hitched down yer truck. I wanted to do it all by water, but . . .

> She trails off, looking past Chris's shoulder to the waves spraying the base of the steep cliffs.

CHRIS: You hungry? Dig in that bag. There's half a burrito from the gas station in Seal Rock.

CLOVE: Thanks.

CHRIS: Wow. Hungry, ay? An' I thought I was adventurous. Shit, I only shot the rapids twenty-five times, climbed Mount McKinley. I killed a bear with a rock once, didn't want to but I had to—

CLOVE: Realistically? God-d-d-d-dess.

what

Chris registers Clove's tick.

CHRIS: Huh. Yeah, but you're sixteen and you've done the open sea from . . . Santa Cruz to. . . . Yaquina Bay! Look, I'm goin' inland, see some friends in Portland. You want to go there? You'll get a ride to Seattle no problem. Tear yourself away from the sproats for twenty-four hours. Ay?

CLOVE: Wull. Okay.

CHRIS: Well, alright. We can bitch about boys all the way. Crank on the radio.

Chris sings along.

CHRIS: "Lea-vin' Las Veegas da-da-da-da—" you like Sheryl Crow?

CLOVE: Not overmuch. I mean, she has a good voice, but I don't see why she had to scarf down all those awards.

CHRIS: Heh. Yeah, well, I like Sheryl Crow. You got a little boy-friend?

CLOVE: Wull, I wax lustful fer this one dude but—

CHRIS: Uh huh?

CLOVE: He met my best friend and fairest cohort Sable the same night.

CHRIS: Oh great, see that? And where is this little two-timer now?

CLOVE: I don't know. After our flickery meetings, he disappeared. But he writes. Sometimes.

CHRIS: Wow, an' I thought the next generation might be a little bit better. Fuck me, 'at's just like Ernie with his Allison and his Jesse. Asshole. You know what kills me?

CLOVE: What?

CHRIS: It's the Marlboro Adventure Team. I mean, we had every-thing but the blankets, you know. I mean, it was just a joke, but it was a good joke when we were together, now it's a bad joke. I actu-ally was holding on to the relationship until we got the blankets. Fuck me, what'll I do?

CLOVE: Die of cancer all solitary an' like that?

CHRIS: Ooo. You are a teenager. That hurt.

CLOVE: Isn't it the realistic truth?

CHRIS: Wow, yeah.

Chris is about to light another cigarette, but tucks it behind her ear instead.

ever

CHRIS: But the truth gets tricky after twenty-one.

CLOVE: What do you mean?

CHRIS: You'll see. Eat that funky apple turnover in the bag too, eat up. You need your strength, girl. I know I need mine.

> Chris hums along to "Leaving Las Vegas" as she expertly wrestles the steering wheel around another hairpin curve.

what

CHAPTER 5

IN WHICH VIOLET STANDS VIGIL

Violet sits in a room at an Upper East Side veterinary hospital. Balzac, minus a leg, lies almost lifeless on a pallet.

VIOLET: Balzac, if you'll just come to, if you'll just come back to your senses and say, Hello Vi, you old fool, thought I was comatose, did you? Damn! Your leg is gone, Balzy, that's all it is. It's just a leg, and an awful shock now, if you'll wake up. Well, here, I'll read you all the headlines. You're famous, you mad wretched little poodle. Here we are. *Daily News*: "Demo Dog Takes Dive for Doc." *Newsdee*: "Prochoice Poodle Plugged by Gunman." *The Post*: "Bow Wow OW!"— Canine Catches Clinic Doc's Bullet," and of course, the paper of record (they didn't give you a headline, they only gave you a small column in the back—th' "Metro" section): "Courageous Toy Poodle Foils Assassination Attempt Outside Manhattan Clinic." Of course, you're *not* a toy poodle, you're an ordin'ry poodle, why must *The Times* invariably get something wrong? All the *other* dailies seem to manage. Ha!

She laughs, now her throat catches.

VIOLET: Balzac, since you were shot, I've scoured my conscience. I've asked myself two questions. One, ought I to have named you afteh the French writer Honoré de Balzac, given the tragic and melodramatic content of his novels, and two, was I right to bring you to the defense of the abortion clinic? About the first, I've decided—what's in a name?

As to the other, I can only tell you this. I myself have had two illegal abortions: one in France, which didn't go badly, that was when I was married to Bill. The other was here in New Yawk during my second marriage. It was an extremely hot day in the middle of August. Pea Soup Days, Kelly called them. Kelly was up at the Tricott Farm in New Hampshire, painting. I'd been waiting half a month for Kelly to leave town so that I could have it. He was an atheist, Kelly, but Irish nonetheless and I knew he'd put his foot down over an abortion. A man could easily have his wife arrested or sent to a ward for such a thing and much as I loved Kel, I could see by that time that our marriage wasn't working and that I'd be left the way Hopper McPherson's wife, Adele, had been left, alone in a flat in the village with a screaming one-year-old while Hopper caroused with artist's models at the Cedar Tavern.

Well, I loved my drink far too much then to give it up for changing diapers so I made my way in a cab to a dirty townhouse in Chelsea where I was blindfolded and put in a car and driven I still have no idea where except it must've been by the seaside in Queens or Brooklyn, because I could hear the surf in the distance. And that's all that kept me alive, Balzy, during the next ten hours, the distant sound of waves, and children playing and bells and an ice cream man calling. Ice creams, ice creams, get your ice creams . . .

I lay on a board, not a hospital gurney, not a cot, but a bare board, no sheet. And there was no fan, flies buzzed about, there was a nauseating stench, and a man with dirty fingers and *dirtier* implements prodded and poked my feminine—organs as though he were deboning a fish! It took twenty times longer than the operation in France had taken, *twenty* times!

And I lay there panting, panting and panting, afraid I was going to die. I could only listen to the sounds of the surf and pray. Please, God, allow me to live long enough not to die here, only allow me enough strength to walk out of this sordid house and follow the salt wind to that seaside. Please, God, I said, I don't care a'*tall* if I die like a feral cat on the boardwalk but please *don't let me* die in here.

Instead I lay in my own blood until I passed out. When I came to, I was back in the townhouse in Chelsea. They wouldn't let me sleep, which was all I wanted to do, but they kept hollering at me, "You've got to leave, this isn't a hotel, you know!"

Violet is quivering with rage. It takes her a moment to get out her next words.

VIOLET: I. Hadn't. Thought. It was.

At last, and I don't know how she knew, but Iris came and fetched me. She was speechless with shock and as well as I know

228

what

her, she was furious, but she got me and she *took* me home and she *nursed* me.

Violet trembles, her eyes water.

VIOLET: And aside from Iris, Balzac, you're the only perso— I mean, creature on earth who knows that story. In fact, the only one, because Iris and I *nev*er discussed it. So you see, deah dog, why I had to escort that girl into the clinic. It was a matter of life and death for me then and, alas, it remains one.

She looks at him. She notices a movement.

VIOLET: Balzac? Balzy? He's awake! Balzac! Hello, deeah, where've you been? You've had loads of people worried sick about you. Look at all the cards. Yes. One from Constantine at the Blue Ship Diner, and all the customers, they send *all* their love and some bacon-and-cheddar quiche, bacon-and-cheddar quiche, you know, what you're always sneaking off Aunt Iris's plate? Hang on, it's only over there, I'll get some.

She gets to her feet with effort, using her cane.

VIOLET: Balzac, you mad, wretched little dog, you-you-you're—

She weeps for joy.

CHAPTER 6

IN WHICH SKEETER RIDES THE RAILS WITH A CURIOUS FELLOW

Late at night, on Amtrak's Silver Zephyr, Skeeter converses with a new companion.

SKEETER: So I'm in the cave by the dead elephant seal with Sable an' she's throbbin' an' grief struck over her best friend Clove an' I'm waxin' masculine-like with, nuh, nuh, she can't be drowned.

JOB: I thought you said you were cryin'?

SKEETER: Tuhh, wull, right, I 'fess up I have yet tuh master th' masculine way o' bein' an' like that, but I'm attemptin' a masculine-like tone through a veil o' tears an' I'm coaxin' her onto as how Clove might not be drowned and *Suicide Watch*—*Actual Deaths* is merely a hoaxish TV show an' fuck 'em an' thur buzzardine curiousity an' like that. And then Sable, how kin I phrase it? She folds inta me, dude, like Just Add Water batter folds inta a cake pan, ahhhh.

JOB: But git back tuh Clove, dude. Did she drown, er?

SKEETER: Don't yuh want t' hear about soft, furry Sable?

JOB: I want tuh hear about Clove. Did she drown?

SKEETER: Nuh. She got found in a brussels sprouts field an' arrested.

JOB: An' what you do then?

SKEETER: Wull, then I stole two fingers on th' inside o' her kneecaps, th' underside, if you ride my thought.

JOB: When? When they were arrestin' her?

SKEETER: Nuh. I'm referring tuh Sable.

JOB: I thought we were on Clove. We're still on Sable.

SKEETER: Wull. I almost was until you 'rupted me.

JOB: Sorry, dude. Just the way you describe that babe, all wild an' spicy. You said her skin was spicy, right?

SKEETER: Right, like her name.

JOB: I just wont tuh know more. It's lak we're here on this train in the dark an' thar's all those freaked rocks out thar on the desert an' each one goes by, I'm seeing her the way you said, her eyes, her hips—the rocks all look lak her runnin' into the water. I cain't believe that. Tell me how she did that agin.

SKEETER: Er, Job dude. You an' me were just acquainted since El Paso. Now it's true we wax most uncannish similar life 'speriences, such as havin' fucked up dads an' both bein' inta our rave 'n like dat, but I fear yur overidentified with my love interests Sable an' Clove. Did I not commence this recountal with the heartfelt pronouncement det I was stricken with love fer both?

Paul, fast asleep across from the two boys, cries out.

PAUL: Polly, Polly, put it down, the mayonnaise jar is empty, don't you see? There's nothing I can do.

JOB: What's his problem?

SKEETER: Paul's a corpret dude losin'. faith in the corpret way o' life an' his marriage an' graspin' onta my Aunt Jeanette, who's rull pretty. Both my ma Linda an' my Aunt Jeanette are *exceed*ingly attractive. You like older women?

Skeeter is discomfited.

JOB: Yeah.

SKEETER: We *do* have most everything in common.

PAUL: Polly, no, throw it away, throw it in the garbage, it's empty. No more sandwiches.

SKEETER: He's dreamin' about his wife, Polly, I surmise.

JOB: Surmise. Thar's good word. You know a word I favor?

SKEETER: What?

JOB: Henchmen.

SKEETER: Tuhh. Yeh-up, 'at's a good word.

JOB: Yeah. I have tuh figure a time tuh use it.

SKEETER: Don't bother with that, dude, take a word of advice, just plug words right on in tuh the goin' vernacular. Those that don't get it won't, an' those 'at *do*'ll tune thur ears most readily.

JOB: Yer thoughts are henchmen tuh my own.

SKEETER: Thur yuh go.

PAUL: Polly! Jeanette!

SKEETER: Tuhh, he's torn 'twixt th' two of 'em.

ever

JOB: You cain't keep two women, you got tuh give one up.

Skeeter gives Job an *un*fond sidelong glance.

SKEETER: Tuhh. What. *Ev*er. Paul dude, wake up.

Skeeter kicks Paul's seat. Paul springs to his feet.

PAUL: Hmm. Where am I?

SKEETER: Yur on the train. Wur in the Arizona desert.

PAUL: Oh. Oh. Hmm.

SKEETER: Paul. I just met this dude, Job. Job, this is Paul.

JOB: Hey dude.

PAUL: He sounds just like . . .

JOB: I know, we were just sayin' how we're all coincidentally re-lated. Lak henchmen.

PAUL: Hench? Hmm. What's your name?

JOB: Job.

PAUL: Don't you mean Jobe?

JOB: That's m' true name, as in th' Bauble book. But m' friends call me Job, as in: *git* one.

PAUL: I see. And where are you headed, young man?

JOB: Santa Cruz.

SKEETER: Er, I thought you said, San Fran*cis*co.

CONDUCTOR: Tickets, please. Ma'am, sorry to disturb you, but we're checking tickets. Thanks.

JOB: Gotta go tuh th' bathroom. See ya, Skeet.

Job bows to them, in courtly fashion.

SKEETER: Er, whur you goin'?

PAUL: Son?

JOB: 'Til we meet agin, henchmen.

He disappears down the train corridor.

SKEETER: But—

PAUL: But—

SKEETER: Tuhhhhh.

PAUL: Am I awake? Did we just meet a kid named Job?

SKEETER: Yeh-up, we did. An' I hazard we'll meet up again.

PAUL: This gets more and more like one of those cheap novels you buy in the airport when your plane is delayed.

SKEETER: Go back tuh sleep, Paul dude. Yur babblin'.

what.

CHAPTER 7

IN WHICH LINDA AND JEANETTE
RESORT TO OLD WAYS

Jeanette, smoking a clove cigarette, stands on her sister's ratty Persian carpet and watches impatiently as Linda limps around in a circle, dispersing a magic powder.

JEANETTE: Linner, when are you going to finish scattering that red powder all around the room so we can hurry up and contact the Goddess already?

LINDA: Jeanette.

Linda stops and fetches *her* clove cigarette from the earthen urn and takes a long toke.

LINDA: Don't try to pull that big-sister spell on me. You come to my domicile, you stay for a month—

JEANETTE: Two weeks, Linner, I've been here two weeks.

LINDA: —and you try to tell me how to practice the craft. Listen, I turned Wicca in '86 back when you were still *escort*-ing members of the Inquisition to your bed.

JEANETTE: What do you mean, Inquisition? They were businessmen, Linner, what is it with you West Coast sorcerists? You think if you keep pretending we're in the Middle Ages that puts you more in touch with Spirit? No amount of velvet money belts and ugly jewelry are going to put you in touch with Spirit any more than—

LINDA: Any more than designer crystals and too much eye shadow—

JEANETTE: These are not designer crystals, they're Mytelene Island cave crone stalagmites from 3000 B.C., Linda, I've been trying to tell you.

LINDA: Alright, alright.

JEANETTE: Besides, am I wearing too much eye shadow?

LINDA: No, no, I'm sorry.

JEANETTE: Tell me, am I, am I—should I wear less?

LINDA: No, no. Just let me finish scattering the griffin's blood.

Linda completes her circle. Then she takes her place beside Jeanette at the altar.

JEANETTE: Touch the crystals.

LINDA: There.

Linda does so grudgingly.

LINDA: Spit over your left shoulder.

Jeanette rolls her eyes and spits.

JEANETTE: Alright.

There is silence.

JEANETTE: I don't feel Spirit.

LINDA: No, but let's read our questions.

JEANETTE: Oh Goddess, please let us invoke you. Let us cooperate. Let us respect each other's *issues* with practicing the craft.

LINDA: Would you just hurry up and read the fucking questions?!

JEANETTE: Okay!

Jeanette reads.

JEANETTE: Will my lover Paul's wife Polly really divorce him? Your turn.

LINDA: Will my son Ezekial—

JEANETTE: Skeeter, Linner. He likes to be called Skeeter.

LINDA: Goddess, his given name is Ezekial Christian Frye. Will he find the answer he's looking for to grow into manhood or will he turn out to be a ne'er-do-well slut like his dad? Your turn.

JEANETTE: Will our mother, buried under the ice in Alaska, find peace—

LINDA: I don't want to ask that! I don't want to go there!

JEANETTE: We'll ask. If it's meant to be answered it will be, if it's not meant to be, it won't be—and will we ever forgive our father's spirit for his crime? You go.

LINDA: Will my ex-husband Bruce ever get paroled out of prison so that he can get a job and pay me all the child support he owes me?

JEANETTE: And he owes me, too.

LINDA: You?

what

JEANETTE: Well, I supported you and Skeeter. You were so coked out during the eighties, no one—

Linda sighs.

LINDA: Let's not spat in the presence of Spirit. Breathe.

There is silence.

LINDA: I don't feel like we're going anywhere.

JEANETTE: Linda, I have an idea!

Jeanette runs to Linda's cleaning-supplies closet and yanks open the door.

JEANETTE: Remember after they took us away from Grandma in Ketchican and took us to the mission school? When the nuns weren't looking, we used to ride the broom. Let's just go back to the old magic ways before either of us *studied*.

Jeanette has the broom ready.

JEANETTE: Come on, climb on, little sis.

LINDA: Okay. Let me get my bad leg over.

They mount the broomstick and stand there in the living room.

JEANETTE: Goddess, take us somewhere.

LINDA: Somewhere.

They begin to take little shuffling steps around the carpet.

LINDA: Oh, I feel we're floating. High above the ground.

JEANETTE: A high up in the celestial space.

LINDA: In the clouds.

They ride, high, high into the sky.

ever

CHAPTER 8

IN WHICH VIOLET FLIES THE AMIABLE SKIES

STEWARDESS: Thank you for flying the amiable skies with Amerways Air. On behalf of the cabin and flight crew on board with you this evening, I'd like to welcome you aboard Flight 303 to Seattle, Washington. I hope—

> They hover, watching. Linda gets off the broomstick and massages her foot.

VIOLET: Well, you see, the poodle had his leg shot to smithereens outside an abortion clinic in New Yawk. Did you hear of it? Yes, he's the famous poodle who saved the doctor. Heah that, Balzy? His full name is Balzac. The gunman, the Bible salesman, did a number of talk shows—did he have marital troubles? I didn't watch. I refused all the talk shows *and* the book deal. I don't like books about horrific events, I prefer lit'rature. I have, however, consented for him to be poster poodle for NARAL. Hmm? That's the NATIONAL ABORTION RIGHTS ACTION LEAGUE, deeah. But first he must recover his strength. I thought the sea air in Seattle would do his legs—the three that remain—some good. D'you think the highball cart will be coming s—What do they call it? Yes, cocktails. Yes, I'd like one as soon as possible. Stewardess, could I have another of your spiffy blankets f' Balzac? The small dog, the poodle? Yes, he's got a ticket, I showed it to the— Thanks *very* much indeed.

> She turns back to her fellow passenger.

VIOLET: No, I've neveh been to the West Coast. Strictly eastern seaboard, and Europe, naturally. I lived in Europe for several yeahs as a young bride. Before the war. I went back after, terrible how it changed after the war. Terrible. Disney, McDonald's, and all the rest. I thought I ought to see the other side of *this* continent before I dropped dead. Well, of course I will, deeah, I'm nearly as *old* as the *century*, look at me. And look at the century! The hat changed? Don't be alarmed, it's a mood-hat, changes four different colors with your moods. I bought it in Soho. Balzac's got one as well. Swell isn't it?

Hmm? Whazat? Balzac, will you be having chicken kiev or salisb'ry steak for your suppah? They'd like to know in advance.

JEANETTE: I know this woman. She lives near me. Park Avenue. Delphi Apartments. She came to my apartment once collecting signatures against the death penalty. Hmm.

LINDA: She seemed like a crone.

JEANETTE: Yeah, that's what I thought. I think she's a crone.

Linda mounts the broomstick and they are off.

LINDA: Well, let's move along, we're going farther east.

ever

CHAPTER 9

IN WHICH POLLY SPEAKS OF SPEAKING IN TONGUES

JEANETTE: East, south, south. Oh, it's nice here—meadows, dogwood, cherry trees. Hmm. Suburban ranch-style homes. Oh no! We're in bed with Paul's wife, Polly, and—a black man?

LINDA: Not bad looking, either.

JEANETTE: Goddess forfend us.

LINDA: Shh. Listen.

They hover.

POLLY: Ooo, look Reuben. The crescent moon. Did you know, Reuben, when I was a sassy young housewife me and my best friend Bunny Peters invented somethin' called Crescent Salad? This was back in Georgia before Paul got promoted and we moved here to Virginia. In the sixties Sheila Marie was three and Derek, he wa'n't even born yet. That ole Christian Coalition he works for wa'n't even around yet. You know? I've been wonderin', my people were Christian, but we didn't see any need for goin' around coalitionin', did your folks? Wey-ell, I mean black folks are Baptists—Reverend Doctor King knew that, and Reverend Jesse Jackson still knows that and that's all that there is to it, right? Oh, don't get prickly, Blackberry Pie, I only brought it up because I was reminded the other day how I loved the black churches when I was a girl. Beverly brought her little gran'-niece in the kitchen? And she was wearin' one of them cute li'l Easter outfits?

And I remembered how we used to have an old aunt in South Carolina, we went to visit her every year at Easter, I just was remembering. Murrell's Inlet. You know those marshes off the coast? The rice plantations? And your folks speak in such a way so as not to be understood by my people? Gullah, that's right! Wey-ell, my old aunt was what we used to call a "high Southern eccentric," and she'd gone and learned to speak it. She did! And on Easter Sundays she would wake me up early early in the day before the humming-birds had hit the feeder on the back porch and she'd say, "Come on, Pollyanna"—she lak'd to call me that 'cause I'm Polly Ann—say, "Pollyanna, we're goin' to the other Easter, come on."

And there we'd go on foot into the saltwater marshes. Ash trees hung with Spanish moss past all the little lonely houses your folks built. There was a fair bit of Negro-owned property in Murrell's In-let. That was another thing special about the area—and Aunt Sister led me waaaaay out past them to a shack—that's all it was, was a shack church, with a cross of Jesus on it. And Aunt Sister had been made an honorary member. So we kneel down and swaaaaayed and it was SPOOOOOOO-KEY. All them little gals in bright dresses 'n lace looked lak little sweet gingerbreads with multicolored frostings! And me just in my nightie with an old coat of Sister's thrown over.

We kneel down and we swayed together and people spoke not in words I'd ever heard or will ever hear again unless you can one day take me to a place lak that, Reuben, but I don't know if you can. All people down that way are strange, black and white alike. Wah, they eat *craw*dads by the *pail*ful. It may be the marsh air, I don't know. Aunt Sister knew a lot of ghosts. I mean, half the fam-ily we visited up in South Carolina were dead people! They were! Some of 'em still had little places set for them at the table, some of 'em set on chairs on the porch, a few of 'em you could see dartin' in and out behind the poplar trees on the driveway, and there was this one, she would set some nights at her old dresser rockin' in her chair, and just coooombin' her hair.

Polly whispers now.

POLLY: So, I was thinkin' of all this as we kneeled there and we swayed and folks stood up, ladies in their colorful skirts and the door was hardly hung from the frame, so wind blew right in through it, and the women stepped around and over some who lay and bumped on the aisle way and the language they spoke was somethin' lak tongues pickled in African jars soaked in American vinegar and out they come tastin' so familiar but you cain't make sense of it, because it's not sensible speech, it's the sounds of words *un*der the sense. And from *un*der the pews I felt the breeze comin'

ever

touchin' my toes and then a biiiiig lady stood up, and she took off a *white* hat with *blue* flowers sewn on and waved it and waved it and I was sure the only breeze was comin' from that hat alone and then she took a BIIIIG breath and we all breathed with her and she was SEIZED and SHAKEN and *carried away*! And I thought she looked just lak a dragonfly I had seen and that the language she spoke was the same as the twir that his dragonfly wings made. That was the first time I ever went to that church. She took me there every Easter 'til I was eight. She died one July when I was eight.

How did I get onto my childhood? You make me go somewhere after we make love. Almost lak a spiritual presence is hoverin' here in the room watchin' us . . . Hee-hee! You know you make me poor Polly parrot just lose herself, Reuben Scott? Wah? Hmm.

Now what was I tellin' you? Oh yes, Crescent Salad. Wey-ell now, Crescent Salad was everything left over in the fridge cut into crescent moons—everything!—celery, potatoes, apples, marsh-hee hee-marshmallows. And then we slathered some mayonnaise on and called it Crescent Salad. Me and Bunny Peters invented it in the sixties when we were bored. Wey-ell, you know how mayonnaise reigned supreme in the sixties. Especially for us gals down in southern Georgia. We didn't know—cholesterol?—we just didn't know!

Maybe that's wah Sheila Marie is such a health nut now. Imagine the amount of mayonnaise I subjected that child to at an early age. Wah did I get on that? The half-moon, that's wah, Blackberry Pie, you make me swoon and half-moon and loony toony wheeeee, I'm Polly the swoony looney tune, hee hee, an' I'm speakin' in tongues!

She falls back next to him on the pillows.

POLLY: Don't ever leave me. And take me to a church one day.

JEANETTE: Hmm. *Quel surprise.* I *like* her.

LINDA: Well, it's not so surprising, you have a lot in common, you're both involved with the same man. For how long? Twelve ye—

JEANETTE: I wonder if she'll give him a divorce?

LINDA: Oh, she'll give him a divorce if she can keep the house.

JEANETTE: Oh, she can *keep* the *house.*

They are off, flying high.

LINDA: We're blowing west across the nation.

what

JEANETTE: Oh, there's Oklahoma City. Look at all the rubble.

LINDA: Ah! It hurts. Should we stop here and do some healing?

JEANETTE: Let's stop for one minute of national mourning.

> They hover in the rubble, feeling a nation of television watchers weep, then reach for the remote.

LINDA: It's too much psychic pain! We'll have to come back. This needs a lot of healing work.

JEANETTE: Let's keep moving.

> They are off.

ever

CHAPTER 10

IN WHICH SABLE CALLS
SKEETER'S BLUFF

LINDA: West. I feel my son. West. West. Here's my son.

They alight in Sable's bedroom. The two young lovers are sitting up naked and facing one another in a chair, legs wrapped around hips.

JEANETTE: Oh! Oh, Linda, he's—he's having sex! Linda. I think we should depart.

LINDA: Oh come on, just one minute. Just one minute.

JEANETTE: Linda, I don't think it's appropriate!

LINDA: Shh. just one minute.

SKEETER: Sssssable, Sable, uh huh yur soo severely sultry.

SABLE: More sultry than Clove?

SKEETER: Nuh nuh nuh yeh-up, more most sultry drippin' most salvacious and copious with sultre.

SABLE: But what about Clove?

SKEETER: What about her? Er er er yur sssssso Sablicious an' sabory, *tú sabes*?

He licks his way up her throat.

Sable pulls away, crossing her legs. They both gasp from the shock of disengagement.

SABLE: No, *no sabe*! Tell me, oh tell me, dude, yer contra-lusting inflexions fer my best friend and fairest cohort Clove.

Skeeter gently pulls apart her legs and reengages them. They shudder.

SKEETER: Er, she is assuredly fair, and enticin' an' like that, and—

SABLE: And?

SKEETER: and—she's not here! And you are! Ahhhh!

He renews his previous efforts.

SABLE: MMMMMMMMMMMMMMMbut a minute ago you were all piteously waxin' tuh go north—ahh!—and retrieve her from her misguided adventure—Ahh!—following Cobain the Friendly . . . GHOST! . . . Ahh!

SKEETER: Yeah, that's true but I wanted you t' accompany me. With you, Sable, with YOU.

SABLE: Then say you love me only and will forsake! Clove!

She flushes scarlet. She digs her fingernails into his shoulders.

SKEETER: Ah!

Now it is Skeeter who pulls back, though he remains engaged.

SKEETER: But then I'd be hazardin' stealth an' mendacity, the two masculine mannerisms most *loathed* by those of yer ferocious sex!

SABLE: Go away, Skeeter, I wish you had never come back to Santa Cruz!

With cruel speed, she abruptly disengages them.

SKEETER: Tuhhhhh.

SABLE: Tuhhhhh.

Skeeter regards the situation, then looks at her.

SKEETER: Au revoir? An' like that.

SABLE: What. *Ev*er.

She looks away.

SKEETER: I'm *go*in'.

He starts to stand.

SABLE: Go!

Suddenly, without either of them expecting it, she is on him, grabbing him to her with her strong thighs.

SKEETER: Anh! Sable yur so—

SABLE: Me or her—which?

SKEETER: Yur a witch, yur a witch, you've bewitched, bothered, and beset me UNH!—

SABLE: ANH! Renounce Clove!

SKEETER: AHHH-AHHHHH I-I-I renoooooounce Clooooove!

SABLE: Renounce her an' her ragin' hectic ways!

SKEETER: Oh Sable—

SABLE: Say it!

SKEETER: I do I do I renounce 'er—

SABLE: Clove and her harpy red hair!

SKEETER: Yehhhhh . . .

ever

SABLE: An' her hexin' tree bark eyes!

SKEETER: Mmmm—

SABLE: Her Tide-white skin.

SKEETER: Skin.

SABLE: Her churnin' brain foam.

SKEETER: Ah!

SABLE: Fuck Clove!

He slows a bit and stares her in the eyes.

SKEETER: No, *you*.

SABLE: Me?

She blushes all over.

SABLE: Meeeeee! PUSH CLOVE OFF A CLIFF!

SKEETER: Yeah.

SABLE: Push!

SKEETER: Oh!

SABLE: Push!

SKEETER: Oh!

SABLE: Push!!

SKEETER: Uh uh uh uh hah un hah!

SABLE: Push! Wait! Is-the-condom-still-clingin'-all-tenaciously-an'-shit?

SKEETER: Yeh-UP!

SABLE: THEN PUSH-CLOVE-OFF-THE-CLIFF!

SKEETER AND SABLE: OH! AYYYYYYYYYYYYYYYYYYYYYYYYYY!

Sable bursts out sobbing.

SKEETER: Sable, Sable, er you? er—

SABLE: Yah, yah. I'm just, it's all all maximated. I'm just all blissed to excess.

SKEETER: Well, then weep most deluvial, sweet Sable.

He strokes her hair.

SABLE: It's just I-I-I—

SKEETER: Yeh-up?

SABLE: I miss Clove! We have to go north to Seattle and retrieve her.

SKEETER: But I thought you wanted me to push 'er off a cliff?

SABLE: No, I miss her! I love her! She's my girl-dude, my—

SKEETER: Tuhh, I know, I know, let's go tuh Seattle then, that

what

corpret dude—I told you about? Paul?—he'll grease our wheels. We'll fly.

SABLE: Put yer mood-hat back on.

SKEETER: Oh yeh, thanks.

He reaches and dons the mood-hat.

SABLE: It changed colors.

SKEETER: It would have to've changed colors.

SABLE: But I still want you to hate her.

SKEETER: Tuhh, null that, I can't be hoaxish with you, I can't hate 'er, I can't renounce 'er, I told you I am stricken with love fer both of you.

SABLE: Still? After . . .

SKEETER: Wull . . . 'at's a most ponderous *pregunta*. I never did *this* with Clove or . . . anybody.

He runs his hands lightly over her small torso, grazing his favorite parts of her with his thumbs.

SKEETER: I am yers, Sable, but I must upheave, I still retain an unfathomed fancy fer that girl-dude. My heart is famished by her, whur you feed it most succulently.

SABLE: I vow I'll win it.

SKEETER: I vow I'll lose it.

SABLE: Let's smoke cigarettes.

SKEETER: Most definitely.

SABLE: All I've got is cloves.

She leans over and brings up a pack of cigarettes, handing him the matches.

SKEETER: What.

He lights her cigarette (incidentally, with the Zippo lighter he stole from Arnie McManus). Sable takes a drag and exhales.

SABLE: Ever.

LINDA: I'm worried. He's *just* like his old man. Exactly.

JEANETTE: I *told* you we shouldn't have watched. Come *on*, get back on the broomstick, Linda, come on!

Jeanette pulls Linda back onto the broomstick and they make off.

ever

CHAPTER 11

IN WHICH BRUCE FRYE OFFERS RESTITUTION

LINDA: We're blowing east, back across the country, to the middle, past it. There's Marion Federal Penitentiary.

JEANETTE: Let's pass in—ooo, the steel is so chilly.

LINDA: How far down do they have him? Poor Bruce.

JEANETTE: Don't pity him, Linda. That's how men control women by exc*i*ting their *pi*ty.

LINDA: Here he is on the lowest bunk. Look at him asleep. He always looked so hapless asleep.

She blows on Bruce's face. His eyelids flutter.

BRUCE: Linda, pretty Linda, is 'at you? You always were one helluva psychic lady. Useta get me real bent outta shape, but now it's useful. Lin, I got a message for you. Back in '83, I buried a shitload uh pot money in th' Seattle area, case I wasn't around when Ezekial came o' age. If you go tuh Seattle in May, one o' my old associates'll find you. You'll know 'im. You know 'im well. Now Ezekial's almost of age I want my son tuh have that bounty.

JEANETTE: Same old Bruce. HIS son? What about my little sister Linda? Same old Bruce. HIS son.

BRUCE: Good tuh dream yuh, Linda. Is that yer foxy spitfire sister Jeanette with ya?

JEANETTE: Hi Bruce, you cad.

LINDA: Would the two of you not flirt! I don't think it's appropriate to flirt on the astral plane.

BRUCE: I dunno. I have some pretty erotic dreams involvin' th' two of y—

LINDA: That's enough. Good-*bye*, ex-husband.

BRUCE: Bye, pretty Linda.

JEANETTE: Bye, Bruce, you burnout.

BRUCE: Bye, Jean. *Ette.*

LINDA: Come on, let's go, Jeanette. Jea*ne*-ette.

JEANETTE: What?

LINDA: *You* know.

JEANETTE: I *don't* know

LINDA: You *do* know.

They fly.

ever

CHAPTER 12

IN WHICH JEANETTE AND LINDA RECEIVE A MESSAGE FROM THE BEYOND

JEANETTE: North to Alaska.

They land in a blue, frozen landscape.

LINDA: Jay—Jay, I hear the ice creaking under the glacier. I can't, I'm frightened.

JEANETTE: Hold my hand, Linner. We must contact Mama.

Linda sobs.

JEANETTE: Mama? Are you there.

LINDA: I see her.

JEANETTE: I see her too.

LINDA: She's frozen. She looks just like she did in that photo from '61. She's wearing the same apron.

JEANETTE: Mama?

LINDA: Ah!

JEANETTE: Stay! Linda, stay still. She's talking.

MAMA: Ullllll ow szzzzzung nyaaaaaaa!*

LINDA: What's she saying?

JEANETTE: Shhhh! She's speaking our Eskimo language.

From behind the blur of ice, their mother raises her arms and wails.

MAMA: Ullllll ow szzzzzung nyaaaaaaa! Ulllll oww szzzzzzung nyaaaaaa.*

JEANETTE: She's saying "bury me." She wants us to go back to Alaska, find her body, and *bury* her.

LINDA: Let's return to Portland.

---

*This is a layman's phonetic spelling of words in the Yupik language of Alaska.

They zip through the heavens and crash-land on Linda's living-room floor.

JEANETTE: Are you okay, little sister?

Linda lies facedown on the floor, shaking. She nods.

JEANETTE: We've got to do it. We've got to go north. We'll stop in Seattle, get that buried money, probably find Skeeter, then we'll go north and excavate Mama from the ice and bury her.

LINDA: Why? Why did Daddy do that?

JEANETTE: Come here, Linda.

She pulls Linda onto her lap and strokes her hair.

JEANETTE: It'll be okay. We'll put her to rest.

LINDA: We will?

JEANETTE: We will. That was some broomstick ride, huh?

She pulls Linda up gently by the shoulders, wipes her cheeks, and smoothes her hair behind her ears.

LINDA: Yeah,

Linda casts an eye around the room.

LINDA: that was one cosmic hitch.

ever

PART SEVEN

EVERYTHING THAT RISES MUST CONVERGE

CHAPTER 1

IN WHICH TIM, THADDEUS, AND STUART ARE UNEMPLOYED AT THE ACRES O' CLAMS TAVERN

A tall guy in fisherman's boots with a Marlboro man mustache walks into a bar and into the dirty, filtered amber light that can be found exclusively in bars in the midafternoon. He is hailed by a short, wiry guy with a beard who stands next to a big bald guy. They are all wearing plaid flannel shirts.

TIM: Hey, huh huh huh huh huhhey, Stuart!

STUART: Tim, you asshole, what're you doin' here in the middle uh th' afternoon?

TIM: Same as you: drinkin'. Stu, dis's my good friend, Thaddeus.

THADDEUS: Aright.

STUART: Aright, hey.

TIM: What ya drinkin', Stuart?

STUART: Aw, I'll take a souza with Olympia chaser.

TIM: Aright, Bingo, get dis dude here his drink, and tequila shots for everyone at dis bar. Get dee old man one too.

He gestures to a wizened figure snoring under a big panama hat at the end of the bar.

TIM: I don't care if he's sleeping, put it by 'im. Yeah, yeah, I got money, just got my unemployment.

He burps loudly.

TIM: Fuck me. Drinkin' my way tuh Nirvana!

STUART: Nirvana? Don't tell me yur another fan uh that sissy—

THADDEUS: No, he means nirvana, not Nirvana.

Thaddeus has a shy and soft-spoken demeanor, in contrast with Tim.

TIM: Yeh-up. Nirvana was always a concept I dug, one uh my favorite words practically. I always, always used it, I'd say he probably stole it off me in high school, 'cept he ain't, well, he wudn't even from—

STUART: He ain't even from Seattle.

THADDEUS: Nah, he's from in-state. Like me.

TIM: Yeh-up.

He burps big again.

TIM: 'At kills me, an' he's got a statue an'-an' it *kill*s me, I mean nothin' against da guy personally, I felt like puttin' a gun in my mouth many's th' time, but, fuck me, all's he did's play guitar and shoot himself, and now dey got dat ugly statue an'—an' more tourists, as if we needed more outta-staters—it's fuckin' incredibly twisted man, you know? Why don't dey got a statue of Hiram Stan-cheon?

THADDEUS: Who?

TIM: Ah, Thad's not from here, he don't know who Hiram was.

STUART: Hiram was a old clam-man, how old was he, Tim?

TIM: He was, I dunno, he was fuckin' old, ag-ed, older'n dat old dude in da corner. Hey dude! Wake up!

Tim pounds the bar, trying to rouse the sleeper.

TIM: He's asleep. He was a beautiful old fart, man, he came up here back way back at da beginnin' when Seattle was just a pioneer town.

STUART: He was a grouchy old stinker when he drank.

TIM: Oh yeh, yeh, he was a old stink fart alright, but he was, man, I had respect for him, I *loved* the dude. He was *real* Seattle. Now why don't dey make a statue for *him*? Why? I'll tellya why. 'Cause da tourists an' all da outta-staters, dey wouldn't understand dat. Dey'd go,

His voice goes falsetto.

TIM: "Whaaaa? I don't get it. Let's go get a Ca*fay* Lah-*tay*, Angie."

He returns to his usual rowdy demeanor.

TIM: Like dat. Am I right or am I right?

STUART: He's right. What's the bartender's name?

TIM: Bingo.

STUART: Bingo! Another round uh souzas for the bar. So how's the boards and nails biz?

what

TIM: Sucks, man. Been unemployed for three months. I'm waitin' here for a friend, Jimmy Scoops. Know him? He might have a side job for me. He's in the

He looks slightly embarassed.

Tim makes a covert gesture indicating the smoking of marijuana.

TIM: real money-makin' biz.

He looks slightly embarassed.

TIM: Yeh-up. Well, meanwhile, you try tuh make an' honest livin'. I'se hopin' wid spring, I don't know, maybe dey'll build a Kurt Museum. Dat'd be six months' work. This country is incredibly twisted.

THADDEUS: Tell me about it.

TIM: Yeah, Thad's messed up, he just came from Snoqualmie. 'Is ole lady left him for another woman.

THADDEUS: For another woman, yeah.

STUART: Yeah? Snoqualmie, what were you doin' out there?

THADDEUS: 'S workin' for the National Forest Service, fire tower lookout. Girlfriend left me for a ranger.

TIM: Tell Stuart da ranger's name, Thaddeus.

THADDEUS: Ah, 'er name was Grunewald.

TIM: Heh heh, can you believe dat? It's incredibly twisted. I tell ya between lesbians and Republicans, guys like us are fucked.

STUART: Yeah.

TIM: You?

STUART: Well, fishin' ain't too frisky. These oceans are gettin' fished out. It's happenin', dudes, I'm seeing it happen. Hell, I'm *makin'* it happen. There's just too many of us and not enough uh them. Know how they say there's always another fish in the sea? Well, turns out, there ain't.

TIM: Sucks. Where's dat Canadian girl you were—

STUART: We broke up.

TIM: Dat's how it is.

STUART: Yeh-up.

TIM: Yeh-up. Did she start wid dat commitment shit?

STUART: Yeh, yeh, but nuh, but that wasn't it so much as . . .

TIM: Yeh-up.

STUART: Wull.

TIM: Go ahead, spit it out, we're all drunk here, Bingo! More tequila! Wha!?

ever

STUART: Well, truth be told, I couldn't get her tuh have an . . . orgasm.

THADDEUS: Orgasm?

TIM: Yeah, Thaddeus, 'at's what da man said. O-R-G-A-S-M! Hell! No wonder yer girlfriend left you for Grunewald!

THADDEUS: Hey!

Thad stiffens.

STUART: Hey!

Stuart clenches his fist.

TIM: Hey! No hard feelin's! Bingo! Cheers!

The drinks arrive just in time to avert a fight and they clink glasses and drink.

TIM: Yeh-up, wull, who knows? Some like fingers, some like a little tongue action, some of 'em just like—

STUART: Tim.

Stuart cocks his head toward the door.

STUART: A little old lady just walked in.

VIOLET: Barman, yes, I'd like— Have you got Glenlivet? Good, I'll have that, neat, and a glass of wateh, no ice, f' the poodle. Thanks very much, keep the change. Don't worry, gentlemen, I've been minding my own business in men's bars for more than *half* a century. I'll just sit at that table in the corner and you can talk as much filth as you'd like. Come on, Balzy.

Violet hobbles off for the tables, drink in hand.

THADDEUS: Thanks, ma'am.

TIM: Cheers!

STUART: You were sayin', Tim?

what

CHAPTER 2

IN WHICH PAUL AND SHEILA WIND UP THE COAST

Paul and Sheila are on a foggy stretch of the coastal highway, in the state of Oregon, heading north.

SHEILA: Dad, could you drive more carefully? This isn't like back home in Virginia, the hairpin curves on Route 101 are really tricky.

PAUL: I know how to drive, She-She.

SHEILA: Please! Don't call me that.

PAUL: Sheila-Marie, I know how to drive. Some view, ay? Quite a coastline you've got out here.

SHEILA: You say that as though it's a commodity, some consumer perk, not a gift of nature.

PAUL: Oh, hell, baby daughter, I thought I just said it.

SHEILA: Hmm. I don't think you treasure nature, that's all. You're an Axnell man, how could you? And please, Dad, don't call me baby daughter either.

PAUL: Well then, hell, don't call me Dad, call me Paul, or-or better yet, Mr. Folsom, god*damn*it. By the way, for your information, Mr. Folsom has been retired from Axnell for three years. And that's not true, I-I-I do, treasure—why, growing up in Wenatchee I used to go for long hikes out in the forest. I'll tell ya, I knew those trees better than I knew the town. They were almost friends to me. And the Wenatchee River, to look at that thing go, in early spring.

SHEILA: You sure you want to go back there, Dad? We could just stick to Seattle, I'll go to my Planet Guard meeting—

PAUL: Your top-secret summit? My daughter, the *eco*-operative!

SHEILA: No, Pops, you're the spook, Axnell Corp. violates the law in tandem with the secret police. We just work to safeguard—

PAUL: I know, I know.

SHEILA: Anyway, we could just go to Seattle, make sure your scruffy little ward—Skeeter?—gets back to your mistress's sister. You could see your mistress, what's her name? Ginger?

PAUL: Jea*nette*.

SHEILA: Right. And then, we could skip driving out to Wenatchee. You might be disappointed, a lot of that area has been deforested. All the old forest is gone.

PAUL: Have you *seen* this with your *very* own eyes or only *heard* it from your *rad*ical friends?

SHEILA: I haven't *been* there, Dad, but I know, okay? I'm an *expert*, I mean, I get *paid* by the University of California in Berkeley to—

PAUL: You get *paid*. See, this environmentalist malarkey is as much a racket as my capitalist imperialism, as you call it.

SHEILA: So you admit you're an imperialist.

PAUL: I don't admit. There you go twisting my words. You're just like your mother.

SHEILA: Whom you've *deserted* after thirty-five years of marriage.

PAUL: I-I-I-I'm not deserting Polly Ann, your mother—she—Polly said to leave her in the house in Middleburg and go away. I told you. Your mother is having an affair with a Negro-black—

SHEILA: PERSON OF COLOR! Why can't either of you use the appropriate ter—

PAUL: Well, she's having one, alright!? Your virtuous martyr housewife mom, the feminist poster-victim, is getting her Southern belles off with a black—colored—*PERSON OF COLOR*!!—apparently ten years younger than she—

SHEILA: You're jealous, Dad, you macho pig. I can't believe after all you did to Mom, you're jealous.

PAUL: Of course I am. I love your mother.

SHEILA: But you're divorcing her.

PAUL: If that's what she wants, yes.

SHEILA: *She* wants. What about you? And this woman Nanette?

PAUL: *Jeanette*. I love. Her.

SHEILA: You— why do men pretend to be passive pawns?

PAUL: Hey, wait a minute, young lady, passive? A minute ago you were calling me a male chauvinist pig!

SHEILA: No, I wasn't. That's an outdated term I would never use.

what

PAUL: Well, you used it.

SHEILA: No, I called you a macho pig.

PAUL: Male chauvinist pig.

SHEILA: Macho pig.

PAUL: Nope.

SHEILA: Well, you're both.

PAUL: Thank you. And you are a belligerent aggressive young woman and it's no wonder no man will have you!

SHEILA: What Is That Supposed to Mean? Is that a patriarchical threat?

PAUL: Patriarchal. Learn to speak English.

SHEILA: Unbelievable. Stop the car! Let me out!

PAUL: She-she, baby daughter, what are you going to do? Jump into the Pacific?

SHEILA: That would be better than staying in a car with you! I'll hitch a ride with your ward, Skeeter, and his little girlfriend's family.

PAUL: We lost them back in Seal Rock.

SHEILA: Well, I'll hitch a ride from a lost member of the Manson family. I don't care, stop the car, and let me out! I hate you! You cipher for corporate America! You clown of a husband to my mother! Ahhh!

PAUL: She-She, pipe down, keep your shirt on—

SHEILA: Dad, watch—

She points out the window at a TV van that is ruthlessly passing them, trying to force them onto a brief shoulder of the road.

PAUL: Calm down, She-She—

SHEILA: Dad, that van!

PAUL: AHHHH!

Sheila grabs the wheel in the nick of time, steering them off the road. The van sails by. They crash into the cliff side.

PAUL: Jesus! Baby daughter, are you okay?

SHEILA: I'm fine, Pops.

PAUL: Thank God, thank God. My She-She, my baby daughter!

SHEILA: I'm not a baby and I'm fine.

She takes the keys out of the ignition.

SHEILA: Turn off the engine and let's get our bearings.

PAUL: But you were my baby once, Sheila, can't you understand?

ever

You were my first child. One night when I was a young man I came home from work and made love to your mother and then that beautiful vivacious Southern belle that this Yankee had married became pregnant and we waited for months and months and months until we took her to the hospital and then I was alone for three days, seventy-two hours. I couldn't concentrate on-on business or-or eating or sleeping and when you *came out* it was the most important thing I'd ever been part of. It was, you were my baby daughter and I knew to deserve that I'd have to work very hard and take care of you as best as I possibly could.

And so I worked, put in all the hours at Axnell. I got promoted. We moved. I tried so hard. I never spent time with you except on some of those weekends but can't you see, I did it FOR you and for Derek when he was born and for your lovely mother, Polly Ann, I didn't know you would all hate me.

He wipes at the corner of his left eye. At first Sheila thinks his eye is irritated.

SHEILA: Are you crying, Dad? Dad? We don't hate you.

PAUL: Yes you do! Derek, that square peg, hates me from over at his Christian Coalition Headquarters in D.C., your mother hates me from out of that sparkling clean home of hers that I *never* felt welcome in, and and what is most painful of all to me, you, my baby daughter, hate me precisely because I worked so hard all my life to succeed in the world and provide as a man should. You hate Axnell Corporation and all that it stands for. But can't you see, it doesn't stand for anything. It's a company composed of men like me who work for it. I'm not Axnell. I'm your *father*!

He pounds his chest.

PAUL: I'm your *pops* and you're my baby daughter!

SHEILA: Pops, goddamnit.

PAUL: What?

SHEILA: I love you, Dad.

PAUL: But do you forgive me?

He is shouting.

SHEILA: Oh Dad, let me hug you.

PAUL: But do you forgive me?!

what

CHAPTER 3

IN WHICH SKEETER AND SABLE RIDE THE RECREATIONAL BUDDHA VEHICLE

Skeeter and Sable rattle around in the back of her parents' recreational vehicle as they drive up the foggy coastal highway. It is pearlescent pink and orange and decorated with hundreds of little beaming Buddhas. Sable's younger siblings run and crawl around the two teenagers.

SKEETER: So when we get tuh Seattle, we'll find my ma Linda, then we'll look fer Clove. I have the presentiment the mood-hats'll sell most heatedly in the Seattle area.

SABLE: I think yur waxin' a tad avaricious over these mood-hats. Perchance you spent too much time with that corpret dude?

SKEETER: Nuh, what er you insinuous on now, sulky Sable? Paul's my friend. I truly b'lieve he's repenting his corpret Amurican ways. You shoulda heard 'im waxin' mournful over Oklahoma City.

SABLE: Wull, everyone waxed all devastated over that.

SKEETER: What lurches? Yer mood-hat's twingin' all puce. 'At means yur angered.

SABLE: Tuhh. I'm just all, why couldn't I run away like you an' Clove do? Why does the total Nugent family—

She trips over one of her toddler siblings.

SABLE: —including scads of my hectic siblings have to come along? Why do my Buddhistic parents have to be so ultra permissive as to overswarm my en*tire rav*ished *life*?

SKEETER: But, but I'm kinda partial tuh this rad recreational Buddha vehicle.

SABLE: What. *Ev*er.

She turns away from him.

SKEETER: Never. Mind.

He turns away from her.

SABLE: And you!

She turns back to him.

SKEETER: Me?

He turns back to her.

SABLE: Yur getting all hectic and capitalized with yer flaccid case of mood-hats.

SKEETER: Flaccid? You said they were rad before.

SABLE: Before what?

SKEETER: Before the penultimate time we . . .

He runs a finger down her arm.

SABLE: Never mind.

She turns away.

SKEETER: What. *Ev*er.

He turns away.

PARENTS: *Nom yoho renge kyo, nom yoho renge kyo—*

Sable marches forward and shouts to her parents in the front.

SABLE: Caroline! Jack! Would you please stop chanting incessant-like while you drive! Yur agging me to excess!

They continue chanting.

SABLE: Ah!

She stalks to the side window and looks out.

SABLE: W-watch out, that van's passing us!

They are narrowly swiped by a passing van.

SABLE: Tuhhhhhh!

SKEETER: Tuhhhhhh.

SABLE: Oh Godddddess, Skeeter, did you see that van?

She clings to him.

SKEETER: Nuh.

SABLE: That was the PO-E-Z-TV Van, fer *Suicide Watch–Actual Deaths.* Godddddess, do you think Clove is skittering all suicidish in Seattle an' thur whisking to report?

SKEETER: Nuh, null 'at fear at the pod, Sabe.

He holds her in his arms.

SKEETER: No doubt thur's another teen suicide threat 'tween here an' our foggy destiny.

what

SABLE: Tuhh. Let's chant a tad.

SKEETER: I succumb if you succumb.

He looks down at her.

SABLE: I succumb.

She looks up at him.

SKEETER: *Nom yoho renge kyo, nom yoho renge kyo.*

SABLE: *Nom yoho renge kyo, nom yoho renge kyo.*

SKEETER: *Nom yoho renge kyo, nom yoho renge kyo.*

SABLE: *Nom yoho renge kyo, nom yoho renge kyo.*

ever

CHAPTER 4

IN WHICH BUSHIE TELLS
THE TRUTH

Bushie sits on a folding metal chair in a circle of folding metal chairs in group therapy. A big toothless guy in a sweatsuit is talking. The group listens.

PETE-O: Aftah my car got totaled, I lost my job wit' my uncle and I was smokin' it day in, day out. I was makin' wit'drawals on the Visa, Stephanie didn't know it. I'd take huh car, take da kids down the Pizza Hut at the mall, an' I'd go to the automatic tellah, score at the video store. My kids, my kids would go, Hey Daddy, hey Daddy, ah . . .

He is close to tears.

PETE-O: I can't, I can't.

COUNSELOR: Thanks, Pete-O. Mollie?

The counselor is a weathered-looking woman with frizzy black hair—mixed race. She has a straight, no-nonsense voice. She breathes out through her nose a lot to indicate empathy.

COUNSELOR: This is how we do it here, we just go around in a circle and stop when we need to.

BUSHIE: I ain't got nuttin' tuh say. I didn't come from dat. Ah, I can't explain it. I didn't come from houses an' cars and da mall. You know? I come from Eleventh Avenue.

COUNSELOR: We all have our own experience.

BUSHIE: Yeah, we all have our own experience, but I come from *dirty-ass* Irish people on da West Side, *Manhattan*, ya know? My pops was killed by da Westies. My stepfadda Henry used tuh lock me in da bafroom wit' his tree vicious-ass Dobahmins fuh punishment. Hated dose fuckin' dogs, whole apahtment stank of 'em. Kids said,

"Dere goes Mollie Bri-ight, she smells like a do-og an' she looks like one too-oo." And I did. An' I still do. Ha-ha.

No one laughs.

BUSHIE: I did one thing wrong at da dinna table, Henry would eithah get out da belt, or lock me in da bafroom wit' dose tree dogs. I useta lie, say I wasn't hungry an' swallow my own spit fuh dinna, ya know? Aw, I'm talkin' too much.

COUNSELOR: Go on.

BUSHIE: I got nuttin' tuh say. Drugs saved *my* life. Drugs was *heav*en fuh me. From eatin' paint off da wall tuh dat deadly-ass glue dey useta have in da seventies? Tuh dust, tuh dope, tuh cracka jacks, I got wacked on it *all* as soon as I could. Me an' my homegirl Magdalena Rigobar, Magenta Rush an' Bushie, dat's when we got tagged, we was, we was like da fuckin' rulers of Forty-fif' Street— takin' rides, makin' cash, an' gettin' wacked. My life be*gan*.

COUNSELOR: So when did you hit bottom?

Bushie looks at her like she is a stupid bitch.

BUSHIE: Dere was no *bot*tom. I was *born* at da bottom. Drugs made me *high*er.

The counselor breathes out through her nose.

COUNSELOR: So why did you come here to try and quit?

Bushie scratches her head and looks around.

BUSHIE: I dunno. I think maybe I hit da top.

ever

CHAPTER 5

IN WHICH A QUESTION IS ANSWERED UNEXPECTEDLY AT THE ACRES O' CLAMS TAVERN

Back at the bar, the discussion of female orgasm continues.

TIM: Guys don't know what women want? What's that Freudian slip thing?

THADDEUS: Nuh, Freud said, what do women want?

TIM: He said dat?

THADDEUS: That's what he said.

TIM: So okay, now so okay, a hundred years later, we made some advancement, okay, now we know dey want tuh come, just like us, okay! So now? What makes 'em come?

THADDEUS: I think it's love.

TIM: But you loved yer girlfriend, Thaddeus.

THADDEUS: Yeah, but she didn't love me.

STUART: I think they like guys who treat 'em like dirt.

TIM: No, we're not talkin' da relationship part.

STUART: Neither am I. I think treat 'em like dirt, it turns 'em on, an'—

TIM: Okay, okay. Bingo, what do you think?

BINGO: What?

TIM: What makes women come?

BINGO: Relaxation. Get 'em drunk an'

He snaps his fingers.

BINGO: . . . 'sall over.

TIM: Yur just pushin' alcohol on us. Pusher!

Tim pounds the bar.

TIM: 'Nother round! Hey, hey Cartlett?

He addresses a middle-aged blond guy in an alcoholic stupor.

CARTLETT: Hm?

TIM: What makes women come?

CARTLETT: Rock stars. Rock stars.

TIM: No, ahhh, ask dee old man. Bingo, wake up dee old man and ask 'im. Hey old man! Wake up, we got a question.

Tim bangs the bar. The oldster looks up from under the brim of the hat and then stands with perfect drunken composure, putting out a cigarette, which has been burning all this while, with the toe of a dainty cowboy boot.

SOPHIE: I can hear you perfectly well, young man, and I'm awake. In answer to your question, I can only tell you this: I've *come* riding horses and *not come* with the best Italian lovers on pillows of white satin. I've *come* sucking rattler poison from an ugly man's arm and *not come* from watching Fred Astaire and Ginger Rogers glide by while teasing myself with a french tickler. I've *come* in *two seconds flat* after sweating for *five days solid* sculpting impossible things, and *not come* from being made love to, at *last*, by the *art*ist I most admired. I've *come* from *spit* on a *finger* and *not come* from cock all aquiver. I've *come* from rolling *naked* in the desert and *not come* from rolling *nude* in the clouds. I've *come* from *slap*ping and *being slapped*, and *not come* from *too much happi*ness and feeling *sapped*, I've *come* from not wanting much and *not come* from wanting too much. In short, gentlemen, I've *come* and *come* and *come* and *come* and *not come* and *not come* and *not come* and *not come*. And now I'm so damn *old* you mistake me for a man, but I tell you, I'm a WOMAN!

The elderly personage rips open her shirt to reveal a very old but very womanly breast.

SOPHIE: And I answer your question, what makes women come, in this way:

Her next words spray them like gunfire at high noon.

SOPHIE: HOW THE HELL SHOULD WE KNOW!? WE'RE HUMAN BEINGS LIKE YOU, THAT'S ALL!!!

VIOLET: Pahdon me, but aren't you the sculptress Sophie Flax?

SOPHIE: I am.

She buttons her shirt with pride, looks at Violet, looks away haughtily, then does a double take.

ever

SOPHIE: Violet *Flan*agan! The Tricott Farm in New Hampshire, 1954!?

VIOLET: Hah! That's right! Violet Smith now. I've been divorced and widowed since. I sawr a piece of yours recently at the Modern, the enormous iron clutch purse and—

SOPHIE: Right, one of them museums they got in New York. Vi, I can't believe you're still alive.

    Violet looks Sophie up and down.

VIOLET: Nor *you*.

SOPHIE: What are you doing out West?

VIOLET: I brought my poodle, Balzac, for a rest cure. He lost a leg to an antiabortion gunman outside a clinic, y'see.

TIM: Hey, I heard about dat on da news.

    Sophie and Violet slowly turn their heads and regard Tim with total disinterest. Balzac barks.

TIM: Uh, can I pat 'im?

VIOLET: Certainly.

SOPHIE: I never read the papers. I live very spare. Work on sculpting out on my land, come in once a week for supplies. And drink. You've got to visit, Vi, old girl. I can't believe it. I always admired you so.

VIOLET: Admired me? But you were grand, Soph, you're an *art*ist.

SOPHIE: Ah! But you weren't, and you lived like one. I needed *art* to fight for me. You fought for your*self*. That takes *true* talent. Come on, hop in my truck, let's go out to my land.

VIOLET: Swell. I'm delighted. Come on, Balzy.

    Balzac barks.

VIOLET: Bye, fellas.

    Tim clown-walks back to the bar.

TIM: Whoooooah. Dose weren't like da little ole ladies on TV commercials.

STUART: Bingo! Another round. Make 'em doubles.

what

CHAPTER 6

IN WHICH A STOWAWAY SLIPS OFF THE SEATTLE FERRY

Gulls swoop and squeal overhead as Linda and Jeanette stand on the deck of a ferry pulling into Seattle's harbor. They are enjoying their cigarettes, cutting the fog with smoke.

JEANETTE: Oh, Linda, I wonder what the gulls are saying.

LINDA: I think they're welcoming us to Seattle, Jeanette, hoping we find what we're looking for.

JEANETTE: I'm so glad we took the ferry.

CLOVE: Tuhh, excuse me, but do you know whur Puget Sound is?

JEANETTE: That way. North.

CLOVE: Tuhh, thanks.

DECKHAND: We're docking.

DOCKHAND: 'Ey, catch that kid! He didn't pay 'is fare—catch 'im!

A young man leaps to the dock from the ferry and flees into the crowd. The dockhand chases after him.

LINDA: Look at him go. Reminds me of Ezekial.

JEANETTE: He does but it can't be. Paul's fax said he was driving up with his new little girlfriend Sable's family. The Nuggets, I think they are.

DOCKHAND: Damn! That kid ran fast, he got away!

CLOVE: Tuhh. He dropped this.

JEANETTE: He did? Linda, that's a mood-hat.

LINDA: What?

JEANETTE: You know, the thing Skeeter had on and they wouldn't let him on the plane.

CLOVE: Whoah, yur acquainted with the dude called Skeeter?

LINDA: Acquainted,

Linda looks Clove up and down.

LINDA: little witch, I'm his mother.

JEANETTE: Who're you, hon?

CLOVE: I'm Clove.

LINDA: Clove!? That's the name of the other one he's in love with. Hmm, the hat looks good on you. *She* reminds me of Ezekial.

JEANETTE: No wonder Skeeter's in love with you. You look like him.

LINDA: Yep, he's a narcissist *just like his dad* Bruce.

DECKHAND: Welcome to the city of Seattle. Please be careful disembarking the ferry. Thank you for riding the *Hiram Stancheon*.

JEANETTE: Here we are.

LINDA: Here we are in Seattle.

JEANETTE: Where are you going, Clove?

Clove turns back and waves a grave good-bye.

CLOVE: To the Space Needle. Farewell.

She runs off.

JEANETTE: Bye, hope to meet again. Linda, did you see that? Her hat just changed colors.

LINDA: That's why they call it a mood-hat, I guess.

JEANETTE: Hmm. Magical.

LINDA: Hmm.

They make their way royally down the gangway.

what

CHAPTER 7

IN WHICH BUSHIE IS ANGERED

The counselor breathes out heavily through her nose and looks Bushie deeply in the eyes.

COUNSELOR: Mollie, did you ever consider that your feelings for Mag might be lesbian? And that's okay.

Bushie stares at her for a long minute. Suddenly, she springs to her feet.

BUSHIE: I can't take dis no more. I'm leavin'!

COUNSELOR: Mollie, Mollie, calm down. You're doing great, come back.

BUSHIE: I am not undah arrest here, I am a free freakin' citizen an' I am leavin' yuh detox centah.

COUNSELOR: Mollie, I think you should consider, where will you go?

BUSHIE: Back on Forty-fif' where I belong!

COUNSELOR: Mollie, wait!

BUSHIE: Da name is BUSHIE, baby!

Bushie slaps her own ass, shaking it in the counselor's face.

BUSHIE: Good-bye, all youse detoxes! I'm gone!

Bushie is gone.

CHAPTER 8

IN WHICH *SUICIDE WATCH* ARRIVES IN SEATTLE

Dawn Malestrella and Harper stand facing the PO-E-Z-TV cameras in front of a coffee bar in Seattle's Seaport Village. Their cameramen frame them so that the Space Needle rises in the background. In fact, it looks as if it is sprouting from Dawn's head.

DAWN: Greetings, siphons of the small screen. You're watching PO-E-Z-TV. I'm your fave rave PJ Dawn Malestrella and you guessed it, morons, now it's time for *Suicide Watch*—

HARPER: *Act*ual Deaths!

DAWN: This week both me and my main man Harper are live on the scene. I am not in the studio because we figured something special is going to happen in Seattle. Yes, in our nation's northmost city we have a hunch there's more than harsh java abrew. Do we sniff mass suicide plans? *Mayyy*-bee. Why?

HARPER: Well as you all know, the anniversary of Kurt Cobain's death triggers—

DAWN: Whoah, it puns!

HARPER: —a slew of fresh suicides and fer the past week, thousands of youths have been washing up in Seattle, looking lost and confused. None of 'em have yet tuh confirm the jumpin' juggernaut rumor, but we think something big is about tuh go down.

DAWN: Do we mean down as in, I'm falling, splat! Harper?

HARPER: Yes, Dawnie baby, I'm afeared that's exactly presentimento aces what we mean.

DAWN: And that's why we're here, live on the scene, to make sure you see whoever knocks themselves off do it for real, raw, right in front of your very eyes. We'll be right back after a Poesy break. Stay suckled for *Suicide Watch*—

They point hip-hop-style fingers at the viewing audience.

HARPER: *Actual Deaths!*

CHAPTER 9

IN WHICH CLOVE ASCENDS

Clove rides the elevator up the Space Needle with a group of vacationing Oklahomans and a cheery guide who speaks into a lavalier mike in a high, sweet voice.

GUIDE: Welcome to Seattle's Space Needle—

CLOVE: Shooting up up up up.

GUIDE: Riding again, huh? You really like it here, don't you?

CLOVE: Tuhh. Let's just say it stokes my curiosity a tad. Up! Up! Up!

GUIDE: The Space Needle was built in 1962 and completed on April 21 in honor of the World's Fair.

CLOVE: Up! Up! Up!

GUIDE: The structure is made of steel and is 520 feet in height—

CLOVE: And to the tip of the needle is 620 feet high.

GUIDE: That's right, she knows the whole talk!

CLOVE: Tuhh, excuse me but is there any way to get all the way to the top?

GUIDE: You're at the top.

CLOVE: Nuh, I mean the tip top of the needle.

GUIDE: No. Only personnel.

CLOVE: Why does personnel go to the top?

GUIDE: Well, they used to burn a torch at the tip of the needle, but that used a lot of gas and was wasteful of resources. So now we just have a light and the guy who goes up to change it climbs a little ladder like the ones you see on telephone poles.

CLOVE: And that takes him all the way to the point of the needle?

GUIDE: Yes it does. She's so curious. She loves this ride. And she won't take off that hat. Why don't you take off your hat? Now, folks, if you look below, you'll see we have a wonderful view of our waterfront. For your enjoyment we have four gift shops located at the base of the needle. Sixty percent of the items sold in these can only be exclusively purchased in the Space Needle, so you really might want to make some purchases while you're here.

CLOVE: Rave on, sister. Rave on.

Clove skulks off to the elevator.

GUIDE: For your dining pleasure, we have two restaurants offering the best in Northwest cuisine, located at the rotating level of the needle. Hey, where'd she go? She used the personnel door. How'd she get it open? Oh shit.

The guide flips open her walkie-talkie.

GUIDE: Leopold, we've got a visitor who's gone off-limits, get somebody up here fast. I'm running a tour. Ladies and gentlemen, if you'll just enjoy the view on your own, we've got a small problem to take care of. Oh my GOD, LOOK! SHE'S CLIMBING THE NEEDLE!

Perhaps it is the high altitude, perhaps the gulls carry a little faery dust in their beaks. Whatever it is, it seems Clove, as she ascends the needle, finds herself on a very different plane of reality:

CLOVE: Rung by rung I climb the needle high

North! I turn into its spacey eye

A needle pokin' in th' celestial arm

A heroine stokin' her way past harm

Cobain the Friendly Ghost was his ID

He saved me from the Cali-fornia sea

There I raved, in ecstatic trance

Learnin' off crabs a luna-tic dance

'Til the ocean's tight bodice laced me o'er

And a prancin' sea horse dude rode me under

Then did pale Cobain rise from the marine

And drag me to a sea garden, most serene

'Twas but a brussels sprout patch across the way

From whur my cohorts danced 'til ravey day

From thence he dumped me nude among the sprouts

Babblin' to excess all on my oceanic bout

Wull, since that time I have haunted been

By this music ghost whose music

—and I'm speaking pellucid-like—

I never waxed all overly interested in

I mean, *In Utero* was a good album,
some songs on it were stoked, I suppose
But it's a ravin' girl-dude I am
Not all yoked by a hoaxish pose
We like to rave all night to a song that isn't there there there . . .
Whur the singer fades like a tree inside a pear, pear, pear . . .
And so, despite my flaccid interest,
I was inflected by this phantom pest
With visions, uncooked dreams and hauntings rare
Which even my best friend Sable mistook fer despair
Until such time as I returned to Fortune's Brow
Borne out in Sable's parents' VW to the same fields whur now
The migrant Mexican farm workers did hectically inform
That they too were all haunted by this "spectro" forlorn
They gifted upon me a brussels sprout
and told me I must put the spirit out
So I planted it in sand at Santa Cruz Beach
And that night was inflected with ultra-visuals
which now, I render as speech.
I saw brussels sprouts twining north underground
And like Jill 'n the Beanstalk I was bound
North on the floodish waves, I floated north
'Til last a ferry put me in this port
Now up up the Spacey Needle I climb
Following the brussels sprouting twine
Vexing one, vexing all
It's Cobain's doing if I fall
Fer he haunts me still up here
High above Seattle's pier
And his friendly ghost will only rest
When my courage has met its test
So to the point I go and wait fer a sign.
    The gulls squeal around her head.
CLOVE: Follow me, gulls, keep my feet sure
I'll not come down, er I'll FIND a CUUUUUURRRE!

what

CHAPTER 10

IN WHICH SOPHIE AMAZES VIOLET

Sophie, Violet, and Balzac are outdoors on Sophie's land, outside a huge old barn.

VIOLET: So, Sophie, now you've shown me everything you've done since the fifties, show me what's inside that barn.

SOPHIE: That, Vi old girl, is my coup de grâce, my fin de siècle, my swan song, if you like. Wait, I hear something. Hand me my shotgun, Vi.

VIOLET: I'll do no such thing. I'm a pacifist now.

SOPHIE: That's a shame. You used to be such a good hunter.

VIOLET: Not since Balzac was shot by that Bible salesman.

SOPHIE: I'll get it.

Sophie grabs her shotgun and levels it at the two intruders.

SOPHIE: Halt! Who goes there!

HELACIO: Excuse me, miss, but we are coming from California looking for work from the floods.

SOPHIE: Where you from?

CARLITO: Mexico.

SOPHIE: I can see that, but where in May-heek-o?

CARLITO: *¿Qué dice ella?*

HELACIO: *No te preoccupa.* We are from the province of Chiapas, lady.

SOPHIE: Oh yeah? I love the pottery from that area, can you make pottery?

HELACIO: No, we no work to make pot grow, we are no safe from *la policía.*

SOPHIE: Naw, naw, not POT—*pot*tery, cera*mi*ca!

CARLITO: *Sí, sí, mi madre fue la mejor en la región entero. Diga-le. Diga-le.*

SOPHIE: La may hor in la entire region, ay? Well, swell, I've been needing assistants in my kiln for years, ever since my last lover, Finian, made off with that berry-farmer. Bisexuals are so unreliable! Go on, you can wash up—there's a pump behind the barn and then we'll all eat something. We'll discuss wages when you've got full stomachs. I don't bargain with hungry people. I used to be hungry in New York, and there was a gallery owner who liked to bargain with me while my stomach was grumbling. After I'd sold my sculptures for a tenth of their worth, given him a huge commission, he'd take me out to eat at the Automat. I vowed that if I ever wore his shoes, I would never never bargain with anyone who had an empty stomach. Because it isn't dignified. Right, Violet?

VIOLET: And aside from that, it stinks!

HELACIO AND CARLITO: *¡Gracias, señora!*

SOPHIE: Sinorita, Sinorita Sophie Flax. This is my old pal Violet Smith, her poocho Balzac and you are—

HELACIO: Helacio.

CARLITO: Carlito. *Gracias.*

HELACIO: *Gracias.*

SOPHIE: Dee nada. Go on.

HELACIO AND CARLITO: *Sí, sí.*

SOPHIE: Poor fellas, they looked as though they'd seen a ghost.

VIOLET: P'rhaps they had. And now I'd like to see this latest work of yours.

SOPHIE: Close your eyes, I'm opening the barn door.

It creaks as she pushes it open. Violet obediently keeps her eyes closed.

SOPHIE: I've been working on it nonstop for months. I only finished it last week, and that's why you found me drunk at the Acres o' Clams Tavern. I always get drunk when I finish something. I'm despondent, really. I tried to make something as explosive as a bomb, but not destructive. Alright, open yer eyes.

Violet looks.

VIOLET: Good Christ! It's enormous. It's, it's grand, hehehehehehe, I've neveh seen anything so green, so firm, and yet so layered, infinite almost, in its—

SOPHIE: Do you know what it is? Is it recognizable?

VIOLET: Of course. I do. It's awfully familiar it's a brussels—no it's femininity itself, it's pleasure, a pahticular sort of pleasure, it's, uh . . .

Balzac barks.

what

SOPHIE: It's a female orgasm!

VIOLET: Yes! I knew it!

For once, Violet seems unsure.

SOPHIE: You did! Are you sure?

VIOLET: Absolutely. Eh, it's amazing. How're you going to exhibit it?

SOPHIE: Well, since you ask . . .

Sophie leans over and whispers in Violet's ear.

even

CHAPTER 11

IN WHICH BUSHIE IS
OVERWHELMED BY
WONDERBREAD

At four o'clock in the morning, Bushie staggers, bent over, bleeding and bruised, onto her home turf of West Forty-fifth Street and Tenth Avenue.

BUSHIE: Terry di'n't hafta do dat, he di'n't have tuh beat Bushie like dat, I told him, Look, Bushie's back from rehab, I ain't wacked out no more, I'm ready tuh work, let me work, he goes, "No Bushie, no whore of mine goes off tuh rehabilitate huhself wit'out my permission, it sets a bad example," I go, "Give me a beatin' den, Terry, you stupid-ass weak-ass pimp, see if I care, you fuck me up den so I can't get no rides, can't make us no money, stupid-ass," an' he goes, "You know I love you, Mollie, why you make me look like dis, no whore of mine could act dis way. It sets a bad example." So he goes tuh work on me, and da Lynchs useta be boxers, Terry had a uncle Francis, he was a champ and Terry goes tuh work on my stomach, bu-bu-bu-bu-bu-bu-bu-bu-bu-bu-bup-bup-bup-baaa, like dat, like bullets. I'm bleedin', people, I think I'm bleedin' from dee inside, but I'm' a get me a ride so help me, an' if it's only five dolliz I'm'a take myself away tuh dat place. Bushie gonna get some huh first night back outta rehab, it's gonna feel good too, 'cause I'm pure-blooded, it's gonna HIT me like a VIRGIN smoke.

Where all my home bitches? Is only 3 A.M., four, four, damn. Bitches have changed, us old bitches useta party all night. Now they all off da streets. Dawn ain't even broke yet. So don't fix it, ah ha ha ha. Where are all da condo-asses? WONDERBREADS? ARE YOU SLEEPIN'? ARE YOU SLEEPIN'? BUSHIE'S BAAAAAACK! BUSH-

IE'S HERE! I bet youse thought you got rid uh Bushie, I bet you thought Bushie was arrested fuh good. No! WAKE UP, PEOPLE. Bushie was in rehab, people, but den she saw da light. She saw you got tuh HAVE a HAB tuh RE-HAB. GET IT? An' Bushie don't got nuttin' but dis street an' it's MINE, people, I don't care how many flashlight patrols an' Save-Our-Neighbah-hood meetins you have.

Bushie shouts at the top of her lungs:

BUSHIE: You could renovate dis block all you fuckin' please, babies, it's still da same *dirty*-ass tenements *my mudda* and *my fadda* grew up in! Bushie's here, people and she ain't *nev*eh *nev*eh gonna go away! WONDERBREADS, DIS IS HELL'S *KITC*HEN. WAKE UP AND SMELL DA DOGSHIT, PEOPLE! Ho-oh!!! Where're all da rides? Aren't dere any perverts? What's wrong wit' perverts dese days?

A white van pulls up. Bushie runs to it.

BUSHIE: Hey baby. I like yuh van. You want a—

She sees two men and a woman in the van—a contingent of her yuppie antagonists are inside.

BUSHIE: Oh, Wonderbreads! You got a van now? Hey, you movin' up from flashlights an' trowin' eggs out yuh windows. Nice van. It's all white. Like you. Oh, I know, I'm white too, I know, I'm white like you.

TED: You're coming for a little ride with us, Bushie. Some people just don't listen if you ask them nicely.

Ted is driving. He is a is a handsome WASP, a bit thin-lipped. His voice is assured and righteous.

BUSHIE: What are you talkin' about, people? You makin' a citizen's arrest like da time you tied me tuh da tree an' called da cops? You killed my tree, you know. Dat tree was *liked*.

MONIQUE: No, unh-uh, Bush, or whatever your dirty name is you call yourself, no, anh-uh, we're not going to the police station this time.

Monique is a cute redhead in her thirties. She has a pinched little Midwestern voice, a voice ideal for television-commercial voiceovers.

BUSHIE: You sound just like da Westies dat killed my fadda, Whoah-oh, da neighbah-hood finally got tuh yuh. It's a shame but it had tuh happen. Bye, condo-asses!

ever

Bushie pounds off down deserted Tenth Avenue, but the two men chase and capture her.

TED: Nate, help me grab 'er!

BUSHIE: AAAAAAHHHHH! Police! Police!

NATE: The police aren't around tonight, B-Bushie.

Nate brushes his lustrous hair back from his forehead, tries to harden his sensual mouth into a grimmer line like Ted's.

TED: Got her?

NATE: Yep.

BUSHIE: TERRY! TERRY! SOMEBODY GET MY PIMP, TERRY, HE'S SPOSETA PROTEC' ME!

They drag her and shove her into the van, facedown.

TED: Get in. Push her down, tie her hands. Get her, get her down. She's violent.

NATE: Now, listen, lady—

MONIQUE: She's *not* a lady! That's the last thing this scum is!

TED: 'Kay, let's keep calm, Monique. Nate, can you calm your wife down?

BUSHIE: Where you takin' me?

TED: To the river where all the other trash goes. We're here. Step down, step out.

Ted pulls her out. They are by the docks, by the Circle Line tour cruise ships.

BUSHIE: Pervert-ass. You like dis! You like tuh tie women up, I seen dat look in da eyes before.

She kicks Ted in the balls.

TED: That bitch!

BUSHIE: Come on, come on, come on.

She dances around like a boxer, though she is drooling blood and her hands are tied behind her back.

BUSHIE: Hit me back, I could take it! Come on, people, you done it now, you Westies now, you wanta fight Bushie? You got it, Wonderbreads.

Ted kicks her in the stomach. She doubles over.

BUSHIE: Oooo, what college you learn dat in, condo-ass?

NATE: We're just here to teach her a lesson, Ted.

what

Nate smoothes back his big hair, as if doing this will help him think more clearly. He massages Ted's shoulders like a coach.

TED: I know that, goddamnit, but she's got to understand she is destroying my life. You just don't know who you're dealing with. Do you know who I work for, babe? You know who I am? Junior Vice President, Axnell Corporation. Ring any bells in that dingy head of yours? And you are disturbing my sleep. You are keeping me up. I cannot concentrate at work. I call in sick because of you.

BUSHIE: Poor yuppo condo-asses.

MONIQUE: Listen, you filthy-mouthed cunt!

BUSHIE: Whoo-oooh!

MONIQUE: I've had about enough of your class warfare bullshit, okay?

NATE: Monique, that's an intellectual concept she doesn't understand—

MONIQUE: I'm going to make her understand. I grew up on a farm in Minnesota, okay?

BUSHIE: Go back tuh Minne*so*-da.

MONIQUE: No, I am not going to go back to Minne*sota*! I grew up working hard and learning self-respect. I am not some rich condo owner. I struggled in this town for fifteen years trying to make it in musical theater and I never lost my self-respect. I worked as a waitress, okay? Not as a filthy low-life cunt whore.

NATE: Monique, calm down.

Nate massages his wife's shoulders. She shakes him off.

BUSHIE: Yeah, Monique, calm down.

MONIQUE: I worked for fifteen years, okay? And now I have finally made it in show business, which believe me, baby, is a lot harder than taking rides with men in cars.

BUSHIE: Oh yeah? Try twenty blow jobs a day for twenty years, den call me.

MONIQUE: Can you believe her? Can you believe her filthy talk? How 'bout a slap in the face, honey? How 'bout that?

She slaps Bushie with a triumphant gleam in her eyes. Bushie looks up at her, blinking but not crying.

BUSHIE: You do dat pretty good wit' my hands tied behind my back.

ever

NATE: Monique, we're just teaching her a lesson.

He strokes Monique's hair; she moves away from him.

MONIQUE: I am teaching her the only way she can learn. Listen, I worked my way up from the bottom, and now I have five national commercials, okay? Hertz, Visa Card, MCI, Kelloggs' Toasted Mini-Wheats, and U.S. Healthcare! OKAY? I earned that money, do you mind, and I bought myself a condo for me and my unemployed-actor-husband, Nate, and my two twin toddlers to live in and I wanted it to be nice. And you make it *NOT NICE*!

Monique is overwhelmed on these last two words and claws Bushie's face twice.

BUSHIE: Fuck. YOU.

Bushie spits in Monique's face. Nate stands stock still. An ugly look transforms his soap-opera-star-handsome features.

NATE: Hey, nobody spits on my wife! Nobody!

Nate swings with all his might, knocking Bushie to the ground. Monique is shrieking and crying.

MONIQUE: Wash her mouth out with soap, wash her mouth out with soap!

NATE: That's it, no more Mr. Nice Guy, you did it to me, you spit on my wife,

Nate repeatedly stomps Bushie in the ribs with his Timberland boots.

NATE: filthy bitch whore crackhead vermin, you vermin, you filthy crackhead vermin! You're sub-human, sub-human *sub*-human! *sub*-human!

There is a soft, airy, crackling sound under his heel. They all stand perfectly still and silent for a solid three seconds. Nate still stands on Bushie's rib cage.

TED: Hey! Hey! Come on! Get off her, guy, get off.

His voice is quiet as he gently pulls Nate away. He looks around. It is getting light out.

TED: Hey hey hey hey! That's enough! Come on, let's go! Nate, Monique! Please do me a goddamn favor and hop in the van!

MONIQUE: Oh my God, did we kill her? Did we kill her?

Ted and Monique are back in the van. Nate stands staring.

TED: I don't think so. Come on.

Nate turns dreamily and looks at Ted and Monique in the van.

what

MONIQUE: Get the rope. It's our recycling twine!

Nate runs and unties Bushie's arms; her body flops limply as he rolls her away.

NATE: I hope we taught you a lesson, Bushie!

His voice is frightened.

TED: COME ON!

Nate jumps in and they screech off. Bushie turns her head to the river. Her mashed lips can barely move.

BUSHIE: Hey, Mistah Hudson. Got a seat wit' a view?

She tries to crawl toward the river but collapses.

BUSHIE: Is dis it?

She tries and fails again.

BUSHIE: Is dis it? Gotta get down by da water.

She musters all her strength and crawls and rolls herself and falls to a cement ledge overhanging the Hudson River.

BUSHIE: Dere we go. Let me touch you, Mistah Hudson.

She dangles her arm over the side and her fingertips touch the water. The sun is rising in the east, behind her.

BUSHIE: At least I got you beside me, Rivah. Dat's bettah dan any people I know except Magenta Rush. Tell Mag, Magdalena Rigobar, dat Mollie Bright loved huh for huhr whole entire life. You know how you tell huh? Just spell it out in da smokestacks over on da Jersey Side. Bushie loves Mag.

She spells with her finger on the Jersey horizon.

BUSHIE: She'll see it. Bushie, you fuckin' stupid-ass.

She laughs and spools of dark blood rush down her chin.

BUSHIE: I thought you could take any beatin' *dey* could give, an' here I am, dawn broke ovah my head like a empty-ass bot'l an' I din't even get high fuh da last time. I feel high, dough, dat las' kick knocked me out somewhere wacked, not like crack, mo' like smack, only bettah. Okay. Dat's okay. I could accept dat. I could live wit' daaaaa—

Bushie's mouth and eyes open wide with amazement, as if she sees some large cosmic breast, finally come to suckle her. A long sigh rattles through her body. She is dead.

ever

PART EIGHT

RAVE ON

CHAPTER 1

IN WHICH POLLY DEMONSTRATES THE WONDERS OF TUPPERWARE

Polly and Reuben stand side by side on the lawn in front of Polly's house on a blazing summer day. A wave of glimmery heat rises from the perfectly cut grass. Cicadas sing. Polly has arranged white picnic furniture under the leaves of the magnolia. A car comes down the driveway.

POLLY: Oh Reuben, I'm nervous.

REUBEN: Don't be, Polly. You doin' great. You look fit to eat.

POLLY: Do I? You look dee-*vine* yourself, Blackberry Pie.

REUBEN: Hush, here they come.

POLLY: Yoo-hoo, Beverly, Beverly, hello, hello.

Polly can't stop smiling out of nervousness. Beverly and her great-grandmother get out of the car. Beverly is in her fifties. No one knows how old her great-grandmother is, but they know she is more than ninety. Four little children scramble from the backseat.

BEVERLY: Hello, ma'am.

POLLY: Oh! Don't call me that. Call me Polly, you're not workin' to-day, I'm the Tupperway-re hostess, *I* have to do all the slavin'! Ain't that right, Granny Louard? Is this your little ole granny?

MRS. LOUARD: Yes it is, Polly Ann. Much obliged.

POLLY: Oh, now, *I'm* much obliged. Look at all these little gran'kee-ids. Aren't they the cutest?

MRS. LOUARD: These my great-great-great-grandkids. They-uh Bev'-ley's gran' kee-ids.

POLLY: Oh, I know. Hello hello!

Polly crouches down and greets the little ones.

POLLY: Y'all lak banana puddin' with Nabisco wafers on top?

GRANDKID: Yeeh.

LITTLE TINY GIRL: Yee-ah! *(Squealing)*

Polly straightens up, pointing toward the special two-foot-high buffet she's set up for the children.

POLLY: Hee-hee! Wey-ell, I know you lak it 'cause your own granny Beverly made it last night for the party. Run over they-ere! There's plastic spoons! Aren't they the cutest?

She turns to Beverly's great-grandmother.

POLLY: Mrs. Louard, you know Mr. Clay?

MRS. LOUARD: Hello, Reuben Scott.

REUBEN: Della, I sure am glad you came.

MRS. LOUARD: You kiddin' me?! I wouldn't miss the firs' nonracialist Tuppaway-uh party in Loudon and Fairfax Counties f'anythin' in the *world*. You *know* I was the first Negro woman in this county to vote. Yes, I was. Ain't that the truth, Bev'ly?

BEVERLY: That's the truth an' she ain't *never* goin' let anyone f'get it. Polly Ann, these are my uncles. They down visiting from up *Noh*-ath, from *New* York. This here's Freddy's daddy's brother on the *Tines* side of the family, this here is Sammy Tines.

Three beautifully turned-out old men, men who were young and handsome in the 1940s and still look good, present themselves to Polly.

SAMMY: How do you do?

Sammy has a fine, debonair, cigarettes-and-whiskey-soaked voice.

POLLY: We'come!

BEVERLY: And this here is Norbert Shields an' Oliver Gaites. If they-uh names sound *famil*iar to you, that's cause they're mu*si*cians. They made quite a name for themselves in jazz.

SAMMY: Oh, they-uh she goes, braggin' on us again.

NORBERT: I know it.

OLIVER: She can brag on *me* all she likes.

POLLY: Wey-ell, what a real honest-to-goodness *ho*nor it is to have you on my li'l ole front *lawn*. We're havin' the party right here on the front lawn for all of Middleburg to see. Hee-hee! Now, you're *all* Beverly's uncles?

SAMMY: Oh, no, rully. *I'm* her uncle, I jest known these other two gentlemen for such an extended period of time that little Beverly cain't tell us one from th'other so she jest refers t'us in a *package* as her uncles.

what

MRS. LOUARD: Oh now, Sammy, don't go teasin' that gal.

POLLY: I am so honored. Now, what instruments do you favor?

Reuben interrupts hurriedly and shakes hands with each of the distinguished gentleman.

REUBEN: Reuben Scott Clay, it's a pleasure. Now, let me see, if I recall correct, bass,

He shakes hands with Sammy.

REUBEN: drums,

He shakes hands with Oliver.

REUBEN: an', uh, an' uh - uh—

He snaps his fingers, trying to remember what Norbert plays. Norbert draws himself up to his full, portly six-foot-two, and states breathlessly but with booming resonance:

NORBERT: Alto sax and clayehnet.

REUBEN: Tha's right. I sure have heard so much about you an' we're so glad you could come by.

POLLY: Oh! Yes! We're just so-so—honored! Reuben, could you just fix them up over there in the shade, I see some folks comin', those folks I invited from the Arcola Trailer Park are here.

She lowers her voice.

POLLY: Finally. I was gettin' afraid no white folks were gonna show.

Reuben whispers back.

REUBEN: They-uh's no quota, Polly Ann.

POLLY: I know!

She waves toward the new arrivals.

POLLY: Hi!

Reuben shields his eyes from the glare and squints down the driveway.

REUBEN: Jes' what are they drivin'?

POLLY: A car, Reuben, angel, a car.

REUBEN: Ye-ah, it looks lak it *was* a car at one time.

POLLY: Oh, Paul, really.

Reuben gives her a sharp look.

POLLY: Whoops! I made a booby! Wah oh wah, Blackberry Pie?

REUBEN: Go on.

He turns to their guests.

REUBEN: Sammy, Norbert, Oliver, Della, whyn't you come over here let me fix you up, set here in the shade.

ever

POLLY: Hello, hello! So glad you could make it. Cammie, right?

CAMMIE: Wey-ell, we shore wouldn't miss a invite here for anythang in the world, Mrs. Folsom.

> Cammie is a weary-looking blonde woman in her forties. A lanky, sinewed, and dark-tanned man in a fresh shirt and blue jeans comes around the side of the ancient station wagon. Kids pile out pell-mell and scatter the lawn.

POLLY: Polly, call me Polly the Parrot, hee hee!

CAMMIE: This here is my husband, Jay.

JAY: Hah.

> They shake hands. Cammie looks over Polly's shoulder. Her voice cracks as she screams.

CAMMIE: Shelly! Cassidy! Don't go tearin' up this lady's fla'wers or I'll smack the livin' shit out you!

> She turns to Polly.

CAMMIE: Sorry. Those're my babies, these're the big ones, Cody and Chrissie. Chris, go get them out the fla'wer bed.

CHRISSIE: Tuhh. Do ah have to?

JAY: Y'heard what yer moms said, git 'em!

CHRISSIE: Whaaat. Ay-ver.

> The teen girl slouches off toward her younger siblings.

POLLY: Hee hee!

> Polly's eyes have gone all shiny.

POLLY: Polly wont a cracker, hee-hee!

> She snaps out of it.

POLLY: No, I'm just jokin'. I'm so glad you came. 'Fore you got here, it was all black folks. Hee hee, now come on over here an' say hello.

> She leads them to the picnic chairs.

POLLY: Yoo hoo, these are the Laffertys from over the trailer park in Arcola? We just met last week, me an' Cammie, at that Better Bean Boutique, the new coffee bar they have top of the mall?

MRS. LOUARD: Now they have the bes' coffee!

CAMMIE: Don't they? Jay has to tear me out of they-ere. He says I'm a coffaholic. I drink four five cups at one time.

SAMMY: Ah, rully, you best watch that.

> Sammy sits smoking a slender brown cigarette. He flicks the long ash on a paper plate and speaks carefully.

what

SAMMY: Lest you awaken one fine day, and find you're an addict and they-uh rully isn't *all* that much you kin do about it.

NORBERT: Now, *what* is he sayin'?

OLIVER: I'm *cert*ain I have no idea in *parti*culah *what* he's talking about.

Oliver has a voice as urbane as they come, and smooth as melted butter.

POLLY: Wah dudn't everyone just sit down. Take a plate, I fixed some extra food other than the food I'm goin' to use to demonstrate the wonder of Tupperway-re.

BEVERLY: Mmm hmm.

REUBEN: She love Tupperware. She do. I've never seen anything lak it.

Beverly looks over toward the children.

BEVERLY: Mnn-mm. Chi'dren, *stop* that wildness now.

JAY: Goddamn, if I have to fuckin' come over there an' whup you?

CAMMIE: Jay! Shh.

JAY: Huh? Oh, 'scuse *me*, 'scuse me.

He looks around at the assembled company.

JAY: We shore are glad to be here.

POLLY: Wey-ell, I'm jest so grateful you could make it.

CAMMIE: We love your hay-ouse? We been drivin' by it for *yeee*ars an' I always say to Jay, I wonder what that house looks like on the inside.

POLLY: Wey-ell, I'll have to give you a li'l ole tour later on, won't I? Hmm, Blackberry—oh, Reuben, d'you think I should start?

They speak quietly while the others get acquainted

REUBEN: I think everyone who's *go*in' to show *has* shown.

POLLY: Do you? What about your daughter and, and, you know, I invited Bunny Peters.

REUBEN: I don't think they-uh comin'.

POLLY: Oh wey-ell. Hmm.

Polly looks sad. She clears her throat and addresses the gathering.

POLLY: Wey-ell, can I, can I have everyone's attention, please? Thank you, kindly. Em, hmm, I'm nervous, uh . . .

REUBEN: Y'alright.

She gives him a trembly, appreciative smile and soldiers on.

POLLY: I wrote myself a little speech, that's what the Tupperway-re Company advises you to— wey-ell, um, I guess I'll just read it.

She produces a crumpled piece of paper and glances at it as she speaks.

POLLY: Ahem. Welcome to the First Interracialist Tupperway-re Party in Loudon and Fairfax Counties in the State of Virginia.

MRS. LOUARD: *Yeah*, yes *sir*! It's about TIME!

POLLY: Hee hee! Thank you, Mrs. Louard. Ahem. In all my years as a citizen of this community, I never questioned the invisible lines of prejudice which separate us all.

She presses her lips together to keep herself under control. Her voice gets very high as she tries to fight back her emotion.

POLLY: Havin' been reared in southern Georgia, I just naturally assumed that things were the way they were and would go on bein' that way. It wa'n't until quite recently—

The paper shakes in Polly's hand.

POLLY: It wa'n't until quite recently—

SAMMY: Ahem.

POLLY: that my family life was disturbed and my world—ahem— was turned upside down—

She smiles at Reuben.

POLLY: —for the better! Now, I'd lak to share. Ohh heeee.

She dabs at tears.

SAMMY: Can I, Can I-er-uh, er-uh. I'd lak to innerject, er-uh, with a story of my own. I, uh, I, uh wasn't *su*re it was, er-uh, ap*pro*priate at first, but, uh, I think *no*w might be the time to share it.

Sammy speaks slowly and resolutely. With the same degree of care with which he speaks, he puts his cigarette out on the sole of his shoe, places the stub on a paper plate, produces a cigarette from a silver case in his breast pocket and leans forward to receive a light from Norbert.

SAMMY: Thank you, Norbert.

He inhales deeply, leans back and continues.

SAMMY: Er-uh, as my niece Beverly's informed you, I've had the privilege of bein' a jazz musician for these past. Several decades. Er-uh, and due to the universiality of jazz music, er-uh, I was afforded the opportunity of mixing with people of various statures and dif-

what

ferent races long before *this* point. In. Racial history. Oh, rully, rully. Now, er-uh, when I was a much younger man, in the 1950s, I had the misfortune of befriending a young, er-uh Caucasian woman by the name of Violet.

Norbert and Oliver make appreciative recognition noises.

SAMMY: Now we spoke the common language of jazz. This young lady, Violet, was what we term a jazz connossieur, she was more than jes' a fan.

NORBERT: Oh yes! She had a, uh, pronounced musicality.

OLIVER: Yes she did. She had what we in the jazz profession commonly refer to as a *perf*ectly *tune*d *ear*.

SAMMY: That's correct. In fact, I don't think either of these gentlemen would find it un*to*-ward of me to state that she most likely could have been an accomplished musician in her own right. Matteh of fact, at one time, I gifted her with a trumpet. I myself favor the bass, but I perceived she might distinguish herself on the horn. Well, you can tell by how I go on, I felt very strongly for this woman. As a matteh of fact, I was in love with her. But in 1958, they-uh wasn't *all* that much a married white lady and a young Negro could do. 'Cept say good-bye an' turn our back on it. Which we did. An' that *cost* me somethin'.

So, er-uh, I bring this up only to say—let's be out in the open here, Reuben, Polly.

He looks each of them solemnly in the eye.

SAMMY: I sup*port* what you doin'. It may be difficult, but if you *care* for one another, then you *doin'* the *right thing*.

Everyone is quiet.

POLLY: Thank you.

REUBEN: I appreciate that.

JAY: Here here! I'm so damn sick uh this racialist shit I could kick some ass, you know? I seen turrible things, stories I could tell'd turn yer stomach, I 'member once down th' back of a bar in Bluemont—

CAMMIE: Jay!

JAY: Sorry.

Jay looks around at everyone, chastised. Then he speaks without shame.

JAY: Just sayin' I agree is all.

ever

POLLY: Wey-ell?

There is silence.

POLLY: Now that we all had our heart-to-heart, how 'bout that Tupperway-re demonstration?

OTHERS: Yeah! Oh yeah!

POLLY: Ready, Reuben? He's got the microwave all wired up so we can wheel it out here on the lawn. Ready?

REUBEN: Oh yeah.

Reuben wheels the microwave out onto the lawn.

POLLY: Okay. Hee hee. This is an extra large, hermetically sealed, Tupperway-re casserole. Inside, I have a brussels sprouts casserole that I prepared late last year an' froze. Feel how hard it is.

She raps it with her knuckles.

POLLY: Knock knock, hee hee! Hard as a nut. Now we just pop it in the microwave and one two three four five—

REUBEN: Ain't that Bunny Peters comin' up the driveway?

Polly turns from the microwave and looks.

POLLY: She came! That ole fat gal changed her mind!

The microwave buzzes. Polly turns back and pops open the door.

POLLY: Ooohh. Here's the brussels sprouts casserole, it's just so fast these microwaves, presto pop it open, now look at that. Lak I just cooked it yesterday!

She holds the steaming casserole under the noses of her guests.

CAMMIE: Amazing.

JAY: That ain't just amazin', it's a fuckin' miracle!

POLLY: Hmm?

CAMMIE: Jay!

Cammie swats her husband.

CAMMIE: Jay said it's a miracle.

Bunny Peters bustles up the walkway toward Polly.

BUNNY: Yoo hoo, Polly Parrot, I'm here. Hope it's not too late. There was a li'l crisis at the Rabbit Lodge, held me up. Hope it's not too late?

POLLY: No no, Bunny, you're not. It's never . . . it's never too late.

Polly stands with her arms open, her eyes shining, ready to receive her friend.

what

CHAPTER 2

IN WHICH BUSHIE'S FRIENDS
MEET BY THE RIVER

On an overcast afternoon by the Hudson River, a gang of whores, two pimps, and other street people convene around the body of Bushie. She is covered in a pale green sheet and a bouquet of plastic blue flowers and surrounded by cheap religious candles in tall jars that can be bought in every corner store in every poor neighborhood in New York City. The religion is Caribbean Santeria, a reconciliation of the Catholic saints and the goddesses and gods of the African Yoruba religion. Colorful depictions of these mixed deities are pasted around the candles. Many of the whores cry quietly. Pam, a light-skinned black whore, who has been around and around the block, tries to make sure everyone gets his turn to speak.

PAM: Is Snapple's turn.
ROSIE: Go, Snapple.
Rosie has not been able to stop crying for one second.
TERRY: GO!
Terry pushes Snapple and she stumbles to the place in front of Bushie.
SNAPPLE: I'd like tuh say dat if she hadda die, Bushie woulda been glad it was hiah by da rivah, 'cause Bushie loved it hiah. She liked tuh get high an' bug out oveh hiah so on da positive side, I just wanna say dat dis was one of huh favorite places. She liked it down by da tracks too, so if she hadda die it coulda been down onna tracks, maybe run ovah by a train, but beat tuh deaf by da rivah is bettah 'cause we got huh body, I guess. And she would be glad too dat we had a wake fuh huh like dis wit' *no* cops, an' no EMS, 'cause she hated cops and she hated hospitals.
TERRY: Hurry up, Snapple!
DE GENOVA: Let her speak, Terry. Damn. Have some respect.

TERRY: 'At's why youse can't control yuh girls, De Genova,

Terry burps and staggers backward.

TERRY: you a pussy.

PAM: *Ter*ry you are *drunk* at Bushie's *fun*eral.

TERRY: Dis ain't no funeral, it's a friggin' WAKE! Youse people don't know. Me an' huh was dee only Irish left.

SNAPPLE: Well, I'm Italian, could I friggin' tawk?

NUTZ: Go ahead, Snapple, f-f-f-f-f-finish what you sayin', finish wh-wh-wh-wh-at you were sayin'.

SNAPPLE: I just wanna say dat I'm'n'a miss Bushie, 'cause da first time, da first time I came out on Forty-fit', nobody wanted tuh say shit tuh me. All youse gave me da cold-shoulder treatment, you wuh like, "Who da fuck is she?" You were, you were. An' I was outta Queens an' I didn't know from nuttin', aright, I'm a'mittin' it! Den Bushie goes, "I'm goin' tuh da store, who wants sometin'" an' she asks everyone down da line, Pam, Nutz, Rosie, and den she goes "You, Angela," 'cause I didn't even have a name yet, she goes, "You want sometin'," just like nuttin', an' I go, "Yiah, a Snapple Ice Tea," 'cause I had tuh say sometin', and she goes, "Okay Snapple," an' afta dat, from dat time on, I was Snapple. She gave me my name! I was Snapple an' everybody treated me normal. But Bushie din't hafta do dat. She din't, dat's all I hafta say.

PAM: Rosie, you go.

Rosie steps forward to speak but is overcome by tears. She steps back.

ROSIE: No, I can't, I can't, I can't.

Terry staggers forward.

TERRY: I got somethin' tuh say. I got tuh say dat I known Mollie from da schoolyahd at P.S. 51 eveh since she was dis high.

He holds his hand up to his waist.

TERRY: An' I been pimpin' huh since she was thirteen an' nobody but nobody could take huh big loud mouf but me. Nobody knows what shit I put up wit' from huh. She ruined my reputation on da West Side. She'd come in wacked outta huh brains an' she'd go Terry, you sonuvabitch Irish asshole, you drunk again, you weak-ass pimp. Ah fuck.

He falls to his knees beside Bushie's body.

TERRY: Mollie, Lit'l Mollie Bright, dat low-life slut, I can't, I can't be-

what

lieve dey beat huh tuh deaf. That woman could take anything, anything I seen huh get beat tree times in one night fuh moufin' off
and walk away laughin'. I told huhr, One day dat mouf will kill you
yet, Bushie! But I di'n't believe nuttin' would eveh kill huh. She's
like dis rivah: it's dirty, it stinks but it's all you got. You grew up
alongside it. She was all I got. I gave huhr a beatin' dat night but it
wasn't me. I neveh beat Mollie tuh kill huh, I knew *just* how much
she could take but somebody else *di'n't* know an' when I find da
bastards, so help, so help me, someone is goin' tuh PAY. BIG. Someone . . . someone I—

He kneels there drooling.

SNAPPLE: Frisco, you want tuh say sometin'?

Frisco, a dark-skinned black man, a street dweller, steps forward. He is
soft-spoken and pensive.

FRISCO: Yeh, Ah jes' want to say Bushie was not a good-lookin'
woman. Matter of fac', she was ugly—

PAM: Now what does *that* have to do with it?

Pam puts a hand to her hip and pulls back her head.

FRISCO: Let me finish—let me finish, Pam. But she was beautiful on
the inside, a'ight? She had a *bad* mouf an' didn't no one never raise
her to re*spec*' herself. But we *all* know she was alright, we *all* had
laughs with Bush, every las' one of us. Is they-uh anyone here
cain't say Bushie didn't make them laugh at one time oh anutha? Is
there?

He looks around at everyone gathered. No one speaks. He looks down
at his feet and steps back.

FRISCO: Tha's all I have to say.

SNAPPLE: Hiah comes da cake man. He looks like he wants tuh say
sometin'. Hey Jippy.

A wild-eyed unshaven old man in a gray suit jacket and sweatpants
joins them. He manages to be intelligible, though he has no teeth.

JIPPY: Dey gimme da cake, dey gimme da cake, was a whole-a bigga
cake, dee Italian, he gimme da cake, da restaurant says "Hee-ah,
you wanna some to eat?" "Wait." I says, I wait, I wait an' he give-a
to me da cake was a bigga cake, was a huge-a cake dey gimme, dey
gimme da cake—

SNAPPLE: Oh friggin' shut up, Jippy. We been hearin' dat cake story

ever

TREE-TOUSAND TIMES! He don't even know she's dead! He's not even mentally a*way*-eh!

FRISCO: Come on, my man, come ovah here come ovah this way.

He sits Jippy down on a crumbling hunk of cement.

FRISCO: You got to tell us later Jippy, later.

JIPPY: Dey gimme da cake.

FRISCO: Tell us 'bout the cake *later*, Jippy, people upset now.

SNAPPLE: Oh!

JIPPY: Da cake!

FRISCO: Bushie dead, tell us 'bout the cake later.

Frisco pats the old fellow on the back until he splutters into silence. Snapple and Rosie cry. A truck on the West Side Highway sounds its horn. The wind blows. The Circle Line cruise repeats its announcement: "Welcome to Circle Line cruise, ding-dong. Welcome to Circle Line Cruises, ding-dong . . ." The traffic on the West Side Highway swooshes by.

SNAPPLE: Anyone else wanna say sometin'? Rosie?

ROSIE: I can't, I can't.

SNAPPLE: Come on, you an' Bushie was tight.

Rosie shakes her head mutely.

PAM: Leave her be, Snapple. Jes' *leave her be*.

There is silence. They listen to the river lap the rotten pier.

SNAPPLE: Well, I guess dat's it. Should we trow huhr inna rivah or should I call da EMS?

A taxi screeches up. Inside Snapple sees a Puerto Rican woman with tons of makeup on.

SNAPPLE: Who da fuck is dis? Lisa Lisa?

Magenta speaks rapid-fire to the cabdriver as she slams out of the cab.

MAGENTA: Lemme-off-hee-ah. Thank-you-very-much.-Keep da change.

PAM: Damn. Is Magenta Rush.

MAGENTA: Am I too late—is this Bushie's wake?

Pam looks her up and down.

PAM: *Yee*-ah.

Rosie sniffles and looks at Pam.

ROSIE: Yeah!

Snapple looks at Pam, then Rosie, then looks Mag up and down.

SNAPPLE: Yup!

what

TERRY: Mag, ya bitch!

Terry staggers toward her.

TERRY: What you doin' back here, ain't you married and born again wit' a coupla mutts?

MAGENTA: Hi, Terry. I was, but I left my husban' because he was violent an' I decided I don't take dat no more. Is da' Bushie?

TERRY: Yeh, dat's Bushie, you never gave a fuck fuh huh when she was alive and now you come when it's too late.

MAGENTA: You drunk, Terry, like you always was. Could someone please tell me is dis a funeral or a wake?

SNAPPLE: It's a wake 'cause she's Irish, ya know, she was from Irish people—

MAGENTA: Well, if dis is a wake, den we gonna dance wit' huh, get dat sheet off huh.

Magenta tears away the sheet that covers Bushie's corpse. Terry tackles her. She flings him away.

TERRY: What da fuck are you doin'?

MAGENTA: Get off me Terry, you Irish! Whyn't you tell dese people what Irish do when somone dies? My husband wouldn't let me do Santeria for my own *abuela* when she passed and I cannot forgive myself for dishonorin' her da' way. But we gonna do huh right. She's Irish people. When huh grandmutha died, dey danced wit' huh. Daz what old-time Irish people do—they dance with they dead. An' I don't cay-uh if I'M A PUERTO RICAN! I'm IRISH today and we gonna make a *hoolie* wit' Mollie Pamela Bright. Come on, Bushie, dance wit' me, homegirl, one las' time.

Coughing from the stench and weeping, Magenta pulls Bushie's body from the ground, wraps her arms around her chest, and begins to do a little merengue step.

MAGENTA: Remembah our song? "Jump on da Jam Slide, do da do da fun-ky glide. Jump on da Jam Slide, do da do da fun-ky glide."

As she turns and and slides back, turns and slides back, she loses her grip on the corpse and it crashes to the cement, disintegrating. A cart full of recyclables crashes into them. Beer and soda cans spill everywhere. From the pile of old cans Bushie rises, vomiting up fountains of blue water. Her blue eyes bug from her skull, as she recognizes her friend.

ever

BUSHIE: Magda*lena* Ri*go*bar!

Bushie backs up.

MAGENTA: Jesus! *¡Dios Mío!*

Magenta backs away from the apparition. Bushie vomits more. Now she straightens up and screams at the top of her lungs:

BUSHIE: BUSHIE'S BACK, PEOPLE! BUSHIE'S BAAAAACK!

SNAPPLE: Bushie, you been dead fuhr a muthafuckin' week!

BUSHIE: I wasn't dead, people! I was sleepin' wit' da fishes. An' dese weren't no cute-ass goldfishes neithah. Dese were big *hairy*-ass Hudson Rivah fishes like Chalie da Tuna or some shit, I dunno.

FRISCO: Shit!

BUSHIE: I was sleepin' an' chillin' wit' da fishes and dey go, "Get outta here, Bushie, you gotta go back tuh Hell's Kitchen! People need you!" I go, me? I'm nuttin' but a loudmouth crackhead whore, a pain in everybody's ass, dat's how I got beat tuh deaf. Dey go, "Dat's why dey need you, Mollie, tuh tell dem what's FUCKED UP ABOUT EVERYTHING." I go, "Why da fuck should I, what's dere fuh me?" Dey go, "Yuh true love, Magenta Rush." I go, "Listen, you faggot-ass fishes, I ain't no homo." Dey go, "Yes, you IS, Bushie! YOU DA *BIGGEST DYKE DAT EVAH LIVED,* SO *GET* USETA IT! DIS IS DA *NINE*TIES!!!! NOW *GET* DA HELL OUUTA HERE!" And den I trew up, an' here I am!

FRISCO: It's a fuckin' miracle!

BUSHIE: I swear tuh God, so help me. I slept wit' da fishes.

TERRY: Quit tawkin' shit, Bushie!

BUSHIE: Terry, you weak-ass pimp—

MAGENTA: BUSHIE! I love you.

Bushie gives all of her attention back to Magenta. A smile spreads across her ravaged face.

BUSHIE: Magenta *Rush*!

MAGENTA: Dance wit' me, Bushie: "Jump on da Jam Slide do da do da funky glide . . ."

BUSHIE: "Jump on da Jam Slide do da do da funky glide, Jump on da Jam Slide do da do da funky glide . . ."

They dance.

what

CHAPTER 3

IN WHICH ALL ENDS WELL
IN SEATTLE

Tim is still drinking at the bar. He shouts out as he sees a big bearded guy in a tie-dyed windbreaker boogie through the doors.

TIM: Scoops, James Scoop Shannon da Third, you funky sunuva-bitch! I been waitin' fer you ferever! I thought you'd never show, dude. I been—

SCOOPS: Not so loud, Timmie baby. How you doin' cat? Somethin' held me up awhile, cat, sorry I'm late.

TIM: LATE? LATE!? I been waitin' fer you here at dee Acres uh Clams Tavern fer three weeks. Ain't dat right, Bingo? SCOOPS MAN, I'm so glad tuh see ya, Seattle ain't da same widout you, brother.

SCOOPS: Shh man, keep it down, brother, keep it down, not so loud. Yur fergettin' what business I'm in.

He hooks a thumb and pulls the skin down under his right eye, to indicate covert activity.

TIM: Ferget? Of course I am, buddy, I fergot everything. Drank m' whole unemployment check. Didn't I, Bingo?

BINGO: Yep, and then he run up a tab, said you'd take care of it. What'll it be?

SCOOPS: Huh? Hmm? Oh gimme a glass uh latte. I'm here on serious crap. I can't mess around wid dee alcohol trip right now.

TIM: Jimmy, I'm drunk. I can't believe it's you, man. You said you had a little side job fer me. 'Nuther souza, Bingo, an uh Olympia.

SCOOPS: No way, no way. Give him a tankard of java, okay? And this oughta cover da tab and den some, okay?

Scoops hooks a thumb and pulls the skin down under his right eye, to indicate covert activities and the necessity to prevent their exposure. He slides a large bill toward Bingo.

SCOOPS: You didn't see me. I wasn't here. Okay?

BINGO: What. Ever.

SCOOPS: Drink dat java, man, sober you up, den I'm'a tell you da mission, dig?

TIM: I dig it, I dig, I dig. Man, am I fucked up. I must be da most fucked-up person in Seattle right now. I mean, kin you imagine anyone more fucked up than me?

Clove hangs from the Seattle Space Needle. It is a foggy day.

CLOVE: Oh Godddddddddddessssssss, what am I doing here all hectic athwart a space needle? How did I allow those brussels sprouts to deludate me again? Blow winds blow, caw gulls caw. Please goddddddddessses if you regurgitate me from this melee, I vow I'll do something different with my life. I'll be all banal and lambish and I'll stop terrorizing my rancid hippie parents. I'll even be all beneficial to my little brother Kyler, just send me a sign oh jolly green goddesses of the brussels sprouts. Let me know what led me here. Let me liquidate my fear. If thur's a tear in the sky that you want me to sew back together er somethin' whul I'm up here, then just be all ferocious an' deitistic an' go, "CLOVE, SEW BACK THE TORN SEATTLE SKY SHORN OF REASONS WHY" er . . . words to that effect. Wait? Did I say that er was that you jolly green goddess of the brussels sprouts? AHHHH, it's too complex! I'm confabulating myself to excess. Ulright, I'm becalmed. I'll just wax all courageous and wait. I know the sprouts would not have led me here if Cobain the Friendly Ghost was not near. By. I'll pray. Blow winds blow, caw gulls caw, grow sprouts grow!

A big crowd mills around the base of the Space Needle. Dawn and Harper are standing by.

DAWN: Greetings, minions of the remote control, you're watching PO-E-Z-TV. I'm your ego-goddess Dawn Malestrella and we're back with *Suicide Watch*—

HARPER: *Actual Deaths!*

what

DAWN: As you know, we are all hangin' by a thread here in the City o' Kurt where thirteen months after the celebrity suicide of the century we've got Clove Carnelian, psycho-teen from where, Harper?

HARPER: Santa Cruz, California, Dawnie baby.

DAWN: Rrrrright. Clove of Cruz is hangin' from the top of—and this is rad!—the Seattle Space Needle, a landmark left over from the days of futurism. Whoah, can you believe how retro and pomo it is? All-at-the-same-time, Harp?

HARPER: No, Dawnie baby, I can't. But maybe these two friends of Clove have a different POV an' like that. Wouldya exploit yerselves fer our viewers, dudes?

SABLE: I'm Sable Nugent.

SKEETER: And I'm Ezekial Christian Frye.

HARPER: And how do you know the soon-to-be-splattered Miss Clove?

SABLE: She is my best friend and fairest cohort.

HARPER: Dynamite. An' you, Zeke?

SKEETER: Skeet.

HARPER: What?

SKEETER: Er.

HARPER: What?

SKEETER: If yur gonna hazard truncacious editions o' my name, I'd prefer tuh be monikered Skeet.

HARPER: What?

SABLE: Er.

SKEETER: Thanks, Sabe, babe.

HARPER: Whoah, babe. So er you two like goin' out?

SABLE: Yah.

SKEETER: Yeh-up. Er most vehemently.

HARPER: That is excellent. And how do you know Clove, Skeet—
   Pause.

HARPER: —er?

SKEETER: Uh, I loathe tuh upheave that I slip on th' amorous side o' the slope fer her most fine person.

HARPER: WHAT, ER YOU SAYIN' YUR IN LOVE WITH HER?

SABLE: No, actually he's in love with me.

ever

SKEETER: Uh, in point of veracity I am stricken with love fer both.

DAWN: Rad, Harper, let me at 'em!

She pushes Harper out of the way.

DAWN: Sable, can you tell us is this a tired love triangle suicide and like that or is it the start of a long weekend here in the City o' Kurt, one that'll end one massive death binge later?

SABLE: If you would tax yer memory gland a tad, Dawn, you'd flash on the time you were last yappin' on my best friend and fairest cohort's ankles with yer hoaxish suicidal contingencies back at a particular rave in Santa Cruz. Remember, you were all, Wull this rave-site become a grave-site? Just spazzing on the fact that Clove'd accidentally walked into the ocean whulst conversing, albeit a tad excessively, with some crustaceans.

SKEETER: Tuhh. An' you may recollect additionally that she emerged most undead from that aquaneous tumult and was subsequentially salvaged in a field o' brussels sprouts, so rest yer houndish slobber glands, dudes, Clove won't be takin' any dives.

DAWN: And how do you know that?

SABLE: Because Clove doesn't want to die. She was pulled from the ocean by Cobain the Friendly Ghost and ever since then she is all haunted by him and she wants to terminate that haunting, not her own life, and plus which she has these fiendish ultra-visuals of brussels sprouts twining everywhur—

DAWN: Well, what hallucination will save her next?

SKEETER: I dunno. But I kin tell yuh it'll be a finer vision than yers. On that account, she's my goddess, *comprendo*?

SABLE: I can't believe you said that! I loathe you to excess, Skeeter Frye!

Sable runs away. Skeeter pursues her.

SKEETER: Sable, wait! Yur my ultra goddess, yur my deity deluxe, wait!

HARPER: Whoah, his hat just changed colors.

DAWN: What are these nauseous-making hats?

HARPER: Dunno, Dawnie uh—

He looks at Dawn. She looks a little green around the gills.

HARPER: Uh, we'll be right back after a poesy break with—

what

DAWN: —*Suicide Watch*—

HARPER: A-*Actual* Deaths!

Tim and Scoops are still at the Acres o' Clams Tavern.

TIM: So old Bruce Frye and you made peace since Bruce been in da slammer? Dat's far out. 'Cause you were good buddies from da git go.

SCOOPS: Yep. An' we got a special funky code we made up back when we were still little wharf brats. Dat's why I'm back home in Seattle. I got a mission from Bruce. He's da only one I'd risk it for: Fed's 're after me, dat's why I was late, cat.

Here's his postcard. Says, "Dear Buddy, Bought a chocolate bar. Watched dee *Exorcist* on TV. Wish I could be in dere in dose sunny mountains. Signed, Yer Good Buddy." And den on the back it's got a picture of dis girl. It says, "Heather Woodbury's *What Ever* (An American Odyssey in 8 Acts). One woman, one hundred characters." Hmm, Bruce corresponds wid all kinds of people. It's lonely in prison, y'know?

Scoops contemplates the advertisement for the obscure performance artist for a moment.

TIM: But get back to da postcard. What's it mean?

SCOOPS: Says I gotta find his ex-old lady Linda and give her da pot money old Bruce buried back in '83 for his son. Linda contacted him telepathically. She always was a wild funky chick. I was crazy about 'er. Dat's what split me an' Bruce's partnership. Naaaaah, don't look at me dat way. I wasn't on no lewd trip wid her. Never even *ball*ed the lady. I-I felt different about 'er, alright? An' Bruce, bless the M.F., he treated her scandalous—ballin' other chicks, knockin' 'em up even, runnin' off to South America. Dat's how he got himself busted by da Feds. I told 'im stick tuh da homegrown product. But anyways, now I'm here an' I gotta find old Lin and give her dat buried dough fer their son Ezekial.

TIM: So how's 'at secret code work?

SCOOPS: Hey, it wouldn't be secret if I told ya. All's I want you tuh do is go here.

ever

Scoops spreads out a map and points to a far corner on it.

TIM: Puget Sound?

SCOOPS: Dat's where my mackerel smack da *Margarita Mama* is moored. Wait in her for three days til I show up. Got it? I'll plunk ya out six months' worth uh carpenter wages. 'Sall you need tuh know.

TIM: Whoah, 'at must be a lotta bread ole Bruce hid from da—

SCOOPS: Shhh, be quiet. Dis cat comin' looks like FBI.

Paul walks in and takes a seat at the bar.

PAUL: Hi, bartender, uh, I'd like a Scotch, rocks, with a twist.

BINGO: Johnny Black?

PAUL: What. Ev-uh, I mean, yah, fine. Thanks.

He drinks down his Scotch.

PAUL: Hey. What's happening?

SCOOPS: Howdy.

TIM: How.

Tim glowers and raises his palm like a stereotype chief in a Western.

PAUL: Heh-heh. Nice weather for Seattle, huh?

TIM: Aah-euuooo! . . . yer not *from* dese parts, hanh?

PAUL: Uh, lived out east for forty years but, tuhh, I was reared in Wenatchee.

SCOOPS: Oh yeah? In-stater? Got cousins in Wenatchee. Lumber town.

PAUL: Yep. Always was.

SCOOPS: Terrible what dey did to it. Stripped all dee old forest.

PAUL: I heard. That. Didn't want to believe it.

SCOOPS: Oh you kin believe it, man, lumber companies messed up Wenatchee. Well, big companies, you know? No concern.

PAUL: Oh yeh-up. Shame. It's a— frankly, I've been a part of that. Chief executive officer of Axnell Corporation for twenty years.

SCOOPS: No shit? Dose oil spill guys?

PAUL: That's right.

SCOOPS: Wull, we all gotta do our thang, I guess. He's gotta do his *thang*. I gotta do my thang. Do your thang! Do your thang! Do your thang!

Scoops executes a little "Doin' Your Thang" prance.

PAUL: No, uh, it wasn't my *thing*, as you say. I just—uh—just went along. Wanted to see how far I could get. When I got there it was too late.

what

Paul drains his glass, sets it down hard on the bar.

PAUL: 'Nother Scotch.

SCOOPS: Wull, dere's still time.

PAUL: Yes. There is. I retired three years ago, uh, but I kept doing the conference circuit, stayed on the board. Huh, it's uh similar to being in the CIA. You can't get out once you're in.

TIM: Huh, dat's funny, 'cause when you walked in Scoops thought you were in da FBI—

SCOOPS: Shut UP, Timmer, man. Drink yer java!

Tim coughs.

TIM: Sorry.

PAUL: Huh. Well, I've known a number of operatives, but, uh, I'm not one. Always envied those fellas.

SCOOPS: Why?

PAUL: Because they were able to change identities. I'd give anything to be someone else. You see, I'm in love with this woman. And-she-I met her in New York when I was a big executive. Things just went haywire, uh, in a good way, but uhhhh, I've left my wife, I chased Jeanette out here—she's visiting her sister, Linda, and then they're going to Alaska—turns out, she's half Eskimo. You know, you fall in love with a person and then you find out who they really are and—then you suddenly want to know—who the hell am I?

SCOOPS: Wait. Jeanette Gladjnois and her little sis Linda Frye? I'm lookin' fer dem! You know where dey are?

PAUL: They're with that crowd by the Space Needle. I just had a spat with Jeanie and came here. She's so distrustful of me. I can't make up to her. Ah—I'm fallin' to pieces here.

SCOOPS: Pull yourself together, man. I got an idea. Listen, fer reasons of my own, I need tuh keep a low profile here in Seattle. I'd feel a whole lot more cool walkin' around in your establishment threads. Meanwhile, you could don my funky garb an' see if your old lady Jeanette took a shine to ya as a different type o' cat. I'll even give you my beard. Bingo, got scissors an' glue?

BINGO: Sure do.

SCOOPS: What do ya say, buddy? Wanna switch? Wanna be James Scoops?

PAUL: Why, hell, okay! And you can be Paul Folsom!

ever

SCOOPS: Far out! Bring on da scissors and glue! Bingo! Latte fer me, Java fer Tim and Scotch fer Paul! To our enterprise.

They raise their glasses and clink.

Sable stands under the Seattle Pier.

SABLE: Here I am, Skeeter. Here. Under the pier starin' at barnacles. I'm totally relieved you found me. I came here to vacate those Suicide Watchers. I'm not all vexated on you anymore. Come down here, jump.

He jumps down.

SABLE: Wh-wh-what happened to yer mood-hat?

JOB: I dropped it slippin' off a ship.

SABLE: Yur not Skeeter.

JOB: Nuh, m' name's Job.

SABLE: You mean Jobe?

JOB: My mom Debbie pronouncees it as in the Bauble but my friends call me Job as in: *git* one. An' you must be Sable.

SABLE: Tuhh, this is so rare, it's uncooked. Are you the ravin' dude Skeeter met on the train going through Texas and then you waxed all Jimmy Hoffa and disappeared and one of his mood-hats was stolen?

JOB: I just lifted it fer luck. Then I lost it.

SABLE: What are you doin' here?

JOB: I came here tuh seduce the spicy Clove.

SABLE: CLOVE? Tuhh. When did you encounter that friskish strumpet—aka my best friend and fairest cohort?

JOB: I never met 'er but Skeeter 'scribed her to me most graphic-like on the train west. How she was at th' rave the night he met 'er an' ever since then I got afflicted sore with th' notion of 'er.

SABLE: Tuhh, so yur in love with Clove too. This is agging me to excess. Why is everybody all obsessive on Clove? What's wrong with me, Sable?

JOB: But Skeeter talked more on you.

SABLE: Realistically? Tuhh. I love Clove too and I want her to be salvaged off the Space Needle an' like that, but then I'm going to PUSH HER IN THE PACIFIC because I desire Skeeter all exclusivistically

what

and now *you* come along and you virtually *dub* him looks-wise. I mean, I thought you *were* him in the shadow and then yur waxin' all Oh Clove, Clove—Rad! Wait, though, you do resemble Skeeter a tad fiendishly. And you scan his vernacular passing well. Do you most truthfully want my best friend and fairest cohort fer yer love interest?

JOB: Most assuredly.

SABLE: Do you vow to love her hotly and pursue her mightily whur-ever her fevered imagination may crash?

JOB: I do.

SABLE: Then tune yer ear, fair dude, if my Clove absconds the nee-dle point without a prick, then from my Skeeter her heart I'll teach you how to nick. Here, take my mood-hat. I'll get another. Now,

> She casts her eye about, then cups a hand over his ear.

SABLE: soak yer brains in this scheme . . .

> At the the other end of the pier, a much-used and yellowed copy of *The Complete Works of William Shakespeare* lies forlorn in the sand. Just now a fierce gust of wind whips through its fragile pages, and they scatter into dust. It is a fine, hardy dust, however, particularly the dust formed from the comedies, and it seems to marry itself to the very mist, to the very air—why, it seems that the very seagulls ingest it. It soon spreads everywhere. It is almost as if, on this particular day and night, little faeries have dusted the entire region of Seattle with these disintegrated writings.

> Back at the Space Needle, Paul, disguised in Scoop's beard and tie-dye regalia, is hawking mood-hats.

PAUL: Mood-hats for sale, mood-hats. Four different colors wich your four different moods. Mood-hats, miss?

JEANETTE: Excuse me, but where did you obtain those mood-hats from? My nephew Skeeter was selling those mood-hats.

> For no good reason Jeanette does not recognize Paul: she is breathing deeply of the damp ocean air.

PAUL: Oh really, miss? You look too young to have a nephew that old. But he's a good-looking kid, guess good looks run in the family. Matter of fact, he made a deal with me to sell them for him. He

ever

got tired of it. Guess he's worried about that girl up there on the needle.

JEANETTE: That's one of his little girlfriends. Clove. Me and my sister met her on the ferry. Skeeter's a good kid, except like all males he can't make up his mind which woman he loves.

PAUL: Well, maybe he'll change. Men mature with age.

JEANETTE: It takes a long time for men to mature. Then they *die*.

PAUL: Well, some men mature a few decades before that. Want a mood-hat on the house?

JEANETTE: I've got one in my purse. Here, I'll—

She puts on her mood-hat.

PAUL: Looks great. It's blushing coral. That means you're in a receptive mood.

JEANETTE: I've got to go. I see that TV crew has got my sis Linda. Bye, nice to meet you.

PAUL: See you again. Mood-hats for sale, mood-hats, four different colors wich your four different moods.

JEANETTE: What an intriguing man. Hmm. Linner, excuse me, this is my sister, excuse me.

She pushes her way through the crowd toward Linda and the PO-E-Z TV crew.

HARPER: So Linda, as a member of the aging generation, would you say Clove is a product of her X-y Age with no commitment to the future, ready tuh plunge from the sky as it darkens in eve, and spark what could be the biggest self-sacrificin' soiree since Jonestown?

LINDA: I think you are laying some very dark magic around this space.

JEANETTE: Needle.

LINDA: What?

JEANETTE: Needle, Linda. Space Needle.

LINDA: Right. Well, it's very dark magic you and what's-her-name, Dawn, are spreading around but I don't think my son Ezekial—

HARPER: You mean Skeeter. He pre*fers* tuh be *called Skeet*er.

LINDA: Right—I don't think *Eze*kial would be smitten by a little Jimina Jones, dig it? I met Clove and I think she's a little witch. Unpracticed, maybe, but I think she's on to some heavy magic and ultimately I think it's going to outweigh yours.

what

JEANETTE: Right on, sister.

Jeanette raises her fist in a power-to-the-people salute.

DAWN: Harper? Why are you talking to these tired thirty-somethings when we've got scads of clueless youths to interview? I've got Alissi here. Alissi, were you a big fan of Kurt Cobain?

ALLISI: Nuh, I rave, dude. I fergot it was all near th'anniversary of his suicide an' like that. I mean, I feel fer the dude 'n all but, I was never overly fixed on his music? I guess *In Utero* was a good album but . . . I like tuh rave?

DAWN: Then why did you come here?

ALLISI: I dunno? It's complex? Just a feelin' in th' air, yah? I heard thur was gonna be a rave? Everyone says thur's spose tuh be one but no one knows fer sure? Do *you* know?

DAWN: No, I don't. Next!

HARPER: Wait, Dawnie baby, one hot second. Uh, Allisi, why're you an' so many other of yer flummoxed co-generators wearin' those nauseous-makin' hats?

ALLISI: Tuhh, Harper, widen yer attention span. These're mood-hats, haven't you heard? They change color wich yer four different moods? Later.

DAWN: Later, Allisi. Hey, you're on *Suicide Watch*, who're you?

KIM: Kim.

Kim gives a friendly bucktoothed grin.

DAWN: Kim, what are you looking for?

KIM: I'm here for the Clown Convention?

DAWN: What?

KIM: The Clown Convention? For people who love anything to do with clowns? Just simply adore clowns? Like pictures of clowns, oil paintings, clown masks, clown shoes, clown faces, disembodied clown heads? Do-you-know-where-it-is?

DAWN: No! Next! Hey, you, you're on *Suicide Watch*. What's your name?

JEMEEL: Jemeel. Tuhh.

DAWN: Jemal, you look grungy. Are you here to emulate 'n self-immolate for the king of grunge?

JEMEEL: Who? Oh, you mean Kurt. Nuh. I mean, th' dude was a good musician, I wager, an' like that, but wur here tuh find out where th' rave is.

ever

DAWN: Rave? What is this rave? What about your dead god? Don't you think it's a strange coincidence that you're all in Seattle so close after the anniversary and now Clove Carnelian is up the needle threatening to jump?

JEMEEL: I guess it's kinda rare, but most assuredly I didn't come here 'cause o' that. I mean, *In Utero* was a good album I suppose but, tuhh, I guess if it was up tuh me an' most of the people I see in this crowd? Kurt coulda stayed underground and we wouldn't a rully noticed?

DAWN: But-but-but-Har-Harper?

HARPER: Dawnie, baby, I've got Dr. Rudolf Snaildrake here, from the famed Public TV program *Nine Brilliant Men*, an' he's got a few words uh wise-dome fer us. Perfesser, what're you doin' here in Seattle? Were you a fan o' Kurt's?

A pale-eyed Brit with frizzy, fly-away hair stands by Harper's side.

RUDOLF: Well, um, actually I'm here to visit a colleague of mine. Personal visit, a, em, marine biologist.

HARPER: What's that dude's name?

RUDOLF: Em, she isn't a "dude," eh, and I'd rather not say. Personal visit. Both married. That sort of thing.

HARPER: So what do you think of all this conflagration 'round the needle o' space? D'ye think the Psycho Teen is goin' tuh plunge?

RUDOLF: Em, if I may, I'd like to differ from that eh, eh, prediction, 'em, I've been given to understand that, em, the girl has eh visions, em, which some call hallucinat'ry, em, of brussels sprouts, em, that would be the, em, twine, the vine as it were of the brussel or, eh, brassica oleracea, gemmifera variety this being North America, and, em, I think if one were to look closely at the needle right now one would note a greenish eh, emanation. So, though I'm certain a great number of my colleagues particularly those mired in the *old* science will quite sharply disagree with what I am about to say, I nevertheless feel compelled to, eh, put for'ard that p'rhaps this girl is neither suicidal nor suffering a form of psychosis but, em, merely vibrating at a more acutely *morphic resonant* frequency than others-of-us.

Sup*pose* for a moment that this needle is less a pin *thrrrust* into

314

what

an inert field of matter and more precisely like the needle of a compass, subject to magnetic fields that girdle the earth's sphere. Whereas Newton once thought that gravitational pull *ema*nated from the heavens, *now* of course we know that 'tisn't the case a *'tall*—now we know that this attraction derives from the *earth's* magnetism. Em, quantum physics has established electromagnetic fields. Thus, just as a piece of iron can gain or lose its magnetism without *w*eighing any less, or more, so, too a *soul* can pass *in* and *out* of a body (or plant), constituting a field around it. I propose that Miss, eh, Carnelian? has reawakened a dormant field around the brussel plant, and that this "field"—or soul, if you prefer—is *morphically resonating* with the soul of the dead, eh guitar player? folksinger?-whatever-he-was in a *most an*imated fashion. In *fact*, she stands a very good chance of transcending OLD style *MECHA*NISTIC physics altogether in a most DRAMATIC and TANGIBLE sense—

DAWN: WHAT is he talking about?!

HARPER: LOOK!

DAWN: It's a bird!

HARPER: It's a, it's a—look look.

Violet is directing Sophie as she backs her truck into the crowd, toward the base of the needle. The giant green sculpture is in the back of the truck, mounted on strings.

VIOLET: Back up the truck, Sophie!

SOPHIE: I'm backing it! Vi old girl, got the strings?

VIOLET: I've got mine. Helacio, Carlito, have you got yours?

HELACIO: *¡Sí!*

CARLITO: *¡Sí!*

SOPHIE: Let 'em go!

They pull, then release the strings and the giant green sculpture rises up out of the truck bed and begins its ascent.

VIOLET: There! Look at it! It's gorgeous.

DAWN: What is it?

RUDOLF: It's big, it's fluffy, it's hard, it's firm, it's infinitely layered, it's giant, it's green, oh, so green it floats. Look, look! It's floating to the needle point. Is it going to burst? It's up there, it's up there. It's to the right, it's listing to the right. Look, she's stepping on it. Clove

ever

Carnelian has stepped onto the giant floating brussels sprout and is descending through the fog, escorted by a cotillion of friendly seagulls. She's descending, descending. Where is she going?

SCOOPS: It's a fuckin' miracle! As near as I can tell the sprout's headed toward Puget Sound. I sure am glad little Clover made it out, I care about dat kid.

Scoops scratches his beardless chin and loosens the tie around his neck. The suit is a little tight.

LINDA: You know her?

SCOOPS: Oh yeah, I had her on my boat, gave her a ride partway up da coast.

LINDA: Really, you own a boat?

SCOOPS: Oh, just a pleasure craft. When I'm, uh uh, away on . . . from my business.

LINDA: Oh, what's your business?

SCOOPS: Uh, agricultural engineering, uh yeh-up.

LINDA: I'm Linda Frye. I'm in occult studies. I practice.

She shakes his hand. For no good reason, she does not recognize him as her ex-husband's old associate. She does feel a little light-headed.

LINDA: Clove is one of my son's little girlfriends.

SCOOPS: Oh really. Pleasure to meet you, Lin.

Jeanette yanks Linda away.

JEANETTE: Linda, come on.

LINDA: Hey!

JEANETTE: That man was giving me scurvy energy. Don't flirt with businessmen, hon, look what happened to me with Paul.

LINDA: He was sort of sexy, Jeanette, I don't usually like establishment types.

JEANETTE: Oh, but look how he dressed. He had on a suit exactly like Paul's. I swear they all dress identically.

LINDA: It was not.

JEANETTE: Was.

LINDA: Was not!

JEANETTE: Was!

HARPER: Dawnie, can yuh believe it? Her mood-hat is changin' colors.

RUDOLF: And if I might interject, it's vibrating not coral, puce, ma-

what

genta, or azul, the four colors for which it is programmed, but i'*tis* in fact a *fifth* color.

DAWN: Green!

HARPER: That's right, Dawnie baby, an' if yuh look around, everybody's mood-hats, including the perfessor's here, is changing tuh that color.

DAWN: I feel sick. How did this happen? Who are these old ladies? Who *are* you?

VIOLET: I'm Violet Smith, deeah, who on earth are you?

DAWN: Dawn Malestrella.

SOPHIE: Hi, Dawn. Sophie Flax, famous artist. Heard of me?

DAWN: Do you have a gallery in New York?

VIOLET: No! This is the sculptress Sophie Flax, all her work has already been *collected in museums! She ought to be *dead* by now. This is her latest piece.

SOPHIE: My final piece, my grace note, my fan-de-see-eyecle.

DAWN: What *is* it?

HARPER: It's a brussels sprout.

SOPHIE: Goddamnit, NO! I was afraid of that! Can't anyone tell? It's female orgasm?! Don't you see how limitless it is? How buoyant and yet so dense, so FREE?

DAWN: Female *what*?

A stunned silence falls on the crowd. All eyes turn to Dawn.

HARPER: Dawnie! *¿Qué pasa?!*

DAWN: I just can't take it. Everything was going so well for a while with the Miami South Beach Fashion Mass Suicides and the Suicide-by-Numbers in New York by that Jeff Jimson—now *he* was a true artist—he killed himself! And now this girl steps onto a *thing* an' just floats away!

VIOLET: What's the trouble, deeah? Aren't you a journalist? Isn't this a good story for you?

DAWN: NO! This is a special *prog*ram.

VIOLET: What is it? Say, aren't *you* on that tedious public television program?

RUDOLF: Yes, I'm afraid so. It is somewhat tedious, but it pays rather handsomely, em . . .

DAWN: Go away, everyone just *go* away!

ever

HARPER: Dawnie? Uh, viewers, uh, we'll be right back after a poesy break.

SOPHIE: What's the program about?

DAWN: When people commit suicide. I need suicide stories not mira-fucking-cles!

VIOLET: Suicide, well, we've got suicide stories, haven't we, Soph! Good Christ, there must've been half a dozen suicides on the Tricott Farm alone, right, Soph?

SOPHIE: Sure. Loads of 'em. The fifties were a good decade for suicide. McCarthy helped with that.

> Dawn looks up brightly from her tears.

DAWN: Really?

VIOLET: Oh yes, people offed themselves all the time. Remember Chad Leventhal, Sophie?

SOPHIE: Yes, he gassed himself in his hotel room, didn't he?

VIOLET: Afteh he wrote that perfectly brilliant novel. It was smashing really. Nobody read it, except for a few.

SOPHIE: Then there was Livonia Holmes.

VIOLET: Hmm, and Everett Thornbull.

SOPHIE: Right, and then the Frenchie—Lillian Quade's lover, what was his name?

VIOLET: Ehhh . . . *Vas*come San-Loup!

SOPHIE: Right! And how'd he do it?

VIOLET: Threw himself off a bridge, if I recall. Though I cahn't remember if it was the Brooklyn Bridge or that, eh, *big* one in Paris.

SOPHIE: Hmmph, at least you remembered it was a bridge, Vi, that's better than I'm doing. Then there was Laramie Potts.

VIOLET: No deeah, he died of an enlarged liver. He drank himself to death.

SOPHIE: Well, hell Vi, that counts.

VIOLET: I'm not sure. Dawn, does it?

DAWN: Sure, that totally counts. Do you have any more suicide stories?

> Jemeel climbs up on on a decorative anchor, cups his hands, and calls out to all.

JEMEEL: Whoah, people, people! Try an' get transport tuh Puget Sound. The sprout is touching down over thar an' word is out that

what

th' mood-hatted rave shall commence soundwards. Rave on, brothers and sisters, rave on.

MISCELLANEOUS RAVERS: Rave on! Rave on! Rave on!

VIOLET: Do you want to go, Soph? If only to get the sprou—eh, female orgasm?

SOPHIE: Hell, let it wash out to sea, I don't want it. I've done what I had to do, I let it go.

BALZAC: Woof, woof.

VIOLET: What's that Balzac? Balzy says he'd like to go. I must confess I'm sort of curious, Sophie. You know what an *id*iot I was—and still am—f' jazz. I'd like to see if this *rav*ing hooey rully swings, what d'you say?

SOPHIE: Yeh-up, sure. Helacio and Carlito'll want to go. Fancy a fiesta fellas?

HELACIO: *Sí, Sí, seguro,*

CARLITO: *El bailando,*

HELACIO: *La música,*

CARLITO: *La luna,*

HELACIO: *Las estrellas,*

CARLITO: *El mar,*

HELACIO: *La playa . . .*

CARLITO: *¿ Por qué no?*

VIOLET: What'd he say, Soph?

SOPHIE: He said why the hell not! Ask what's-her-name if she's coming.

VIOLET: Dawn, you want to rave?

DAWN: NO! All those loathsome youths are happy! No one will commit suicide tonight.

VIOLET: I've no idea why I like you, deeah, because you're a perfectly horrid girl. But for some reason I do. Perversity. My last husband, Elliot, said I was perverse. Not per*vert*ed, per*verse.*

DAWN: Did he commit suicide?

VIOLET: NO, he did NOT!

SOPHIE: But hop on in the truck, gal. We know plenty more who did.

DAWN: Yah? Will you tell me more suicide stories on the way?

VIOLET: Certainly!

ever

DAWN: Come on, Harper. Let's go. Maybe we can do a retrospective.

Dawn's tears are almost dried now and she smiles through her sniffles.

HARPER: Who-okay, Dawnie, whatever ya say.

SOPHIE: Anyone who wants to, hop in the back of my truck. We're going to the RAVE!!!

Clove wafts through the fog on the giant green sculpture.

CLOVE: Oh immortal sprout waft soft to the sandy sweep

It's there I'll sleep having finished my quest

Oh friendly gulls guide me sweet to the beachy keep

In Puget Sound's gray arms I'll rest

Now smooth as I glide,

Let restless Cobain be pried

From the moon, released from his reign

No more a king, a fad, or a thing

But lapsed at last in a mortal swoon

It's underground you'll sleep and dwell

Far beneath earth's hectic hell

So if, in Life, the hounds of fame did bloody yer soul

Now, in Death, we resurrect yer obscuuuurity

Play on, brother, play on, in that garage beneath the foam

Fix lattes fer a living

And never get a record contract fer th' rest of eterrrrnity

I thank yer friendly ghost fer sparing me a watery grave

By bringing on about this most authenticated rave.

She lands on the beach.

CLOVE: Whoah! I'm here capsized, oh fine spray, salt haze

Oh ocean! O! O! O! O!

Lull to peace the restless prince of grunge

Rock him to sleep with periwinkle, mollusk and sponge

And now, by this capsized ball I, too, must doze

Until Ravers come and pull my toes.

She falls fast asleep beside the sculpture, snoring quite loudly. From over the dunes, two figures emerge. Individually they skulk up to the shoreline and then bump into each other.

SCOOPS: Paul!

what

PAUL: Scoops!

SCOOPS: What're you doin' here?

PAUL: I came here to sell mood-hats at the rave. They're selling like hotcakes. I think there's a genuine future in them. But, uh, I'm looking for Jeanette. Have you seen her? What are you doing here?

SCOOPS: Uh uh, just so happened tuh have something tuh dig up. I'll fess up to ya, Paul. Y'ain't in the FBI?

PAUL: I promise you I'm not.

SCOOPS: I got a bud in Marion Pen, buried some pot money out here. Linda's ex-husband.

PAUL: You mean Skeeter's dad? The one in Marion Federal Prison?

SCOOPS: Yep, dat's the one. Bruce Frye. He buried some money he made smugglin' out here back in '83, and now I've come tuh undig it, dig? And give it tuh Linda tuh give their son, Ezekial.

PAUL: Ezekial. That's Skeeter.

SCOOPS: Huh?

PAUL: His true name is Ezekial Christian Frye.

SCOOPS: 'At's right.

PAUL: But his friends call him Skeeter 'cause he annoys 'em in a mosquito-type fashion. I love the boy. He's my ward. I took him across the country on the train. We had a blast. It was his idea to sell the mood-hats. Incipient little entrepreneur, is what he is. A real self-starter! All he needs is a little capital. Hey, fantastic! Where's his inheritance buried?

SCOOPS: Fer some cosmic fuckin' reason, if my calculations an' memory serve me correct, which dey always do, it's buried right under dis sprout.

PAUL: Female orgasm.

SCOOPS: What?

PAUL: Ever. You want me to help you move it?

SCOOPS: Th' hairs on the back uh my neck tell this old sea dog that he better ride out dis rave 'fore we go movin' dat thing. Dere's something cosmic 'n' funky 'n' mysterious goin' down an' I don't mess wid dat.

PAUL: You're right, you're right. My girlfriend, Jeanette, is always telling me to be more spiritually tuned.

SCOOPS: Hey, ain't that Linda and Jeanette comin' over da rocks?

ever

PAUL: It is. Quick! Let's hide behind this sculpted spasm and see what happens.

SCOOPS: Good idea.

They hide behind the giant green sculpture.

LINDA: Ezekial? Ezekial?

JEANETTE: No one's here yet. I wonder where Clove is? I hope she didn't get smushed by that giant sprout.

LINDA: She probably wandered off to some cave. Do you think she was a crone in a past life, Jeanette?

JEANETTE: I think she was something. What magic. But I don't think she's right for Skeeter.

LINDA: Why not, if she's a witch, I'd be glad for Ezekial.

JEANETTE: No, a mother and an aunt in the augury crafts are enough. Believe me, he needs to get away from females like us, it's too incestuous.

LINDA: I don't believe you.

JEANETTE: Listen, baby sister, your son tried to make out with me once in the back of a cab in New York City, okay?

LINDA: Goddess forfend us! Maybe you're right. Maybe Sable is the one. She doesn't even resemble us!

PAUL: Hey!

JEANETTE: Oh you again. Did you sell any more mood-hats?

PAUL: Thousands.

JEANETTE: Hmmm.

PAUL: Beautiful night, hmm?

JEANETTE: It is. The sea is so calm and yet so seething.

PAUL: So passive and yet so full of rage.

JEANETTE: Exactly! You have a nice voice. It reminds me of someone.

PAUL: Do you want to go for a walk?

JEANETTE: Sure. Linda, I'll be back in a little while.

Jeanette goes off arm in arm with the mood-hat man.

LINDA: Hmmph, and she told me not to flirt with that guy wearing the suit. Then she flits off with some mood-hat cat!

JOB: Thar's the sprout, whar is she?

Job, disguised as Skeeter, appears from over the dunes.

JOB: 'Scuse me, ma'am, did yuh happen tuh see whar th' one they call Clove went?

what

LINDA: Ezekial. There you are. Jeanette and I have been looking all over for you. Where's little Sable?

JOB: Uh, dunno, dunno.

LINDA: Listen, you can't vacillate between girlfriends like this. You're turning out just like Bruce. Now listen, I've got something heavy to lay on you. I acknowledge you had a messed-up childhood trip, okay? And I'm sorry. I'm sorry, boy o' mine.

JOB: Gotta go, gotta go, Mama.

He runs off down the shore.

LINDA: Ezekial! Come back. You're acting strange. What's hexing him? He's not himself. Hmm. I think I have an uncrossing candle in my purse. There. I'll light it. Please Goddess, uncross my relationship with my son and his relationship with those two girls and Bruce's relationship to him. And those two girls' relationship with one another and—Oh Goddess! JUST UNCROSS ALL THESE CROSSED RELATIONSHIPS!!!! Glackhverrrgwth Wick Braganenjumblingque euerk squaw leee!

She spits thrice and pentacles herself, then raises high the candle and limps after him.

LINDA: Ezekial? Ezekial? Ezeeeekial!

Sable climbs over the dunes.

SABLE: Clo-ove! Clove, whur are you, Clove? Oh my Godddddddess. Have all my jealous hexings caused her to get all smushed? Clove? Clove? There you are Clove! My ravished soul sister. Strumpet of the high seas! It's me, yer best friend and fairest cohort, Sable. What's this? Tuhh. She's snoring most extravagantly. Poor Clover, yur massively depleted, aren't you? Boing boing boing, who wouldn't be? Snore on, raging wench, snore on. Tuhh. Pause. I'll trade IDs with her, whul she naps on the shore.

Sable strips off her own clothes, and then begins undressing Clove.

SABLE: Then I'll hide behind this giant fiendish spore. When Skeeter comes, I'll test his love. Will he choose Sable er will he choose Clove? Yah! Clove, girl-dude, I'll bury you here with friendly care. You'll be most snuggish thus out of sight,

Sable finshes donning Clove's clothing and buries her naked sleeping friend in the sand.

SABLE: and when you wake up, we won't have to fight! Yah! Ta-ta!

ever

Sable then hides behind the giant green sculpture.

SKEETER: Sable? Sable? Whur in the fuck are ye, my savage Sabe-babe? Tuhh. I'm prone tuh despairin' o' ever retrievin' her. Sable?

Sable pops out from behind the sculpture, holding her nostrils shut, so that she will sound like Clove. She remains in the shadows.

SABLE: Sly Skeeter, you seek my friend?

SKEETER: Whoah. Is that you, Clove?

SABLE: Yah!

She answers in her own voice, then catches herself, replugging her nose.

SABLE: Yah. It is me, Clove, harlot of the surf!

SKEETER: Tuhh, I fear I'm taxed fer th' optimo word at this junket in time. (How rare.) But at th' risk o' waxin' antique, let me state det it is a marvel tuh behold you after all these months.

SABLE: Ahem, were you looking fer Sable?

SKEETER: I was.

SABLE: You were?

SKEETER: Er, I am, but I'll righteously tarry a tad with *yer* auspicious person.

SABLE: Tuhhhhhh, is not *Sable* auspicious?

SKEETER: Sable's delicious! Er, but, t'amend that observance I add that I'm yer humble servant.

He bows to her in a courtly manner.

SABLE: Why? Aren't you stricken with love fer Sable? Didn't you tell her that?

SKEETER: Er, I told her I was stricken with love fer two. Sable 'n you. Why do you stand so far away?

SABLE: I want to comprehend yer attentions to my friend. It's me you met first.

SKEETER: And her I knew segundo. O, O, O! But fer you I nurse the greater thirst.

SABLE: Alas, but not poor Sable?

SKEETER: Nuh, no need. Fer Sable satiates me most severely, 'til I'm near disabled.

SABLE: And me? Clove?

SKEETER: Steppin' on that sprout was unsurpassable. Now I fear you're untrespassable.

what

SABLE: You fear? Take me, Skeeter, I'm yers.

SKEETER: Come closer then, yur most obscure.

He backs away.

SABLE: Here I am.

Sable throws herself at him, grinding her hips.

SABLE: Yer Clove, yer love, now wax all Johnny Depp. Unsheathe yer sword.

SKEETER: Tuhh . . . I'm fiended out. I can't. My mood-hat's dizzyin' me.

Skeeter half faints and falls to the sand. She cries out in her real voice.

SABLE: Skeeter! Er, are you tweaked?

Perhaps because he feels so strange, he doesn't notice her voice change. He avoids looking at her, and tries to get his bearings.

SKEETER: Nuh nuh, it's just, when I hitched across this nation, I landed 'round Thanksgiving on a reservation and th'elder dudes there ceremonized me. Scattered hamburger an' Marlboros an' smoked a rag-pipe with me. An' as I slipped down that psycho acti-vated slope, I looked in a slice o' light an' saw my face an' yers re-semblin' an echo. I'm fiended, Clove. I can't be yer love. This is rare, I want tuh find Sable.

He tries to crawl off, but Sable, resuming her trickery, pulls him to her.

SABLE: Come here, Skeeter.

SKEETER: I can't, Clove, you feel too rare, too mmmm hmmm.

He burrows his head in her thighs, her belly, her breasts.

SKEETER: Mmmmmm-hmmmmm, you feel most alarmingly famil-iar, you feel so luscious and er—like Sable!

SABLE: I am Sable, Skeeter, you scurvy knave!

She hurls him away. He leaps to his feet.

SKEETER: You decepted me, you hoaxish wench! Whur's Clove, have you slaughtered her?

SABLE: Nuh. I buried her in the sand over there. Go be with her and wax all Jason Priestley, who gives a care?

SKEETER: Clove? Clove?

He looks at Clove's head, snoring in the sand.

SKEETER: She snores most fiercely. Tuhh. Thur's somethin' in her countenance that disequilibrates my unconscious.

SABLE: Wake her up, then. Boing boing boing, be all, "Cluh-ove! Cluh-ove!"

ever

He looks up and moves toward Sable.

SKEETER: But that disequilibriation notwithstanding, Sable, I vouch-safe my heart in yer most able care.

SABLE: Realistically?

SKEETER: Without an ounce o' mendacity.

SABLE: You pledge yer heart to me to exclusive excess?

SKEETER: Yeh-up. Fer now.

SABLE: What?

SKEETER: No, I do. I do. Most devotedly an' undubiously I do. Take my hand. We'll go search out a curvy cave and there I'll warm you, ere we rave.

SABLE: Rave on!

SKEETER: Rave on!

Hand in hand, the young lovers skip off.

Paul and Jeanette are in a cave, madly making out.

JEANETTE: Oh you're so wild, so hairy, so unrepressed. You're more like the pipeline men I used to run around with when I was a girl in Anchorage. Not like this tight-mouthed businessman I've been deal-ing with.

PAUL: The hypocrite CEO?

JEANETTE: Right. It's uncanny how spot on you are. I swear I know you from another life.

PAUL: I think so.

JEANETTE: You do? Hmm. Ever since I saw you selling the mood-hats, this strange thought has been in my mind. Is this the man who'll make me forget Paul Folsom?

PAUL: And why do you want to forget him?

JEANETTE: Because he always betrays me. As all men have always done.

PAUL: I can make you forget him.

JEANETTE: Prove it, show me.

PAUL: I can make you forget him, Jeanie, because I AM HIM!

He rips off his beard.

JEANETTE: Paul!

PAUL: I am him and I've forgotten him. He betrayed me too. He be-

what

trayed the boy from Wenatchee, the boy who loved the green, green forests of the Olympic Mountains and the Wenatchee River. I've forgotten him, Jeanie, and I've remembered me. And I, I will never leave you again.

JEANETTE: Paul!

PAUL: Jean?

JEANETTE: I liked you better with a beard.

PAUL: I'll glue it back on. I'll grow one of my own. I love you, Jeanette!

JEANETTE: Oh Paul!

Back at the beach, Job creeps toward the giant green sculpture.

JOB: Man, that lady was hord to git rid of. Hmm . . . Thar's the sprout, whar's my Clove? Hm hm hm.

CLOVE: SNORE SNORE SNORE, buzz ye bees an' buy him a ticket passage to th' real underground. Farewell! Good-bye! Now release the thicket of fans, release the thicket! SNORE SNORE SNORE.

JOB: Whut's 'at? Hm hm hm—

He trips on her.

JOB: Who's this? Snoring seashell? Is it she they call Clove? I think it'd do me well tuh wake 'er up an' ask.

He kneels beside her and blows in her ear.

JOB: Clo-ove. Cuh-lo-ove. Coo-lo-ove.

CLOVE: Tuhh huh uh what thwacks? Who's 'at?

JOB: It is I, Skeeter, come to claim yer eye.

CLOVE: What am I doing all buried up to my neck in sand and whur're all my clothes? Why do I always wind up denuded at the end of my adventures?

JOB: Wah oh wah? Hmm, here's a fake fur cape, will that clothe yuh?

CLOVE: I'll take it. Hmm. Smells like Sable. Whur is that scurrilous tart?

She sniffs the breeze.

CLOVE: I whiff her. Skeeter, is that totally you?

JOB: Most verily it is me

He gives her his hand and helps her to her feet.

ever

CLOVE: You've altered a tad since that night at the rave. Yer voice twinges all tobaccoish and slithery.

> She follows him as he backs away.

JOB: Is that good, er—

> She abruptly turns her back to him.

CLOVE: I dunno. It's complex. It doesn't matter, nevermind. I suppose yur all salivating after my best friend and fairest cohort, otherwise known as the poaching paramour Sable?

JOB: No, I've got no time fer sultry whispery girls.
I want to be the henchman of she who whirls
in foamy margents of the sea
and hurls herself off needles,
she who sows orgasmic seeds
and sleeps in sand-holes,
curled and fetal.

CLOVE: Tuhh. How do you rhyme like that?

JOB: Dunno. You inspire me, I guess. Do you desire me?

CLOVE: Yes! More than ever. Skeeter!

JOB: Clove!

> Clove inclines her head one way, Job the other, her lips part just slightly. His lips move toward these parted lips.

SCOOPS: Wait just one hot second! Hold it!

> Scoops comes rushing out from behind the giant green sculpture. Clove recognizes his jolly gravelly voice immediately.

CLOVE: Captain Scoops!

> He stops, surprised.

SCOOPS: Hey kid, dat's pretty good. See, no beard.

> He flaps his hands under his chin.

SCOOPS: Clove, kid, I hate to tell ya dis, but you can't— dis Skeeter here is—

> Sophie's truck pulls up through the dunes.

VIOLET: Here we are, Sophie. There's your swell, eh, female eh, there it is!

SOPHIE: Let it float away. Where's the rave?

VIOLET: I see the people coming from down the shore.

> Violet calls out.

what

VIOLET: Hello there.

Linda comes back, heads for Job.

LINDA: There you are, Ezekial.

Jeanette and Paul rejoin the others.

JEANETTE: Linda! Sorry I was gone so long. Look! I've met a new man, but it's the same old one!

PAUL: Yep, I traded identities with this man.

SCOOPS: Well, I guess da game is up here. Linda, it's me, Scoops. See? Wid da beard?

He flaps his hand under his chin.

SCOOPS: An' I got some news fer ya from Bruce, but first I got tuh raise an objection here. Me an' little Clove here met when she hitched a ride from me on my fishin' smack, da *Margarita Mama*.

CLOVE: Yah, that was rad, the cellular phone. The radar detector running from the Coast Guard an' like that.

SCOOPS: Shh shh shh, Clove, little darlin', shut yer trap. But anyways, me an' little Clover here rapped a whole heap and bonded really good an' let me tell you dis is one wild funky little lady wid a whole lotta dreams and I wish she were my own, but she ain't. An' I wish she were da kid uh Nick Carnelian, but she ain't. See, we got tuh rappin' an' it turns out I knew 'er parents from back in da seventies. Knew 'em real well. An' back in '78, we had us da last o' da cocaine campin' trips out down near Malibu an' it happened, little Linda Frye here can tell ya dat her old man Bruce Frye balled just about every chick on dat campin' trip. Includin' Clove's mom, Judy Carnelian.

LINDA: Wait, this is Judy Carnelian's little accident?

CLOVE: Tuhh.

SCOOPS: So, Clove, I hate tuh break yer little heart, but you can't do da sideways samba wid old Skeeter here, 'cause he's your HALF-BROTHER BY BRUCE FRYE!

CLOVE: Oh, God-duh-duh-duh-duh-duh-dddddddesssss!

Sable comes running down the beach to join her friend.

SABLE: Duh-duh-duh-duh-duh

CLOVE AND SABLE: Duh-duh-ddddddess!

They embrace.

ever

CLOVE: Sable, girl-dude, at long last!

SABLE: Clove, oh Clove. I'm in love with Skeeter. It's so right on. I'm truly in love.

CLOVE: But this is Skeeter.

Sable points to her love, then to the imposter.

SABLE: No, *this* is Skeeter. *That* is Job.

SKEETER: Job?

PAUL: Jobe?

SCOOPS: Jobe? Job?

JOB: Wull, I dressed up like Skeeter tuh seduce th' spicy Clove, but I now confess, m' true name is Jobe Shannon Serreli, as in the Bauble book. I'm from Texas. I ran away west to look fer my fuck-up dad. An' also 'cause I heard the raves were pretty stoked in Cali an' I'm a ravin' boy 'til the day I die.

LINDA: Wait a minute! Goddesses, faeries, sprites, nymphs, nyads, dryads, druids, and wee elfin things be with us all! This is Debbie Serreli's kid from that same cocaine camping trip. Remember, Scoops? You got her pregnant and she moved out to Texas?

SCOOPS: SMALL FUCKIN' COSMOS, man! I'm yer DAD, James Scoops Shannon da Third!

He vigorously pumps Job's hand and gives him a bear hug.

JOB: Dad, it's about time. Better late than never, I guess.

SKEETER: But what I don't get is why are me an' Job so doppel-ganged an' like that?

SCOOPS: Uhhh, 'cuz me an' Bruce came up together, we were best friends, like brothers. Soul-brothers. So you two're like soul-cousins. An' dat makes me almost like yer uncle, I guess.

SKEETER: Uncle Scoops!

SCOOPS: Nephew Skeet!

SKEETER: Cousin Job!

JOB: Cousin Skeet!

CLOVE: Brother Skeeter!

SKEETER: Sister Clove!

ALL: WHAT. EVER!

CLOVE: And so sweet day slip into night

And make this rave so ultra bright

That even Kurt in his pale shroud

what

Can pierce the silent Puget Sound
Oh rest ye well, musician fair
Brother to us children of flat despair
Rest ye, rest ye, while we dance
A synthopop liquidated trance
Rest ye, suicides and sacrifices
May our mood-hats beam a color that entices
The very demons from thur tanks
Waving white flags, and giving thanks
Rejoice, make noise
Fuck girls, fuck boys
The time fer the end has come
Let us sing and dance every last one!

VIOLET: Must you speak in verse all the time, deeah? Other than that you're a perfectly pleasant girl. Balzac! Fetch me Sammy Tine's trumpet!

> Balzac comes running up, drops the trumpet case on the sand, and flips it open.

VIOLET: *Good* poodle!

> Violet lifts the trumpet to her lips, hesitates, then gathers up all of her breath and blows the horn.

ever